A W
WEST

BRENDA JACKSON

AND

CLAIMING HIS
ROYAL HEIR
BY
JENNIFER LEWIS

MILLS & BOON

Dear Reader,

It's hard to believe that *A Wife for a Westmoreland* is the nineteenth book in THE WESTMORELANDS series and the fourth book about the Denver Westmorelands. Time sure flies when you're having fun, and I've really had a ball bringing you stories about such gorgeous men and women.

I knew Derringer Westmoreland was going to be a challenge when he appeared on the scene in *Hot Westmoreland Nights*. Besides being a man too handsome for his own good and a man used to playing the field, he's ruggedly seductive and can talk the panties off any woman. He's also a man who believes in getting whatever it is that he wants, no matter what it takes to get it, and he's decided he wants Lucia Conyers. That would be all fine and dandy for Lucia, since she's loved Derringer most of her life, but she wants him to want her for all the right reasons and refuses to settle for anything less. So what does this Westmoreland man have to do to get the woman he wants? I think you're going to enjoy the results.

All the best,

Brenda Jackson

A WIFE FOR A WESTMORELAND

BY
BRENDA JACKSON

Published in Great Britain 2011
by Mills & Boon, an imprint of Harlequin (UK) Limited,
Eton House, 18-24 Paradise Road, Richmond, Surrey TW9 1SR

© Brenda Streater Jackson 2011

ISBN: 978 0 263 89094 5

51-1211

Harlequin (UK) policy is to use papers that are natural, renewable and
recyclable products and made from wood grown in sustainable forests. The
logging and manufacturing processes conform to the legal environmental
regulations of the country of origin.

Printed and bound in Spain
by Blackprint CPI, Barcelona

Brenda Jackson is a die "heart" romantic who married her childhood sweetheart and still proudly wears the "going steady" ring he gave her when she was fifteen. Because she's always believed in the power of love, Brenda's stories always have happy endings. In her real-life love story, Brenda and her husband of thirty-eight years live in Jacksonville, Florida, and have two sons.

A *New York Times* bestselling author of more than seventy-five romance titles, Brenda is a recent retiree who now divides her time between family, writing and traveling with Gerald. You may write Brenda at PO Box 28267, Jacksonville, Florida 32226, USA, by e-mail at WriterBJackson@aol.com or visit her website at www. brendajackson.net.

THE DENVER WESTMORELAND FAMILY TREE

Raphel and Gemma Westmoreland

Stern Westmoreland (Paula Bailey)

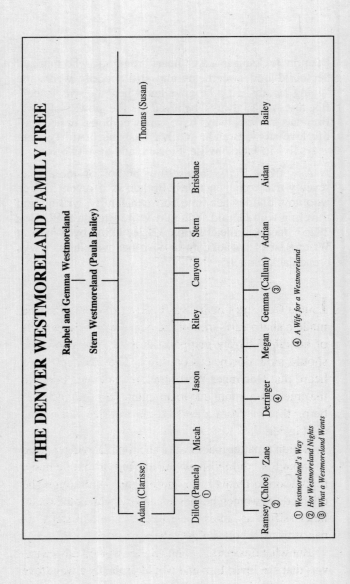

Thomas (Susan)

Adam (Clarisse)

Dillon (Pamela) ①

Micah   Jason   Riley   Canyon   Stern   Brisbane

Ramsey (Chloe) ②

Zane   Derringer ④   Megan   Gemma (Callum) ③   Adrian   Aidan   Bailey

① *Westmoreland's Way*
② *Hot Westmoreland Nights*
③ *What a Westmoreland Wants*
④ *A Wife for a Westmoreland*

One

Lucia Conyers's heart was beating like crazy as she made a sharp turn around the curve while the wheels of her SUV barely gripped the road. She knew she should slow down, but couldn't. The moment she'd heard that Derringer Westmoreland had been taken to the emergency room due to an injury he sustained after being thrown from a horse, a part of her had nearly died inside.

It didn't matter that most of the time Derringer acted as though he didn't know she existed or that he had a reputation in Denver as a ladies' man—although she doubted the women he messed around with could really be classified as ladies. Derringer was one of Denver's heartthrobs, a hottie if ever there was one.

But what did matter, although she wished otherwise, was that she loved him and would probably always love him. She'd tried falling out of love with him several times and just couldn't do it.

Not even four years of attending a college in Florida had changed her feelings for him. The moment she had returned to Denver and he had walked into her father's paint store to make a purchase, she'd almost passed out from a mixture of lust and love.

Surprisingly, he had remembered her. He'd welcomed her back to town and asked her about school. But he hadn't asked her out, or offered to share a drink somewhere for old time's sake. Instead, he had gathered up the merchandise he'd come to the store to buy and left.

Her obsession with him had started back in high school when she and his sister Megan had worked on a science project together. Lucia would never forget the day that Megan's brother had come to pick them up from the library. She'd almost passed out when she first laid eyes on the handsome Derringer Westmoreland.

She thought she'd died and gone to heaven, and when they were introduced, he smiled at her, showing a pair of dimples that should be outlawed on anyone, especially a man. Her heart had melted then and there and hadn't solidified since. That introduction had taken place a few months after her sixteenth birthday. Now she was twenty-nine and she still got goose bumps whenever she thought about that first meeting.

Ever since her best friend, Chloe, had married Derringer's brother Ramsey, she saw more of Derringer, but nothing had changed. Whenever he saw her he was always nice to her. But she knew he really didn't see her as a woman he would be interested in.

So why wasn't she getting on with her life? Why was she risking it now by taking the roads to his place like a madwoman, needing to see for herself that he was still in one piece? When she'd gotten the news, she'd rushed to the hospital only to receive word from Chloe that he'd been released and was now recuperating at home.

He would probably wonder why she, of all people, was showing up at his place to check on him. She wouldn't be surprised if some woman was already there waiting on him hand and foot. But at the moment it didn't matter. Nothing mattered but to make sure for herself that Derringer was okay. Even the threat of possible thunderstorms this evening hadn't kept her away. She hated thunderstorms, and yet she had left her home to check on a man who barely knew she was alive.

It was a really stupid move, but she continued to speed down the road, deciding she would consider the foolishness of her actions later.

The loud sound of thunder blasting across the sky practically shook the house and awakened Derringer. He immediately felt a sharp pain slice through his body, the first since he'd taken his pain medication, which meant it was time to take more.

Wrenching at the pain, he slowly pulled himself up in bed, reached across the nightstand and grabbed the pills his sister Megan had laid out for him. She'd said not to take more before six, but a quick glance at his clock said that it was only four and he needed the relief now. He was aching all over and his head felt as if it had split in two. He felt sixty-three instead of a mere thirty-three.

He had been on Sugar Foot's back less than three minutes when the mean-spirited animal had sent him flying. More than his ego had gotten bruised, and each and every time he breathed against what felt like broken ribs he was reminded of it.

Derringer eased back down onto the bed and laid flat on his back. He stared at the ceiling, waiting for the pain pills to kick in.

Derringer's Dungeon.

Lucia slowed her truck when she came to the huge wooden marker in the road. Any other time she would have found it amusing that each of the Westmorelands had marked their property with such fanciful names. Already she had passed Jason's Place, Zane's Hideout, Canyon's Bluff, Stern's Stronghold, Riley's Station and Ramsey's Web. She'd heard when each Westmoreland reached the age of twenty-five they inherited a one-hundred-acre tract of land in this part of the state. That was why all the Westmorelands lived in proximity to each other.

She nervously gnawed on her bottom lip, finally thinking she might have made a mistake in coming here when she pulled into the yard and saw the huge two-story structure. This was her first time at Derringer's Dungeon and from what she'd heard, most women only came by way of an invite.

So what was she doing here?

She brought her car to a stop and cut off the engine and just sat there a moment as reality set in. She had acted on impulse and of course on love, but the truth of the matter was that she had no business being here. Derringer was probably in bed resting. He might even be on medication. Would he be able to come to the door? If he did, he would probably look at her as if she had two heads for wanting to check on him. In his book they were acquaintances, not even friends.

She was about to back out and leave, when she noticed the rain had started to come down harder and a huge box that had been left on the steps of the porch was getting wet. The least she could do was to move it to an area on the porch where the rain couldn't touch it.

Grabbing her umbrella out the backseat, she hurriedly got out of the truck and ran toward the porch to move the box closer to the door. She jumped at the sound of thunder and drew in a sharp breath when a bolt of lightning barely missed the top of her head.

Remembering what Chloe had once told her about how the Westmoreland men were notorious for not locking their doors, she tried the doorknob and saw what her best friend had said was true. The door was not locked.

Slowly opening the door, she stuck her head in and called out in a whisper in case he was downstairs sleeping on the sofa instead of upstairs. "Derringer?"

When he didn't answer, she decided she might as well bring the box inside. The moment she entered the house, she glanced around, admiring his sister Gemma's decorating skills. Derringer's home was beautiful, and the floor-to-ceiling windows took full advantage of the mountain view. She was about to ease back out the door and lock it behind her when she heard a crash followed by a bump and then a loud curse.

Acting on instinct, she took the stairs two at a time and stumbled into several guest bedrooms before entering what had to be the master bedroom. It was decorated in a more masculine theme than all the others. She glanced around and then she saw him lying on the floor as if he'd fallen out of bed.

"Derringer!"

She raced over to him and knelt down beside him, trying to ignore the fact that the only clothing he had on was a pair of black briefs. "Derringer? Are you all right?" she asked, a degree of panic clearly in her voice. "Derringer?"

He slowly opened his eyes and she couldn't stop the fluttering of her heart when she gazed down into the gorgeous dark depths. The first thing she noticed was they were glassy, as if he'd taken one drink too many… or probably one pill too many. She then took a deep breath when a slow smile touched the corners of his lips and those knock-a-girl-off-her-feet dimples appeared in his cheeks.

"Well, now, aren't you a pretty thing," he said in slurred speech. "What's your name?"

"Puddin' Tame," she replied smartly. His actions confirmed he'd evidently taken one pill too many since he was acting as if he'd never seen her in his life.

"That's a real nice name, sweetheart."

She rolled her eyes. "Whatever you say, cowboy. Would you like to explain why you're down here and not up there?" She motioned toward his bed.

"That's easy enough to answer. I went to the bathroom and when I got back, someone moved the bed and I missed it."

She tried keeping the smile from her face. "You sure did miss it. Come on and hold on to me while I help you back into it."

"Someone might move it again."

"I doubt it," she said, grinning, while thinking even when he was under the influence of medication, the deep, husky sound of his voice could do things to her. Make the nipples of her breasts strain against her damp shirt. "Come on, you have to be hurting something awful."

He chuckled. "No, in fact I feel good. Good enough to try riding Sugar Foot again."

She shook her head. "Not tonight you won't. Come on, Derringer, let me help you up and get you back in bed."

"I like it down here."

"Sorry, pal, but you can't stay down here. You either let me help you up or I'll call one of your brothers to help you."

Now it was he who shook his head. "I don't want to see any of them again for a while. All they know how to say is, I told you so."

"Well maybe next time you'll listen to them. Come on."

It took several attempts before she was able to help Derringer to his feet. It wasn't easy to steer him to the bed, and she suddenly lost her balance and found herself tumbling backward onto his bed with him falling on top of her.

"I need you to shift your body a little to get off me,

Derringer," she said when she was able to catch her breath.

He flashed those sexy dimples again and spoke in a voice throaty with arousal. "Um, why? I like being on top of you, Puddin'. You feel good."

She blinked and then realized the extent of her situation. She was in bed—Derringer's bed—and he was sprawled on top of her. It didn't take much to feel the bulge of his erection through his briefs that was connecting with the area between her legs. A slow burn began inching from that very spot and spreading all through her, entering her bloodstream and making her skin burn all over. And if that wasn't bad enough, the nipples of her breasts, which were already straining, hardened like pebbles against his bandaged chest.

As if sensing her body's reaction to their position, he lifted his face to stare down at her and the glassy eyes that snagged hers were so drenched with desire that her breath got caught in her throat. Something she'd never felt before, a pooling of heat, settled between her legs, wetting her panties, and she watched his nostrils flare in response to her scent.

The air between them was crackling more than the thunder and lightning outside, and his chest seemed to rise and fall with each and every beat of her heart.

Fearing her own rapid reaction to their predicament, she made an attempt to gently shove him off her, but found she was no match for his solid weight.

"Derringer…"

Instead of answering her, he reached up and cupped her face into his hands as if her mouth was water he needed to sip, and before she could turn her mouth away from his, with perfect aim, he lowered his mouth and began devouring hers.

Derringer figured he had to be dreaming, and if he was, then this was one delusion he didn't care to ever wake up from. Feasting on Puddin' Tame's lips was the epitome of sensual pleasure. Molded perfectly, they were hot and moist. And the way he had plunged his tongue inside her mouth, devouring hers was the sort of fantasy wet dreams were made of.

Somewhere in the back of his lust-induced mind he remembered getting thrown off a horse; in that case, his body should be in pain. However, the only ache he was feeling was the one in his groin that signaled a need so great his body was all but trembling inside.

Who was this woman and where did she come from? Was he supposed to know her? Why was she enticing him to do things he shouldn't do? A part of him felt that he wasn't in his right mind, but then another part didn't give a damn if he was in his wrong mind. The only thing he knew for sure was that he wanted her. He could eat her alive and wouldn't mind testing that theory to see if he really could.

He shifted his body a little and brought her in the center of the bed with him. He lifted his mouth only slightly off hers to whisper huskily against her moist lips, "Damn, Puddin', you feel good."

And then his mouth was back on hers, sucking on her tongue as if he was a man who needed to taste her as much as he needed to breathe, and what was so shocking to him at that moment was that he was convinced that he did.

* * *

Lucia knew she had to put a stop to what she and Derringer were doing. He was delirious and didn't even know who she was. But it was hard to stop him when her body was responding to everything he was doing to it. Her mouth had never been kissed like this before. No man had consumed her with so much pleasure for her not to think straight. Never had she known a woman could want a man with such magnitude as she wanted Derringer. She had always loved him, but now she wanted him with a need that had been foreign to her.

Until now.

"I want you, Puddin'..."

She blinked as he slightly leaned up off her and the reality of the moment hit her. Although he was delusional, Lucia realized that the honorable part of Derringer would not force her into doing anything she didn't want to do. Now was her chance to slide from beneath him and leave. Chances were, he wouldn't even remember anything about tonight.

But something wouldn't let her flee. It kept her rooted in place as she stared up at him, caught in a visual exchange that not only entrapped her sight but also her mind. A part of her knew this would be the one and only time she would have his attention like this. Sadly, it would be the one and only time he would want her. She pushed to the back of her mind that it had taken an overdose of pain medication to get him to this state.

If she didn't love him so much, she probably would have been able to fight this sexual pull, but love combined with lust was a force she couldn't fight, and a part of her truly didn't want to. She would be thirty in ten months and as of yet, she hadn't experienced how it would feel to be with a man. It was about time she did and it might as well be with the one and only man she'd ever loved.

She would take tonight into her soul, cradle it in her heart and keep it safe in the deep recesses of her brain. And when she saw him again she would have a secret he wouldn't know about, although he would have been the main person responsible for making it happen.

Captured by his deep, dark gaze, she knew it was only a matter of minutes before he took her silence as consent. Now that she'd made up her mind about what she wanted to do, she didn't want to wait even that long. And as more liquid heat coiled between her legs, she lifted her arms to wrap around his neck and tilted her mouth to his. The moment she did, pleasure between them exploded and plunged her into a mirage of sensations that she'd never even dreamed about.

He began kissing her senseless and in her lust-induced mind she was barely aware of him pulling her blouse over her head and removing her lace bra from her body. But she knew the exact moment he latched on to a nipple and eased it between heated lips and began sucking on it as though it was just for his enjoyment.

Waves of pleasures shot through every part of her as if she'd been hit with an atomic missile that detonated on impact. She caught his head between her hands to keep his mouth from going anywhere but on her. Several moans she hadn't known she was capable of making eased from her lips and she couldn't help but writhe the lower part of her body against him, needing to feel the hardness of his erection between her thighs.

As if he wanted more, she knew the moment his fingers eased up her skirt and tracked their way to the part of her that was burning more than any other part— her moist, hot center. He slid one hand beneath the edge of her panties and, as if his finger knew exactly what it was after, it slowly and diligently trekked toward her throbbing clitoris.

"Derringer!"

Her entire body began trembling and with all the intent of a man on a mission he began stroking her with fingers that should be outlawed right along with his dimples. Her womanly core was getting more attention than it had ever gotten before, and she could feel sensations building up inside her at such a rapid rate she was feeling dizzy.

"I want you," he said in a low, guttural tone. And then he kissed her again in a deep, drugging exchange that had him sliding his tongue all over her mouth, tasting her as if doing so was his right. Just the thought made her powerless to do anything other than accept his seduction with profound pleasure.

She was so into the kiss that she hadn't realized he had worked his briefs down his legs and had removed her panties, until she felt them flesh to flesh. His skin felt hot against hers and the iron-steel feel of his thighs resting over hers was penetrating through to every pore in her body.

And when he broke the kiss to ease his body over hers, she was so overcome with desire that she was rendered powerless to stop him.

He lowered his eyes to her breasts and smiled before his eyes slowly returned to her face and snagged her gaze. The look he gave her at that moment was so sexual that she was willing to convince herself that she was the only woman on earth he'd ever given it to. And she was just that far gone to believe it.

Then he leaned down and captured her mouth at the same time he thrust into her body. She couldn't help but cry out from the pain and, as if he sensed what had happened and just what it meant, his body went completely still. He eased his mouth away from hers and glanced down at her while still deeply embedded within her. Not sure just what thoughts were going through his mind about her virginal state and not really wanting to know, she reached up and wrapped her arms around him. And when she began using her tongue to kiss him the way he'd done to her earlier, she felt his body tremble slightly before he began moving inside her. The first time he did so, she thought she would come apart, but as his body began thrusting into hers, smoldering heat from him was being transferred to her, building a fire she could not contain any longer.

He released her mouth long enough for her to call his name. "Derringer!"

He was devouring her in a way she'd never been devoured before and she couldn't help but cry out as his tongue took over. The lower part of him was sending waves of pleasure crashing through her that had her sucking in sharp breaths.

She had heard—mainly from Chloe during one of their infamous girl chats—that making love to a man, especially one you loved, was a totally rewarding and satisfying experience. But no one told her that it could be so mind-consuming and pleasurable. Or that it could literally curl your toes. Maybe Chloe had told her these things and she hadn't believed her. Well, now she believed. And with each hard plunge into her body, Derringer was making all the fantasies she'd ever had of him a reality.

He released her mouth to look down at her while he kept making love to her, riding her the way he rode those horses he tamed. He was good. And he was also greedy. To keep up with him, she kept grinding her hips against his as sensations within her intensified to a degree that she knew she couldn't handle much longer. She cried out again and again as sensations continued to spiral through her.

And then something happened that had never happened to her before and she knew what it was the moment she felt it. He drove deeper and deeper into her, riding her right into a climax of monumental proportions. He lifted his head and met her gaze and the dark orbs gazing at her pushed her even more over the edge.

And when he whispered the name Puddin', thinking it was hers, she accepted it because it had sounded so good coming from him, and it was all she needed to hear to push her into her very first orgasm.

"Derringer!"

He lowered his head again and his tongue slid easily inside her mouth. She continued to grind against him, accepting everything he was giving. Moments later, after breaking off the kiss, he threw his head back and whispered the name again in a deep guttural tone, and he continued to stroke her into sweet oblivion.

* * *

Lucia slowly opened her eyes while wondering just how long she'd slept. The last thing she remembered was dropping her head onto the pillow. She'd been weak, spent and totally and thoroughly satisfied after making love to the sexiest man to walk the face of the earth.

He was no longer on top of her, but was asleep beside her. She missed the weight of him pressing down on her. She missed how his heart felt beating against hers, but most of all she missed the feel of him being inside her.

Remnants of ecstasy were still trickling through her when she thought of what they'd done and all they'd shared. Being gripped in the throes of orgasm after orgasm for several long moments was enough to blow anybody's mind and it had certainly done a job on her. And the way he had looked down at her—during those times he wasn't kissing her—had sent exquisite sensation after exquisite sensation spiraling through her. Even with the bandages covering his chest and parts of his back, she had felt him—the hardness of his shoulders and the way the muscles in his back had flexed beneath her fingertips.

There was no way she could or would forget tonight. It would always be ingrained in her memory despite the fact that she knew he probably would not remember a single thing. That thought bothered her and she fought back the tears that threatened her eyes. They should be tears of joy and not of sorrow, she thought. She had loved him for so long, but at least she had these memories to cherish.

The rain had stopped and all was quiet except the

even, restful sound of Derringer's breathing. Day was breaking and she had to leave. The sooner she did so the better. She could just imagine what he would think if he woke and found her there in bed with him. Whatever words he might say would destroy the beautiful memories of the night she intended to keep.

And her guess was that someone—any one of his brothers, sisters or cousins—might show up any minute to check up on him. They, too, would be shocked as heck to find her there.

She slowly eased out of bed, trying not to wake him, and glanced around for her clothes. She found all the items she needed except for her panties. He had taken them off her while she was in bed, so chances were they were somewhere under the covers.

She slowly lifted the covers and saw the pair of pink panties were trapped beneath his leg. It would be easy enough to wake him and ask him to move his leg so she could get them, but there was no way she could do such a thing. She stood there a moment, hoping he would stir just a little so she could pull them free.

Lucia nervously gnawed on her bottom lip, knowing she couldn't just stand there forever, so she quietly began getting dressed. And only when the sun began peeking over the horizon did she accepted that she had to leave quickly...without her panties.

Glancing around the room to make sure that was the only thing she would be leaving behind, she slowly tiptoed out of the room, but not before glancing over her shoulder one last time to look at Derringer. So this was how he looked in the early mornings. With his shadowed face showing an unshaven chin while lying on the pillow, he looked even more handsome than he'd been last night.

He would probably wonder whose panties were left in his bed, but then he might not. He bedded so many women that it wouldn't matter that one had left a pair of their panties behind. To him it might not be any big deal. Probably wouldn't be.

Moments later while driving away, she glanced back in her rearview mirror at Derringer's home, remembering all that had taken place during the night in his bedroom. She was no longer a virgin. She had given him something she had never given another man, and the only sad part was that he would never, ever know it.

TWO

Some woman had been in his bed.

The potent scent of sex brought Derringer awake, and he lifted his lids then closed them when the sunlight coming through his bedroom window nearly blinded him. He shifted his body and then flinched when pain shot up one of his legs at the same time his chest began aching.

He slowly lifted his head from the pillow, thinking he needed to take some more pain pills, and dropped it back down when he remembered he might have taken one too many last night. Megan would clobber him for taking more than he should have, but at least he'd slept through the night.

Or had he?

He sniffed the air and the scent of a woman's perfume and of sex was still prevalent in his nostrils. Why?

And why were clips of making love to a woman in this very bed going through his brain? It was the best dream he'd had in years. Usually a dream of making love to a woman couldn't touch the reality, but with the one he'd had last night, he would beg to differ. He could understand dreaming about making love to a woman because it had been a while for him. Getting the horse business off the ground with his brother Zane, his cousin Jason and their newfound relatives, those Westmorelands living in Georgia, Montana and Texas, had taken up a lot of his time lately. But his dream had felt so real. That was one hell of an illusion.

Nevertheless, he thought, stretching his body then wishing he hadn't when he felt another pain, it had been well worth the experience.

He reached down to rub his aching thigh, when his hand came in contact with a lacy piece of material. He brought up his hand and blinked when he saw the pair of lace bikini panties that carried the feminine scent he had awakened to.

Pulling himself up in bed, he studied the underthings he held in his hand. Whose were they? Where had they come from? He sniffed the air. The feminine scent was not only in the panties but all over his bed as well. And the indention on the pillow beside him clearly indicated another head had been there.

Monumental panic set in. Who the hell had he made love to last night? Since now there was no doubt in his mind he'd made love to someone. All that pleasure hadn't been a figment of his imagination, but the real thing. But who had been the woman?

He closed his eyes and tried to come up with a face

and couldn't. It had to have been someone he knew; otherwise, who would have come to his house and gotten into his bed? He had messed around with some pretty brazen women in his lifetime, but none would have dared.

Hell, evidently one had.

He opened his eyes and stared at the wall, trying to recall everything he could about yesterday and last night. He remembered the fall off Sugar Foot's back; there was no way he could forget that. He even remembered Zane and Jason rushing him to the emergency room and how he'd gotten bandaged up and then sent home.

He definitely recalled how his brother and cousin kept saying over and over, "We told you so." He remembered that after he'd gotten into bed, Megan had stopped by on her way to the hospital where she worked as an anesthesiologist.

He recalled when she'd given him his pain medicine with instructions of when to take it. The pain had come back sometime after dark and he'd taken some of the pills.

Hell, how much of the stuff had he taken? He distinctly recalled the E.R. physician's warning that the painkillers were pretty potent stuff and had to be taken when instructed. So much for that.

Okay, so he had taken more pain medicine than he was supposed to. But still, what gave some woman the right to enter his home and take advantage of him? He thought of several women who it could have been; anyone who might have heard about his fall and decided to come over and play nursemaid. Only Ashira would have been bold enough to do that. Had he slept with her last night? Hell, he sure hoped not. She might try to pull something and he wasn't in the market of being any baby's daddy any time soon. Besides, what he'd shared with his mystery woman had been different from anything he'd ever shared with Ashira. It had been more profound with one hell of a lasting effect.

He then remembered something vital. The woman he'd slept with had been a virgin—although it was hard to believe he could remember that, he did. And it was pretty far-fetched to think there were still any of them around in this day and time. But there was no way in hell he could have imagined her innocent state even with a mind fuzzy with painkillers. And he knew for certain the woman could not have been Ashira since she didn't have a virginal bone in her body. Besides, he had a steadfast rule to leave innocents alone.

Derringer sighed deeply and wished, for his peace of mind, that he could remember more in-depth details about last night, including the face of the woman whose virginity he had taken. The thought of that made him cringe inside because he knew for certain he hadn't used a condom. Was last night a setup and the result would be a baby just waiting to be born nine months from now?

The thought of any woman taking advantage of him that way—or any way—made his blood boil. And anger began filling him to a degree he hadn't known was possible. If the woman thought she had gotten the best of him she had another thought coming. She had not only trespassed on his private property, but she had invaded his privacy and taken advantage of him when he'd been in a weakened, incoherent state.

If he had to turn over every stone in Denver, he would

find out the identity of the woman who'd had the nerve to pull one over on him. And when he found her, he would definitely make her pay for her little stunt.

"Lucia, are you all right?"

It was noon and Lucia was sitting behind the desk of her office at the Denver branch of *Simply Irresistible*, the magazine designed for today's up-and-coming woman.

The magazine, Chloe's brainchild, had started out as a regional publication in the Southeast a few years ago. When Chloe had made the decision to expand to the West and open a Denver office, she had hired Lucia to manage the Denver office.

Lucia loved her job as managing editor. Chloe was editor in chief, but since her baby—a beautiful little girl named Susan—was born six months ago, Chloe spent most of her time at home taking care of her husband and daughter. Lucia had earned a business-management degree in college, but when Chloe had gotten pregnant she had encouraged Lucia to go back to school and get a master's degree in mass communications to further her career at *Simply Irresistible*. Lucia only needed a few more classes to complete that degree.

Lucia figured it would only be a matter of time before Chloe and Ramsey decided they would want another baby, and the running of *Simply Irresistible's* Denver office would eventually fall in her lap.

"Lucia!"

She jumped when Chloe said her name with a little more force, getting her attention. "What? You scared me."

Chloe couldn't help but smile. It had been a long time

since she'd seen her best friend so preoccupied. "I was asking you a question."

Lucia scrunched up her face. "You were?"

"Yes."

"Oh, what was your question?"

Chloe shook her head, smiling. "I asked if you were all right. You seem preoccupied about something and I want to know what. Things are looking good here. We doubled our print run for April's issue since the president is on the cover, so that shouldn't cause you any concern. What's going on with you?"

Lucia nibbled on her bottom lip. She needed to tell someone about what happened last night and since Chloe was her best friend, she would be the logical person. However, there was a problem with that. Chloe was married to Ramsey, who was Derringer's oldest brother. There was no doubt in Lucia's mind Chloe would keep her mouth closed about anything if she asked her to, but still...

"Okay, Lucia, I'm only going to ask you one more time. What's wrong with you? You've been acting spaced out since I got here, and I doubt you were listening to anything Barbara was saying during the production meeting. So what's going on with you?"

Lucia breathed in deeply. "It's Derringer."

Frowning, Chloe stared. "What about Derringer? Ramsey called and checked on him this morning and he was doing fine. All he needed was a dose of pain medication and a good night's sleep."

"I'm sure he got the dose of pain medication, but I don't know about the good night's sleep," Lucia said drily, before taking a long sip of cappuccino.

"And why don't you think he got a good night's sleep?"

Lucia shrugged, started to feign total ignorance to Chloe's question and then decided to come clean. She looked up and met her friend's curious gaze.

"Because I spent the night with him and I know for certain we barely slept at all."

She could tell from the look that suddenly appeared on Chloe's face that she had shocked her friend witless. Now that she had confessed her sins, she was hoping they could move on and talk about something else, but she should know better than to think that.

"You and Derringer finally got together?" Chloe asked. The shocked expression had been replaced by a smile.

"Depends on what you mean by got together. I'm no longer a virgin, if that's what you mean," Lucia said evenly. "But he was so over the top on painkillers he probably doesn't remember a thing."

The smile dropped from Chloe's lips. "You think so?"

"I know so. He looked right in my face and asked me for my name."

She took the next ten minutes and told Chloe everything, including the part about the panties she had left behind. "So that's the end of it," Lucia finished her tale by saying.

Chloe shook her head. "I really don't think so for two reasons, Lucia. First, you're in love with Derringer and have been for a very long time. I don't see that coming to an end any time soon. In fact, now that the two of you have been intimate, you're going to see him in a whole new light. Whenever you run into him, your hunger for him will automatically kick in."

Chloe's expression became even more serious when she said, "And you better hope Derringer doesn't find your panties. If he does find them and can't remember the woman he took them off of, he will do everything in his power to track her down."

Lucia preferred not hearing that. She gripped the handle of her cup tightly in her hand. Turning away to look out the window to view downtown Denver, she drew in a deep ragged breath before taking a sip of her coffee. She hoped Chloe was wrong. The last thing she needed was to worry about that happening.

"With his reputation with women it will be like looking for a needle in a haystack."

"Possibly. But what happens if he finds that needle?"

Lucia didn't want to think about that. She had loved Derringer secretly for so long, she wasn't sure she wanted that to change, especially when he didn't love her back.

"Lucia?"

She turned and looked at Chloe. There was a serious expression on her best friend's face. "I don't know what will happen. I don't want to think that far. I want to believe he won't remember and let it go."

A few moments passed. "What I said earlier was true. Whenever you see Derringer, you're going to want him," Chloe said softly.

She shrugged. "I've always wanted him, Clo."

"Now it will be doubly so."

Lucia opened her mouth to deny Chloe's words and

decided not to waste her time because she knew Chloe
was probably right. She had thought about him all that
day, barely getting any work done. She kept playing over
and over in her mind just what the two of them had done
together. "I will fight it," she finally said.

Chloe bristled at her words. "It won't be that simple."

She could believe that. Nothing regarding Derringer
had ever been simple for her. "Then what do you suggest
I do?" Lucia said with resignation in her voice.

"Come out of hiding once and for all and go after
him."

She wasn't surprised Chloe would advise her to do
something like that. Her best friend was the daring one.
She never hesitated in going after anything she wanted
and she'd always envied Chloe for being so bold and
brave.

Chloe must have seen the wistful look in her eyes
and kept pushing. "Go after him, Lucia. Go ahead and
take Derringer on. After last night, don't you think it's
about time you did?"

A week later, Jason Westmoreland glanced over at
his cousin and grinned. "Was that supposed to be a trick
question or something?"

Derringer shook his head as he eased back in the
chair. He'd done nothing over the past few days but stay
on his pain medication and get plenty of sleep. Each
time he awoke he would reach under his pillow and pull
out the panties he had placed there just to make sure
he hadn't dreamed the whole thing. They proved that

he hadn't. And the name Puddin' Tame, the alias the woman had given him, kept going through his mind.

This morning he woke feeling a whole lot better and decided to lay off the pills. He hoped clearing his head would trigger something in his memory about what happened a week ago. So far it hadn't.

Jason had dropped by to check on him and the two were sharing early-morning coffee at the kitchen table. "No, it's not a trick question. I figured I'd ask you first before moving on to Riley, Zane, Canyon and Stern. Afterward, I'll compare everybody's answers."

Jason inclined his head with the barest hint of a nod. "Okay, I'll give your question a shot, so go ahead and repeat it to make sure I heard you right."

Derringer rolled his eyes and then leaned closer to the table. His expression was serious. "What can you tell about a woman from the panties she wears, both style and color?"

Jason rubbed his chin a moment. "I would have to say nothing in particular unless they are white, granny-style ones."

"They aren't." He hadn't told Jason why he was asking, and Jason, the easygoing Westmoreland, wouldn't ask... There was no doubt in Derringer's mind that everyone else would.

"Then I really don't know," Jason said, taking a sip of his coffee. "I think some pieces of clothing are supposed to convey messages about people. I picked white because it usually means innocence. But then again, Fannie Nelson had on a pair of low-riding jeans one day that showed her white panties, and she is a long way from being innocent."

"Aren't you curious as to why I want to know?"

"Yes, I'm curious, but not enough to ask. I figure you have your reasons and I don't want to come close to thinking what they might be."

Derringer nodded, understanding why Jason felt that way. His cousin knew his history with women. And what Jason said was true. He had his reasons, all right.

"So what do you plan to do today now that you've returned to the world of the living? I heard the E.R. doc tell you to take it easy for at least a week or so to recuperate, so you're still under restrictions," Jason reminded him.

"Yes, but I'm not restricted from driving. I'm going to hang around here and take it easy for a few more days before venturing out anywhere."

"I'm glad you're following the doc's advice. Although things could have been worse, that was still a nasty fall you took. And as far as your question regarding women's undergarments, I suggest you talk to Zane when he gets back from Boulder." Jason chuckled and then added, "And be prepared to take notes."

Two days later Derringer left home for the first time since his accident and drove to Zane's Hideout. He was glad to see his brother's truck parked in the yard, which meant he was back. Jason was right. He should have been prepared to take notes. Zane, who was only fourteen months older but a heck of a lot wiser where women were concerned, had no qualms about telling him what he wanted to know.

According to Zane, the color and style of a woman's panties said a lot about her. Sexually liberated women wore thongs or barely-there panties, all colors except white, and they rarely wore pastel colors. Most of them preferred black.

Zane further went on to say that women who liked to tease men wore black lace. Women who preferred lace to any other design were women who liked to look and feel pretty. And bikini panties weren't as popular these days as thongs and hipsters, so a woman still wearing bikini panties weren't as sexually liberated as others.

Derringer smiled when Zane, with a serious look on his face, advised him to steer clear of women who wore granny panties. Zane furthermore claimed that women who wore red panties gave the best blow jobs. Those with yellow panties the majority of the time weren't afraid to try anything and were pretty good with a pair of handcuffs. Blue panties–wearing women were loyal to a fault—although they had a tendency to get possessive sometimes, and those who preferred wearing green were only after your money, so the use of double condoms was in order.

It had taken his brother almost an hour to make it to pink panties and, according to the Laws of Zane, women who wear pink panties were the ones you needed to stay away from because they had the word *marriage* written all over them, blasting like neon lights. They were a cross between innocent and a woman with an inner hunger for getting laid. But in the end she would still want a wedding ring on her finger.

"Okay, now that you've taken up more than an hour of my time, how about telling me why you're so interested in a woman's panties," Zane said, eyeing him curiously.

For a moment Derringer considered not telling his brother anything, but then thought better of it. He, his five brothers and all his cousins were close, but there was a special bond between him, Zane and Jason. Besides, it was evident that Zane knew a lot more about women than he did, so maybe his brother could give him some sound advice about how to handle what had occurred that night, just in case he had been set up.

"Some woman came over to my place the night I was injured and let herself in. I can't remember who she was, but I do remember making love to her."

Zane stared at him intently for a moment. "Are you absolutely sure you made love to her and didn't imagine the whole thing? When we took you home from the hospital—right before I had to take off for the airport—you were pretty high on those pain meds. Megan figured that you would probably sleep through most of the night, although she set out more medicine for you to take later."

Derringer shook his head. "Yeah, I was pretty drugged up, but I remember making love to her, Zane. And to prove I didn't dream the whole thing, I found her panties in bed with me the next morning." What he decided not to say was that as far as he was concerned, it had been the best lovemaking he'd ever experienced with a woman.

Zane drew in a deep breath and then said on a heavy sigh. "You better hope it wasn't Ashira. Hell, man, if you didn't use a condom she would love to claim you're her new baby's daddy."

Derringer rubbed the ache that had suddenly crept into his temples at the thought. "It wasn't Ashira, trust me. This woman left one hell of an impression. I've never experienced lovemaking like it before. It was off the charts. Besides, Ashira called a few days after hearing about the accident. She left town to go visit her sick grandmother in Dakota the day before the accident and won't be back for a few weeks."

"You do know there's a way for you to find out the identity of your uninvited visitor, don't you?" Zane asked.

Derringer glanced over at him. "How?"

"Did you forget about the video cameras we had installed on your property to protect the horses, the week before your fall? Anyone pulling into your yard would be captured on film if they got as far as your front porch."

Derringer blinked when he remembered the video camera and wondered why he hadn't recalled it sooner. He got up from Zane's table and swiftly strode to the door. "I need to get home and check out that tape," he said without looking back.

"What happens when you find out who she is?" Zane called out.

He slowed to a stop and glanced over his shoulder. "Whoever she is, she will be sorry." He then turned and continued walking.

He meant what he said. Thanks to Zane, the mystery might have been solved. But once Derringer discovered the woman's identity, her nightmare for what she'd done would just be beginning, he thought, getting into his truck and driving away. He had a feeling *his* nightmare would continue until he found her—their night together had been so good, it haunted his dreams.

He made it back to Derringer's Dungeon in record time, and once inside his house he immediately went to his office to log on to his computer. The technician who had installed the video camera had told him he had access to the film from any computer anywhere with his IP address. This would be the first time he had reason to view the footage since the cameras had been installed.

A year ago his Westmoreland cousins from Montana had expanded their very successful horse-breeding and training business and had invited him, Jason and Zane to join as partners. Since all three were fine horsemen—although you couldn't prove how good he was, considering what had happened on Monday—they had jumped at the chance to be included. In anticipation of the horses that would be arriving, they had decided to install cameras on all three of their properties to make sure horse thieves, which were known to pop up every so often in these parts, didn't get any ideas about stealing from a Westmoreland.

Derringer hauled in a deep breath when the computer came to life and he typed in the code to get him to the video-camera channel and almost held his breath as he searched for the date he wanted. He then sat there, with his gaze glued to the computer screen, and waited with bated breath for something to show up.

It seemed it took forever before the lights of a vehicle came into view. The time indicated it wasn't early afternoon, not quite dark, but there had been a thunderstorm brewing. He then recalled it had been raining something awful with thunder and lightning flashing all around. At one point the intensity of it had awakened him.

He squinted at the image, trying to make out the truck that turned into his yard in the torrential rain. It seemed the weather worsened and rain started to pour down on the earth the moment the vehicle pulled into his yard.

It took only a second to recall whose SUV was in focus and he could only lean back in his chair, not believing what he was seeing. The woman who got out of her truck, battling the weather before tackling the huge box on his porch by dragging it inside his place was none other than Lucia Conyers.

He shook his head trying to make heads or tails of what he was seeing. Okay, he had it now. He figured, for whatever reason, Lucia had come by—probably as a favor to Chloe—to check on him and had been kind enough to bring the box inside the house, out of the rain.

He sat there watching the computer screen, expecting her to come back out at any minute and then get in her truck and pull off. He figured once she left, another vehicle would drive up, and the occupant of that car would be the woman he'd slept with. But as he sat there for another twenty minutes or so viewing the screen, Lucia never came back out.

Lucia Conyers was his Puddin' Tame?

Derringer shook his head, thinking that there was no way. He then decided to fast-forward the tape to five o'clock the next morning. His eyes narrowed suspiciously when a few minutes later he watched his front door open and Lucia ease out of it as if she was sneaking away from the scene of some crime. And she was wearing the same clothes she had on when she'd first arrived the night before. It was obvious she had dressed hurriedly and was moving rather quickly toward her SUV.

Damn. He couldn't believe it. He wouldn't believe it if he wasn't seeing it for himself. She was the one woman he would never have suspected, not in a million years. But from the evidence he'd gotten off his video camera, Lucia was the woman he had slept with. Lucia, his sister-in-law's best friend. Lucia was innocent—at least his assumption of that had been right. His mystery lover had been Lucia, the woman who would shy away from him and act skittish whenever he came around her.

Last month he recalled hearing Chloe and his sisters tease her about this being the last year of her twenties and challenge her to write a list of everything she wanted to do before hitting the big three-oh. He couldn't help wondering if she had added something outlandish like getting pregnant before her biological clock stopped ticking or ridding herself of her virginity.

Anger filled him, seeped through every pore in his body. Lucia Conyers had a hell of a lot of explaining to do. She better have a good reason for getting into bed with him that night two weeks ago.

He pulled his cell phone out of his pocket and punched in the number to his sister-in-law's magazine.

"*Simply Irresistible,* may I help you?"

"Yes, I'd like to speak to Lucia Conyers, please," he said, trying to control his anger.

"Sorry, but Ms. Conyers just stepped out for lunch."

"Did she say where she was going?" he asked.

The receptionist paused and then asked. "Who may I ask is calling?"

"This is Mr. Westmoreland."

"Oh, Mr. Westmoreland, how are you? Your wife and baby were here a couple of days ago, and your daughter looks just like you."

Derringer shook his head. Evidently the woman thought he was Ramsey, which was okay with him if he could get the information he wanted out of her.

"I take that as a compliment. Did Lucia say where she was going for lunch?"

"Yes, sir. She's dining at McKay's today."

"Thanks."

"You're welcome, sir."

Derringer hung up the phone and leaned back in his chair as an idea formed in his mind. He wouldn't let her know he had found out the truth about her visit. He would let her assume that she had gotten away with it and that he didn't have a clue that she was the woman who'd taken advantage of him that night.

And then when she least expected it, he would play his hand.

Three

Something, Lucia wasn't sure exactly what, made her glance over her menu and look straight into the eyes of Derringer Westmoreland. She went completely still as he moved in fluid precision toward her, with an unreadable expression on his face.

Staring at him, taking him all in, all six-three of him, while broad shoulders flexed beneath a blue Western shirt, and a pair of jeans clung to him like a second layer of skin and showed the iron muscles in his thighs. And then there was his face, too handsome for words, with his medium-brown skin tone, dark coffee-colored eyes and firm and luscious-looking lips.

For the moment she couldn't move; she was transfixed. A part of her wanted to get up quickly and run in another direction, but she felt glued to the chair. But that didn't stop liquid heat from pooling between her thighs when her gaze locked onto his face and she looked at the same features she had seen almost two weeks ago in his bed.

Why was he here and approaching her table? Had he found her panties and figured out she was the woman who had left them behind? She swallowed, thinking there was no way he could have discovered her identity, but then she asked herself why else would he seek her out?

He finally came to a stop at her table and she nervously moistened her lips with the tip of her tongue. She could swear his gaze was following her every movement. She swallowed again, thinking she had to be imagining things, and opened her mouth to speak. "Derringer? What are you doing here? Chloe mentioned you had taken a nasty fall a couple of weeks ago."

"Yes, but a man has to eat sometime. I was told McKay's serves the best potpie on Thursdays for lunch and there's always a huge crowd. I saw you sitting over here alone and thought the least we can do is help the place out," he said.

She was trying hard to follow him and not focus on the way his Adam's apple moved with every word he said, as if it was on some sensuous beat. She lifted a brow. "Help the place out in what way?"

He gave her a smooth smile. "Freeing up a table by us sharing one."

Lucia was trying really hard not to show any emotion—especially utter astonishment and disbelief—as well as not to let the menu she was holding fall to the floor. Had he just suggested that they share a table during lunch? Breathe the same air?

She was tempted to pick up the glass filled with ice water and drink the whole thing in one gulp. Instead, she drew in a deep breath to stop her heart from pounding so hard in her chest. How could spending only one night in his bed cause her to want to let go of her sensibilities and play out these newfound urges at the sight of him?

Of course, there was no way she would do something like that. In fact, a part of her was shaking inside at the thought he wanted to join her for lunch. She quickly wondered how Chloe would handle the situation if she was in her place. The answer came easy, but then she wasn't Chloe. However, she had to keep her cool and respond with the confidence Chloe possessed. The confidence that she lacked.

Lucia forced a smile to her lips. "I think that's a good idea, Derringer."

His lips eased into a smile right before her eyes. "Glad you agree," he said, taking the chair across from her.

She forced herself to breathe and belatedly realized just what she'd done. She had agreed to let him sit at her table. What on earth would they have to talk about? What if she let something slip and said something really stupid like, *"Oh, by the way, when can I drop by and get the panties I left behind the other night?"*

She sighed heavily. For all she knew, he might have figured things out already. Seriously, why else would he give a royal flip whether or not McKay's was crowded for lunch? That in itself was suspect because he'd never sought out her attention before.

She glanced over at him and he smiled at her, flashing those same dimples that he'd flashed that night she almost melted in her chair. He looked the same, only thing was that his eyes no longer had a hungover look. Today his gaze was as clear as glass.

The waitress saved them from talking when she walked up to take both their lunch orders. When she left, Lucia wished she had a mirror to see how she looked. She would die if she didn't at least look halfway decent. Absently, she ran a finger through her hair and pressed her lips together. She was grateful to feel her lipstick still in place, although she was tempted to get the tube of lipstick from her purse and apply a fresh coat.

"I understand you're back in school."

She was watching his mouth and his lips moved. She realized he'd said something. "Excuse me?"

He smiled again. "I said I heard you were back in school."

"Yes, I am. How did you know?"

"Chloe mentioned it."

"Oh." She wondered why Chloe would mention such a thing unless he'd asked about her. Had he? She shook her head, finding the idea unlikely. Her name must have popped up for conversational purposes and nothing more than that. If there had been anything more, Chloe definitely would have told her.

"Yes, I'm back at school taking night classes to get my master's degree in mass communications." Then, without missing a beat, she said, "You seem to be doing well from your fall." No sooner had the words left her mouth than she wished she could take them back.

Why on earth would she bring up anything relating to that day?

"Yes, but I'm doing better now. I've been taking it easy for the past week or so and sleeping most of the time. It helped. I feel in pretty good shape now."

She didn't know how to tell him that as far as she was concerned, he'd been in pretty good shape that night as well. His movements hadn't been hindered in any way. The thought of all he'd done to her sent heat soaring all through her body.

"So, what else have you been up to lately?"

Lucia felt her heart give a loud thump in her chest and wondered if he'd heard it. Dragging her gaze from her silverware, she thought that she could remember in vivid detail just what she'd been up to lately with him. Sitting across from her was the man who'd taken her virginity. The man who'd introduced her to the kind of pleasure she'd only read about in romance novels, and the man whom she'd loved forever. And knowing he probably had no idea of any of those things was the epitome of insane. But somehow she would fake it and come off looking like the most poised person that ever existed.

"Not a whole lot," she heard herself saying. "School and the magazine keep me pretty busy, but because I enjoy doing both I won't complain. What about you?" His gaze seemed to linger on her lips.

He chuckled. "Other than making a fool of myself with Sugar Foot, I haven't been up to a whole lot either."

She inclined her head. "What on earth would entice

you to ride that horse? I think everyone has heard how mean he is."

He chuckled and the sound was a low, sexy rumble that made goose bumps form on her arms. "Ego. I figured if Casey could do it then so could I."

She knew his cousin Casey and her husband, along with his cousin Durango and his wife, Savannah, had come visiting a few weekends ago. She'd heard everyone had been amazed at the ease with which Casey had gotten on Sugar Foot's back and held on even when the horse had been determined to get her off.

"I'm a pretty good horseman," Derringer said, breaking into her thoughts. "Although I'd be the first to admit I wasn't personally trained by the renowned and legendary Sid Roberts like Casey and her brothers while growing up."

Lucia nodded. His cousins Casey, Cole and Clint were triplets, and she had heard that they had lived with Roberts, their maternal uncle, while growing up. "We can all learn from the mistakes we make," she said, taking a sip of her water to cool off.

"Yes, we sure can."

Deciding she needed to escape, if only for a short moment, Lucia stood. "Would you excuse me for a moment? I need to go to the ladies' room."

"Sure, no problem," he said, standing.

Lucia drew in a deep breath, wishing she was walking out the restaurant door with no intention of returning and not just escaping to the ladies' room. And as she continued walking, she could actually feel Derringer staring at her back.

* * *

Derringer watched Lucia leave, thinking she looked downright sexy in her below-the-knee skirt and light blue pullover sweater. And then he couldn't help but admire her small waistline and the flare of her hips in the skirt as she walked. Standing about five-seven, she had a pair of nice-looking black leather boots on her feet, but he could recall just what a nice pair of legs she had and remembered how those legs had felt wrapped around him the night they'd made love.

He would be the first to admit that he'd always thought Lucia was pretty, with her smooth brown skin and lustrous shoulder-length black hair that she usually wore pulled back in a ponytail. Then there were her hazel eyes, high cheekbones, cute chin and slim nose. And he couldn't forget her luscious-looking mouth, one that could probably do a lot of wicked things to a man.

He leaned back in his chair remembering how years ago when she'd been about eighteen—about to leave home for college—and he had been in the process of moving back home from university, she had caught his eye. In memory of his parents and his aunt and uncle, who'd died together in a plane crash while he was in high school, the Westmorelands held a charity ball every year to raise money for the Westmoreland Foundation, which had been founded to aid various community causes. Lucia had attended the ball that year with her parents.

He had been standing by the punch bowl when she had arrived, and the sight of her in the dress she'd been wearing that night had rendered him breathless. He hadn't been able to take his eyes off her all evening. Evidently others had noticed his interest, and one of those had been her father, Dusty Conyers.

Later that same night the older man had pulled him aside and warned him away from his daughter. He let Derringer know in no uncertain terms that he would not tolerate a Westmoreland sniffing behind his daughter, creating the kind of trouble that Carl Newsome was having with Derringer's cousin Bane.

Bane had had the hots for Crystal Newsome since junior high school, and since Bane had a penchant for getting into trouble, Newsome hadn't wanted him anywhere near his daughter. Unfortunately, Crystal had other ideas and had been just as hot for Bane as he'd been for her, and Crystal and Bane managed to get into all kinds of naughty trouble together. Once, they'd even tried their hand at eloping before Carl Newsome had found his daughter and shipped her off to heaven knows where. A brokenhearted Bane had decided to take charge of his life by going into the Navy.

Derringer knew that although he didn't have Bane's badass reputation, he was still a Westmoreland, and a lot of mamas and daddies were dead set on protecting their daughters from what they thought was a Westmoreland heartbreak just waiting to happen. A part of him couldn't fault Dusty Conyers for being one of them; especially since Derringer had made it known far and wide that he had no plans to settle down with any one woman. A wife was the last thing on his mind then as well as now. Making a success of the horse-training business he'd just started was his top priority.

"I'm back."

He glanced up and stood for her to sit and thought that Lucia was even more beautiful up close. She had a nervous habit of licking her lips with her tongue. He would do just about anything to replace her tongue with his the next time she did it. And he also liked the sound of her voice. She spoke in a quiet yet sexy tone that did things to his insides, and he decided to keep her talking every chance he got.

"Tell me about the classes you're taking at the university and why you decided to go back and get your master's degree."

She lifted a brow and then her lips curved into one of her smiles again. Evidently, he'd hit on a subject she liked talking about. "Although Chloe hasn't made any announcements about anything, I can see her spending less and less time with *Simply Irresistible*. Whenever she does come into the office she has the baby with her, and it's obvious that she prefers being home with Susan and Ramsey."

He nodded, thinking he'd had that same impression as well. Whenever he paid Ramsey and Chloe a visit, they appeared to be a content and very happy couple who thoroughly enjoyed being parents. He'd heard from his other brothers that already Ramsey and Chloe were thinking about having another child.

"And I want to be prepared if she decides to take a leave of absence for a while," Lucia continued. "She and I talked about it, and because my bachelor's degree was in business, we thought it would be a good idea for me to get a degree in communications as well."

The waitress chose that moment to return with their

food, and once the plates had been placed in front of them, she left.

"I understand Gemma is adjusting to life in Australia."

He couldn't help but smile. Although he missed his sister, it seemed from all the phone calls they got that she *was* adjusting to life in Australia. He'd known Callum, the man who used to be the manager of Ramsey's sheep farm, had loved Gemma for a while, even if his sister had been clueless. He'd always known Callum's feelings for Gemma had been the real thing and not for the sole purpose of getting her into bed. He'd wholeheartedly approved of Gemma and Callum's relationship.

"Yes, I talked to her a few days ago. She and Callum are planning to come home for the Westmoreland Charity Ball at the end of the month." He wondered if she planned to go and if so, if she already had a date.

"Are you dating anyone seriously?" he decided to ask and set his plan into motion.

She looked over at him after popping a strawberry into her luscious mouth, chewed on it a moment, and then she swallowed it before replying. "The only dates I have these days are with my schoolbooks."

"Um, what a pity, that doesn't sound like a lot of fun. How about a movie this weekend?"

She cocked a surprised eyebrow. "A movie?"

He could tell his suggestion had surprised her. "Yes, a movie. Evidently, you're not spending enough time having fun, and everyone needs to let loose now and then. There's a new Tyler Perry movie coming out this weekend that I want to see. Would you like to go with me?"

Lucia's heart began pounding in her chest as she quickly reached the conclusion that Derringer had to have figured out that she was the woman who'd brazenly shared his bed. What other reason could he have for asking her out? Why the sudden interest in her when he'd never shown any before?

Their eyes held for what seemed like several electrifying moments before she finally broke eye contact with him. But what if he *didn't* know, and asking her out was merely a coincidence? There was only one way to find out. She glanced back over at him and saw he was still staring at her with that unreadable expression of his. "Why do you want to take me out, Derringer?"

He gave her a smooth smile. "I told you. You're spending too much time studying and working and need to have a little fun."

She still wasn't buying it. "We've known each other for years. Yet you've never asked me out before. In fact, you've never shown any interest."

He chuckled. "It wasn't that I didn't want to show an interest, Lucia, but I love my life and all my body parts."

She raised a brow and paused with the fork halfway to her mouth. "What do you mean?"

He took a sip of his iced tea and then his mouth curved ruefully. "I was warned away from you early on and took the warning seriously."

She nearly dropped the fork from her hand and had

to tighten her grip to place it back down. "What do you mean you were warned away from me?" That was impossible. She'd never had a boyfriend jealous enough to do such a thing.

A grin flashed across his face. "Your dad knows how to scare a man off, trust me."

Her head began spinning at the same time her heart slammed hard against her rib cage. "My dad warned you away from me?"

He smiled. "Yes, and I took him seriously. It was the summer you were about to leave for college. You were eighteen and I was twenty-two and returning home from university. You attended the Westmoreland Charity Ball with your parents before you left. He saw me checking you out, probably thought my interest wasn't honorable, and pulled me aside and told me to keep my eyes to myself or else…"

Lucia swallowed. She knew her dad. His bark was worse than his bite, but most people didn't know that. "Or else what?"

"Or else my eyes, along with another body part I'd rather not mention, would get pulled from their sockets. The last thing he would put up with was a Westmoreland dating his daughter."

Lucia didn't know whether to laugh or cry. She could see her father making a threat like that because he was overprotective of her. But she doubted Derringer knew how much his words thrilled her. He had been checking her out when she was eighteen?

She nervously moistened her lips with the tip of her tongue and couldn't help noticing the movement of his gaze to her mouth. Her skin began burning at the thought that he had been attracted to her even when she hadn't had a clue. But still…

"Aw, come on, Derringer, that was more than ten years ago," she said in a teasing tone.

"Yes, but you probably don't recall a few years ago I dropped by the paint store to make a purchase and you were working behind the counter and waited on me."

Oh, she definitely remembered that day, and three years later hadn't been able to forget it. But of course she couldn't tell him that. "That was a long time ago, but I think I remember that day. You needed a can of paint thinner." She could probably tell him what brand it was and exactly how much he'd paid for it.

"Yes, well, I had planned to ask you out then, but Mr. Conyers gave me a look that reminded me of the conversation we'd had years before and that his opinion of me pursuing you hadn't changed."

She couldn't help but laugh and it felt good. He had actually wanted to talk to her then, too. "I can't believe you were afraid of Dad."

"Believe it, sweetheart. He can give you a look that lets you know he means business. And it didn't help that he and Bane had had a run-in a few years before when Bane swiped a can of paint on display in front of the store and used it to paint some not-so-nice graffiti all over the front of Mr. Milner's feed store and signed off by saying it was a present from your father."

Lucia wiped tears of laughter from her eyes. "I was away at college, but I heard about that. Mom wrote and told me all the details. You're right, Dad was upset and so was Mr. Milner. Your cousin Bane had a reputation for getting into all kinds of trouble. How are things going with him and the Navy?"

"He's doing fine at the Naval Academy. It's hard to believe he's been gone for almost two years already, but he has."

"And he hasn't been back since he left?"

Derringer shook his head sadly. "No, not even once. He refuses to come back knowing Crystal isn't here, and he's still angry that he doesn't know where she is. The Newsomes made sure of that before they moved away. We are hoping he'll eventually forget her and move on, but so far he hasn't."

In a way, she knew how Bane felt. She hadn't looked forward to returning to Denver either, knowing she was still harboring feelings for Derringer. It was hard running into him while he was dating other girls and wishing they were her. And now to find out they could have been her. Her father had no idea what he'd done and the sad thing was that she couldn't get mad at him. Bane hadn't been the only Westmoreland with a reputation that had made it hard on the other family members. Derringer's younger brothers—the twins, Adrian and Aidan—as well as his baby sister Bailey had been Bane's sidekicks and had gotten into just as much trouble.

Needless to say, it had gotten to the point everyone in town would get up in arms when they saw any Westmoreland headed their way. But she had heard her father say more than once lately that considering everything, he thought Dillon and Ramsey had done a pretty good job in raising their siblings and in keeping the family together, and that he actually admired them

for it. She knew that several people in town did. All
the Westmorelands were college-educated and in some
sort of business for themselves or holding prestigious
jobs. And together they were the wealthiest family in
the county and the largest landowners. People no longer
feared them, they highly respected them.

"Just look how things turned out, Derringer," she
heard herself say. "The twins are at Harvard. Bailey
will be finishing up her studies at the university here in
a year, and Bane is in the hands of Uncle Sam. Ramsey
mentioned that Bane wants to become a Navy SEAL.
In that case, he has to learn discipline, among other
things."

Derringer chuckled. "For Bane, even with Uncle
Sam, that won't be easy to do." He picked up his glass
to take a sip of his iced tea. "So do we have a date for
Saturday night or what?"

A date with Derringer Westmoreland…

She couldn't stop herself from feeling all giddy
inside. She almost trembled at the thought. But at the
same time she knew she had to be realistic. He would
take her out on Saturday night and probably some other
girl on Sunday. He'd asked her out to the movies, not a
trip to Vegas to get married.

She would take the date for what it was and not put
too much stock in it. She hadn't been born yesterday and
she knew Derringer's reputation around town. He dated
a lot, but let it be known that he didn't like women who
clung or got too possessive.

Still, she couldn't help but smile at the thought
that he was attracted to her and had been since she

was eighteen. Didn't that account for something? She decided that it did.

"Yes, I'd love to go to the movies with you Saturday night, Derringer."

Four

Derringer frowned the moment he pulled into his yard and saw his sister Bailey's car parked there. The last thing he needed was for her to drop by to play nursemaid again. Megan was bad enough, but his baby sister Bailey was worse. She had only been seven when their parents had gotten killed. Now at twenty-two, she attended college full-time, and when she didn't have her nose stuck in some book it was stuck in her five brothers' personal affairs. She liked making it her business to know anything and everything about their comings and goings. Now that Ramsey was married, she'd given him some slack, but she hadn't let up with him, Zane and the twins.

He wondered how long she'd been there waiting on him and figured she probably wouldn't like the fact that he hadn't been home and had driven into town.

Since she wasn't out on the porch, that meant she had let herself inside, which wouldn't be a hard thing to do since he never locked his doors. His sister flung open the door the moment his foot touched the step. The look on her face let him know he was in trouble. She was there when the doctor restricted him from doing almost anything, other than breathing and eating, for two weeks.

"Just where have you been, Derringer Westmoreland, in your condition?"

He walked past her to put his hat on the rack. "And what condition is that, Bailey?"

"You're injured."

"Yes, but I'm not dead."

He regretted the words the moment they left his mouth when he saw the expression that suddenly appeared on her face. He and his brothers knew the real reason Bailey was so overprotective of them was that she was afraid of losing them the way she'd lost their parents.

But he could admit to having the same fears, and if he were to analyze things further, he would probably conclude that Zane had them as well. All of them had been close to their parents, aunt and uncle. Everyone had taken their deaths hard. The way Derringer had managed to move on, and not look back, was by not getting too attached to anyone. He had his cousins and his siblings. He loved them, and they were all he needed. If he were to fall in love, give his heart to a woman, and then something were to happen to her—there was no telling how he'd handle it, or even if he could. He liked things just the way they were. And, for that reason, he doubted he would ever marry.

He crossed the room and placed a hand on her shoulder when he saw her trembling. "Hey, come on, Bail, it wasn't that bad. You were there at the hospital and heard what Dr. Epps said. It's been almost two weeks now and I'm fine."

"But I also heard him say that it could have been worse, Derringer."

"But it wasn't. Look, unless you came to cook for me or do my laundry, you can visit some other time. I'm going to take a nap."

He saw the sad look on her face turn mutinous and knew his ploy had worked. She didn't like it when he bossed her around or came across as if she was at his beck and call. "Cook your own damn meals and do your own laundry, or get one of those silly girls who fawn all over you to do it."

"Whatever. And watch your mouth, Bailey, or I'll think you're slipping back to your old ways and I'll have to wash your mouth out with soap."

She grabbed the remote off the table, dropped down on the sofa and began watching television, ignoring him. He glanced at his watch and fought to hide his smile. "So, how long are you staying?" he asked. Because she hadn't yet inherited her one hundred acres, she had a tendency to spend time at any of their places. Most of the time she stayed with Megan, which suited all her brothers just fine because Bailey had a tendency to drop in unannounced at the most inconvenient times.

Like now.

She didn't even look over at him when she finally

answered his question. "I'm staying until I'm ready to leave. You have a problem with it?"

"No."

"Good," she said, using the remote to flip to another channel. "Now go take your nap and I hope when you wake up you're in a lot better mood."

He chuckled as he leaned down and planted a brotherly kiss on her forehead. "Thanks for worrying about me so much, kid," he said softly.

"If me, Megan and Gemma don't do it, who will? All those silly girls you mess around with are only after your money."

He lifted a brow in mock surprise. "You think so?"

She glanced up at him and rolled her eyes. "If you don't know the truth about them then you're in real trouble, Derringer."

Derringer chuckled again thinking yes, he knew the truth about them...especially one in particular. Lucia Conyers. He didn't think of her as one of those "silly girls" and knew Bailey wouldn't either. He would be taking Lucia to the movies Saturday night. He intended to return her panties to her then. He looked forward to the moment her mouth fell open and she realized he knew what she'd done and had known all this time. He couldn't wait to see what excuse she would come up with for what she had done.

Before heading up the stairs, he decided to feel his sister out about something. "I ran into Lucia Conyers a few moments ago at McKay's."

Bailey didn't take her gaze off the television and for a moment he thought that possibly she hadn't heard him, but then she responded. "And?"

He smiled. "And we shared a table since McKay's was crowded." He paused a moment. "She's pretty. I never realized just how pretty she is." The latter he knew wasn't true, because he'd always known how pretty she was.

He watched as Bailey slowly turned toward him with a frown on her face. "I hope you're not thinking what I think you're thinking."

He smiled. "Oh, I don't know. What do you think I'm thinking?"

"That you plan to hit on Lucia."

He grinned. "If by 'hit on her' you mean ask her out, I've already done so. We have a date to go to the movies this Saturday night."

Bailey's eyes widened. "Are you crazy? That's Chloe's best friend."

Now it was his turn. "And?"

"And everybody around these parts knows how most of the single male Westmorelands operate. You're used to those silly girls and wouldn't know how to appreciate a woman with sense like Lucia."

"You don't think so?"

"I know so and if you end up doing something stupid like hurting her, Chloe would never forgive you for it."

He shrugged at the thought. Chances were, Chloe had no idea what her best friend had pulled that night. And as far as what Bailey said about Lucia's having sense, he didn't doubt that, which made him uneasy about just what she would gain from tumbling into bed with him.

"Lucia is an adult. She can handle me," he said.

He wouldn't break it down and tell her that Lucia *had* handled him and had done a real good job doing so. He got a hard-on every time he thought about that night.

"I'm still warning you, Derringer. And besides being Chloe's best friend, Megan, Gemma and I like her as well."

He cocked an amused brow. "I guess that means a lot. The three of you never like any of the girls I date. I'll have to keep that in mind."

Without giving his kid sister time to say anything else, he quickly moved up the stairs for his nap.

Lucia couldn't wait to get back to her office to give Chloe a call and tell her about her date on Saturday night with Derringer.

"I'm happy for you," Chloe said with a smile in her voice that Lucia heard. "Falling off that horse must have knocked some sense into him. At least you know why he never approached you before. I can see your dad warning him off. I heard the Westmorelands had quite a reputation back in the day."

Lucia nodded. "And you think I did the right thing in agreeing to go out with him?"

"Come on, Lucia, don't you dare ask me that. You've loved the guy forever. You've even gone so far as to sleep with him."

She drew in a deep, ragged breath. "But he doesn't know that. At least I don't think he does."

"You honestly think he doesn't know?"

"I assumed he did and that was the only reason he wanted to share my table."

She heard Chloe bristle at that assumption. "Why

do you continue to think you're no match for Derringer when you're classier than all those other women he messes around with?"

"But that's just it, Chloe. I'm not the kind of woman he prefers, the kind he has a history of dating. I can't hold a candle to someone like Ashira Lattimore. And everyone knows she has been vying for his attention for years."

"I've met her and she's spoiled, self-centered, possessive and clingy. Definitely not wife material."

"Wife material?" Lucia laughed. "A wife is the furthest thing from Derringer's mind. You know that as well as I do."

"Yes, but I'm sure a lot of people said the same thing about Ramsey before I arrived on the scene. So that means a man's mind can change with the right woman. All you have to do is convince Derringer you're the right woman."

Lucia cringed at the thought of trying to do that. She wouldn't even know where to begin. "That's easy for you to say and do, Chloe. You've always been sure of yourself in everything you did."

"In that case, maybe you ought to try it for yourself. Just think, Lucia. Evidently Derringer is on your hook and now you have the chance to reel him right on in. You know how I feel about missed opportunities. How would things have turned out had I accepted Ramsey's refusal to be on the cover of my magazine? I saw what I wanted and decided to go after it. I think you should use that same approach."

"I don't know," Lucia said on a heavy sigh. This wasn't the first time Chloe had made that suggestion.

A part of her knew her friend was right, but what she was suggesting was easier said than done. At least for her it was.

"Think about it. Saturday is only two days away and if I were you, when Derringer arrived at my place to pick me up I'd make sure he would take one look at me and know he would enjoy every minute of his time in my presence. Now's your chance, Lucia. Don't let it go by without taking advantage of it."

A few moments later, after hanging up the phone with Chloe, indecisiveness weighed heavy in her chest. More than anything she would love to pique Derringer's interest, but what if she failed in her efforts to do so? What if she couldn't get the one man she loved to want to love her back? Was there a possibility that she was wrong about the type of women Derringer actually preferred?

One thing Chloe had said was true. No one would have figured that Ramsey Westmoreland would have fallen for any woman. The man had been set in his ways for years and the last woman he'd attempted to marry had announced she was pregnant from another man in the middle of the wedding. Yet, he had fallen in love with Chloe, whether he had wanted to or not. So maybe there was hope for all those other single Westmorelands; but especially for Derringer.

"I've heard you're interested in women's under-garments these days, Derringer. Is there a reason why?"

Derringer slowly turned away from the pool table with a cue stick in his hand to gaze at each man in the dimly lit room inside his basement. Now that he knew who his late-night visitor had been, he wouldn't tell anyone, not even Zane, her identity.

"No reason," he answered his cousin Canyon who was four years younger.

Canyon smiled. "Well, you never got around to asking me anything, but just so you know, the women I date don't wear underwear."

Derringer shook his head and chuckled. He didn't find that hard to believe. He studied the other men who had gone back to sipping their beers while waiting their turn at shooting pool—his brother Zane and his cousins Jason, Riley, Canyon and Stern. They were as close as brothers. Zane knew more than the others about the situation with him and the underwear, but Derringer was confident his brother wouldn't say anything.

"So, what's this I hear about you going on a date with Lucia? I thought old man Conyers pretty much scared you off her years ago," Jason said, chuckling.

Derringer couldn't help but smile. "He did, but like you said, it was years ago. Lucia isn't a kid anymore. She's an adult and old enough to make her own decisions about who she wants to date."

"True, but she's not your type and you know it," Riley piped in.

Derringer lifted a brow. That was the same thing Bailey had alluded to earlier that day. "And what, supposedly, is my type?"

"Women who wear black panties," Canyon said, chuckling.

"Or no panties at all," Riley added, laughing.

"Hmm, for all you all know, my taste in women

might have changed," he said, turning back to the pool table.

Zane snorted. "Since when? Since you got thrown off Sugar Foot's back and hit your head?"

Derringer frowned as he turned back around. "I didn't hit my head."

"Makes us wonder," Riley said. "First you're going around asking about women's underwear and now you're taking Lucia Conyers out on a date. You better treat her right or Chloe will come gunning for you."

"Hell, we'll all come gunning for you," Zane said, taking a sip of his beer. "We like her."

Derringer turned back to the pool table and proceeded to chalk his stick. At the moment, he didn't give a royal flip how his family felt about Lucia. He still planned to deal with her in his own way and if they didn't like the outcome that was too bad.

Five

By the time seven o'clock came around on Saturday night, Lucia was almost a nervous wreck. She had pulled her father aside that week to verify what Derringer had told her. With a sheepish grin on his face, Dusty Conyers hadn't denied a thing, and had laughingly agreed he had intentionally put the fear of God in Derringer. He didn't regret doing so and was glad it had worked.

He did agree that now she was old enough to handle her own business and wouldn't butt in again. She had ended up giving him a kiss on his bald head after telling him how much she loved him, and that he was the best dad in the whole wide world.

His confirmation meant that what Derringer had said the other day was true. He had shown interest in her years ago, but her father had discouraged him. Although she knew she would always wonder how things might have gone if her father hadn't intervened, she was a firm believer that things happened for a reason. Besides, at eighteen she doubted she would have been able to handle the likes of Derringer Westmoreland and was even doubtful she could have at twenty-two. She wasn't even confident she had the ability to handle him now, but was determined to try. She was convinced there was a reason she had shared his bed that night.

She just wished she had a clue what that reason was.

She was grateful that one didn't have anything to do with the other. The reason he had asked her out had nothing to do with them sleeping together and she felt good about that. She had played the details of their night together over and over in her mind so many times that she knew practically every single movement by heart.

All week she had found herself going to bed but unable to sleep until she replayed in her mind every sensation she'd felt that night. It didn't take much to remember how it felt to grip his iron-steel shoulders beneath her fingers while he thrust in and out of her. The thought of making love with a man like Derringer sent sensuous chills up her spine.

She knew the exact moment Derringer pulled into her driveway. From the smooth hum of the engine she could tell he was driving his two-seater sports car instead of his truck. That meant the car's interior would be that much cozier. The thought of being in such proximity to Derringer stirred all kinds of feelings inside.

She had spoken to Chloe earlier and her best friend had said the Westmorelands were torn as to whether or not her dating Derringer was a good idea, considering his history with women. Bottom line was that no one wanted to see her get hurt. But what they didn't know was that she had loved Derringer so long that to her tonight was really a dream come true. And if he never asked her out again that would be fine because she would always have memories of tonight to add to those she had of that Monday night. Not that she expected things would get as heated tonight as they had in his bedroom, mind you. But she couldn't wait to see what was in store for her tonight. Just knowing she was Derringer's date made her feel good inside, and knowing he had no ulterior motive in taking her out made it that much more special.

Derringer smiled when he pulled into Lucia's driveway, thinking her house was the brightest on the block with floodlights in every corner, the porch light on and a light pole shining in the front of the yard. He thought it was a real nice neighborhood with beautiful trees on both sides of the street and the silhouette of mountains in the background. But he felt crowded. One of the pitfalls of being a Westmoreland was that because each of them owned a hundred acres of land, living anywhere else would seem restrictive and too confining.

As he walked up to the porch, he felt as if he was under the bright lights and wouldn't be surprised if some of her neighbors were watching him. In fact, he was certain he saw the front curtain move in the house across the street. He chuckled, thinking if she could deal with her nosy neighbors then he certainly could.

Besides, he had enough on his plate dealing with his own nosy relatives. Maybe it had been a bad idea to mention his date to Bailey. She hadn't wasted time spreading the word. He'd gotten a number of calls warning him he had best behave tonight—whatever that meant. And yet, the one call he'd expected, the one from Chloe, had never come. That made him wonder if she knew a lot more than he thought she did.

He glanced at his watch before ringing Lucia's doorbell. It was seven-thirty exactly. He'd made good time and since he'd already reserved tickets online, they wouldn't have to stand in line at the theater. He had thought of everything, including when would be the best time to drop the bomb on her about that night. He had decided that they would enjoy the movie first before dealing with any unpleasantness.

He heard the lock turn on her door and then seconds later she was standing there, illuminated in the doorway. He blinked in surprise when he gazed down at her. She looked different. She'd always been a pretty girl, but tonight she looked absolutely stunning.

Gone was the ponytail. Instead, her hair was curled and fell in feathered waves to her shoulders. And she had done something with her eyes that made them look more striking and the entire look somehow showcased her dazzling sophistication.

And then there was the outfit she was wearing. Not too daring, but enough to keep him on the edge all evening. Her sweater dress was a plum color and she had black suede boots on her feet. She wasn't overly dressed for the movie and he thought her attire was perfect... and it fit her just that way, emphasizing her small waist, and falling above the knees, it definitely showed off a beautiful pair of thighs encased in tights.

A second passed and then several before he was able to open his mouth to speak, and from the smile that touched her lips she was well aware of the effect she was having on him. He couldn't help but smile back. She had definitely pulled one over on him. Gone was just the "pretty" Lucia and in her place stood a creature so gorgeous that she took his breath away.

"Derringer."

He exhaled an even breath. At least he tried to. "Lucia."

"I just need to get my jacket. Would you like to come in for a second?" she asked.

He felt another smile pull at his lips. She was inviting him in. "Sure."

When he brushed by her, he almost buckled to his knees when he took a whiff of her perfume. It was the same scent he had awakened to that Tuesday morning. The same scent that was all in his head. She was the one woman who had him sleeping each night with her panties under his pillow. He took in a deep breath to pull more of the fragrance into his nostrils. There was just something potent about the scent of a woman.

"Would you like a drink before we leave?"

"No, but thanks for the offer," he said, glancing around her living room.

"It won't take but a minute to grab my jacket."

"Take your time," he said, watching as she walked away, appreciating her movements in the dress, especially how it fit her from behind. He forced his gaze away from her when she entered her bedroom and continued his study of her house, thinking it was small but just the right size for her. And it was tidy, not a single thing out of place, even the magazines on the table seemed to lie in a perfect position. He liked her fireplace and could imagine how it would look with a fire blazing in it. He could imagine her on the floor, stretched out in front of it on one of those days that was cold, snowy and dreary outside.

On the drive over, he did notice that this particular subdivision was centrally located to just about every-thing; shopping, fast-food places, grocery stores and a dry cleaner. That had to be pretty advantageous to her. He rolled his eyes wondering why the heck he cared if it was or not.

"I'm ready now, Derringer."

He turned and glanced back at her. She was standing beside a floor lamp and the lighting totally captured her beauty. For a moment he just stood there and stared, unable to tear his gaze away from her. What the hell was wrong with him? He knew the answer when he felt blood rush straight to his groin. It would be so easy for him to suggest that they forget about the movie and hang here instead. But he knew he couldn't do that.

However, there was something he could do, some-thing he definitely felt compelled to do at that moment. He slowly moved toward her with his heart pounding hard in his chest with every step he took. And when he stood directly in front of her, he said the only words he could say at that moment. Words he knew were totally true. "You look simply beautiful tonight, Lucia."

Lucia didn't know what to say. His compliment caused soothing warmth to spread all through her. In the back of her mind something warned her that the man was smooth, sophisticated and experienced. Like most men, he would say just about anything to score. But at that moment she didn't care. The compliment had come from Derringer Westmoreland and to her that meant everything.

"Thank you, Derringer."

He lowered his head a little, bent low to murmur in her ear, "You're so very welcome."

He kept his head lowered to that angle and she knew without a shadow of a doubt that he intended to kiss her. And that knowledge caused several heated anticipatory sensations to flow from the toes of her feet to the crown of her head.

"Lucia?"

The throaty tone of his voice seemed to stroke everything within her and was doing so effortlessly.

"Yes?"

He lifted his hand to cradle her chin and tilt her face up to his. Her pulse rate increased when a slow smile touched his lips the moment their eyes connected. "I need to kiss you." And before she could draw her next breath, he lowered his mouth to hers.

He had kissed her that night numerous times in the throes of passion, but she immediately thought this kiss was different. The passion was still there, but unlike before it wasn't flaming out of control. What he was doing was slowly and deliberately robbing her senses of any and all control.

His tongue eased between her lips on a breathless moan and he seemed in no hurry to do anything but stand there, feed on every angle of her mouth, every nook and cranny. His kiss burned her in its wake, sharing its heat. He tasted like the peppermint candy he'd obviously been sucking on earlier.

But now he was sucking on her—her tongue at least; and he wasn't letting up as he probed deeply, gently but thoroughly, plunging her into an oasis of sensations as his tongue continued to sweep over her mouth.

She felt something roll around in her belly at the same time he moved his body closer, and automatically the cradle of her thighs nestled the hard erection pressing against her, causing an ache that was so engaging she couldn't do anything but moan.

This was the sort of kiss most men left a girl with after a date and not before the start of their evening. But evidently no one told that to Derringer and he was showing her there was no particular order in the way he did things. He made his own rules, set his own parameters. Now she knew why he was so high in demand with women, and why fathers warned him not to pursue their daughters. And why heat could resonate off his body like nobody's business.

But tonight he was making it her *business.*

He shifted the intensity of the kiss without warning and the hands that were already wrapped around her waist tightened in a possessive grip. The probing of his tongue deepened and she could only stand there and continue to moan while her pulse throbbed erratically in her throat. Her hips moved instinctively against his and the heat that spread lower all through her belly didn't slow down any.

There was no telling how long they would have stood there, going at each other's mouths, if she hadn't pulled back for air. She closed her eyes and took a deep breath, licking her lips and and tasting him on her tongue. The pleasure she felt just being kissed by him was almost unbearable. She slowly opened her eyes to calm the turbulent emotions inside her.

For the second time that night, his hand lifted to capture her chin, lifting her face to meet his gaze. The look in his eyes was dark, intense, sexually hungry. At that moment, he looked as rugged as the landscape in which he lived. Westmoreland country. She never realized until now just how much that had defined him. She continued to hold his gaze. Mesmerized. Falling deeper and deeper in love.

"You, Lucia Conyers, are more than I bargained for," he said in a deep, husky tone that sounded intimate and overwhelming at the same time.

She chuckled unevenly while wondering if this was how a kiss could easily get out of hand. Was this how a couple could take a kiss to another level without realizing they'd done so until it was too late to do anything about it?

"Is being more than you bargained for a good thing or a bad thing, Derringer?" she asked him.

He laughed softly at her question and released her chin, but not before lowering his head and brushing his lips across hers. "I'll let you decide that later," he whispered hotly against her lips. "Come on. Let's get out of here while we can."

Tonight was not going the way he'd planned, Derringer thought. Even the smell of popcorn couldn't get rid of her scent. His nostrils were inflamed with it. This was their first date and he had fully intended for it to be their last.

But…

And there was a *but* in there someplace. For him there were probably several and each of them were messing with his mind. Making him not want to end their evening together. Or to spoil just how good things were going between them.

After the movie he suggested they go to Torie's for coffee. She was everything a man could appreciate in a date, while at the same time not fully what a man expected—but in a positive way. She had the ability to ease into a conversation that wasn't just about her. And as he maneuvered his sports car through downtown Denver, he quickly reached the conclusion that he liked the sound of her voice and in the close confines of the car, her scent continued to overtake his senses.

Derringer couldn't help but wonder if there was something with this "scent of a woman" theory that men often talked about behind closed doors and in dimly lit, whiskey-laden poolrooms. Over his lifetime he had encountered a lot of women who smelled good, but the one sitting next to him right now, whose eyes were closed as she took in the sound of John Legend on his CD player, not only smelled good but was good to smell. And he decided then and there that there was a difference. He chuckled and shook his head at his conclusion.

"Um, what's so funny?" she asked, opening her eyes and turning her head to glance over at him.

"I was just thinking about the movie," he lied, knowing there was no way he would tell her what really had amused him.

She laughed lazily. "It was good, wasn't it?"

When the car slowed in traffic, he gave her a sidelong glance. "Yes, it was. Are you comfortable?"

"Yes. And thanks. This car is nice."

"Glad you like it." He was certain his smile flashed in the dimly lit interior. He appreciated any woman who liked his car. A number of his former dates had complained that although his car was sleek and fast, it was not roomy enough.

"Can you believe they are expecting snow next weekend?"

He chuckled. "Hey, this is Denver. Snowstorms are always expected." They passed a moment in silence. "Did you enjoy living in Florida those four years?"

She nodded. "Immensely."

"Then why did you return to Denver?"

She didn't answer right away. "Because I couldn't imagine living anywhere else," she said finally.

He nodded, understanding completely. Although he had enjoyed living in Phoenix while attending college, he never could wait to return home...to see her again. He hadn't been back a week when Ramsey had sent him into town to pick up a can of paint thinner and he'd seen her again.

At first he'd been taken aback, nearly not recognizing her. She had gone from the gangly young girl to a twentysomething-year-old woman who had grown into a beauty that he had noticed right away. It was a good thing her father had been on guard and had intervened again, because there was no telling where his lustful

BRENDA JACKSON   79

mind would have led him that day. She had gotten spared from being added to the list as one of Derringer's Pleasers. When he'd returned home it seemed women had come out of the woodwork vying for his attention.

They soon arrived at Torie's, an upscale coffee shop that was known for its signature award-winning coffee and desserts. He helped her out of his sports car, very much aware of the looks they were getting. But now, unlike the other times, he wasn't so sure the focus was on his specially-designed Danish car and not on the woman he was helping out of it. For the first time since he could remember, he relinquished the car to the valet without giving the young man a warning look and strict instructions to be careful on how his prize was handled.

"Mr. Westmoreland, it's nice to see you," the maître d' greeted when they entered the coffee shop.

"Thanks, Pierre. And I'd like a private table in the back."

"Most certainly."

He cupped Lucia's arm as they were led to a table that overlooked the mountains and a lake. The fire that was blazing in the fireplace added the finishing touch. A romantic setting that for even someone like him—a man who probably didn't have a romantic bone in his body until it suited him—was clearly defined. "We can have just coffee if you like, but their strawberry cheesecake is good," he said, smiling when they were seated.

Lucia chuckled. "I'm going to take your word for it and try some."

The waiter came to take their drink order. She ordered a glass of wine and when he ordered only a club soda she glanced over at him curiously. "I'm driving, remember? And I'm still on medication," he said by way of explanation. "And the doctor was adamant about me not consuming alcohol while I'm taking them."

She nodded. "Are you still in pain?"

A rueful smile touched his lips. "Not unless I move too fast. Otherwise, I'm doing fine."

"I guess you won't be getting on Sugar Foot's back again any time soon."

"What makes you say that? In fact, I plan to try him again tomorrow."

Her look of horror and disbelief was priceless, he thought, and he chuckled as he reached across the table to engulf her hand in his. "Hey, I was just kidding."

She frowned over at him. "I hope so, Derringer, and I certainly hope you've learned your lesson about taking unnecessary risks."

He laughed. "Trust me, I have," he said, although he knew she was a risk and he had a feeling spending too much time with her wasn't a good thing. It was then that he realized he was still holding her hand, and with supreme effort he released it.

He should know better than to get too attached to a woman like Lucia. She was the kind of woman a man could become attached to before he knew it. His attraction to her seemed too natural, but way too binding. She was a woman who seemed to be created just for the purpose of making a man want her in ways he had never wanted a woman before. And that wasn't good.

After their initial drinks, they ordered coffee and then shared a slice of strawberry cheesecake, and while they sat there she had his undivided attention. They conversed about a number of topics. More than once he caught his gaze roaming across her face, studying her features and appreciating her beauty. Whether she knew it or not, her facial bone structure was superb and any man would definitely find her attractive. But he knew there was more to her than just her outside beauty. She was beautiful on the inside as well. Derringer listened as she told him about a number of charities and worthwhile events she supported, and he was impressed.

A couple of hours later while driving her back home, he couldn't help but reflect on how the evening had gone. Certainly not the way he had planned. When the car came to a traffic light, he glanced over at her. Not surprisingly, she had fallen asleep. He thought about all the things he wanted to do to her when he got her back to her place, and knew the only thing he should do was walk her to her door and then leave. Something was going on with him that he didn't understand and he was smart enough to know when to back off.

That thought was still on his mind when he walked her to the door later. For some reason, he was being pulled in another direction and frankly he didn't like it. Her kiss alone had shot his brain cells to hell and back and knocked his carefully constructed plans to teach her a lesson to the wind. Even now the taste from her kiss was lingering in his mouth.

"Thanks again for such a wonderful evening, Derringer. I had a great time."

He'd had a great time, too. "You're welcome." He forced his lips closed to stop from asking her out again. He simply refused to do that. "Well, I guess I'll be going now," he said, trying to get his feet to step back and trying to figure out why they wouldn't budge.

"Would you like to come inside for more coffee?"

He shook his head. "Thanks, but I don't think my stomach can hold much more. Besides, my restrictions are over and I can return to work soon. I'll be helping Zane and Jason with the horses in the morning. I need to get home and get to bed."

"All right."

He made a move to leave but couldn't. Instead, his gaze settled on the face staring at him and he felt something pull at his gut. "Good night, Lucia," he whispered, just seconds before leaning down and brushing a kiss across her lips.

"Good night, Derringer."

He straightened and watched as she let herself inside the house. When the door clicked locked behind her, he turned to move down the walkway toward his car. He opened the door and slid inside. He needed to go home and think about things, regroup and revamp. And he had to figure out what there was about Lucia Conyers that got to him on a level he wasn't used to.

Six

Zane stopped saddling his horse long enough to glance over at his brother. "What's going on with you, Derringer? Last week you were inquiring about women's panties and now this week you want to know about a woman's scent. Didn't you get that mystery solved by viewing the tape on that video camera?"

Derringer rubbed his hand down his face. He should have known better than to come to Zane, but the bottom line was his brother knew more about women than *he* did and right now he needed answers. After he got them he'd be able to figure out what was going on with him when it came to Lucia. It had been almost a week after their date to the movies and he still didn't have a clue. And he had yet to confront her about being his late-night visitor.

He glanced over at Zane across the horse's back.

"There's nothing going on with me. Just answer the damn question."

Zane chuckled. "Getting kind of testy, aren't you? And how did your date go with Lucia Saturday night? I haven't heard you say."

"And I'm not going to say either, other than we had a nice time."

"For your sake I think that's all you better say or Chloe, Megan and Bailey will be coming down on you pretty hard. You might get a reprieve from Gemma since she's out of the country, but I wouldn't count on it if I were you, because she's coming home later this month for the charity ball."

Derringer grunted. The women in his family ought to stay out of his business and he would tell them so if the topic of Lucia ever came up with any of them again. So far, he'd been lying low this week, and when he had dropped by to see Ramsey, Chloe and baby Susan, the topic of Lucia hadn't come up. He could inwardly admit the reason he'd made himself scarce was his fear of running into her at Ramsey's. It was unheard of for Derringer Westmoreland to avoid any woman.

"So, will you answer my question?"

Zane crossed his arms over his chest. "Only after you answer mine. Did you or did you not watch that video footage?"

He glared over at his brother. "Yes, I watched it."

"And?"

"And I'd rather not discuss it."

A smirk appeared on Zane's face. "I bet you'll be glad to discuss it if you get hit with a paternity suit nine months from now."

Zane's words hit Derringer below the belt with a reminder that Lucia could be pregnant with his child. They'd had unprotected sex that night. She had to know that as well. Was she not worried about that possibility? He met his brother's intense gaze. "I'll handle it if that were to happen, now answer the question."

Zane smiled. "You're going to have to repeat it. My attention span isn't what it used to be these days."

Like hell it's not, Derringer thought. He knew Zane was trying to get a rise out of him and he didn't like it, but since he needed answers he would overlook his brother's bad attitude for now. "I want to know about the scent of a woman."

Zane smiled as he leaned back against the corral post. "Um, that's an easy one. Every woman has her own unique scent and if a man is attentive enough he's able to tell them apart by it. Some men will know their woman's location in a room before setting eyes on her just from her scent alone."

Derringer pulled in a deep breath. He knew all that already. He tilted his Stetson back off his head. "What I want to know is the effect that scent can have on a man."

Zane chuckled. "Well, I know for a fact that a woman's natural scent is a total turn-on for most men. It's all in the pheromones. Remember that doctor I dated last year?"

Derringer nodded. "Yes, what about her?"

"Man, her scent used to drive me crazy, and she damn well knew it. But it didn't bother me one bit when she took that job in Atlanta and moved away," Zane said.

Derringer decided not to remind Zane of the bad mood he'd been in for months after the woman left. "Every woman has her unique scent, but many douse it with cologne," Zane continued. "Then every woman that wears that cologne practically smells the same. But when you make love to a woman, her natural scent will override everything."

Zane paused a minute and then said, "And the effect it can have on a man depends on what degree of an attractant her scent can be. A woman's scent alone can render him powerless."

Derringer lifted his brow. "Powerless?"

"Yes, the scent of a woman is highly potent and sexually stimulating. And some men have discovered their own male senses can detect the woman who was meant to be their mate just from her scent. Animals rely on scent for that purpose all the time, and although some people might differ with that theory, there are some who believes it's true for humans as well. So if the scent of some woman is getting to you, that might be your cue she's your mate."

Derringer studied his brother's gaze, not sure if Zane was handing him a bunch of bull or not. The thought of his future being shared with a woman because of her scent didn't make much sense, but he'd watched enough shows on *Animal Kingdom* to know that was basically true with animals. Was man different from other animals?

"Some woman's scent has gotten to you," Zane taunted.

He didn't answer. Instead, he looked away for a second, wondering about that same thing. When he looked back at Zane moments later, his brother was grinning.

"What the hell do you find amusing?"

"Trust me, you don't want to know."

Derringer frowned. Zane was right; he didn't want to know.

"And you haven't heard from Derringer since your date Saturday night?"

A lump formed in Lucia's throat with Chloe's question. It was Friday night, late afternoon, and she sat curled on her sofa. Although she really hadn't expected Derringer to seek her out again, the notion that he didn't still bothered her, especially because she thought they'd had such a good time. At least she knew for a fact *she* had, and he'd seemed to enjoy himself as well. But she figured when you were Derringer Westmoreland, you could have a different girl every day.

When he had brought her home Saturday night, she had expected him to accept her invitation to come inside for coffee, although she would be the first to admit they had drunk plenty of the stuff at Torie's. He had declined her offer and given her a chaste kiss on the lips then left.

"No, I haven't heard anything, but that's okay. I was able to write in my diary that I had a date with him and that's good."

"One date isn't good when there can be others, Lu. You do know that women don't have to wait for the man to call for a date, we have that right as well."

Yes, but Lucia knew she couldn't be that forward with a man. "I know, but—"

There was a knock at her door. "Someone's at the door, Chloe. It's probably Mrs. Noel from across the street. She bakes on Fridays and uses me as her guinea pig, but I have no complaints. I'll call you back later."

When the knock sounded again, she called out after hanging up the phone. "I'm coming."

She eased off the sofa and headed to the door, thinking she would chow down on Mrs. Noel's sweets and get her romance groove on by watching a romantic movie on Lifetime. If you couldn't have the real thing in your life then she figured a movie was second best.

She nearly choked when she glanced out her peephole. Her caller wasn't her neighbor. It was Derringer. She suddenly felt hot when she realized he was staring at the peephole in the door as if he knew she was watching him. She closed her eyes trying to slow down the beating of her heart. He was the last person she expected to see tonight. In fact, she'd figured he wouldn't appear on her doorstep any time soon, or ever again. She assumed they would get back into the routine of running into each other whenever she visited Chloe, Ramsey and the baby.

Forcing her brain cells to stop scrambling, she turned the doorknob to open the door and there he stood in a pair of jeans, a sweater, a leather jacket and boots. He looked good, but then he always did. He was leaning against a post on her porch with his hands in his pockets.

She cleared her throat. "Derringer, what are you doing here?"

He held her gaze. "I know I should have called first."

She stopped herself from saying that he could appear on her doorstep anytime. The last thing a woman should do is let a man assume she was pining for him…even if she was. "Yes, you should have called first. Is anything wrong?"

"No, I just needed to see you."

She tried to ignore how low his voice had dropped and how he was looking at her. Instead, she tried to focus on what he'd said. *He just needed to see her.*

Yeah, right. She thought he could really do better than that, especially since he hadn't done so much as picked up a phone to call her since their date on Saturday night. Was she to believe needing to see her had brought him to her door? She wondered if his date tonight had canceled and she had been his backup plan. Curious about that possibility, she decided to ask him.

Crossing her arms over her chest, she said. "Um, let me guess, your date stood you up and I was next on the list." After saying the words, she realized her mistake. First, she doubted very seriously that any woman stood him up and she really thought a lot of herself to even assume she was on any list he had.

He tilted his head as if he needed to see her more clearly. "Is that what you think?"

She shook her head. "To be honest with you, Derringer, I really don't know what to think."

He made a slow move and inched closer to her face. He then leaned over and whispered against her ear. "Invite me in and I promise you won't be thinking at all."

And that was what she was afraid of.

She drew in a deep breath, thinking she would be

able to handle him. She opened the door and stepped back, hoping at that moment that she could.

What the hell am I doing here? Derringer wondered as he brushed by her. He had caught a whiff of her scent the moment she had opened the door, and as always it was playing hard on his senses.

He turned when he heard her close the door behind him and his gaze studied her. For some reason he didn't have the strength or inclination to tear his eyes away from her. What was wrong with him? When had he ever let a woman affect him this way? She was standing there leaning back against the door in her bare feet and a pair of leggings and a T-shirt. Her hair was back in that signature ponytail. She looked comfortable. She looked sexy. Damn, she looked good enough to eat.

He cleared his throat. "What are your plans for tonight?"

She shrugged. "I didn't have any. I was just going to watch a movie on Lifetime."

He was familiar with that channel, the one that was supposed to be for women that showed romance movies 24/7. His sisters used to be glued to their television sets, and in Bailey's case, sometimes to his.

"How would you like to go roller skating?"

The glow from a table lamp captured the expression of surprise on her face. "You want us to go out again?"

He noted that there was a degree of shock in her voice. There was a note of wariness as well.

"Yes, I know I should have called first, and I am sorry about that. And just to set the record straight, when I left home I didn't have a date. I didn't have any plans for tonight. I got in my car and I ended up here. What I said earlier was true. I needed to see you."

Serious doubt was etched in her features. "Why, Derringer? Why did you need to see me?"

It should be so easy to use this moment and come clean and say because I know who you are. I know you are the woman to whom I made love in what should have been a weak and crazy moment, but it ended up being the one time I slept with a woman that I remember the most. That no matter what I do or where I go, your scent is right there with me. You are responsible for the lust that rages through my body every time I think of you, whenever I see you. Even now there is a throbbing in my groin that you're causing and I want more than anything to make love to you again.

"Derringer?"

He realized at that moment that he hadn't answered her. Instead, he had been standing there and staring at her like a lust-crazed maniac. He slowly crossed the floor, pinning her in when he braced his hands on both sides of her head, and leaned in close to her mouth.

"I really don't know why I needed to see you tonight," he whispered huskily against her lips. "I can't explain it. I just needed to see you, be with you and spend time with you. I enjoyed Saturday night and—"

"Could have fooled me."

He noticed her voice had barely been audible, but he'd heard that, and he'd heard the hurt in her tone. He hadn't called her. He should have. He had wanted to. But he had fought the temptation. If only she knew to what degree he had fought it. A part of him knew being here with her now wasn't good; especially when he was thinking of all the things he wanted to do to her right now—against the door, on the floor, on her bed, the table, the sofa, every damn place in her house. But even more important was that he knew more about the situation than she did. He had yet to tell her that he knew about her visit to his home that night.

He had spent the last few days going over the video time and time again. It was evident from viewing the footage and seeing how she had merely stuck her head in the door that initially she'd had no intention of staying. Then she had glanced back at the box and decided to put it inside. She must have heard him fall once she was inside, because this week he remembered that part—missing the bed when he'd gotten up to use the bathroom and falling flat on his behind when he was returning to bed. He remembered someone, his Puddin' Tame, helping him back into bed, and the only thing he remembered after that was making love to a woman.

And the woman he had made love to had been her.
Things were still kind of fuzzy, but he remembered that much now. "I apologize for not calling you this week. I should have," he murmured.

She shook her head. "You didn't have to. I'm the one who should be apologizing. I should not have given you the impression that you should have called, just now."

His heart beat hard in his chest. That statement alone showed how different she was from the other women he messed around with. And that difference, among other things, he was convinced, was what had him here with her now.

"I don't want any apologies from you," he said,

leaning in closer, drawing one of her earlobes between his lips. "This is what I want." He then brushed his tongue across her lips and when she gave a sharp intake of breath, he did it again. And again.

"Why, Derringer...why me?" she whispered moments before she began trembling against the door.

"Why not you?" he breathed huskily against her lips before bending close to taste them again. Her flavor as well as her scent was getting to him on a level that made him want to push forward instead of drawing back.

Then deciding they had done enough talking for now, he sidled up closer to her and pressed his mouth to hers.

By rights she should send him away, Lucia's mind screamed over and over again. But it was hard to listen to what her mind was saying when Derringer was causing so much havoc with her body. This was the kind of kiss that could knock the sense out of a woman. It was long, deep and downright greedy. He was eating at her mouth as if it were his last meal, and there was no doubt in her mind this kiss was definitely X-rated.

And if that wasn't bad enough, his erection was pressing into her right at the juncture of her thighs, cradled against her womanly mound as if it had specifically sought out that part of her. And then there were the nipples of her breasts that were piercing his chest through the material of her T-shirt. She couldn't help but remember how it felt when they had been flesh to flesh, skin to skin. If he was seducing her then he was certainly going at it the right way.

He suddenly pulled back. Puzzled as to why, she

nervously chewed on her bottom lip—a lip he'd just released from devouring—and stared up at him. He was staring back. "I think we need to take time and think through a few things," he said huskily.

She arched a bemused brow. He evidently was speaking for himself. As far as she was concerned there was nothing to think through. She knew what she wanted and had a feeling that he did, too. So what was the problem? She knew the score. Nothing was forever with Derringer Westmoreland and she was okay with that. Although she was hopelessly in love with the man, she knew her limitations. She had accepted them long ago. She had made more strides within the last twelve days than she'd expected in her entire lifetime. They had made love, for heaven's sake, and he had kissed her senseless a week ago tomorrow.

But still…she was no longer a teenager with fantasies of him marrying her and living happily ever after with each other. She totally understood that was not the way the ball would bounce. She was not entering into anything with him blindly; she had both eyes wide open. Bottom line was that she didn't have to safeguard her heart. Although she wished otherwise, the man had her heart, lock, stock and barrel, and it was too late to do anything about it but gladly take whatever she could and live the rest of her life on memories.

"I think I need to give you time to get dressed so we can get to the skating rink."

She couldn't help but smile softly. "Do you really want to do that?"

He shook his head. "No, but if you knew what I really want to do you would probably kick me out."

"Try me."

He threw his head back and laughed. "No, I think I'll pass. I'll wait out here until you change clothes."

She moved around him to head down the hall and stopped right before crossing the threshold into her room. "You know it would probably be more fun if we stayed here, don't you?"

He smiled then said in a firm voice, "Go get dressed, Lucia."

Laughing, she entered the bedroom and closed the door behind her. While removing her clothes, Lucia made a decision about something.

For the first time ever she intended to try her luck at seducing a man.

Seven

Derringer glanced over at Lucia, who was across the room standing in line to check out their roller skates. He had two words to describe the jeans she was wearing— snug and tight. And then the first two words that would describe her overall appearance tonight were hot and sexy.

Deciding he needed to stop staring at her every chance he got, he glanced around. He had expected the place to be crowded since it was a Friday night, but why were there more kids than adults? Granted, it had been years since he'd gone skating, but still, he would think it was past these kids' bedtime.

He laughed recalling how some smart-mouthed preteen had come up to him a few minutes ago and said he hoped he and Lucia were fast enough on the skates to keep up and not get in anyone's way. Hell, he and Lucia weren't *that* old.

"What's so funny?"

He glanced down to see Lucia had returned with their skates. He then told her about the smart-mouthed kid and she smiled. "Doesn't this city still have a curfew?" he asked her.

She shook her head. "Not anymore."

He lifted a brow. "When did they do away with it?" He figured she would know because her dad had been a member of Denver's city council for years.

She smiled sweetly up at him. "They did away with it when Bane turned eighteen."

He stared at her for a second, saw she was serious and threw his head back and laughed so hard they couldn't help but get attention. "You're making a scene, Derringer Westmoreland," she whispered.

He shook his head and pulled her closer to him. "Is there anywhere Bane didn't leave his mark?"

"According to my father, the answer to that question is a resounding no. Now, come on, *old man,* or that kid will return and ask us to step aside."

He took her teasing of his age in stride, but still he reached out and grabbed her around the waist. "I'll show you who's old and who's not," he said, and then he took off, pulling her with him.

It was past three in the morning when Derringer returned Lucia home, and he smiled as he escorted her inside her home. It had taken a while, but he'd eventually shown that smart-mouthed kid why he once had earned the reputation of being hell on wheels with roller skates. And then when the kid had found out he was a Westmoreland—a cousin to the infamous Bane Westmoreland—he had to all but sign autographs.

"Can you believe those kids actually think Bane is some kind of hero?" he said, dropping onto Lucia's love seat.

She chuckled as she sat down on the sofa across from him. "Yes, I can believe that. Bane was bold enough to do some of the horrific things they would probably love to try but know that they can't get away with doing. Tell me, who in their right mind would take off in the sheriff's car while he's giving someone a ticket other than Bane? He became something of a legend if you were to read some of the stuff the girls wrote all over the walls in the bathroom at the local high school. He and the twins."

He glanced over at her. "How do you know about those walls? That was after your time."

She smiled as she settled back against the cushions, wrapping her arms across the back. "I have a young cousin who used to have a crush on Aidan and he's all she used to talk about then, in addition to all the trouble Aidan, Adrian and Bane would get into."

Derringer shook his head and chuckled, remembering those times. "And let's not forget Bailey—she was just as bad. At one time we considered sending all four of them to military school, but that would be like giving up on our own, and we knew we couldn't do that."

A serious expression touched his features before he said, "I don't tell Ramsey and Dillon enough how much I appreciate them keeping our family together. Losing my parents and my aunt and uncle at the same time was hard on everyone, but they helped us get through it." Derringer inwardly struggled with what he'd just told

her, realizing he had never shared those emotions and
feelings with anyone, certainly not any of his women.

"I'm sure they know you appreciate what they did,
Derringer. The proof is in the successful, law-abiding
men and women you all became. That's a testimony in
itself. The Westmorelands are getting something now
the townspeople figured they wouldn't ever get after
your parents and aunt and uncle passed away."

He lifted a brow. "And what's that?"

"Respect." A smile touched her lips when she added,
"And admiration. I wish you would have noticed the
look on that kid's face tonight when he realized you
were a Westmoreland."

Derringer snorted. "Yes, but he was admiring me for
all the wrong reasons."

"It doesn't matter."

He knew deep down that Lucia was right—it didn't
matter, because in the end what Dillon and Ramsey
had done was indeed a success story in his book. He
stretched his legs out in front of him thinking how
throughout the evening he had enjoyed the time he was
spending with Lucia. It had been the first time he'd
spent with a woman when he'd had honest-to-goodness
fun. She had been herself and hadn't gone out of her
way to impress him and draw all the attention on her.

Even on the drive to and from the skating arena he
had enjoyed their conversation, and although it was hard
to believe, they had a lot in common and shared the
same interests. They both enjoyed watching Westerns,
they enjoyed a good comedy every once in a while and
were huge fans of the Wayans brothers, Bill Cosby and

Sandra Bullock. She also rode horses and enjoyed going hunting.

But more than anything, he had enjoyed being with her, sharing her space and breathing the same air that she did. And he smiled, thinking she wasn't too bad on roller skates either. He had enjoyed going around the rink with her, often hearing her throaty laugh, looking over at her and seeing the huge smile on her face; and he especially liked wrapping his arms around her waist when they skated together.

"I had a wonderful time tonight, Derringer. I really enjoyed myself."

He glanced over at her. At some point, she had removed her boots and shifted position on the sofa to tuck her jeans-clad legs beneath her. But still, it didn't take much to remember how her long, curvy legs looked in a pair of shorts, a skirt or a dress. But most of all, he could recall those same legs wrapped around his waist while they had made love. The more time he spent with her, the more things were coming back to him that he had forgotten about their night together.

"I enjoyed myself as well," he responded.

"You were pretty good on those skates."

"You weren't so bad yourself." He wondered why he was sitting here making small talk with her when what he really wanted to do was to cross the room and join her on that sofa. His attention was trained directly on her and he could tell by the way she was moving her fingers on her knee he was making her nervous.

"Lucia, does my being here bother you?"

"What makes you think that?"

"Because you're over there and I'm here," he didn't

hesitate to say. He watched as she nervously licked her bottom lip, and immediately the lower part of his body—directly behind his zipper—responded in a hard-up way.

"There's nothing keeping you over there, Derringer," she said softly.

He couldn't help but smile at her deduction. She was right. There was nothing keeping him on this love seat when more than anything he wanted to be on that sofa with her. Knowing what he should do was stand up, thank her again for a good time and head toward the door and leave, never to return again, he remained seated for a minute. But he knew, just as much as he knew that tomorrow would bring another day, he wasn't going to do that.

And he also knew that she didn't know, she didn't have a clue just what she did to him, what being here with her was doing to him. He figured his intense attraction to her had everything to do with the night they had made love. But that wouldn't make sense since he'd made love to a number of women before and none had left the kind of lasting impression that she had. So why had the time with her been different, and why was he so quick to accept that it was?

The answer nearly made him tremble inside. It made his chest clench and made blood rush through his veins. She was deeply embedded in his system and he knew only one way to get her out of there. When they'd made love before, he hadn't been completely coherent and maybe that was the problem. Now he needed to make love to her in his right mind, if for no other reason than to purge her from his thoughts, mind and body. Then he could get on with his life and she could get on with hers. But before it was all over, he intended to let her know he was well aware that she had been his visitor that night.

Deciding he was doing too much thinking and not delivering enough action, he eased off the love seat.

Nowhere to run and nowhere to hide.

Deep down, Lucia knew she didn't want to do either as she watched Derringer slowly move toward her. Why was she getting all tense and nervous? Hadn't she made up her mind to seduce him tonight? But it seemed as if he had beat her to the punch and he was about to take things into his own hands. Literally.

His visit had been a surprise. She hadn't expected him tonight. He was the most unlikely person to show up at her place tonight or any other time. Not only had he shown up, but he'd taken her out again. Skating. It was their second date and he claimed the reason he was here was because he had needed to see her.

She knew needing to see her had only been a line and men like Derringer were good at saying such things. They said whatever they thought a woman wanted to hear. But that hadn't stopped her from allowing herself to be taken in, relish the moments spent with him and be greedy enough to want more. She would take whatever part of Derringer she could get. Tomorrow she would wake up and hate herself for being such a weakling where he was concerned, but she would also wake wearing the blush of a satisfied woman all over her face.

There was no doubt in her mind that he intended

to make love to her. He'd done it before, and from the dark, intense look in his eyes, he planned to do so again. And tonight he wouldn't get any resistance, because she loved him just that much and was secretly grateful for this time with him.

He slid down beside her on the sofa. "There is just something tantalizingly sweet about your scent, Lucia."

Another line, she was sure of it. "Is there?"

"Yes. It makes my body burn for you," he said, wrapping his arms around her shoulders.

She drew in a deep breath, thinking she would love to believe what he was saying, but knew better. However, tonight it was all about make-believe. Besides, it was hard not to melt under the intense look he was giving her and the way his arm felt around her shoulders. And he was sitting so close, every time he spoke his warm breath blew across her lips.

He then pulled back slightly and gazed at her thoughtfully. "You don't believe a word I've said, do you?"

She began nibbling on her bottom lip. She could easily lie and assure him that she did, but deep down she knew she didn't believe him. She tilted her chin upward. "Does it matter whether or not I believe you, Derringer?"

He continued to stare at her for a moment with an unreadable expression on his face, and for a split second she thought he was going to say something but he didn't. Instead, he reached out and cupped her chin with his fingertips before slowly lowering his mouth to hers.

Sensations ripped through her the moment their lips

touched. She closed her eyes when his tongue eased into her mouth and he began kissing her with a hunger that had her groaning deep in her throat.

Her heart thundered when he captured her tongue with his and began doing all kinds of erotic things to it, sucking on it as if there was a time limit to get his fill, mating their tongues as if all they had was the here and now. This was the kind of kissing that made a woman forget that she was supposed to be a lady.

She wanted this. She wanted every mind-blowing moment because she knew there *was* a time limit on this fantasy. Everyone around town knew of Derringer's reputation for getting tired of his women quickly. There was only a chosen one or two who were determined to hang in for the long haul no matter what—by their choice and not his. She refused to be one of those women. She would take this and be satisfied.

When he broke off the kiss to shift their positions to press her back against the sofa cushions, she moved willingly with him. She gazed up at him when his body eased on top of hers. She could feel his hard erection between her thighs.

He lowered his head and began nibbling around her throat, taking the tip of his tongue and licking around her chin. "Too many clothes." She heard him utter the word moments before he leaned up and, without warning, pulled the sweater over her head. He tossed it to the floor. He then proceeded to tug her jeans down her legs.

He looked down at her and smiled at her matching red lace bra and panties. She wondered what was going through his mind and why he was so captivated by her lingerie. He then glanced back up at her. "I like a woman who wears lace," he whispered huskily before leaning down and taking her mouth once more.

His lips seemed incredibly hot and he had no problem sliding his tongue where he pleased while kissing her with slow, deep strokes. And when she felt his fingers move toward her breasts, ease under her bra to stroke a nipple, she nearly shot off the sofa when sensations speared through her.

"Derringer..." she whispered in a strained voice.

This was getting to be too much and she began quivering almost uncontrollably, knowing what she'd heard for years was true. Derringer Westmoreland was almost too much for any woman to handle.

She was wrong. It did matter to him that she believed what he said.

That thought raged through Derringer's mind as he continued to kiss her with a hunger he could not understand. What was there about her that made him want to taste her all over, make her groan mercilessly and torture her over and over again before exploding inside her? The mere thought of doing the latter made his groin throb.

He pulled back slightly, wanting her to watch exactly what he was doing. What he was about to do. When he released the front fastener of her bra, his breath quickened when her breasts came tumbling out. They were full, firm and ripe and the nipples were dark and tightened even more into hard nubs before his eyes. And when he swooped his mouth down and captured a peak between his lips, she moaned and closed her eyes.

"Keep them open, Lucia. Watch me. I want you to see what I'm doing to you."

He saw her heavy-lidded eyes watch as he tugged a nipple into his mouth and begin sucking on it, and the more he heard her moan the more pressure he exerted with his mouth.

But that wasn't enough. Her scent was getting to him and he needed to touch her, to taste her, to bury himself in a feminine fragrance that was exclusively hers. He left one breast and went to another as he lowered a hand underneath the waistband of her lace bikini panties. And when his fingers ran over the wetness of her feminine folds, she writhed against his hand and let out a deep moan and whispered his name.

He lifted his head to stare down at eyes that were dazed with passion. "Yes, baby? You want something?"

Instead of answering, she began trembling as his fingers slipped inside her and he began stroking her while watching the display of emotions and expressions appear on her face. The breathless wonder drenched with pleasure that he saw in her gaze, in response to his touch, was a sight to behold and the sweetest thing he'd ever seen.

Lust thundered through him with the force of a hurricane and he knew he had to make love to her in the most primitive way. Leaning back, he eased to his feet and continued to hold her gaze while he tugged off his boots, pulled off his socks and unzipped his jeans. He took the time to remove a condom from the back pocket and held it between his teeth while he yanked down his jeans, careful of his engorged erection.

"Derringer…"

If she said his name like that, with that barely-there voice, one more time, he would lose it. The sound was sending splendorous shivers up his spine and there was a chance he would come the minute he got inside her, without making a single thrust. And he didn't want that. He wanted to savor the moment, make it last for as long as he could.

When he was totally naked, he stood before her and watched her gaze roam over him, seeing some parts of him that she probably hadn't seen their other night together. There was no shame in his game, but he knew deep down this wasn't a game with him. He was serious about what was taking place between them.

Thinking he had wasted more than enough time, he bent over her to remove the last item of clothing covering her body. Her panties. He touched the center of her and she sucked in a deep breath. He tossed aside the condom packet he'd been holding between his teeth. "You're drenched, baby," he said in a low, rough voice. "I know you don't believe me, but there is something about you that drives me crazy."

When he began tugging her panties down her legs, he whispered throatily, "Lift your hips and bend your legs for me."

She did, and when he removed her panties, instead of tossing them aside, he rubbed the lacy material over his face before he bent to the floor and tucked them into the back pocket of his jeans. He knew she was watching his every move and was probably wondering what on earth possessed him to do such a thing.

Instead of mounting her now, as he wanted to do,

there was something he wanted to do even more. Taste her. He wanted to taste all that sweetness that triggered the feminine aroma he enjoyed inhaling. It was a scent he was convinced he had become addicted to.

He lowered his body to his knees and before she could pull in her next breath, he pressed an open mouth to the wet, hot feminine lips of her sex. She groaned so deep in her throat that her body began trembling. But he kept focused on the pleasure awaiting him as he leisurely stroked her with his tongue, feasting on her with a hunger he knew she could not understand, but that he intended her to enjoy.

Because he was definitely enjoying it.

He'd been of the mind that no other woman had her scent. Now he was just as convinced that no other woman had her taste as well. It was unique. It was hers. And at the moment, as crazy as it sounded, he was also of the mind that it was also *his,* in a possessive way he'd never encountered before with any woman. The mere thought should have scared the hell out of him, but he was too far gone to give a damn.

When heat and lust combined and resonated off his mind he knew he had to be inside her or risk exploding then and there. He tore his mouth from her and threw his head back and released a deep savage groan. He then stared down at her while licking her juices from his lips. He felt as if he was taking part in a scorching-hot, exciting and erotic dream, and it was a dream he was dying to turn into a reality. And there was only one way he knew to do that.

He would take her and now.

Without saying a word, he leaned over and spread

her thighs and placed a kiss on each before moving off his knees to shift his body over hers. Instinctively she arched her back and wrapped her arms around his neck. Their gazes held as he eased his body down, the thick head of his shaft finding what it wanted and working its way inside her wet tightness. He paused when he'd made it halfway, glorying in the feel of her muscles clamping down on him, convulsing around him.

He wanted to take things slow, but the feel of her gripping him had him groaning deep in his throat, and when in a naughty, unexpected move she licked out her tongue and flicked his budded nipple before easing it into her mouth with a hungry suck, he took in a sharp breath at the same time he thrust hard into her.

When he heard her cry out, he apologized in a soothing whispered voice. "I'm sorry. I didn't mean to hurt you. Just lie still for a moment."

He used that time to lick around her mouth, nibble at the corners, and when she parted her mouth on a sweet sigh, he eased his tongue inside and sank right into a hungry kiss filled with more urgency and desire than he'd ever known or had ever cared knowing. Until now.

And then he felt the lower part of her body shift beneath the weight of his. He pulled back from the kiss. "That's it, baby," he crooned close to her ear. "Take it. All that you want."

His body remained still as she moved her body, grinding against him, dipping her hips into the sofa cushions before lifting them up again, arching her back in the process. Then she began rotating her hips, pushing up and lowering back down.

Derringer's body froze when he remembered the condom he'd tossed aside and he knew he needed to pull out now. But heaven help him, he couldn't do so. Being inside of her like this felt so darn right. He kept his body immobile until he couldn't stay still any longer and then he joined her, driving his erection deeper into her. He thrust in and out with precise and concentrated strokes that he felt all the way to the soles of his feet.

He had thought their first time together had been off the charts, but nothing, he decided, could compare to this. Nothing could compete with the incredible feeling of being inside her this way. Nothing. Desperate to reach the highest peak with her, he took total possession of her, kissing her with urgency while their bodies mated in the most primitive pleasure known to humankind.

He whispered erotic things in her ear before reaching down and cupping her face in his hands to stare down at her while his body continued to drive heatedly into hers. Their gazes locked and something happened between them at that moment that nearly threw him off balance. Somewhere in the back of his mind a voice was taunting that this had nothing to do with possessing but everything to do with claiming.

Denial froze hard in his throat and he wanted to scream that it wasn't possible. He claimed no woman. Instead, he grunted savagely as his body exploded, and then he heard her scream as she cried out in ecstasy. He kept thrusting into her, pushing them further and further into sweet oblivion and surging them beyond the stars.

Eight

Lucia moved her head slowly, opened her eyes and then came fully awake when a flash of sunlight through her bedroom window hit her right in the face. It was then that she felt the male body pressed tightly against her back and the heated feel of Derringer's breathing on her neck.

She then remembered.

They had made love on the sofa before moving into her bedroom where they had made love again before drifting off to sleep. Sometime during the wee hours of early morning they had made love again. The entire thing seemed unreal, but Derringer's presence in her bed assured her that it had been real.

Her body felt sore, tender in a number of places, but mostly between her legs, and she wouldn't be surprised if her lips were swollen from all the kissing they had done. Her cheeks flooded with heat thinking about a number of other things they'd gotten into as well. She had proven to him in a very sexual way that she definitely knew how to ride a stallion. He had taunted her to prove it and she'd done so.

Her eyes fluttered closed as she thought how she would handle things from here on out. She knew last night meant more to her than it had to him, and she could handle that. But what she wouldn't be able to handle was letting things go beyond what they'd shared these past few hours. She loved him and for him to ever make love to her again would turn things sexual, into a casual relationship that would tarnish her memories rather than enhance them. She was smart enough to know when to let go and move on. Now was the time.

Tears flooded her eyes. Derringer would always have her heart, but the reality was that she would never have his. And being the type of person that she was, she could never allow herself to become just one in a long line of women vying for his attention. She preferred letting things go back to the way they were between them before they'd become intimate.

The way she saw things, if she never had him then there was no way she could lose him. She couldn't risk a broken heart because of Derringer and she knew her place in his life. She didn't have one. If she began thinking of developing something serious with him knowing the kind of man he was, she was setting herself up for pain from which she might never be able to heal.

She would continue to love him like this—secretly. She had gotten used to doing things that way and, no matter what, she couldn't let their sexual encounters—no matter how intense they'd been—fill her head and mind with false illusions.

She swallowed when she felt Derringer's penis swell against her backside and tried to convince herself it wouldn't be a good idea to make love to him one last time. But she knew the moment he pulled her closer to his hard, masculine body that she would. This would be saying goodbye to the intimacy between them. She knew it even if he didn't.

"You're awake?" He turned her in his arms to face him.

Desire rippled through her the moment she looked into his face. Propped with his head on her pillow, his eyes had the same desire-glazed look they'd had that first night they'd made love. It was a sexy, drowsy look, complete with a darkened shadow on his chin. No man had a right to look this good in the morning. He looked so untamed, wild and raw. His rumpled look was calling out to her, arousing her and making her want him all over again.

"Sort of," she said, yawning, and couldn't help the anticipation she heard in her voice. And when he gave her a dimpled cowboy smile, sensations shot through her entire body, but especially in the area between her thighs.

"Then let me wake you up the Derringer West-moreland way." He then captured her mouth at the same time he tossed his leg over hers, adjusting their positions to ease inside her body.

"Oh," she whispered, and when he locked his leg on her and began slowly moving in and out of her and capturing her lips with his, she figured there was nothing wrong with one for the road...even though she knew she would end up in heaven.

Derringer's smile faded as he buttoned up his shirt and stared at Lucia. "What do you mean we can't ever make love again?"

He saw the flash of regret that came into her eyes before she stopped brushing her teeth long enough to rinse out her mouth. "Just what I said, Derringer. Last night was special and I want to remember it that way."

He was confused. "And you don't think you can if we make love again?"

"No. I know about the women you usually sleep with and, personally, I don't want to be one of them."

He frowned, crossing his arms over his chest, not sure he liked what she'd said. "Then why did you sleep with me last night?"

"I had my reasons."

His frown deepened. He couldn't help but wonder if those reasons were the same ones he had initially suspected her of having. And it didn't help matters to know that every time he had made love to her they had been unprotected. The first time had been a slip-up, and then after that, he'd deliberately chosen not to think about it. Why he'd done such a thing, he didn't know. He usually made it a point to always use protection. Even now, Lucia might be pregnant with his child.

"And just what are those reasons, Lucia?"

"I'd rather not say."

Anger ignited inside him. That response wasn't good enough.

"Oh!" she cried out in surprise when he reached

out, snatched her off her feet and tossed her over his shoulders like a sack of potatoes and strode out of the bathroom.

"Derringer! What in the world is wrong with you? Put me down."

He did. Tossing her on the bed and glaring down at her. "I want to hear these reasons."

She glared back. "You don't need to know them. All you need to know is that I won't be sharing a bed with you again."

"Why? Because you think you're pregnant now and that's what this is about?"

Shock leaped into her face. "Pregnant? What are you talking about?"

"Are you on the pill or something?"

He could tell his question had surprised her. "No."

His frown deepened. "There's only one reason I can think of for a woman to let a man come inside her. Are you going to deny that sleeping with me this time around…as well as the last time…has nothing to do with you wanting a Westmoreland baby?"

He saw her throat tighten. "The last?"

"Yes," he said between clenched teeth. "I know all about your little visit that night when I was drugged up on pain medication."

She blinked. "You know?"

"Yes, and I couldn't figure out why you, a virgin, would get into my bed and take advantage of me. And, yes, I do remember you were a virgin even if I couldn't recall your identity."

She angrily reared up on her haunches. "I did not take advantage of you! I was helping you back into bed after you fell. If anything, you're the one who took advantage of me."

"So you say." He could see fury consume her body. and smoke was all but coming out her ears, but he didn't care.

She rolled off the bed and stood in front of him, almost nose to nose. "Are you insinuating I slept with you that night to deliberately get pregnant? And that I only slept with you last night and this morning for the same reason?"

"What am I supposed to think?"

She threw her hair over her shoulders. "That maybe I am different from all those other women you spend your time with, and that I would not have an ulterior motive like that," she all but screamed at him.

"You said you had your reasons."

"Yes, I have my reasons and they have nothing to do with getting pregnant by you, but everything to do with being in love with you. Do you have any idea how it is to fall in love with a man knowing full damn well he won't ever love you back?"

"In love with me," he said in a shocked stupor. "Since when?"

"Since I was sixteen."

"Sixteen!" He shook his head. "Hell, I didn't know."

She placed her hands on her hips and her eyes sparked with fire. "And you weren't *supposed* to know. It was a secret I had planned to take to my grave. Then like a fool I rushed over to your place when I heard you'd gotten hurt. And when you fell, I rushed up the stairs to help you back into bed and you wouldn't get off me."

He lifted a brow. His head was still reeling from her admission of love. "Are you saying I forced myself on you?"

"No, but I would not have gotten into bed with you if you hadn't fallen on top of me. And then, when you began kissing me, I—"

"Didn't want me to stop," he finished for her. Her cheeks darkened and he knew he'd embarrassed her. "Look, Lucia, I—"

"No, *you* look, Derringer. You're right. The thought of pushing you off me only entered my mind for a quick second, but I didn't set out to get pregnant by you that night or any other night."

"But you let me make love to you without any protection." He remembered all too well that he hadn't used a condom this time either.

"Then I can accuse you of the same thing. Trying to *get* me pregnant," she all but snarled.

"And why would I do something like that?"

"I don't know, but if you're willing to think the worst of me, then I can certainly do the same thing with you. You had taken the condom out of your wallet last night, why didn't you put it on?"

Derringer tensed. To say he'd been too carried away with making love to her would be to admit a weakness for her that he didn't want to own up to. "I think this conversation has gotten out of hand."

"You're right. I want you to leave."

He arched his brow. "Leave?"

"Yes. And my front door is that way," she said as she pointed to the door.

He narrowed his eyes. "I know where your door is located and we haven't finished our conversation."

"There's nothing else left to say, Derringer. I've already told you more than I should have and I'm ashamed of doing it. Now that you know how I feel, I won't let you take advantage of those feelings. For me it's even more important to protect my heart more than ever. Nothing has changed from the way you've always looked at me. Most of the time you acted like I didn't exist."

"That's not true. I told you I was attracted to you a few years back."

"Yes, and I honestly thought it meant something and that you were seeking me out after all that time. Now I know you only did so because you knew I was the one who slept with you that night."

She didn't say anything for a moment and then asked, "How did you know? I figured you wouldn't remember anything."

He jammed his hands into his jeans. "Oh, I remembered just fine, and you left a little something behind that definitely jogged my memory. Something pink and lacy. I just couldn't remember who they belonged to. My security system gave me the answers I needed. I had video cameras installed outside my place last month. You were the woman I saw entering my house that evening and the same one I saw sneaking out the next morning with a made-love-all-night-long look all over you."

Lucia tightened her bathrobe around her. "Like I said, that wasn't the purpose of my visit. I just wanted to make sure you were okay."

"It had been storming that night. You hate storms. Yet you came to check on me," he said.

That realization touched something within him. The reason he knew about her aversion to storms was because of something Chloe had once teased her about from their college days in Florida that involved a torrential thunderstorm and her reaction to it.

"Doesn't matter now."

"And what if I say it matters to me?" he all but snarled.

"Then I would suggest you get over it," she snapped back.

"I can't. I want to be with you again."

She narrowed her gaze. "And I told you that we won't be together that way ever again. So get it through that thick head of yours that I won't become just another woman you sleep with. You have enough of those."

Emotions he had never felt before stirred in Derringer's stomach. He should leave and not come back and not care if he ever saw her again, but for some reason she had gotten in his blood and making love to her again hadn't gotten her out. Instead the complete opposite had happened; she was more in his blood than ever before.

"I'll give you time to think about what I said, Lucia." He turned to leave the room knowing she was right on his heels as he moved toward the living room.

"There's nothing to think about," she snapped behind him.

He turned back around after snagging his Stetson off the rack. "Sure there is. We will be making love again."

"No, we won't!"

"Yes, we will," he said, moving toward the door. "You're in my blood now."

"I'm sure so are a number of other women in this town."

There was no point in saying that although he'd had a lot of women in the past, none had managed to get into his blood before. When he got to the door, he put on his hat before turning back to her. "Get some rest. You're going to need it when we make love again."

"I told you that we—"

He leaned forward and swiped whatever words she was about to say from her lips with a kiss, effectively silencing her. He then straightened and smiled at the infuriated face staring back at him and tipped the brim of his hat. "We'll talk later, sweetheart."

He opened the door and stepped outside and it didn't bother him one bit when she slammed the door behind him with enough force to wake up the whole neighborhood.

Chloe leaned forward and kissed Lucia on the cheek. "Hey, cheer up. It might not be so bad."

Lucia covered her face with both hands. "How can you say that, Clo? Now that Derringer knows how I feel, he's going to do everything in his power to find a weakness to get me back in his bed. I should never have told him."

"But you did tell him, so what's next?"

She lowered her hands and narrowed her eyes. "Nothing is next. I know what he's after and it's not happening. And just to think he knew I was the one who slept with him that night, when silly me thought he didn't have a clue. And now he wants to add me to his list."

Chloe raised a brow. "Did he actually say that?"

"He didn't have to. His arrogance was showing and that was enough." She doubted she could forget his exit and his statement about their talking later. She was so angry with him. The only good part about his leaving was the mesmerizing view of his backside before she slammed the door shut on him.

"I've known Derringer a lot longer than you, Chloe, and he doesn't know the meaning of committing to one woman," she decided to add.

Chloe shrugged. "Maybe he's ready to change his ways."

Lucia rolled her eyes. "Fat chance."

"I don't know," Chloe said, tapping her finger against her chin. "Of the three die-hard-bachelor Westmoreland men who hang tight most of the time—Jason, Zane and Derringer—I think Jason will get married first...then Derringer...and last, Zane." She chuckled. "I can see Zane kicking, screaming and throwing out accusations all the way to the altar."

Lucia couldn't help but smile because she could envision that as well. Zane was more of a womanizer than Derringer. Jason didn't have the reputation the other two had, but he was still considered a ladies' man around town because he didn't tie himself down to any one woman.

"Derringer is so confident he's getting me back into his bed again, but I'm going to show him just how wrong he is."

Chloe took a long sip of her iced tea. She had been out shopping and had decided to drop by Lucia's. Unfortunately, she had found her best friend in a bad mood and it didn't take long for her to get Lucia to spill her guts about everything.

"Now, tell me once more your reason for not wanting to sleep with Derringer again."

Lucia rolled her eyes as she sat back on the sofa. "I know how those Westmoreland brothers and cousins operate with women. I don't want to become one of those females, pining away and sitting by the phone hoping I'm next on the list to call."

"But you've been pining away for Derringer for years anyway."

"I haven't been pining. Yes, I've loved him, but I knew he didn't love me back and I accepted that. I was fine with it. I had a life. I didn't expect him to phone or show up on my doorstep making booty calls."

Chloe laughed. "He didn't make a booty call exactly. He did take you out on a date."

"But that's beside the point."

Chloe leaned forward, grinning. "And what is your point exactly? I warned you that once you had a piece of a Westmoreland you'd become addicted. Now you've had Derringer more than once, so watch out. Staying away from him is going to be easier said than done, Lucia."

Lucia shook her head. "You just don't understand, Chloe."

Chloe smiled sadly. "You're right, I don't. I don't understand how a woman who loves a man won't go after him using whatever means it takes to get him. What are you afraid of?"

Lucia glanced over at Chloe. "Failing. Which will lead to heartbreak." She drew in a deep breath. "I had a cousin who had a nervous breakdown over a man. She was twenty and her parents sent her all the way from Nashville to live with us for a while. She was simply pathetic. She would go to bed crying and wake up doing the same thing. It was so depressing. I hate to say this, but I couldn't wait until she pulled herself together enough to leave."

"How sad for her."

"No, that's the reality of things when you're dealing with a man like Derringer."

Chloe quirked a brow. "I still think you might be wrong about him."

Lucia figured she couldn't change the way her best friend thought; however, she intended to take all the precautions where Derringer was concerned. Now he saw her as a challenge because she was the woman not willing to give him the time of day anymore.

Some men didn't take rejection well and she had a feeling that Derringer Westmoreland was one of them.

Nine

Jason snapped his fingers in front of Derringer's face. "Hey, man, have you been listening to anything I've said?"

Derringer blinked, too ashamed to admit that he really hadn't. The last thing he recalled hearing was something about old man Bostwick's will being read that day. "Sort of," he said, frowning. "You were talking about old man Bostwick's will."

Herman Bostwick owned the land that was adjacent to Jason's. For years, Bostwick had promised Jason if he ever got the mind to sell, he would let Jason make him the first offer. The man died in his sleep and had been laid to rest a couple of days ago. It didn't take much to detect from the look in Jason's eyes that he wanted the land and Hercules, Bostwick's prize stallion. A colt from Hercules would be a dream come true for any horse breeder.

"So who did he leave the land to?" Derringer asked. "I hope it didn't go to his brother. Kenneth Bostwick is one mean son of a gun and will take us to the cleaners if we have to buy the land and Hercules from him."

Jason shook his head and took a sip of his beer. "The old man left everything to his granddaughter. Got Kenneth kind of pissed off about it."

Derringer lifted a brow. "His granddaughter? I didn't know he had one."

"It seems not too many people did. I understand that he and his son had a falling-out years ago, and when he left for college the son never returned to these parts. He married and settled down in the South. He had one child, a girl."

Derringer nodded and took a sip of his own beer. "So this granddaughter got the land and Hercules?"

"Yes. The only good thing is that I heard she's a prissy miss from Savannah who probably won't be moving here permanently. More than likely she'll be open to selling everything, and I want to be ready to buy when she does."

Jason then slid down to sit on the steps across from him, and Derringer looked out across his land. It was late afternoon and he still couldn't get out of his mind what had happened earlier that day with Lucia. If she thought he was done with her then she should think again.

He glanced over at his cousin. "Have you ever met a woman that got in your blood, real good?"

Jason just stared at him for a long moment. It didn't take much to see that Derringer's question had caught his cousin off guard. But he knew Jason; he liked mulling things over—sometimes too damn long.

"No. I'm not sure that can happen. At least not with me. Any woman who gets in my blood will end up being the one I marry. I don't have a problem with settling down and getting married one day, mind you. One day, when I'm ready, I want to start a family. I want to will everything I've built up to my wife and kids. You know what they say, 'You can't take it with you.'"

Jason then studied Derringer. "Why do you ask? Have you met a woman that's gotten deep in your blood?"

Derringer glanced away for a moment and then returned his gaze to Jason. "Yes...Lucia."

"Lucia Conyers?"

"Yeah."

Jason stood, almost knocking over his beer bottle. "Damn, man, how do you figure that? You only had one date with her."

Derringer smiled. "I've had two. We went skating last night." He didn't say anything and wanted to see what Jason had to say. Jason sat back down without opening his mouth.

"She's different," Derringer added after a moment.

Jason glanced over at him. "Of course she's different. You're not talking about one of your usual airheads or Derringer's Pleasers. We're discussing Lucia Conyers, for heaven's sake. She used to be one of the smartest girls at her school. Remember when Dillon and Ramsey paid her to tutor Bailey that time so she wouldn't be left back? Lucia was only seventeen then."

Derringer smiled. He had almost forgotten about that time. And if he wanted to believe what she'd told him earlier, she had been in love with him even then. "Yes, I remember."

"And remember the time Megan got her first A on a science project because she was smart enough to team up with Lucia?"

Derringer chuckled, recalling that time as well. "Yeah, I recall that time as well." At least he did now.

"And you actually think someone that smart is destined to be your soul mate?"

"Soul mate?"

"Yes, if a woman is in your blood that much then it means she's destined to be your soul mate. Someone you want to be with all the time. Think about it, Derringer. Like I said, Lucia is not some airhead, she's pretty smart."

He didn't say anything for a moment as he studied his boots, grinning, thinking Jason's question had to be a joke. Then he lifted his gaze to find a serious-looking Jason staring at him, still waiting for a response. So he gave him the only one he knew. "Yes, I'm not exactly a dumb ass, Jason, so what does her being so smart have to do with anything? And as far as being my soul mate if that means sharing a bed with her whenever I want, then I intend to do everything in my power to convince her that she is the one."

Jason rolled his eyes and then rubbed his chin thoughtfully as he stared at Derringer. "So are you saying you've fallen in love with Lucia?"

Derringer looked taken aback. "Fallen in love with her? Are you crazy? I wouldn't go *that* far."

Jason appeared confused. "You have no problem

wanting to claim her as your soul mate and sleep with her, but you aren't in love with her?"

"Yes. That's pretty much the shape and size of it."

Jason shook his head, grinning. "I hate to tell you this, but I'm not sure that's how it works."

Derringer finished off his beer and said, "Too bad. That's the way it's going to work for me."

On Monday morning, Lucia stood in the middle of her office refusing to let the huge arrangement of flowers get to her. They were simply gorgeous and she would be the first to admit Derringer had good taste. But she knew just what the flowers represented. He wanted her back in his bed and would try just about anything to get her there. She wished things could go back to how they used to be when he hadn't had a clue about her feelings. But it was too late for that.

Six hours later, Lucia glanced over at the flowers and smiled. They were just as beautiful as they had been when they'd been delivered that morning. She glanced at her watch. She would leave in a couple of hours to go straight to class. Mondays were always her busiest days with meetings and satellite conference calls with the other *Simply Irresistible* offices around the country during the day and class at night.

She kicked off her shoes, leaned back in her chair and closed her eyes. The office would be closing in less than twenty minutes and since she would be there long after that, she figured there was no reason she couldn't grab a quick nap.

With her eyes shut, it didn't surprise her when an image of Derringer came into view. Boy, he was gorgeous. And arrogant. She frowned, thinking he was as arrogant as he was gorgeous Still…

She wasn't sure how long she slept. But she remembered she was dreaming of Derringer, and wherever they were, she had whispered for him to kiss her and he had. She heard herself moan as the taste of him registered on her brain, and she couldn't help thinking how real her dream was. And was that really the feel of his fingertips on her chin as he devoured her mouth with plenty of tongue play. She could actually inhale his scent. Hot, robust and masculine.

They continued kissing in her dream and she simply melted while he leisurely explored the depths of her mouth. Nobody could kiss like him, she thought as he probed his tongue deeper. She had dreamed of him kissing her many times before, but for some reason this was different. This was like the real deal.

Her eyes flew open and she squealed when she realized it wasn't a dream! It was the real deal! She jerked forward and pushed him away from her. "Derringer! How dare you come into my office and take advantage of me."

He stood back, licked his lips and smiled. "The way I assume you took advantage of me that night? Just for the record, Lucia, you asked me to kiss you. When I entered your office, you were whispering my name. And I distinctively heard you ask me to kiss you."

"I was dreaming!"

He gave her an arrogant smirk. "Nice to know I'm in your dreams, sweetheart."

She eased out of her chair and crossed her arms over her chest. When she saw where his gaze went—directly to where her blouse dipped to reveal more cleavage than she wanted—she dropped her arms, scowling. "What are you doing here and who let you into my office?"

He jammed his hands into the pockets of his jeans. "I came to see you and I arrived when your administrative assistant was leaving. She remembered me from Chloe and Ramsey's wedding and let me in."

His smile widened. "She figured I was safe. I did knock on the door a few times before I entered, and would not have come in if I hadn't heard you call out my name."

Lucia swallowed. Had she really called out his name? She ignored that possibility. "Why are you here?"

"To make sure you liked your flowers."

She dragged her gaze from him to the huge floral arrangement she had been admiring all day. In fact, everyone in the office had admired it, and she knew they were wondering who'd sent the flowers. She glanced back at Derringer. Okay, maybe she should have called and thanked him; she hadn't wanted to give him any ideas, but it seemed he'd gotten plenty without her help.

"Yes, they're beautiful. Thank you. Now you can leave."

He shook his head. "I figured while I'm here I might as well drop you off at school. You do have class tonight, right?"

"Yes, but why would I want you to drop me off at school when I can drive myself? I do have a car."

"Yes, but I wouldn't want you to get a ticket. You told me all about your Monday-night professor and how he hates it when anyone is late. You also mentioned that tonight is your final. You're going to be late."

Lucia glanced down at her watch and went still. She wasn't aware she had slept that long. She needed to be in class in twenty minutes and it would take her longer than that to get through town. Professor Turner had already warned the class that he would close his door exactly at seven, and Derringer was right, tonight she was to take her final.

She slipped into her shoes and quickly moved around the desk to grab her purse out of the desk drawer. "And just how are you supposed to get me there any sooner than I can drive myself?" she asked, hurrying out the office door. He was right behind her.

"I have my ways." He then pulled his cell phone out of his back pocket. "Pete? This is Derringer. I need a favor."

She glanced over her shoulder as she was locking the door. He was calling Pete Higgins, one of the sheriff's deputies and also one of his good friends.

"I need escort service from *Simply Irresistible* to the U, and we need to be there in less than fifteen minutes." Derringer smiled. "Okay, we're on our way down."

He glanced over at her when he put his phone in his back pocket. "We'll leave your car here and come back for it after class."

She frowned over at him as they stepped into the elevator. "Why can't I drive my own car and your friend Pete can just give me escort service?"

He shook his head. "It doesn't work that way. He knows I'm trying to impress my girl."

"I am not your girl, Derringer."

"Sure you are. Why else would you moan my name in your sleep?"

Lucia turned her head away from him, deciding that question didn't need an answer. Besides, what response could she give him?

Once they reached the bottom floor, things moved quickly. He took her laptop bag off her shoulder and put it in the backseat of his truck. By the time he escorted her to the passenger side, Pete pulled up in the patrol car with his lights flashing and a huge grin on his face. He nodded at her before giving Derringer a thumbs-up.

Luckily, she got to school in one piece and was able to make it to class on time. An hour or so later, after she'd finished her exam and placed her pencil aside, instead of glancing back over her exam to make sure she didn't need to do any last-minute changes, her mind drifted to Derringer.

Lucia shook her head. What some men wouldn't do for a piece of tail, she thought. Regardless of what Chloe assumed, she knew that was probably all she was to him. Of course he was trying to impress her just to prove a point, and just the thought that he had caught her dreaming about him, and that in her sleep she had asked him to kiss her, was enough for her to wear a brown bag over her head for the rest of the year.

And what was even worse was that he would be picking her up when class was over. She had no choice if she wanted to get home without taking the bus. A part of her steamed at the thought of how things had worked out nicely for him in that regard. He would be driving her to get her car and nothing more. If he thought there would be more, he had another think coming.

The moment she stepped out of the Mass Communications Building, she glanced around. Derringer's truck was parked in a space in a lighted area and he was leaning against it as if he was expecting her, which was odd since he hadn't known when her class would let out. Had he been here the entire time?

She quickly crossed to where he stood. "How did you know I was about to walk out?"

He glanced over at her as he opened the truck door for her. "I didn't. I figured that you would catch a cab to get your car if I wasn't here, so I thought the best thing to do was to be here when you came out."

She frowned at him before stepping up into the truck. "You've been here the whole time?"

"Yep."

"Don't you have anything better to do?" she asked coolly.

"Nope." He then closed the door and moved around the front of the truck to get into the driver's side.

He closed the door, buckled his seat belt and turned the key in the ignition. "Don't you think you're getting carried away with all this, Derringer?"

He chuckled. "No."

She rolled her eyes. "Seriously. I couldn't have been that great in bed."

His mouth tilted in a slow, ultrasatisfied smile. "Trust me, Lucia. You were."

She crossed her arms over her chest as he pulled out of the parking lot. "So you admit this is only about sex."

"I didn't say that, so I won't be admitting anything. I told you what I wanted."

She glanced over at him. "To sleep with me again."

"Yes, but not just a couple more times. I'm talking about the rest of my life. You're my soul mate." Derringer smiled thinking that sounded pretty darn good and had to thank Jason for putting the idea into his head.

Her mouth dropped. "Soul mate?"

"Yes."

"That's insane," she threw out

"That's reality. Get used to it," he threw back.

She turned around in her seat as much as her seat belt would allow. "It's not reality and I won't get used to it, because it doesn't make sense. If this has anything to do with you thinking I got pregnant from our previous encounters you don't have that to worry about. My monthly visitor arrived this morning."

"That wasn't it, although that would have definitely been important to me if you had gotten pregnant. But like I told you before, you're in my blood now. You were a virgin and I'd never been with a virgin before."

"Whoop-de-do," she said sarcastically. "No big deal."

"For me it is."

She just stared at him, deciding not to argue with him anymore. Doing so would give her a friggin' headache. She shifted positions to sit straight in her seat and closed her eyes, but she wouldn't go to sleep for fear of waking up with her lips locked to his again.

Each time she felt herself being lulled to sleep by the smooth jazz sounds coming from the CD player, she would open her eyes to gaze out the window and study all the buildings they passed. She thought Denver was a beautiful city and there was no other place quite like it.

Due to the lack of traffic, they returned to her office building sooner than she had anticipated. And, she tried convincing herself, not as quickly as she would have liked. But she knew that was a lie. She liked the fact that she was the woman riding in the truck with him tonight. She had been the one he had waited for outside her classroom building. And she was the one for whom he had ordered a special escort service to get her to school on time. Then there were the flowers. A girl could really succumb to him if she wasn't careful.

"How do you think you did on your test tonight?"

His question surprised her and she glanced over at him when he parked his truck behind her car. She couldn't help but smile. "I think I aced it. I'm almost sure of it. There were a lot of multiple-choice questions, but there was one essay question to test our writing skills."

"I'm happy for you then."

"Thanks."

She watched as he opened his door and then walked around the back of the truck to open the door for her. Once he helped her out, they stood there facing each other. "I appreciate all you did tonight, Derringer. Because of you I got to school on time."

"No problem, baby."

The term of endearment sent sensations rippling through her. "Don't call me that, Derringer."

"What?"

"Baby."

He leaned against his truck. "Why?"

"Because I'm sure I'm not the only woman you've called that."

"No, you're not, but you're the only one I've called that when it meant something."

She shook her head as she walked slowly to her car with him strolling beside her. The April air was cold and everyone was talking about a snowstorm headed their way this weekend. "You just won't give up, will you?"

"No."

"I wish you would."

They came to a stop next to her car. The smile he gave her was slow and sexy. "And I wish you would let me make love to you again, Lucia."

She was certain that irritation showed on her face. "Yet you want me to believe it's not just about sex?"

She shook her head sadly, thinking he just didn't get it. She loved him and now that he knew how she felt, she refused to settle for anything less than being loved in return. She knew for him to fall in love with her was something that wouldn't happen—not in her wildest dreams—so all she wanted to do was get on with her life without him being a part of it. "Good night, Derringer."

He moved out of the way when she got into her car and quickly drove away.

Later that night, Derringer tossed and turned in his bed. Finally, he pulled himself up and reached out to turn on the light. Brightness flooded the room and he rubbed his hands down his face.

Tomorrow would be a busy day for Denver's branch

of D&M Horse-Breeding and Training Company. In fact, the rest of the week would be hectic. His cousin Cole would be delivering more than one hundred horses from Texas at the end of the week and they needed to make sure everything was ready. It didn't help matters that a snowstorm was expected this weekend. That made things even more complicated as well as challenging.

He reached behind him and lifted his pillow and smiled when his hand touched the lacy items. He had two pairs of Lucia panties. Added to the pink pair were the red ones he'd taken off her last weekend. He wondered if she'd missed them yet and figured she probably hadn't; otherwise, she would have mentioned it.

And she wasn't pregnant. He'd actually been disappointed when she'd made that announcement. He had gotten used to the idea that perhaps she could be pregnant with his child. He knew that kind of thinking didn't make much sense, but he had.

He settled back down in bed thinking she just wouldn't let up with this "only sex" thing. He had all but told her she was his soul mate so what else did she want?

He knew the answer without thinking much about it. She wanted him to love her, but that wouldn't and couldn't happen. What if she got real sick or something and he couldn't get her to the hospital in time? What if she was in a car accident and didn't survive? What if she got stampeded by a herd of horses? What if…he lost her like he had his parents? His aunt and uncle? They were here one day and had been gone the next. He rubbed his hand down his face, not liking how his thoughts were going. He was freaking out for no reason; especially when he didn't intend to get attached to her like that.

He liked things just the way they were and didn't intend for any woman, not even Lucia, to start messing with his mind…and definitely not with his heart. But he wanted her.

There had to be a middle ground for them, something they could both agree on. It would have to be something that would satisfy them both.

He would come up with a plan. Because, no matter what, he had no intention of giving up on her.

Ten

Lucia closed the lid to her washing machine and leaned back against it thinking that Derringer had not given her back the panties he'd taken off her the other night. The red pair. Now he had two. What was he doing with them? Collecting them as souvenirs?

She strolled to the window and glanced out. It looked totally yucky outside. The forecasters' predictions had been correct. She had awakened to see huge snowflakes falling outside. That's the only thing she missed about the time she lived in Florida. This was the middle of April, spring break in most states and it was hard to believe that in some other place the sun was shining brightly. A week spent on Daytona Beach sounded pretty darn good about now. At least the snow had waited for the weekend and most people didn't have a reason to venture outside.

Her parents had gotten smart and decided to fly to Tennessee for a few weeks to visit her mother's sister. Chloe had called this morning to chat and to tell her how she, Ramsey and the baby were snuggled inside in front of the roaring fireplace and planned to stay that way. Lucia sighed deeply, thinking this was the only time she regretted being an only child. Things could get lonely at times.

She moved away from the window to go into the kitchen to make herself a cup of hot chocolate and watch that movie she had planned to watch last week, and she remembered why she hadn't.

Derringer had dropped by.

She hadn't heard from him since the night he had taken her to school. Maybe he had finally admitted to himself that he only wanted one thing from her and had moved on to some other willing female. The thought of him making love to someone else had her hurting inside, but she could deal with it the way she'd always done. It wasn't the first time she'd known the man she loved was sleeping with others and it wouldn't be the last. But it hurt knowing someone else was the recipient of his smile, his look and his touch. More than anything, a part of her wished she hadn't experienced any of it for herself. But then a part of her was glad that she had and would not trade in a single moment.

Moments later, with a cup of hot chocolate in her hand, she moved toward the living room to watch her movie. She had a fire blazing in the fireplace and it added soothing warmth to the entire room. Why she wanted to watch a romantic movie when she lacked romance in her own life was beyond her. But then, women had their dreams and fantasies, didn't they?

Lucia had settled back against her sofa with a cup in one hand and a remote in the other when the doorbell rang. She frowned, wondering what on earth could get Mrs. Noel to come across the street in this weather, unless her heating unit was on the blink again. Standing, she placed the cup and the remote on the table and headed for the door. She looked out the peephole and caught her breath.

Derringer!

Denying the rush of heat she immediately felt between her thighs, seeing him standing there and looking sexier than any man had a right to look—this time of day and in this horrid weather—she drew in a deep breath and fought the anger escalating in her chest. She would not hear from him for a week or so and then he would show up at her place unannounced. It didn't matter that she had told him to leave her alone. That was beside the point. The only point she could concentrate on was that he evidently thought he could add her to his booty-call list. Well, she had news for him.

She snatched the door open and was about to ask what he was doing there, but wasn't given the chance to do so.

Derringer didn't give Lucia the chance to ask any questions, but leaned in and covered her mouth with his. He not only wanted to silence her, he also wanted the heat from his kiss to inflame her as they stood just inside with a frigid snowstorm raging outside. There was no doubt in his mind the kiss had enough spark, power and electricity to light the entire city of Denver. And he felt it all rush through his body.

She didn't resist him, and at the moment that was a good thing. He didn't need her resistance, what he needed was this—the taste of her all over his tongue.

He had tried not thinking about her all week. Hell, with the delivery of those horses he'd had enough to keep his mind and time occupied. But things hadn't happened quite that way. She'd still managed to creep into his thoughts most of the time, and he had awakened that morning with a need to see her so intense that he just couldn't understand it. And nothing, not elephant snowflakes nor below-zero-degree temperature would keep him from her. From this.

He finally pulled back from the kiss. Somehow they had made it inside her house and closed the door behind them and that was a good thing. Having an X-rated kiss on her doorstep would definitely have given her neighbors something to talk about for years.

She gazed up at him and he thought at that moment she was the most beautiful person he had ever seen. No other women he'd messed around with before could claim that. He inwardly flinched when he thought of what he'd just done. He had compared her with all the other women in his womanizing life and in essence none could compare to her. In fact, her biggest beef about having an affair with him were those other women in his life. But he knew at that moment he would give them all up for her.

The reality of him willingly doing that hit him below the belt and he nearly tumbled over. Derringer Westmoreland would give up his lifestyle for a woman?

Make a commitment to be only with her? He drew in a sharp breath. He'd never made such an allegiance with any female. Had never intended to be dedicated or devoted to one. There were too many out there and he enjoyed being footloose and fancy-free. Was she worth all of that? He knew in that instant that she was.

"What are you doing here, Derringer?"

He could tell she had regained control of the senses they'd both lost when she had opened her door. He had initiated the kiss, but she had reciprocated, which told him that although she wished otherwise, she had enjoyed it as much as he had.

"I needed to see you," he said simply.

She rolled her eyes. "That's what you said the last time."

"And I'm saying it again."

She drew in a deep breath and then turned and walked toward the sofa. He followed, thinking at least she hadn't asked him to leave…yet. She sat down on the couch and he dropped down on the love seat.

"If you had to venture out in this blasted weather, why not go visit Ashira Lattimore? I'm sure she has a bed warming for you."

The last thing he needed to do was to admit there was a strong possibility the woman did. As far as he knew, Ashira had gotten it into her head that she would eventually become Mrs. Derringer Westmoreland. He wouldn't marry Ashira if she was the last woman on earth. She was too possessive and clingy. On the other hand, the woman sitting across from him wasn't possessive and clingy enough. Yet she claimed to love him, when he knew all Ashira wanted was the Westmoreland name and all his worldly possessions.

"She isn't the woman I want warming a bed for me," he said quietly, glancing over at her intently. Not only did she look good as usual, she smelled good, too. He was so familiar with her scent that he could probably pick her out of any room even if he was blindfolded.

"Do most men care what woman warms their bed?"

He'd never cared until now.

"Don't answer, Derringer, you might incriminate yourself," she said bitterly.

That should have gotten him off the hook, but he felt a need to respond anyway. "Those who find the woman they want care. Then they are willing to give up all the others."

She lifted a brow and he knew the moment she thought she had boxed him into the perfect corner, one she figured he wouldn't be able to get out of because there was no way he would give up his other women for her. It amazed him that he could discern just how his woman thought.

His woman?

He smiled thinking that yes, she was definitely *his* woman.

"And you want me to believe you're willing to give up all other women for me," she said, chuckling with a look on her face that said the whole idea of him doing such a thing was simply ridiculous.

"Yes, I'd give up all other women for you," he said, meeting her gaze with a look that told her he was dead serious. She almost dropped the cup she was holding in her hand.

She shook her head. "Don't be silly."

"I'm not," he responded. "I'm as serious as a Bugatti Veyron on an open road."

"No, you're not."

"Oh, yes, sweetheart, I am."

She simply stared at him for a moment and then asked in a cautious and quiet tone, "Why?"

"Because you are the only woman I want," he said.

"But love has nothing to do with it?"

He knew he had to be completely honest with her. He didn't want to give her false hope or misguided illusions. "No. Love has nothing to do with it. But we'll have something just as important."

"What?"

"Respect for each other and a sense of caring. I do care for you, Lucia, or I wouldn't be here." There. He'd painted her the picture he intended for her to see. She loved him and had admitted to doing so and he had no reason not to believe her. But he knew a woman's love went deep and things could get rather messy if she expected or anticipated those feelings in return. She wouldn't get them.

"Are you willing to accept being the only woman in my life in a long-term exclusive affair, Lucia?"

She stared at him, not saying anything and then as if to be certain she'd heard him correctly and clearly understood the perimeters of what he'd proposed, she asked, "And during that time you won't be involved with any woman but me?"

"Yes, I give you my word on it. Something I've never given any woman I've been involved with in the past.

You are the first woman." It was on the tip of his lips to add, *Just like I was your first man.*

Lucia sat there, staring at Derringer and searching his face for any signs that he was being anything but aboveboard. Was he giving her a line? She drew in a deep breath. He had given her his word, and most people knew that the Westmorelands' word meant everything to them. But could it withstand temptation? What if he got tired of her and was tempted to test the waters elsewhere with someone else?

"And if you change your mind about this exclusivity thing, you will let me know? I wouldn't find out from others?"

He shook his head. "No, you wouldn't find out from others. I wouldn't do you that way, Lucia. If and when I get ready to end things between us, you will be the first to know."

He paused for a moment and then inclined his head. "So, if you fully accept those terms, please come over here for a second," he murmured in seductive invitation.

She hesitated, still uncertain. She knew there was sexual chemistry between them, she could feel the snap, crackle and pop even now with the distance separating them. On what was probably the coldest day in Denver this year, he was sitting over there looking hotter than any man had a right to look, and he got finer and finer each time she saw him. His dark eyes were pulling her in, mesmerizing her down to her panties. And that luscious mouth of his seemed to be calling out to her, tempting her in ways she really didn't need to be tempted; especially when she went to bed each night dreaming of him.

She would be the first to say that his offer of an exclusive affair surprised her because she knew that's not how he operated. In fact, that was not how any of the single Westmorelands handled their business with women. So why was he treading off the beaten track?

One thing was for certain; his blatant honesty about the kind of relationship he wanted with her had caught her off guard. He wasn't promising love, although he was well aware of how she felt about him. Instead of offering her love in return, he was offering her an exclusive affair.

Suddenly something happened that she hoped she didn't live to regret. At that moment, she began listening to her heart and not her mind. Her heart was telling her that she loved him too much not to take him up on the offer he'd laid out to her. She would be entering the affair with both eyes open and no expectations except one. He would give her advance notice when he was ready to end things between them.

That meant that while things lasted she would spend all the time with him she desired. She would be the only woman sharing his bed. The one and only woman claiming Derringer Westmoreland's full attention. She glanced down at her hand and accepted the fact that the only drawback was that he would never put a ring on her finger.

She glanced back up and her gaze returned to the deep, dark eyes that were staring at her. And waiting. And as she returned his stare, she was getting wet just thinking about all the things they would probably spend their time doing together as an exclusive couple.

She moistened her lips with the tip of her tongue and watched his gaze take in her every movement as she slowly stood. And then he stood and at that moment she realized what he was doing. Something she hadn't expected. He was meeting her halfway.

He began walking toward her the moment she began walking toward him and they met in the center. "I wasn't sure you were going to take those steps," he whispered throatily when they stood face-to-face, his mesmerizing dark gaze locked on hers.

"I wasn't sure either."

He then cupped her face in his hands and took possession of her mouth in the way she'd gotten used to him doing.

When Lucia began responding to his kiss that had liquid heat flaming inside him, he knew what they both wanted and needed. And this was the perfect day for it. He broke off the kiss and swept her off her feet and into his arms and purposefully moved toward her bedroom. Wanting her this much was the epitome of insanity, but he might as well get used to it.

He placed her on the bed and stepped back to quickly remove his clothes, sending them flying all over the place. And then for the first time since they'd made love, he took the time to use a condom.

When he returned to the bed, he captured her hand and drew her toward him to remove her clothes, slowly stripping her bare. Today she was wearing a pair of white panties, but they weren't of the granny style. They were bikinis. But the style or color of her undergarments didn't matter to him.

"Nice panties," he said, picking up his jeans and placing the panties in the back pocket.

"Why are you doing that? You have two pairs of mine already. Is there something I should know?" she asked when he tossed his jeans back to the floor and eased down onto the bed to join her.

"Yes," he said, pulling her into his arms. "I go to sleep every night with them under my pillow."

Her mouth dropped. "You're kidding, right?"

He smiled. "No, I'm not kidding, and before you ask, the answer is no. I've never collected the underwear of other women, Lucia. Just yours."

He saw the confused look on her face and thought she could dwell on what he'd confessed at another time. He needed her full concentration for what he intended to do to her right now.

Now that she was his, he wanted to get to know each and every inch of her body. Reaching out, he cradled her chin in his hand, forcing her to meet his gaze again. He could tell she was still trying to understand what he'd said earlier about her panties.

He smiled, thinking this was where he needed to shift her focus.

Lucia saw the sexy-curvy smile that touched Derringer's lips and knew she was in trouble in the most sensual way. For some reason, she knew this lovemaking session would be different, but she didn't know in what way.

"We're staying in all weekend," he whispered in a

voice so low and hot that a burning sensation began at the tips of her toes and moved upward through her body.

She was trying to understand what he'd said about staying in all weekend. Was he letting her know that he intended to keep her here, in this bed, the majority of the time? Before she could think further about it, he lifted his hand and went straight to her breasts and his fingers began toying with a darkened nipple.

"I like your breasts. I especially like how well defined they are and how easy they can slip into my mouth. Like this."

He lowered his head and his stiffened tongue laved the nipple, licking all around it a few times before easing the firm pebble between his lips, and began sucking.

Her eyes fluttered closed as a multitude of sensations pulled at the juncture of her thighs in response to the pulling motion to her breasts. His mouth was like a vacuum, drawing her nipple more and more into his mouth as his hot tongue did all kinds of wicked things to it. He switched breasts, to take on nipple number two, and she watched through hooded eyes as he continued to devour her this way.

Moments later, he drew away to lean back on his haunches to look down at her with a satisfied smile on his lips. It was then that she sensed a need in him, and the thought of him wanting her that much sent a rush of excitement through her bloodstream.

"Now for your pillows," he said, reaching behind her and grabbing both to place under her hips. She didn't have to ask what he was about to do and groaned softly at the vision that flowed through her mind. When he'd gotten her in the position he wanted, with the lower part of her elevated to his liking, he just continued to gaze at that part of her.

"You're beautiful," he whispered. "All over. But especially here," he said, reaching out and gently tracing a hand inside her inner thigh, slowly letting his fingers work their way toward the feminine folds that she knew were wet and ready for his touch.

She couldn't help but respond, and moaned as his fingers continued to lightly skim over her most intimate parts, causing sensuous shivers to flow through her. By the time he inserted two fingers inside her, she let out a deep groan and threw her head back, unable to help the way her hips rolled against the pillows cushioning them. And when he lowered his head, her fingers sank into the blades of his shoulders.

"Scent is closely linked to taste," he whispered, his breath hot against her womanly folds. "You're so wet here," he said softly, and proceeded to blow air through his lips onto her. "Since I can't blow you dry, that means I'm going to have to lap you up."

His words turned every cell in her body into a wild, unrestrained state. Instinctively, she bucked wildly against his mouth and he retaliated by grabbing her hips and diving his tongue between her womanly folds.

"Derringer!"

Her hands left his shoulders to grab hold of his head. Not to push him away, but to keep him there. Right there at that perfect angle, that most sensuous position as his mouth devoured her as if she were the tastiest meal he'd ever consumed.

She continued to cry out his name over and over,

but there was no stopping him. He used his mouth to brand the woman he wanted. And the mere thought that that woman was her made her become more and more deeply entranced with every stroke of his tongue.

And when she couldn't take any more and her body began shuddering violently in the wake of one gigantic orgasm, he wouldn't let up, but continued to make love to her this way until the last jolt passed through her body. It was then that he quickly removed the pillows from beneath her body before mounting her.

"Lucia."

Her name was a whispered hunger from Derringer's lips. Hunger that had only slightly been appeased. And when she opened glazed eyes to look up at him the exact moment he slid into her, his nostrils flared and he felt his shaft thicken even more inside her. He knew she felt it the moment that it did.

"Take me, baby, hold me, clench me. Get everything out of me that you want," he prodded in a deep, guttural voice.

And from the way her inner muscles began clenching him, clamping down tight, compressing him, he could only throw his head back, knowing he was about to enjoy the ride of his life. This was one mating he would never forget.

He began moving, thrusting in and out of her, and when she began moving in rhythm with him, the sound of flesh smacking against flesh, he let out a ragged groan. And when she locked her legs around him and rubbed her breasts against his chest, he leaned close to her mouth and captured her lips with his.

There was nothing like kissing a woman while you made love to her, he thought. Knowing your body was planted deep in hers, knowing sensual aches were being satisfied and an earth-shattering climax was on the horizon. And when she moaned deep within his mouth, he pulled back, looked down at her, wanting to see the exact moment an orgasm ripped through her.

He watched in breathless fascination as the pleasure he was giving her contorted her features, made her tremble, almost took her breath away. It was then that he felt his own body explode, and he thrust into her deeper than he'd ever gone before.

"Lucia!"

No woman had ever done this to him; reduce him to a ball of fiery sensations that had him bucking wildly all over the place. He gripped her hips as sensations continued to tear into him, enthrall him, and each desperate thrust only called for another.

And when she came again, he was right there with her and together their bodies quaked violently as unrestrained pleasure took them over the edge.

"How are we going to explain things to your family, Derringer?"

His eyes popped open and he shifted his gaze to look over at Lucia. They had taken a nap after their last lovemaking session and she was leaning down over him, still naked and with strands of her hair hanging in arousing disarray around her shoulders. He glanced beyond her to the window to look outside. Was it getting dark already? He hadn't eaten breakfast or lunch yet.

"Derringer?"

His gaze returned to her and he saw the anxiety in her eyes and the way she was nervously biting her lower lip. "We don't owe them any explanations, Lucia. We're adults."

"I know that, but..."

When she didn't complete what she was going to say, he decided to finish it off for her. "But they're going to think you've lost your mind for getting involved with me."

He knew it was true and really didn't like the way it sounded. His family knew of his reputation more than anyone, and for him to have talked Lucia into an affair wouldn't sit too well with them. But as he'd told her, he and Lucia were adults.

"They're going to think you'll eventually hurt me," she said quietly.

"Then I guess it will be on me to prove otherwise, because I'm not letting what they think cause a rift between us. Besides, they know we've been out a couple of times, and once they see how taken I am with you, they'll start minding their own business."

And he *was* taken with her, he'd admit that much. He was taken with her in a way no other woman could claim. He couldn't help but smile when he then said, "But I'm not the one they need to be concerned about. Zane's and Canyon's womanizing ways are probably right up there with Raphel's."

"Your great-grandfather? The one who was married to all those women?" she asked.

"Well, we're still trying to figure out what's fact and what's fiction. So far, the women we thought were his first two wives actually weren't. Dillon gave all the records he'd accumulated to Megan. She's determined to find out the truth as to whether Raphel actually lived all those lives," he said, pulling her down to him before he would be tempted to take one of her nipples into his mouth. As much as he loved tasting her, he figured they needed to eat something more nourishing now.

"I think I'll shower and then go into your kitchen to see what I can throw together for us," he said.

She looked surprised. "You're going to feed me?"

He couldn't help but smile, thinking that wasn't all he intended to do to her. "Yes, but trust me, I have a reason for doing so. I meant what I said earlier about keeping you inside all weekend, sweetheart."

And then he leaned down and locked his mouth with hers. This was one snowstorm that he would never forget.

Eleven

"So how are things going with you and Derringer?"

Sensations of excitement rippled in Lucia's stomach at the mention of Derringer's name. She and Chloe had decided to do lunch at McKay's, and as soon as the waitress had taken their orders and moved away, Chloe had begun asking Lucia a number of questions.

The weather had started clearing up a little on Sunday night, and Derringer had talked her into going to his ranch and leaving for work on Monday morning from there. He had even helped her pack an overnight bag. What she hadn't expected was his siblings and cousins showing up early Monday morning to check on him because no one had seen or heard from him all weekend. She hadn't missed the look of surprise on their faces when she'd come down the stairs dressed for work, giving everyone a clear idea of how he'd spent those snowed-in hours and with whom.

That had been a couple of weeks ago. "So far, so good. I enjoy spending time with him."

And truly she did. He'd taken her to the movies several times and picked her up from work on several occasions, and had spent the night over at her place a number of times as well.

Chloe beamed. "I'm glad. Ramsey is too. Already he's seen a change in Derringer."

Lucia raised a brow as she took a sip of her iced tea. "What kind of change?"

"Peace. Calm. He seems more focused. Less untamed and wild. Not only Ramsey but the other Westmorelands think you're good for him."

Lucia nervously nibbled at her lower lip. "I hope they aren't getting any ideas. I told you what's between me and Derringer is only temporary. He made sure I understood that, Chloe."

Chloe waved her words away. "All men think nothing is forever at first, only a few have love on their minds initially. Callum was an exception. He knew he loved Gemma before she had a clue."

"But Derringer doesn't love me. He's said as much. I'm in this relationship with both eyes open."

Later, back in her office, she recalled her words to Chloe as she sat staring at the huge arrangement of flowers that was sitting on her desk that had been delivered while she was at lunch. The card had simply said, *I'm thinking of you.*

Just the thought that he was thinking of her made everything inside her rock with anticipation to see him again. It was Friday and they were going skating again tonight and she couldn't wait.

The intercom on her desk went off, almost startling her. "Yes?"

"Someone is here to see you, Ms. Conyers."

Excitement flowed in her stomach. The last time she'd received flowers from Derringer, he had shown up at her office later. Was he here to see her now? "Who is it, Wanda?"

"Ashira Lattimore."

Lucia's throat tightened. Why would Ashira Lattimore be visiting her? There was only one way to find out. "Thanks, Wanda, ask her to come in."

Lucia clicked off her intercom and glanced at the flowers on her desk. Something about them gave her inner strength to deal with what was about to take place. She wasn't exactly sure what would happen, but she figured it had something to do with Derringer.

It wasn't long before the woman knocked on her door. "Come in."

Ashira walked in and just like all the other times Lucia had seen her she looked beautiful. But Lucia knew that beauty was merely on the outside. She had heard a number of stories about the spoiled and reckless woman who had long ago stamped ownership on Derringer. In a way she was surprised Ashira hadn't confronted her before now.

"Ashira, this is a surprise. What can *Simply Irresistible* do for you?" Lucia plastered a smile on her lips.

The woman didn't bother returning her fabricated smile. "I've been gone, Lucia, visiting a sick relative in Dakota, and thought I'd let you know I'm back."

Lucia placed her arms across her chest. "And that's supposed to mean something to me?"

The woman glanced at the flowers on Lucia's desk, paused a minute and then said, "I think it would where Derringer is concerned. Not sure if he told you, but the two of us have an understanding."

"Do you?"

"Yes. No matter who he dallies with, I'm the one he'll always come back to. I'm sure you've known him long enough to know our history."

"Unfortunately, I don't, and for you to pay me a visit to stake a claim you think you have speaks volumes. It makes me think you're not as confident as you want to claim," she said with more bravado than she actually felt.

"Think whatever you want. Just remember, when he's done with you he'll come back to me. He and I have plans to marry one day."

Lucia's heart dropped at the woman's announcement. "Congratulations on your and Derringer's future plans. Now, if you've said everything you've come here to say, I think you should leave."

It was then that Ashira smiled, but the smile didn't quite reach her eyes. It didn't come close. "Fine, just remember my warning. I'm trying to spare you any heartbreak." The woman then walked out of her office.

Derringer's gaze flickered over Lucia's face. "You okay? You've been quiet most of the evening."

They had gone skating with what he was now beginning to think of as the regular crowd. Most of the kids and teens had gotten used to him and Lucia invading their turf. And now they were back at her place, but she hadn't said a whole lot since he'd picked her up that evening.

She smiled over at him. "Yes, I'm fine. This has been a busy week at work and I'm just glad it's the weekend. I need it."

He pulled her into his arms. "And I need it as well. More horses are arriving this week and then all our relatives start arriving the week after that for the Westmoreland Charity Ball. You are going to the ball with me, aren't you?"

He watched her features and she seemed surprised he'd asked. Her next question proved him right. "You really want to take me?"

"Of course I do."

"Thanks."

He stared down at her for a moment. "Why are you thanking me?"

"Um, no reason. I just wasn't sure what your plans would be."

It was on the tip of his tongue to say that whatever his plans were they would always include her, but he didn't. Lately, he was encountering feelings and emotions when it came to Lucia that he didn't quite understand and didn't want to dwell on.

"I hear Gemma is coming home in a few days," she said, cutting into his thoughts.

A smile touched his lips. "Yeah, and I miss her. I'd gotten used to Gemma being underfoot and wasn't sure how I'd handle her up and moving to Australia. But

Callum loves her and we know he's taking good care of her. Besides, homecomings are good."

"Yes, he does love her."

There was something about her tone of voice that sounded contemplative and reflective, as if she was wondering, considering just how that would be for a man to love her that way. For a moment he didn't know what to say, so he decided not to say anything.

Instead, he did something he always enjoyed doing to her. He touched her chin, making rotary motions with his thumb on her soft skin before tilting her head back to lower his mouth to kiss her.

The sound of her sensual purr fueled his desire, making him so aroused his erection thickened painfully against the zipper of his jeans. And when she wrapped her arms around his neck as he deepened the kiss, he went crazy with lust for her.

Not able to hold back any longer, he swept her off her feet into his arms and carried her upstairs to the bedroom.

"Why haven't you mentioned Ashira's visit to Derringer, Lucia?"

Lucia glanced over at Chloe. They had just finished a business meeting and she'd known something had been on her best friend's mind all morning. "And how do you know I haven't?"

"Trust me, had you told him, all hell would have broken loose. He's never appreciated Ashira's possessiveness."

Lucia shrugged. "For all I know they could have an understanding just like she claims."

"I can't believe you would think that."

"In all honesty I'm trying not to think about anything regarding Derringer and Ashira. I'm just taking one day at a time."

Chloe frowned. "She would never have come into *my* office with that haughty I'm-Derringer's-real-woman foolishness, trust me."

"Because you know Ramsey loves you, I can't say that for Derringer and me. I know he doesn't love me," she said softly.

Later that night she lay in Derringer's arms with her naked body spooned intimately to his. His arm was thrown over her and he slept with his hand cupping her breast. His warm body and the scent of his musky masculinity surrounded her and she became aroused by it. That was something she couldn't help.

Since becoming sexually involved with Derringer, she had become more aware of herself as a woman, particularly her needs and wants, mainly because he made her feel as if she was the most enticing and alluring woman he'd ever met. And coming from a man like Derringer, that meant a lot.

She then thought about her conversation with Chloe earlier that day. Maybe she should have mentioned Ashira's visit to her office to Derringer. And yet a part of her didn't want to draw him into any women-over-man drama. Besides, time would tell if what the woman said was true.

She knew the moment he'd awakened by the change in his breathing. The other telltale sign was the feel of his erection beginning to swell against her naked backside. And then he began touching her. With the hand that wasn't cupping her breast he started at the dip in her thigh and let his fingers do a little walking, tracing a line toward her waist. It then followed the curve toward the juncture at her inner thighs.

"Shift open your legs for me, baby," he leaned over to whisper in her ear. "I need to touch you there."

She did what he asked and moments later she was moaning at his exploratory touch. And then when the hand cupping her breasts began doing its own thing by torturing her nipples, she clenched her lips to keep from crying out his name.

"You're so passionate," he murmured close to her ear. "You are the most sensuous woman I know."

She wanted so much to believe him. She wanted to believe it was her that he wanted and not Ashira. And when she couldn't take his torture any longer, she cried out for him to make love to her.

"My pleasure."

He then eased her onto her back and straddled her, and before she could draw her next breath, he entered her, melding their bodies as one. And each time he stroked into her and retreated, she ground her body against him ready for his reentry.

Over and over, back and forth, performing the mating dance the two of them had created as he thrust in and out of her and all she could do was continue to groan out her cries of pleasure. And when a guttural moan flowed from Derringer's lips, she knew they had been tossed into the turbulent waves of pure ecstasy.

Incredible.

Derringer pulled in a deep breath. That's how he

always thought of making love with Lucia. Each and every time was simply incredible. And she was incredible. He glanced over at her and saw she had fallen asleep with her body spooned against his.

The room was quiet as images flickered in his mind of all the things they'd done together over the past few weeks, and not all of them had been in the bedroom. He enjoyed taking her places, being seen with her and spending time with her. Exclusivity was working, but he knew it was only because the woman was Lucia.

No other woman crossed his mind. He didn't want any other woman but her. And his inner fear of something happening to her lessened more and more each day. When he considered all the possibilities, weighed all his options and thought of what could happen, none of it was more significant than spending time with her, being with her. For the rest of his life. He loved her.

Derringer drew in a sharp breath because at that moment he couldn't imagine being without her…. He wanted to live each day to the fullest with her, loving her completely. She was the only woman he wanted. For his soul mate and then one day for his wife.

His wife.

A smile touched his lips. No other woman deserved that title. And he was determined that Lucia—only Lucia—would wear it. He knew he couldn't rush her. He had to take things slow and believe that one day she would realize she was the only woman who could be a wife for this Westmoreland.

The following days passed quickly and everyone was excited when Gemma returned home and confirmed the rumor that she and Callum would become parents in seven months. It was decided that a cookout was in order to welcome the couple home and to celebrate their good news. Another Westmoreland baby was on the way.

Derringer, his brothers and cousins were playing a friendly game of horseshoes when someone rang the bell letting them know it was time to eat. The men went into Dillon's kitchen to wash up, when Zane leaned over and whispered, "Lucia looks just like she belongs with the Westmorelands, Derringer."

His gaze moved across the yard to where she was helping Chloe and Megan set the table. Zane was right. She did look as if she belonged, mainly because she did belong. In a way, he'd always known that. And now he was waiting patiently for her to realize it as well.

They had been spending a lot of time together lately. It had become his regular routine to go home and shower after working with the horses and then head on over to her place each day. School was out, so she was home most evenings now. They cooked dinner together, on occasion they would go out to take in a movie or shoot pool—something he had shown her how to do. Then on Friday nights they went roller skating. But he also enjoyed those times they would stay inside to cuddle on the sofa and watch videos.

As if she felt him looking at her, she glanced over at him and an intimate connection, as well as sexual chemistry, flowed between them the way it always did. A slow, flirty smile touched his lips and he tipped his hat to her. She returned his smile and nodded before returning to what she was doing.

"I think you like her," Zane said, reminding Derringer he was there.

Derringer smiled at his brother, refusing to let Zane bait him. "Of course I like her. We all do."

"Hey, don't be an ass, Derringer. You're in love with the woman. Admit it."

Derringer only smiled and glanced back to where Lucia was sitting. The women were crowded together on the porch listening to Gemma share stories about her Australian adventure and how she was settling into her role as Mrs. Callum Austell.

He couldn't help it, but he kept looking at Lucia. Each and every time he saw her, spent time with her, he fell more and more in love with her. Now he understood how Dillon could have left home to investigate all the rumors they'd heard about Raphel and return less than a month later an engaged man. At first he thought his cousin had needed to have his head examined, but once he met Pam and had seen how Dillon would light up around her, he sort of understood. But he'd figured nothing like that would ever happen to him.

He had been proven wrong.

He loved everything about Lucia, including her interaction with his family. But mainly he loved the way she made him feel whenever they were together.

His thoughts were pulled back to the present when Jason took a minute to provide an update on old man's Bostwick's granddaughter from Savannah. Folks were saying the woman was supposed to arrive in town to claim her inheritance in a couple of weeks. Jason was anxious about that and he was hoping his offer for the land and Hercules was the one the woman would accept.

"Looks like we have a visitor," Canyon whispered. "At least, she's *your* visitor, Derringer."

Derringer frowned when he saw the sports car driven by Ashira Lattimore pull up in the yard. He couldn't help wondering what she wanted since he knew she hadn't been invited. Also, Ashira and his sisters didn't get along. But that had never stopped Ashira from thinking her lack of an invite was merely an oversight on someone's part. She was her parents' only child and was spoiled rotten. In contrast, he thought, Lucia was her parents' only child, yet she was sweet as wine. The difference in the two women was like night and day.

"Hello, everyone," she called out, waving, while glancing around as if she had every right to show up at a family function uninvited. Her face lit up in a huge smile when she saw Derringer, and she immediately headed toward him.

"Derringer, sweetheart, I've missed you." She leaned over, wrapped her arms around his neck and placed a kiss on his lips in full view of everyone.

He took her arms from around his neck and stared down at her. "What are you doing here, Ashira?"

She gave him a pouty look. "I came to see you."

"This is not where I live," he said in an annoyed voice.

"I know, but you weren't home and we need to talk."

"About what?"

She leaned up on tiptoe and whispered close to his ear, "About that horse you're trying to sell Daddy. Since he's buying it for me, I think we need to discuss it, don't you?"

"I'm busy right now, Ashira."

"But you want to make that sale, don't you? Daddy is ready. He wants to see you now, at the ranch."

Derringer knew he needed to put Ashira in her place once and for all, but here was not the place to do it. "Okay, let's go," he said, gripping her hand and pulling her with him toward her car. "I'll be back later," he called over his shoulder to everyone. "I've got some business to take care of."

He was angry. He didn't care about the horse sale as much as Ashira assumed that he did. If she thought it was a carrot she could dangle in front of him to make him do what she wanted then she had another thought coming. What ticked him off more than anything was her underhanded behavior. He should have put her in her place regarding him years ago.

He was so intent on taking her off somewhere to give her a piece of his mind, that he didn't notice the haughty look of victory the woman shot over her shoulder at Lucia.

Chloe drew in a deep breath. "I don't think you should leave, Lucia."

Lucia wiped the tears from her eyes. "There's no reason for me to stay," she said, gathering up her things. "You saw it for yourself. Ashira shows up and he leaves. She wanted to prove what she told me that day was true and she did."

Chloe shook her head. "But I don't think that's the way it was. According to Zane and Jason, Derringer said it was about business and probably had to talk to her about that horse he's trying to sell her father."

"And it couldn't wait? Please don't make excuses for what I saw with my own eyes, Chloe. She snaps her finger and he takes off. He was leading her over to the car and not the other way around. And I truly don't want to be here when they come back."

She reached out and hugged Chloe and whispered in a broken voice, "I'll call you later."

Lucia knew it would be hard telling the others goodbye. They would see the hurt in her eyes and they would pity her. Or it might be one of those you-should-have-known-better-than-to-fall-in-love-with-Derringer looks. In her book, one was just as bad as the other.

Somehow she made it through, but nearly broke when Zane pulled her into his arms and asked her to stay a while longer. She forced a smile up at him and told him she couldn't, before rushing to her car, getting inside and driving away.

Derringer returned over an hour later. He hadn't meant to be gone that long, but when he'd arrived at the Lattimores' place he had encountered more drama. Ashira had given her father the impression things were serious between them and he had to first break the news to Phillip Lattimore that they weren't. And then he had to let Ashira know that he didn't consider her a candidate as a wife, at least not for him since there was no way in hell he would ever get shackled with someone as spoiled and selfish as she was. Those words hadn't been too well received, and Derringer had found himself stranded on the Lattimore land. He'd had to call Pete to give him a lift back here.

The moment he got out of Pete's patrol car he knew something was wrong. He could understand everyone staring at him, probably wondering why Pete, instead of Ashira, had brought him back. But they weren't just staring at him. They were openly glaring.

"Looks like your family is pissed off at you for some reason," Pete said.

"Yes, looks that way," he responded. "Thanks for bringing me here."

Once the patrol car had driven off, Derringer's gaze roamed over the group that were outside in the yard cleaning up from today's activities. He looked for one person in particular, but he didn't see her. "Where's Lucia?"

It was Canyon who answered in a belligerent tone, "Oh, so now you remember that she does exist?"

Derringer frowned. "What are you talking about?"

Dillon folded his arms over his chest. "You invited Lucia here, yet you took off with another woman without giving her a backward glance. I expected better of you, Derringer."

Derringer's frown deepened. "That's not the way it was."

It was Ramsey who spoke up. "That's the way we saw it."

"And that's the way Lucia saw it," Bailey snapped, losing her cool. "I can't believe you would leave here with one of those 'silly' girls—in fact, the silliest of them all—deserting Lucia and then showing back up an hour later expecting her to still be here waiting on you. You are so full of yourself."

"Like I said, that's not the way it was," he said, glancing around at all his family circling around him.

"You're going to have a hard time convincing Lucia of that," Chloe said, not with the same snappish tone Bailey had used, but there was no doubt in everyone's mind that if given the chance she would clobber this particular brother-in-law right about now.

"Especially when just a couple of weeks ago Ashira paid Lucia a visit at *Simply Irresistible* and warned her that she could get you back anytime she wanted, and that the two of you have an understanding and that she would be the one who would eventually become your wife," Chloe added in disgust.

"Like hell," Derringer snarled.

"Doesn't matter. Ashira came here today to prove a point and in Lucia's eyes, she did."

"But like I said, it wasn't that way," Derringer implored. He then outlined everything that had happened once he'd left with Ashira and the reason that he'd left with her in the first place. "And I won't let that sort of misunderstanding come between me and Lucia," he said, moving toward his truck. "I need to go see her."

She wasn't home when Derringer got there, but according to her neighbor, Mrs. Noel, she had been there, rushing in and then leaving with an overnight bag. Derringer had no idea where she had gone. And she wouldn't answer her cell phone, although he had left several messages for her. He knew her parents were still in Tennessee and wouldn't be returning for another week or so. Thinking she'd possibly driven out to their place to stay for the night, he had gone there too, only to find the Conyers's homestead deserted.

It was after midnight when he returned to his place and rushed over to his phone when it began ringing the moment he opened the door. "Hello?"

"This is Chloe. I just got a call from Lucia. She's fine and asked that you not try seeing her or calling her. She needs time."

"No, she needs me just like I need her. She should have told me about Ashira's visit and I would have straightened things out then. I need to talk with her, Chloe. I can't stand to lose her."

"And why can't you stand to lose her, Derringer? What makes her so different from the others?"

He knew why Chloe was goading him. He was well aware what she was trying to get him to admit, not only to himself, but to her as well, just how he felt about Lucia. "I love her." He drew in a deep breath. "I love her so damn much."

"Then somehow you're going to have to convince her of that, not only in words, but with actions. Good night, Derringer."

Chloe then hung up the phone.

Twelve

Lucia sat behind her desk and stared at the beautiful arrangement of flowers that had arrived that morning. She then glanced around her office at the others that had arrived during the week. The cards all said the same thing: *You are the only woman I want.*

She drew in a deep breath wishing she could believe that, but for some reason she couldn't. Maybe it had to do with the haughty I-told-you-so look Ashira had had on her face when she had left that day with Derringer. The two of them had a history. The woman had been after Derringer for years and it seemed as if she had him. And according to Ashira, no matter who he messed around with, *she* would be the woman he married.

So, Lucia couldn't help asking herself, why was she wasting her time and her heart? The latter she knew there was no answer for. She would continue to love him, no matter what. Always had and always would. But she could do something about the former. To spend any more time with him was heartbreak just waiting to happen. Of course, he wouldn't see it that way. Men had a tendency to look at affairs differently. They didn't have a clue when it came to emotions.

At least he was respecting her wishes and hadn't tried contacting her again. She figured he and Ashira were now a hot item, although Chloe insisted otherwise. Of course, she had come up with an excuse for the reason he'd left, which Lucia was certain was the one he'd told everyone. Little did he know that Ashira was spreading another story. She wanted to make sure word got back to Lucia through mutual acquaintances that she and Derringer had left the party to go to his place and have hot, blazing sex. It deeply pained Lucia that he could leave her bed that morning and hop into bed with another woman less than twelve hours later.

Lucia glanced up when she heard the knock at her office door. "Come in."

Chloe stuck her head in and smiled. "Word is around the office that you got more flowers."

She came in and closed the door behind her, admiring the arrangement sitting on Lucia's desk. "They are gorgeous, but then, all the bouquets Derringer has sent have been gorgeous. You have to admit that."

Lucia smiled slowly. "Yes, they've all been gorgeous, but they don't mean a thing."

Chloe took the chair across from her desk. "Because of what Tanya McCoy called and told you yesterday? That she'd heard Ashira and Derringer left my place and had hot, rousing sex over at Derringer's Dungeon?

I don't believe that and neither should you. Ashira is just trying to save face. I was there when Derringer returned in Pete's patrol car. Don't let Ashira continue to mess with your mind like that. You need to take Derringer's message on those cards you've been getting with the flowers to heart."

Lucia fought back tears. "I wish I could, but I can't. All these years I've loved him and was fine with loving him from a distance. But then I had to go ruin everything by admitting I loved him and letting him into my space. From now on it's going back to status quo."

"Does that mean you won't ever visit your god-daughter at my place, for fear of running into Derringer?"

"No, but I'm trying to get beyond that."

"Then I think this coming Saturday is the perfect way to start. I suggest you change your mind about coming to the Westmoreland Charity Ball. If you see Derringer, no big deal. Now is your time to show him once and for all that you've gotten over him and you're moving on and won't be hiding out to avoid him."

Lucia nervously nibbled on her bottom lip. "And what if he's there with Ashira?"

"And what if he is? It's his loss. And if he wants her instead of you then more power to him. But if I were you, I would definitely let him see what he gave up. Um, I think you and I should go shopping."

Lucia wasn't convinced making an appearance at the charity ball this weekend would be the right thing to do.

"Just because you think one Westmoreland acted like

an ass is no reason to ostracize yourself from the rest of us," Chloe added.

Lucia knew what Chloe just said was true. Gemma had called her this morning and she had yet to call her back. So had Megan and Bailey earlier in the week. They had been friends long before she'd met Derringer. It wasn't their fault that she had fallen head over heels in love with their brother, a man who would never settle down, fall in love and marry any woman. Except maybe Ashira one day when he got tired of playing the field.

She tossed her pen on the desk and met Chloe's gaze. "Maybe you're right. I can't avoid the other Westmorelands just because my affair with Derringer went sour."

A smile touched Chloe's lips. "No, you can't. So are we going shopping this weekend?"

Lucia chuckled. "Yes, and I know this is more about you than me, Chloe Burton Westmoreland. You'll do anything, come up with any excuse, to shop."

Chloe stood, smiling. "Hey, what can I say? A woman has to do what a woman has to do."

Derringer glanced around. He was surrounded by Westmorelands and he couldn't help but smile. Once a year all the Westmorelands—from the south and west— got together for a family reunion rotating between Atlanta, rural Montana and Denver. At other times they got together to support each other for various events. Earlier this year they had traveled to Austin to be with their cousins: Cole, Clint and Casey Westmoreland had honored their deceased uncle during the Sid Roberts Foundation annual charity ball. And usually every year there seemed to be a Westmoreland wedding. The last one had been Gemma's a few months back.

And now all the Atlanta and Montana Westmorelands were gathered here in Denver with their wives for the Westmoreland Charity Ball. They had begun arriving a few days ago and were all accounted for as of noon today when Thorn and Tara had arrived. Thorn had come straight from Bikers' Week in Myrtle Beach, South Carolina.

"Thanks for putting us up for the next couple of days, Derringer."

He glanced around and smiled at his cousins, the twins—Storm and Chase. But then there were several sets of twins in the Atlanta Westmorelands' group. Storm and Chase's father had been a twin, and his cousins, Ian and Quade, were twins as well.

"Hey, no problem. If there's anything you need, just let me know." At that moment his cell phone went off and when he saw it was Chloe he smiled. "Excuse me while I take this."

He went outside to sit on the porch. "Yes, Chloe?"

"You owe me big-time, Derringer, and I swear, if you screw up, I'm coming after you myself."

He believed her. "Trust me, I've got everything planned. I'm just grateful you got Lucia to agree to come to the charity ball."

"It wasn't easy. Ashira and her girls are out spreading lies, claiming that when you left the cookout, you took her to Derringer's Dungeon and got busy."

Derringer's mouth dropped. They hadn't gone near his home. "That's a lie."

"I know, but she's intent on spreading that rumor. I

don't know what you have planned for the ball, but it better be good, and hopefully it will put a stop to Ashira once and for all."

Derringer nodded. "Trust me. It will."

"You sure you're all right, sweetheart?"

Lucia glanced over at her parents, namely, her dad, who had a concerned look on his face. "Yes, Dad, I'm fine."

He smiled. "Well, you look simply beautiful."

And considering everything, she felt beautiful. Chloe had nearly worn her out last weekend. They hadn't just shopped in Denver but had caught one of those commuter planes to Boulder to do some shopping there as well. In the end, she felt like Cinderella entering the ball. And just like good ole Cinderella she feared she would leave the ball without her man.

The moment she and her parents entered the huge ballroom she drew in a deep breath at the number of people in attendance. But then, she really wasn't surprised. The Westmoreland Foundation provided funds to a number of charities and for that very reason the people of Denver were always supportive.

It didn't take long to pick out all the Westmorelands, especially the males. Whether they were from the north, south, east or west, they had similar looks and builds. In their black tuxes, they were all tall, dashing and ultrahandsome and, not surprisingly, even with their wives on their arms most of the other women present had their eyes on them with wishful expressions on their faces.

She had met all of them at Chloe's wedding and

again at Gemma's. They were a nice group of people and she thought Chloe was blessed to be a part of the Westmoreland clan.

It seemed Chloe spotted her the moment she arrived and eagerly pulled her from her parents' side, telling her over and over just how ravishing she looked. So did Bailey, Megan, Gemma and a number of the other Westmoreland women. All the men spoke to her and as usual Zane gave her a naughty wink, which made her chuckle.

She released a deep breath, glad no one was acting or behaving any differently toward her, although all that might change once Derringer arrived with Ashira on his arm. She was just speculating and couldn't help doing so when both he and Ashira didn't appear to be present. No sooner had that thought left her mind than she glanced up and Ashira walked in with a couple of her girlfriends. Lucia was surprised she wasn't with Derringer.

A short while later, Lucia was dancing with Jason when Derringer cut in. She glanced up and tried her best not to narrow her gaze at him. The last thing she wanted was to let him know just how badly he had hurt her, although she was sure he had a clue, which was the reason for the flowers. But if he thought he could woo her and sleep with Ashira at the same time then he had another thought coming.

"Lucia."

She wished he didn't say her name quite that way. With that same throatiness she remembered so well. "Derringer."

"You look beautiful."

"Thanks. You look handsome yourself." That was no lie. For some reason, tonight he looked more handsome than ever.

"I'm glad you came."

"Are you?"

"Yes, and I hope you liked the flowers."

"I did, but they mean nothing as far as rekindling our relationship. It's over, Derringer."

He shook his head. "Things will never be over between us. If you read all those cards then you know you're the only woman I want."

She rolled her eyes. "Yeah, right, go tell that to someone else."

He smiled. "I don't have a problem telling anyone else. In fact, I think I will tell everyone."

He turned and gave the orchestra a cue to stop playing and everything got quiet. Also, as if on cue, someone handed him a microphone. "May I have everyone's attention, please?"

Aghast, she tried tugging her hand from his. "What do you think you're doing?" She wanted to run and hide when her words got captured on the mic for all to hear. She was certain before the night was over she would die of shame.

"I'm about to speak from my heart," he said, holding tight to her hand.

"When it comes to the ladies, I didn't know you had a heart, Derringer," Pete called out.

She tried not to glance around since she knew all eyes were on them. They were in the middle of the ballroom's dance floor, and everyone, curious as to what was going on, had moved closer to watch. The

Westmorelands, she noted, were standing in a cluster behind Derringer as if to show a united front.

A smile touched Derringer's lips, but when he turned around and met her gaze, his expression got serious. Then he said in a loud and clear voice, "I didn't know I had a heart either until Lucia captured it." He paused and then added, "And that is something no other woman has been able to do."

She glanced away, refusing to believe what she thought she heard him saying. She didn't want to make a mistake about what he was saying. There was no way it could be true.

As if he'd read her thoughts, he tugged on her hand to make her look back at him. "It's true, Lucia. I am so hopelessly in love with you I can't think straight. You are so filled with goodness, warmth and love, I can't imagine not loving you. And it's not anything I discovered upon waking this morning. I knew that I loved you for a while, but didn't want to. I have this fear of loving someone and then losing that person. I think a number of us Denver Westmorelands can't help but feel that way due to the catastrophic losses we've endured in the past. It can do something to you. It can make you not want to take a chance and get attached to anyone.

"But I want to get attached to you. I have to get attached to you. You make me whole. Without you I am nothing."

Lucia couldn't stop the tears that began falling from her eyes. She couldn't believe what he was saying. Derringer was declaring his love and his need for her in front of everyone. His family. Her parents. Their neighbors and friends. Ashira. Ashira's girlfriends. Ashira's parents. Everyone who wanted to hear it.

Evidently, Ashira and her girlfriends didn't. Lucia watched them walk out. It didn't matter to her. The man she had loved for a lifetime was letting her know in front of everyone that he loved her back.

"And when a man has that much love for any woman," Derringer was saying, bringing her attention back to him, "he will choose that woman as his mate for life. The woman he wants for his wife."

She then watched in shock as he eased down on bended knee, gripped her hand tighter and then held her gaze. "Lucia, will you marry me? Will you take my name? Have my babies? And continue to make me happy? In turn, I will be the best husband to you. I will love you. Honor you and cherish you for as long as I live. Will you marry me?"

While she was still swooning from his public proposal, she felt a ring being slid onto her finger. She glanced down. The diamond sparkled so brightly it almost blinded her. She could only stare at it in amazement.

"You have a proposal on the table, Lucia. Please answer the man," someone called out from the crowd.

She couldn't help but smile as she swiped her tears. That had been her father's voice. She met Derringer's gaze. He was still on his knees waiting. "Oh, Derringer," she said through her tears. "Yes! Yes! I will marry you!"

Smiling, he got to his feet and pulled her into his arms in a deep, passionate kiss. She was not sure how long the kiss lasted. The only thing she did know was that the orchestra was playing music again and others were dancing all around them. They didn't care. Tonight was their night and they were going to take full advantage of it.

Hours later, Derringer and Lucia lay together naked in the bed where their adventure all began at Derringer's Dungeon. Upon hearing her wake up during the night, he was ready and leaned up on his elbow and looked down at her, his gaze hot as it roamed over every inch of her naked body.

He leaned down and kissed her and moaned deep in his throat when she returned the kiss with the same hunger he was giving her. Moments later when he pulled back he could only draw in a deep breath in total amazement. Would he always want her to this extreme? He smiled, knowing that yes, he would.

"I love you," he whispered softy. "I regret all the years I didn't make you my one and only girl."

Lucia smiled up at him. "You weren't ready for that type of serious move back then, and in a way I'm glad." She chuckled. "Besides, you needed to impress my dad."

"And you think I did?"

Her smile brightened. "Yes. Going to him and asking for his permission to marry me scored you a lot of brownie points for sure. You're going to be a son-in-law for life."

"Baby, I intend to be a husband for life as well. And you will be my wife for life."

He ran his fingers through her hair as he leaned down

and captured her mouth with his. She was definitely a wife for a Westmoreland. She was his, and their love was just the beginning.

Epilogue

A month and a half later

"Okay, Derringer, you may kiss your bride."

A huge smile lit Derringer's features when he pulled Lucia into his arms. She was the woman he wanted, the wife he desired, and as he captured her mouth with his he knew they would share a long and wonderful life together.

He finally released her and turned to their guests as the minister presented them to everyone as Mr. and Mrs. Derringer Westmoreland. He loved the sound of that and wondered why he'd let his fear keep him away from the altar for so long. But as Lucia had said, he hadn't been ready until now.

A short while later, with his wife's hand tucked in his, they made their way around his property, which the women of the family had transformed from Derringer's Dungeon to Derringer and Lucia's Castle. Gemma had returned the week before the wedding and had worked alongside the wedding planner to give Lucia the wedding she deserved.

He glanced down at her and tightened her hand in his. "Happy?"

She smiled up at him. "Immensely so."

He thought she looked beautiful and doubted he would ever forget how he felt the moment he saw her walking down the aisle to him on her father's arm. She was the most beautiful vision in white that he'd ever seen. They had decided to travel to Dubai for their honeymoon, and while they were across the waters they planned to visit Callum and Gemma in Australia before returning home.

"Time for you to throw your bouquet to the single ladies, Lucia," the wedding planner came up to say.

Lucia turned to Derringer and placed a kiss on his lips. "I'll be back in a moment," she whispered.

"And I'll be right here waiting," was his response. He watched her walk to an area where over thirty women— that included his sisters—stood waiting.

"I've never seen you so happy, Derringer," Jason said, smiling as he walked up. "Congratulations."

"Thanks, and I'm going to give you the same advice I gave Zane, Riley, Canyon and Stern this morning at breakfast, although I could tell they didn't want to hear it. Being single is nice, but being married is much sweeter. Trust me, two is better than one."

Derringer figured if he could get any of his single cousins to take his advice it would be Jason. He had been standing with Jason at the charity ball the moment old man Bostwick's granddaughter had made her entrance. It had been obvious that Jason had been spellbound, entranced by the woman's beauty.

He looked over at Jason. "So, have you officially met Bostwick's granddaughter yet?"

Jason smiled. "Yes, I introduced myself at the ball. Her name is Elizabeth but she prefers being called Bella."

Derringer nodded. "Did you let her know you were interested in her land and in Hercules?"

"Yes, we spoke briefly before Kenneth Bostwick interrupted us. I hear she's trying to make up her mind about what she wants to do. I don't think she's interested in hanging around these parts. This is no place for a Southern belle and besides, she knows nothing about ranching."

"But you do. You can always show her the ropes."

Jason looked shocked at the suggestion. "Why would I want to do something like that? She has two things I want—her land and that stallion. The sooner she decides to sell and return to Savannah, the sooner I can get both. I'd do just about anything to get the land and that horse."

Derringer glanced up at Jason and saw his cousin was serious. "Just remember what I said, Jason. Worldly possessions aren't everything. The love of a good woman is."

He then watched as Lucia began walking back over toward him. She was a good woman. She was his life and now she was his wife.

* * * * *

"Here we'll have all the time in the world."

His smile broadened. "And we can do *anything* you like."

The emphasis sent a shiver down her spine. Already her body had a few suggestions, mostly involving peeling those well-cut clothes off Vasco's tanned physique.

What was it about this guy that set her on fire? Maybe him being Nicky's father had something to do with it. There was already a bond between them, forged in blood, a connection with him that went far beyond their brief acquaintance.

"When you look out the window tomorrow and see the sunrise, you'll know you've come home." Vasco's voice startled her out of her thoughts. He looked at her, heavy lidded, over a sparkling glass of white wine.

"I'm not at all sure I'll be awake at sunrise."

"I could come rouse you." His eyes glittered.

"No thanks!" She said it too fast, and a little too loud. She needed to keep this man *out* of her bedroom.

Which might be a very serious challenge.

Dear Reader,

When I set out to write this book, I wasn't entirely sure where Vasco's kingdom would be. At first I thought of the Basque country of Northern Spain, with its fiercely proud culture. I even picked the name Vasco with this association. Shortly before I started writing, however, I took a trip to Barcelona. What an amazing city. It has everything—winding streets dating back to the Roman empire, medieval palaces, grand Parisian-style avenues of elegant apartments, Gaudi's unique organic architecture, even a long stretch of beach!

I was especially enchanted by the Catalan culture of the area. The Catalan language has survived decades of repression and is thriving. To the uneducated ear (mine!) it's an intriguing mix of Spanish and French, and is utterly unique. Everywhere you go there's an infectious sense of the majesty and heritage of the people and their culture. I immediately knew that Vasco's nation would be a Catalan country, like the tiny nation of Andorra nestled in the Pyrenees mountains. Using creative licence I kept the name Vasco because I liked it and thought it suited him!

I hope you enjoy Vasco and Stella's story, and enjoy your visit to the mythical nation of Montmajor.

Jen

CLAIMING HIS
ROYAL HEIR

BY
JENNIFER LEWIS

Published in Great Britain 2011
by Mills & Boon, an imprint of Harlequin (UK) Limited,
Eton House, 18-24 Paradise Road, Richmond, Surrey TW9 1SR

© Jennifer Lewis 2011

ISBN: 978 0 263 89094 5

51-1211

Harlequin (UK) policy is to use papers that are natural, renewable and recyclable products and made from wood grown in sustainable forests. The logging and manufacturing processes conform to the legal environmental regulations of the country of origin.

Printed and bound in Spain
by Blackprint CPI, Barcelona

Jennifer Lewis has been dreaming up stories for as long as she can remember and is thrilled to be able to share them with readers. She has lived on both sides of the Atlantic and worked in media and the arts before she grew bold enough to put pen to paper. Happily settled in England with her family, she would love to hear from readers at jen@jenlewis.com. Visit her website at www. jenlewis.com.

For Lilly, my good friend and companion
in many adventures.

Acknowledgements:

Many thanks to the lovely people who helped improve
this book while I was writing it: Anne, Jerri, Leeanne,
my agent Andrea and my editor Charles.

One

"Your son is my son." The strange man looked past her into the hallway, searching.

Stella Greco wanted to slam the front door in his face. At first she'd wondered if he was a strip-a-gram like the one her friend Meg hired for her surprise party two years ago. But the expression on this man's face was too serious. Tall, with unruly dark hair that curled around his collar, stern bronzed features and stone-gray eyes, he filled her doorway like a flash of lightning.

Now his words struck her like a harsh bolt. "What do you mean...your son?" Her mother lion instincts recoiled against him. "Who are you?"

"My name is Vasco de la Cruz Arellano y Montoya. But I go by Vasco Montoya when I'm abroad." A smile flickered at the corner of his wide, sensual mouth, but not enough to reassure her in any way. "May I come in?"

"No. I don't know you and I'm not in the habit of letting unknown men into my house." Fear crept up her spine. Her son didn't have a father. This man had no business here. Could she simply shut the door?

The sound of nursery-rhyme music wafted toward them, betraying the presence of her child in the house. Stella glanced behind her, wishing she could hide Nicky. "I have to go."

"Wait." He stepped forward. She started to push the door shut. "Please." His voice softened and he tilted his head. A lock of dark hair dipped into his eyes. "Perhaps we could go somewhere quiet to talk."

"That won't be possible." She couldn't leave Nicky, and she certainly didn't intend to bring him anywhere with this man. She prayed Nicky wouldn't come crawling down the hallway looking for her. Every maternal instinct she possessed still urged her to slam the door in this man's too-handsome face. But apparently she was too polite. And there was something about this strange man that made it hard. "Please leave."

"Your son…" He leaned in and she caught a whiff of musk mingled with leather from his battered black jacket. "My son…" his eyes flashed "…is heir to the throne of Montmajor."

He said it like a proclamation and she suspected she was supposed to fall down in surprise. She kept a firm hold on the door frame. "I don't care. This is my private home and if you don't leave I'll call the police." Her voice rose, betraying her fear. "Now go."

"He's blond." His brow furrowed as he looked over her shoulder again.

Stella spun around, horrified to see Nicky scooting along the floor with a huge grin on his face. "Ah goo."

"What did he say?" Vasco Montoya leaned in.

"Nothing. He's just making sounds." Why did people expect a barely one-year-old to be speaking in full sentences? She was getting tired of people asking why he couldn't talk properly yet. Every child developed at his own pace. "And it's none of your business, anyway."

"But it is." His eyes remained fixed on Nicky, his large frame casting a shadow that fell through the doorway.

"Why?" The question fell from her lips as a frightening possibility occurred to her.

"He's my son." He peered at her boy.

She swallowed. Her gut urged her to deny his claim. But she couldn't—not really. "What makes you think that?"

The intruder's gaze stayed riveted on Nicky. "The eyes, he has the eyes." Nicky stared back at him with those big gray eyes she'd tried to attribute to her maternal grandmother. Her own eyes were a tawny hazel.

Nicky suddenly darted past her, reached out a chubby hand and grabbed one of Vasco's fingers. The big man's face creased into a delighted smile. "It's a pleasure to make your acquaintance."

Stella had snatched Nicky back into the hallway and clutched him to her chest before she took a breath.

"Ga la la." Nicky greeted the man with a smile. Somehow that just made it worse.

"This is a gross invasion of my privacy. Of our privacy," Stella protested, clutching her son tighter. A horrible feeling in the pit of her stomach told her this really was the father of her son. She lowered her voice. "The sperm bank assured me that donor identity was confidential and that my information would never be shared with anyone."

His eyes met hers—ocean-gray and fierce. "When I was young and foolish I did a lot of things I now regret."

She knew Nicky had the right to contact his father once he came of age, but she'd been assured the father did not have the same rights.

"How did you find me?" She wanted her child to be hers alone, with no one else around to make demands and mess things up.

If this even was the father. How could he know?

He cocked his head. "A donation or two in the right pocket reveals most things." He had a slight accent, not a strong one but a subtle inflection warming his voice. He certainly had an old-world sense of entitlement and the importance of bribery.

"They gave you the names of the women who bought your samples?"

He nodded.

"They could have lied."

"I saw the actual records."

He could be lying right now. Why did he want Nicky? Her son wriggled against her, squawking to be put down, but she didn't dare release her grip.

"He might not be yours. I tried sperm from several donors." She clutched Nicky close. Now she was lying. She'd become pregnant the first cycle.

He lifted his chin. "I saw your records, too."

Her face heated. "This is outrageous. I could sue them."

"You could, but it doesn't change the one really important fact." He looked down at Nicky and his harsh gaze softened. "That's my son."

Tears sprang to her eyes. How could a perfectly ordinary day turn into a nightmare so fast?

"You must have fathered loads of children through the bank. Hundreds even. Go find the others." She grasped at straws.

"No others." He didn't take his eyes off Nicky. "This is the only one. Please may I come in? This is no conversation to have in the street." His tone was soft, respectful.

"I can't let you in. I don't truly have any idea who you are and you freely admit that you're here because of information you obtained illegally." She straightened her shoulders. Nicky wriggled and fussed in her arms.

"I regret my mistake and wish to make amends." His wide gray eyes implored her.

An odd tender feeling unfurled in her stomach. She shoved it back down. Who was this man to play on her feelings? With his looks, he was probably used to women rolling over every time he asked. Still, she couldn't seem to shut the door on him.

"What's his name?"

The stranger's question, asked with a tender half smile at Nicky, startled her.

She hesitated. Telling him Nicky's name would give him the right to call him by it. Almost an invitation. But what if he was Nicky's real donor? His father...the word made her quake deep inside. Did she have the right to drive him away?

"Can I see some ID?" She was stalling as much as anything. A man capable of paying for information could pay for fake ID. But she needed time to think.

He frowned, then reached into his back pocket and pulled out a money clip. He plucked a card from it. A

California driver's license. "I thought you were from Mont…" What was the name he'd said again?

"Montmajor. But I lived in the U.S. for a long time."

She peered at the picture. A slightly younger, less world-weary version of her visitor stared back. Vasco Montoya was indeed the name on the card.

Of course, you could buy driver's licenses on every street corner these days, so it didn't prove anything. She hadn't seen the donor's name at any time, so she still had no idea if Vasco Montoya was the man whose frozen semen she'd paid for.

It was all so…ugly. People had laughed when she told them how she planned to conceive her child. Then they'd frowned and clucked about turkey basters and told her to just find a man. She'd wanted to avoid that complication. Frozen semen seemed safer at the time.

"Which sperm bank did you donate to?" Maybe he was bluffing.

He took his license back from her trembling fingers and shoved his money clip back in his pocket. "Westlake Cryobank."

She gulped. The right place. She hadn't told anyone, not even her best friend, where she went. Somehow that made the whole clinical procedure easier to forget. Now this tall, imposing male was here to shove it back in her face.

"I know you don't know me. I didn't know how to approach you other than to come in person and introduce myself." His expression was almost apologetic, accompanied by a Mediterranean hand gesture. "I'm sorry to shock you and I wish I could make this easier."

He shoved a hand through his dark hair. "You know my name. I've made my fortune in gemstone mining.

I have offices and employees all over the world." He pulled another card from his money clip. She took it with shaky fingers, which wasn't hard, since she still held Nicky clamped to her chest with the other arm.

Vasco Montoya, President
Catalan Mining Corporation

Catalan. The word struck her. She'd chosen her donor partly because he'd proudly proclaimed his Catalan ancestry. It seemed exotic and appealing, a taste of old Europe and a proud culture with a glorious literary history. She'd always been a sucker for that kind of thing.

And those eyes were unmistakable. The same slate-gray—with a hint of stormy ocean-blue—as her son's.

"I don't want to hurt you. I just want to know my son. As a mother, I'm sure you can imagine what it would be like to have your own child out there, walking around, and you've never met him." Again his gaze fixed on Nicky, and powerful emotion crossed his face. "You would feel like part of your heart, of your soul, is out there in the world, without you."

Her heart clenched. His words touched her and she recognized the truth in them. How could she deny her son the right to know his own father? Vasco's attitude had softened, along with his words. Her maternal instincts no longer screamed at her to shove him back down her steps. Instead she felt an equally powerful urge to help him. "You'd better come in."

Vasco closed the front door and followed Stella Greco down the hall and into a sunny living room with colorful toys scattered on the wood floor and on the plump beige sofa.

Strange emotions and sensations tightened his muscles. He'd come here from a sense of duty, keen to tie up a loose end that could cause succession problems in a future he didn't want to think about.

He'd wondered how much money she'd take to give him the child. Most people had their price, if it was high enough, and he knew he could promise the boy a good life in a loving environment.

Then those big gray eyes met his, wide with the innocent wonder of childhood. Something exploded in his chest at that moment. Recognition, at a gut level.

This was his son and already he felt a connection with him stronger than anything he'd ever experienced. She'd put the boy down and the toddler had crawled up to him. While his anxious mother watched, Vasco crouched and held out his finger again. His heart squeezed as the toddler took a tight hold of it.

"What's his name?" She never had answered his question.

"Nicholas Alexander. I call him Nicky." She said the words slowly, still reluctant to let him into their private world.

"Hello, Nicky." He couldn't help smiling as he said it.

"Hi." Nicky's grin showed two tiny white teeth.

"He said hi." Stella's face flushed. "He said a real word!"

"Of course he did. He's greeting his father." His chest swelled with pride. Though he could take no credit for Nicky other than providing half his DNA. Shame crept through him at the callous act of donating something as precious as the building blocks of life for a few dollars.

At the time he'd been glad to throw away the royal seed as he'd rather have died than dip into the royal coffers.

He glanced at Stella. He'd had his reasons for donating his sperm ten long years ago, but what were her reasons for buying it? His preliminary research told him Stella Greco worked at the local university library, restoring books. He'd expected a pinched spinster type, older and forbidding. What he found instead was a total surprise.

She was pretty, too pretty to need to purchase sperm at a store. Her hair was cut in a shiny, golden-brown bob. Freckles dotted her neat nose and her hazel eyes were wide and kind. He'd be surprised if she was even thirty, certainly not old enough to get desperate over her biological clock expiring. Did she perhaps have a husband who was infertile?

He glanced at her hand and was relieved to see no ring. He didn't need another person in the mix. "You must move to Montmajor with Nicky." Thoughts of paying her to give him the child seemed foolish, now. If he'd connected so forcefully with his own flesh and blood in only a few seconds, the maternal bond was not something that could be dissolved by any amount of cold cash.

"We're not moving anywhere." Still standing, she hugged herself. The living room of the little Arts and Crafts bungalow was small but pleasant. She wasn't rich. He could tell that from the simple furnishings and the tiny blue car parked outside.

"You'll have a comfortable home in the royal palace

and you'll want for nothing." The palace he loved with his soul, and that he'd once been cruelly driven from, was the perfect place. She'd know that once she saw it.

"I like California, thank you. I have a good job restoring rare books at the university, and I love our little house here. The schools are excellent and it's a nice, safe, friendly community for Nicky to grow up in. Believe me, I did a lot of research."

Vasco glanced around. Sure, the house was pleasant, but the sound of nearby traffic marred the peace and California was filled with temptations and traps for a young person. "Nicky would be far better off in the hills and fresh air of Montmajor. He'd have the best teachers."

"We're staying here, and that's final." She crossed her hands over her chest. She wasn't tall, maybe five foot five, but she had an air of authority and determination that amused and intrigued him. He could tell she had no intention whatsoever of changing her carefully thought-out plans.

Luckily, he had decades of experience in negotiation, and rarely failed. He could offer financial incentives or other temptations she'd be loath to resist. Although she might not have her price in purely financial terms, everyone had dreams and if he could tap into those she'd eventually be persuaded.

Or he could seduce her. Now that he'd seen her this possibility held tremendous appeal. Seduction offered the benefits of instant intimacy and unlimited enjoyment. Definitely something to consider.

But this wasn't the right time. His appearance was a shock and she needed a chance to digest the idea that her son's father would be involved in his life. He'd give her a day or two to accommodate herself to the new reality of his presence.

Then he'd return and entice her into his arms and his plans.

"I'll bid you adieu." He made a slight bow. "Please do some research into me." He gestured at his business card, held between his fingers. "You'll find that everything I've told you about myself is true."

She frowned, which caused her nose to wrinkle in a rather adorable way.

Stella blinked. She looked surprised that he'd chosen to leave without securing a deal. "Great."

"I'll be in touch to discuss matters further."

"Sure." She tucked a strand of hair behind her ear. Suspicion hovered in her eyes. He suspected she'd be locking all the doors and windows tonight. He had to admit that she seemed an excellent and protective mother to his child.

Little Nicky sat on the floor, engrossed in putting plastic rings onto a fat plastic stick. Emotion filled Vasco's chest at the sight of the sweet young boy that was his flesh and blood. "Nice to meet you, Nicky."

The toddler glanced up, obviously aware of his own name. "Ah goo."

Vasco grinned, and Nicky grinned back. He looked at Stella. "He's wonderful."

"I know." She couldn't help smiling, too. "He's the most precious thing in the world to me. I think you should know that."

"Trust me, I do. And I respect it." Which is why he intended to bring Stella back to Montmajor along with Nicky. A boy should be with his mother as well as his father.

As he fired up the engine of his bike, now hot from standing in the California sun outside Stella's house, he congratulated himself on a successful first encounter with his son's mother. She'd started by wanting to throw him out, and ended by giving him her phone number.

He gunned the engine and took off up the hill toward the Santa Monica freeway. A very promising start.

Stella bolted the door as soon as Vasco was gone. She wanted to let out a huge sigh of relief, but she couldn't. It wasn't over.

It wouldn't ever be over.

Her son's father—the one she never wanted or needed—had come into both of their lives and if he checked out after testing they'd never be the same again. The best she could hope for was that he'd go back to wherever he came from—Montmajor, was it? She'd never even heard of the place—and leave them in relative peace.

She wanted to believe that he was an impostor and that his country was the invention of an overactive imagination. He certainly looked like something out of a Hollywood movie with his worn leather jacket, faded jeans and scuffed leather boots. His looks were pure glam.

He didn't look like a king of anything at all, except maybe King of the Road. Especially since she'd seen him climb on a big, black motorbike right in front of her house. What kind of king went around on a hog?

Maybe he was a fake. Or some kind of crazy. California had enough of those.

Whoever he was, something told her he was Nicky's father. His hair was dark, almost black, and his skin tanned and scorched by the sun, but his eyes were unmistakably Nicky's. Slate-gray and intense, they'd surprised the nurses at the hospital who insisted a blond baby should have blue eyes. They'd never changed color and they were the first place she could read his mood.

Vasco's eyes were hooded by suspicious lids and dark lashes, while Nicky's still had the bold innocence of childhood, but they were the same eyes. Vasco Montoya was Nicky's father.

She settled Nicky into his high chair with some Cheerios and a cup of watered-down apple juice.

She hated that they'd had the whole conversation in front of him. How much could a one-year-old comprehend? Just because he didn't say much didn't mean he couldn't understand at least some of what was going on.

Two

A faint ray of sunlight snuck through the wall of miniblinds in the office of the customer relations manager at Westlake Cryobank. Stella watched the wand of light stretch across the neat gray desk toward the woman behind it. The finger of accusation?

Three days had passed since Vasco Montoya had appeared in her life, and she hadn't heard from him again. Maybe the whole thing was a dream—or rather, a nightmare—and nothing would come of it. She'd been preoccupied with "what ifs" and spent hours online reading about other people's experiences with absent fathers reappearing in their lives. Her brain was boggling with possibilities and problems, and now he'd vanished.

Still, she needed to know where she stood.

"As I said, madam. We assure confidentiality for

all our clients." The woman's voice was crisp and businesslike, her hair styled into a golden blond helmet.

"So how do you explain the arrival of this man on my doorstep?" She flung down the page she'd printed from a website on sapphire mining. An interview with Vasco Montoya, head of Catalan Mining and—as he'd claimed—king of the sovereign nation of Montmajor. Apparently he'd grown his business from a small mine in Colombia to an international concern with billions in assets. In the picture, he wore a pinstriped suit and a pleased expression. Why wouldn't he? He was the man who had everything.

Except her son.

The woman swallowed visibly, then shone a fake smile.

It's her, I can feel it. He probably seduced her into it. Rage swelled in her chest. "He knows where I live and that I used his donation. He wants us to move back to his country with him." The idea was laughable—except that it wasn't funny. "How much did he pay you?"

"It's not possible for him to obtain the information from us. All our records are kept in a secure, offsite location."

"I'm sure they're computerized, as well."

"Naturally, but…"

"I don't want to hear any *buts*. He said that he paid money to obtain the information, so you have a leak in your security somewhere."

"We take the greatest precautions and we have top-notch legal advice." Her words contained a veiled threat. Did they expect her to sue? That wouldn't help.

She sat back in the hard plastic chair. "I guess what I really want to know…" She thought of Nick, happily playing at the university day care. She'd hurried to Westlake after dropping him off early. "Does he have any rights, or did he sign those away when he donated the sperm?"

"Our donors do sign away all rights. They have no say in the child's future and no responsibility to support it."

"So I can tell this man that, legally, he's not my son's father."

"Of course."

Relief trickled through her. "Has he fathered any other children?"

"That information is confidential." The cool smile again. "However I can tell you that Mr. Montoya has pulled his donations and will not be doing further business with Westlake Cryobank."

"Why? And when did he do this?"

"Just last week. It's not unusual for a donor to find themselves in a new situation—married, for example— and to decide to withdraw themselves from our database."

"But how did he find my identity?"

She could hear her own breathing during the silence that followed.

Debbie English tapped on her keyboard for a minute, then leaned back in her chair. "Okay, I can't see there's any harm in telling you that you are the only one who used his sample."

"So if he hacked into your database…"

"Impossible." The woman's face resembled a finely made-up stone wall.

She drew in a breath. "Why was I the only one in ten years who used his sample?"

"We have a very large database. More than thirty thousand donors. Just glancing at his file, I can see that he's not American, and that he wrote in Catalan ancestry rather than checking a box for a more popular heritage. Those things alone might have turned buyers off. We advise our donors to…" Debbie English's voice trailed on and she remembered the excitement and confusion of her trip to Westlake Cryobank.

There it was again. His Catalan ancestry—unusual and intriguing to find in the prosaic database—had attracted her. Probably most people didn't even know what Catalan meant, or thought it was somewhere in China. She knew it was a unique culture with its own language and customs, a mixture of French and Spanish, charming and romantic with strong roots in a colorful past.

Just like Vasco Montoya.

"PACIFIC COLLEGE IN FUNDING CRISIS AFTER STATE SPENDING SLASHED."

The article headline caught Stella's eye as she marched past the newsstand on her way from the parking lot to the library. Rushed and scattered by her unsatisfactory visit to Westlake Cryobank, she had to stop and read it three times. She was sitting out in the garden on her swing seat while Nicky napped in the stroller after a walk. Three days had passed since Vasco Montoya had appeared in her life, and she'd heard nothing.

Pacific College was her employer.

She handed over some coins and scanned the article about a fifty percent cut in state spending on the small liberal arts college. Fifty percent? The college president was quoted saying that he planned to protest and also to raise money from the private sector, but that programs would have to be cut.

In her office, there was a message on her phone asking her to visit Human Resources at her earliest convenience. She sank into her chair and her breathing became shallow.

A knock on the door made her jump and she half expected to see Vasco Montoya respond to her murmured, "Come in."

"Hi, Stella." It was Roger Dales, dean of the fine arts department. Her boss. "I just want you to know how sorry I am."

"What do you mean, you're sorry."

"You haven't heard from HR?" He sounded surprised.

"I had an…outside appointment this morning. I just got in. I saw an article about funding cuts but I haven't had time to…" She hesitated, a sense of doom growing inside her. "Am I fired?"

He came into the room, a whiff of pipe smoke clinging to his tweed jacket, and closed the door behind him. "We've lost all funding for the books and prints archives. It's devastating news for all of us." He hesitated, and she saw the regret in his eyes. "I'm afraid your job has been eliminated."

Words rose to her lips, but not ones she'd want to say to a college dean. An odd fluttering, panicky sensation gripped her stomach.

"As Human Resources is no doubt about to tell you, you'll receive two weeks' pay and your benefits will continue until the end of the month. I'm sorry there isn't a better severance package but with the current financial situation…"

His words continued but her brain ceased to register them. Two weeks' pay? She had some savings but not enough to last more than six months, and that's if nothing went wrong with the car or their health or—

"If there's anything I can do, please don't hesitate to call me."

"Do you know of anyone looking for a rare book restorer?" Her voice had an edge that she hadn't planned. Jobs like this were scarce at the best of times.

"Perhaps you could approach some private libraries."

"Sure. I'll try that." She'd lose the university day care, too. Now she'd have to pay for child care or renovate precious and fragile items on her kitchen table while Nicky crawled around her feet.

Disbelief warred with shock and confusion as he opened the door and slipped from her office. How could her whole life fall apart so fast?

Stella spent three days sending out carefully composed résumés to every university library, museum and private library she could dig up on the internet. When one in Kalamazoo, Michigan, offered her an interview, she realized that even applying for a job with a very young child was challenging. She couldn't take him with her, but he was too young to leave for more than a few hours with even her most devoted friends. Her mom had died three years ago in a skiing accident, leaving her with no close family to count on.

"Maybe I should call Vasco and tell him I need him to babysit," she joked on the phone to her pal Karen, who sat for her occasionally during the day, but worked nights as a bartender in a downtown club, leaving her own three- and eight-year-olds with her mom.

"That would be one way to get rid of him. In my experience men lose interest in anything that involves changing diapers."

"Why didn't I think of that before? I should have invited him in and handed Nicky to him after a poop."

"Has he called?"

"No." She frowned. Now that he'd gone several days without calling, she was actually ticked off at him. Who was he to waltz into her life—and Nicky's—and announce his right to be there and then just disappear without a trace?

"Hmm. He did sound a bit too good to be true. Tall, dark, handsome, leather-clad and royal?"

"Trust me, none of those things appeal to me."

"Yes, I know. You prefer short, fickle redheads."

"Trevor had sandy hair, not red."

"Same diff, sweetie. Either way, he seems to have put you off men for good. Have you even dated since you guys broke up?"

"I don't have time for dating. I'm busy with Nicky." And work, she would have said until two days earlier. She'd been told, very gently, to collect her belongings immediately after her HR discussion. Apparently newly laid-off employees were not encouraged to mess with rare books.

"It's been nearly three years, Stell."

"I'm not interested. I have a very full life and the last thing I need is a man to screw it up for me."

"The right man will come along. Just don't be so busy slamming the door in his face that you don't recognize him when he does. Hey, look at it this way. Vasco already wants you to move to his country—that's a bit of a change from Trevor who wasn't even ready to live with you after eight years."

"Vasco wants Nicky to move to his country. He couldn't care less about me. Besides, he hasn't called. Maybe I'll never hear from him again." Annoying how his face had imprinted itself in her mind. She kept seeing those steel-gray eyes staring at her from everywhere.

"Oh, he'll call. I have a feeling." Karen laughed. "The question is, what will you say to him?"

Stella drew in a breath. "I'll let him spend time with Nicky if he wants, and let them get to know each other. It would probably be best for Nicky to have a relationship with his father."

"Aren't you worried he'll try to take over and tell you what to do?"

"He can't. He doesn't have any legal rights. I could tell him to go away at any time."

"He doesn't seem like the type who takes orders. But here's a thought, wouldn't a European royal have a large collection of old books that need fixing up? You might be able to find some nice work through him."

"Oh, stop. My job search is a disaster. Everything's so far away and the pay is dismal. Barely enough to pay for diapers, let alone support us both. Soon I'll be asking people if they'd like fries with that—hang on, there's someone at the door." The familiar chime sounded and the glass pane darkened as a large silhouette loomed outside.

Stella's stomach contracted. Although she couldn't

see much through the dimpled glass, she knew—every single part of her knew—that Vasco Montoya stood on her doorstep.

Three

Stella said goodbye to Karen and shoved the phone in her pocket. To her annoyance she found herself smoothing her hair as she walked up the hallway to the door. Ridiculous! Still, she might as well be civil since she'd decided that if he was Nicky's father she couldn't in good conscience try to keep him entirely out of Nicky's life.

She'd always wished for the kind of family you saw on TV, with the smiling mom and dad doting on their kids. Instead she had the awkward and hard to explain reality of a dad who had disappeared when she was a baby and never gotten in contact again. There'd always been a gap in her life, a thread of pathetic hope that he'd remember her—that he'd love her—and come back for her. When her mom died suddenly when Stella was in her twenties she'd even tried to look for him, until friends persuaded her that might bring more heartache rather than the resolution and affection she craved. They'd told her she was too nice, too anxious to please, too hopeful that she could put everything right and make everyone happy, when sometimes that wasn't possible.

Didn't stop her from trying, though, which was probably why she couldn't drive Vasco Montoya away without at least finding out the truth. Deep down she just wanted everyone to be happy.

She pulled open the door to find him standing there—even taller and more infuriatingly handsome than she remembered—his arms laden with wrapped gifts and a big spray of flowers.

"Hi, Stella." His mouth flashed a mischievous grin.

She blinked. "Hello, Vasco. Please come in." Mercifully she sounded calmer than she felt. What did he have in all those shiny packages?

"These are for you." His gray gaze met hers as he handed her the bouquet. Her heart jumped and she snatched them from him and turned down the hallway. The arrangement was beautiful—a mix of wildflowers and exotic lilies. The scent wafted to her. "I'll just put these in water."

"Where's Nicky?"

"He's upstairs having a nap. He'll wake up soon." She wanted him to know she wasn't going to disturb her son's routine for an unscheduled visit.

"That's fine. It gives us a chance to talk."

She filled a green glass vase with water and slid the flowers into it. Later she'd take the time to trim the stalks and arrange them. Right now her hands were shaking too much. "Would you like some…tea?"

It was impossible to imagine Vasco Montoya sipping tea. Swigging rum from an open bottle, maybe.

He smiled as if he found the idea amusing, too. "No, thanks." He unleashed the pile of packages onto the kitchen table, then pulled out a small rectangular present wrapped in dark red paper and ornamented with a slim white ribbon. "This is also for you."

She took the present from his outstretched hand, then realized she was frowning. Obviously he was trying to curry favor with her, which rubbed her the wrong way. "You shouldn't have."

"I've done a few things I shouldn't have." Humor danced in his eyes. "I'm trying to put that right. I appreciate your giving me the chance to try."

She softened a bit, more from his hopeful expression than his words. "Should I open it now?"

"Please do." He sat in a kitchen chair, apparently relaxed despite the strange situation.

Her hands shook a bit as she plucked at the ribbon and carefully pulled the wrapping paper off by lifting the tape. She was constitutionally unable to rip paper. Probably an occupational hazard.

The wrapping peeled back to reveal a black paper book jacket with an abstract picture. Her eyes widened as she realized that she now held in her hands a 1957 first edition of Jack Kerouac's Beat Generation classic *On the Road*.

"I know you like books."

"Where did you get this?" This edition retailed for nearly ten thousand dollars. In near-mint condition like this, possibly far more.

"A friend."

"I can't accept it. It's far too valuable." Still, she

couldn't help turning it over to look at the back, and peer inside. The pages were in such good condition, no yellowing or wear, that it must have been in a box for over fifty years.

"I insist. I like finding the right gifts for people."

She stared at him. How could he know about her interest in that era—music and art as well as literature—and that her life revolved around rare books?

His easy grin revealed that he knew he'd scored a hit. "I know you restore books, so I had to give you one in perfect condition or it would be like handing you work." He had dimples in his right cheek and chin when he smiled.

"How did you know what I do?"

He shrugged. "I searched for your name on Google."

"Oh." She'd done the same thing with his, which had informed her that not only was he the king of a tiny country in the Pyrenees, but that he'd amassed a fortune in the mining industry over the last ten years. At least he could afford the gift.

It seemed a shame to even touch the cover, when she knew how every fingerprint caused fabric and paper to deteriorate. Still, what was the point of a book if not to be looked at and enjoyed? "Thank you."

Still, there were a lot of unanswered questions, most of them hard to ask and undoubtedly awkward to answer. Like this one: "Would you be willing to take a paternity test?"

"Absolutely."

"Oh." For some reason she'd expected him to resist. "I found a lab locally. They said you and Nicky have to go in and they'll take swabs from your cheek."

"I'd be glad to." His expression was perfectly serious.

"Why did you donate your sperm?" She was on a roll now.

For once he looked uncomfortable. He leaned forward, frowned, shoved a tanned hand into his hair. "It's complicated. Mostly it had to do with being turned away from the land and family that meant everything to me, and finding myself here in the land of plenty without fifty dollars to my name. Not very heroic, huh?"

She shrugged. His honesty appealed to her. "I suspect money trouble is a pretty common reason. Most of the donors seemed to be college students. I guess it's a painless way to earn some extra cash."

"Sure, until you grow up and realize the consequences."

He regretted it now. Somehow that hurt. "Your donation has brought the greatest joy into my life. Don't wish that away."

He tilted his head, thoughtful. "You're right. Nicky was meant to be here. It's just a strange situation to find oneself in." A smile lit his eyes.

Stella's toes curled as a hot sensation unfurled in her belly. She wished he'd stop looking at her like that. As if he'd found the woman of his dreams, or something.

Definitely *or something*.

"I've decided that you and Nicky should visit Montmajor. Then you can see and decide for yourselves whether it's the right place for you to live." His easy pose and confident expression suggested that he already knew what their decision would be.

The urge to say no was flattened by the reality of her bleak economic prospects in California right now. "That sounds like a good idea."

His eyes widened. Apparently he'd expected at least

some resistance. "Fantastic. I'll arrange the flights. Is next week too soon to leave?"

Should she pretend she needed to "take time off work" or did he already know her job was gone? She didn't want to appear too much of a pushover. "Let me check my book."

She rose and walked into the living room, where she pretended to flip through her datebook, which was alarmingly empty. As she walked back into the kitchen his gaze drifted over her in a way that was both insolent and arousing and made her suck in her breath.

"After Wednesday would be fine. How long would you like us to visit for?"

He propped one ankle on his knee and his smile widened. "Forever would be ideal, but why don't we start with a month."

"I'm afraid I can't take a month away from work." Or at least from looking for a job. Even if he was paying for everything in his country she needed something to come back to.

Vasco's expression softened. "I know you lost your job at the university."

"How do you know that?" Suspicion pricked her. Was he behind it somehow?

He shrugged. "I called them to see if you were affected by the cuts. I'm sorry."

Her face heated. "Me, too. I need to find more work right away. I can't have a big gap on my résumé." He wasn't behind it. Local finances were. All the stress was making her paranoid.

"No need for any gap at all." He leaned forward. "The palace library has over ten thousand books, some of them so old they were handwritten by monks. As far as I know they have seen no restoration efforts in generations, so you will be amply supplied with work if you'd be kind enough to turn your attentions to them."

Funny how his speech could get so formal and princely sometimes.

"That does sound interesting." She tried to contain her excitement. It sounded like every book restorer's fantasy. Old libraries could contain gems that no one even knew existed. Visions of medieval manuscripts and elegant editions of, say, Dante's *Commedia* danced in her mind.

"You'd be well paid. Since I'm not familiar with the field you can set your own rate. Any supplies and equipment you need will be furnished."

"I'll bring my own tools," she said quickly, then realized she sounded a little too keen. "A month should give me time to assess the condition of the collection and plan preliminary repairs to those volumes most in need."

"Excellent." His dimples deepened.

Today Vasco wore faded jeans and black boots with a suit jacket and casual white shirt. He could have stepped right out of the pages in *GQ*. Stella became conscious of her less than scintillating ensemble of black yoga pants and a striped T-shirt that might well be stained with baby food. She resisted the urge to look down.

Besides, one set of eyes on her body was quite enough. Vasco's gaze heated her skin. Was he flirting with her? She was so out of practice she couldn't even tell. Trevor had scoffed at romantic overtures and seductive gestures, and she'd grown to think of them as childish.

But the way Vasco was looking at her right now felt

anything but infantile. "Glass of water?" She didn't know what else to say and the temperature in the room was becoming dangerously uncomfortable.

"Why not?" He raised a brow.

She busied herself filling a glass and was relieved to hear Nicky's voice rising in a plea for freedom from upstairs. "He's up."

At least now she wouldn't be alone with Vasco, and those penetrating gray eyes would have someone else to look at. Vasco stood up to come with her.

"Why don't you wait here?" She didn't want him upstairs in their personal space, knowing where Nicky's crib was. She didn't much like leaving him alone in the kitchen, either. Not because she had a bad feeling about him—at least not that she could put her finger on—but it was all way too much, too soon.

She'd committed to visiting his country for a month. Which gave her a queasy feeling of being swept away on a tide of destiny. For now, at least, she wanted to keep her feet—and Nicky's—firmly planted in their own little reality.

He was still standing as she left the room, possibly ready to go snooping through the opened mail on the sideboard or peering into her fridge and discovering that she'd eaten three out of the six Boston cream donuts inside it. She grabbed Nicky out of his crib and hurried back down as fast as she could.

The expression on Vasco's face when he saw Nicky almost melted her suspicious heart. Delight and wonder softened his hard features. Part of her wanted to clutch Nicky to her chest and protect him from this stranger who hoped to love her son like she did, and part of her wanted to put Nicky in Vasco's arms so he could experience the happiness she'd known since he came into her life.

She lowered Nicky to the floor, where he took off at a high-speed crawl.

"I think he's been awake for a while. He seems full of beans."

"Maybe he was listening in on our conversation." Vasco's eyes didn't leave Nicky. Apparently she was way less fascinating now that he was in the room.

Stella's stomach tightened. She'd actually agreed to head off to Montmajor with Nicky. "Will we stay in a hotel while we're there?"

"The royal palace has more than ample room. You'll have your own suite—your own wing, if you like—and plenty of privacy."

A palace. Somehow she hadn't thought of that part. A royal palace where Nicky might be heir to the throne. The whole idea made her feel nauseous. And Nicky's diaper smelled. "He needs changing."

Karen's idea of asking Vasco to change him crossed her mind but she quickly dismissed it. Far too intimate. She didn't want Vasco assuming fatherly duties, at least not until after the DNA test proved he was Nicky's father.

And she suspected he'd be willing and able to rise to that and any other challenge she could throw at him.

Vasco followed her into the dining room, where she had a changing mat on the floor. "When do they stop wearing those things?"

"It depends. When we were kids our moms would be trying to take them off already. These days it's common for kids to wear them until three or four. Everyone has a theory on what's right."

Vasco seemed like the kind of guy who'd let his kid run around naked outdoors and discover things the old-fashioned way. She'd probably try that if she didn't live in the corner lot on a busy street in full view of half the neighborhood. She wasn't sure they'd appreciate the view.

This thought reminded her how little she knew about Vasco and what his life in Montmajor was like. She'd seen plenty of pictures of him with his arm around different women on the internet, but no hard information about his personal life. "Are you married?"

He laughed. "No."

"Why not?" The question was bold, but she couldn't resist asking. He was old enough, over thirty, certainly. Wealthy, gorgeous and royal, Vasco Montoya must have women trailing him like stray cats after a fish truck.

His throaty chuckle made her belly tighten. "Maybe I'm not the marrying kind. What about you? Why aren't you married?"

His question heated her face. "Maybe I'm not the marrying kind either." It was hard to sound cool and hard-boiled while wiping a rosy bottom.

"You do seem like the marrying kind." His voice was soft, suggestive, even.

"Maybe I would be if I ever met the right man. I was engaged for a long time, but eventually I decided I was better off on my own."

She'd probably still be engaged to Trevor, still childless and living alone, if she hadn't made a clean break. It was an easy relationship, if not an exciting one.

"You're independent. Don't need a man to take care of you. I like that."

Don't I? The sudden evaporation of her income and

career prospects had made her feel dangerously alone. It wasn't just herself she needed to support—Nicky was counting on her, too.

She fastened up his tiny dungarees and let him squirm off the mat and crawl away. She and Vasco both watched him scoot out of the dining room and back into the kitchen.

"Wassat?" A delighted cry accompanied by rustling alerted them that he'd discovered the wrapped gifts Vasco brought.

"Is he allowed to open them?"

"That's what they're for." They followed him into the kitchen where he'd already pulled the shiny silver paper off a large box containing a Thomas the Tank Engine starter set that must have cost almost as much as her book. Nicky put the corner of the box in his mouth.

Vasco laughed. "I bought the most delicious train I could find."

"He'll love it." She pulled the box out of Nicky's arms. "Let me open it up, sweetie."

Nicky reached for the next gift, a sparkly blue one.

Vasco shrugged. "I missed his first birthday." He watched with joy in his eyes as Nicky skinned the present, an elaborate construction set made from pieces of carved wood.

"You're good at picking age-appropriate stuff." She was relieved nothing so far looked like a choking hazard.

"I'm good at asking for and taking expert advice." His eyes met hers, and an annoying shiver sizzled down her spine. Again his voice had been almost suggestive.

Shame her body was so keen to pick up on the suggestion.

He'd removed his jacket, and she was chagrined to discover that his jeans hugged his well-formed backside in an appetizing way. Unfortunately, every time she looked at him something inside her lit up like Christmas tree lights, which was not at all appropriate to the situation.

Maybe Karen was right and she needed a little romance—or at least sex—in her life. Just to take the edge off, or something.

But not with Vasco. Since he was the father of her child, that would be way too heavy. And it was unlikely that a dashing royal bachelor would be interested in a short, frumpy book restorer. He probably looked at everyone like that.

The third gift, wrapped in green shimmery paper, proved to be a stuffed purple dinosaur. Not one with its own PBS show, happily, but rather an expensive, handmade-looking one with plush fur. "I don't know what kind of toys he likes, so I got a mix."

"Very sensible." She pulled apart the stiff plastic of the train packaging and set some cars down on the floor. Nicky spun them across the polished wood with a whoop of glee. "That one's a hit."

Vasco assembled the track, complete with bridges and a tunnel and two junctions, and helped Nicky get the train going around it.

Stella watched with a mix of quiet joy and stone-cold terror. Nicky was already getting attached to Vasco. She could see from the look of curiosity in his big, gray eyes that he liked the large new man in his kitchen. So far Vasco seemed to be thoughtful and kind. She'd worried about Nicky not having a father in his life, particularly if he needed male guidance as he got older.

Vasco's appearance seemed to offer a lot of exciting possibilities for him. And some rather worrying ones, too. Was Nicky expected to be king of Montmajor someday?

She'd better confirm that Vasco was Nicky's biological father before this situation went any further. "I need to take Nicky out and run some errands. How about we stop by the lab on the way and drop off the DNA samples."

Would he go there with her? That way she'd know he was serious, and wasn't going to pay someone off to produce the results he wanted.

He stood up and his dark brows lowered over narrowed eyes. For a moment she thought he'd say no or find an excuse. Doubts sprang to her mind—who was this man she'd allowed to play on the floor with her son, who she'd promised to move in with for a full month?

Then he nodded. "Sure. Let's go."

The DNA test results which arrived three days later confirmed what Vasco knew in his heart from the moment he saw Nicky—the boy was his flesh and blood.

He arrived on their doorstep that afternoon laden with more packages. Not the silly toys he'd brought last time, but luggage for their journey. He knew Stella was strapped for cash and it was easier to give her things than offer her money. She'd already turned that down when he'd offered at their last meeting.

He hadn't bothered to phone ahead, so she was surprised, and answered the door in a rather fetching pair of bike shorts and a tank top. She gasped when she saw him. "I was working out." She looked like she wanted to cover herself with her hands. "Pilates." She blushed.

"No wonder you look so good." Her body was delicious. Fit without being too slim, with high, plump breasts that beckoned his palms to cup them.

Lucky thing his palms were wrapped around suitcase handles. "I bought some bags for the trip and printed copies of your eTickets. I'll come by to pick you up when we leave for the airport."

Stella's pink mouth formed a round O.

"You did say you could leave anytime after Wednesday, so I booked us on a flight for Thursday. Plenty of time to pack."

"Did you book the return trip?" Her voice sounded a bit strained.

"Not yet, since we don't know how long you'll be staying." He smiled, in a way that he hoped was reassuring. He did not intend for them to come back, but it was far too early for her to know that. "Where shall I put these?"

Her eyes widened further at the sight of the luggage in his hands. "I didn't know Coach made suitcases."

"They're good quality." He decided to walk in and put them down. Maybe she was a little flustered by her Pilates workout. "Where's Nicky?"

"Napping."

"He naps a lot."

"They do at this age, which is a blessing since it's the only way I can do anything for myself. I can't take my eyes off him for an instant lately before he's climbing onto the back of the sofa or tugging on the lamp cords."

"In Montmajor you'll have plenty of time to yourself.

All the ladies in the palace are fighting with each other for the chance to take care of him."

"Ladies?" Her face paled.

"Older ladies with gray hair." He fought the urge to chuckle. Had she seen them as competition? "They won't try to take him away from you, just to squeeze his cheeks a lot and cluck over him."

She blew out a breath. "It's a lot to take in. Nicky has the advantage of being too young to worry about everything."

He wanted to take her in his arms and give her a reassuring hug, but right now he could see that would be anything but reassuring. Her whole body stiffened up whenever he came within about five feet of her.

There'd be plenty of time for caressing and soothing once they arrived in Montmajor. "Don't you worry about anything. I'll take great care of both of you."

Four

The journey to Montmajor was an adventure in itself. Naturally everyone assumed they were a family. Stella was called Mrs. Montoya twice at the airport, even though her ticket and passport were in her own name.

Vasco carried Nicky at every opportunity, and the little boy looked quite at home in his strong arms. Vasco himself beamed with paternal pride, and handled each situation from Stella's overweight luggage to Nicky running around the airport—he'd started walking that Monday, and quickly progressed to sprinting—with good humor and tireless charm.

And then there were the stares.

Every woman in the airport, from the headphone-wearing teenagers to the elderly bathroom attendants, stared at Vasco wherever he went. His easy swagger and piratical good looks drew female attention like a beacon. He wore a long, dark raincoat—it was pouring when they left—and army green pants with black boots, so no one would have guessed he was a king. His passport was black and larger than hers, bearing an elaborate seal, and she wondered if all his royal titles were listed inside.

He still had to go through security like everyone else, but he'd bought them some kind of VIP tickets that entitled them to fly past most of the lines and get right onto the plane with almost no waiting.

Stella tried to ignore the envious looks. She certainly didn't feel smug about strolling around with Vasco. Probably none of these people would covet the situation she was in, her future uncertain and her son's affections at stake.

The long plane ride passed quickly. Nicky sat between them in the wide first-class seats, and they were both so busy keeping him entertained, or being agonizingly quiet while he napped, that she didn't have to worry about keeping a conversation going.

A small private plane met them at Barcelona Airport for the rest of the journey to Montmajor, whose airport wasn't large enough for commercial jets.

Suddenly things felt different. Men in black jackets with walkie-talkies swept them onto the plane, bowing to Vasco and generally treating him like a monarch. The inside of the plane was arranged like a lounge, with plush purple leather seats and a well-stocked bar. Except for takeoff and landing, Nicky was allowed the run of the plane, and two stern male attendants indulged his every whim. Vasco smiled and watched.

Stella felt herself shrinking into the background. They were now in Vasco's world and she wasn't at all sure of her place there.

Once they'd landed, a black limo drove them from the airport through some hilly countryside, then up toward an imposing sandstone castle with a wide, arched entrance. Inside the arch, the castle spread out around them, long galleries of carved stone columns lining a paved courtyard.

People rushed out from all directions to greet them. Vasco put his arm around her and introduced her—in Catalan she presumed, since it sounded somewhere between Spanish and French—with a proprietary air that made her stomach flip.

Did he want people to think they were a couple? His arm around her shoulders set alarm bells ringing all over her body. She gripped Nicky's hand with force. She hadn't got used to him toddling beside her rather than traveling in her arms.

"Stella, this is my aunt Frida, my aunt Mari and my aunt Lilli." Three women, all dressed in black and too old to be literally his aunts, nodded and smiled and gazed longingly at Nicky. She'd presumed that his father was dead, or he wouldn't be king, but it hadn't occurred to her to ask about his mother or any siblings. How blindly she'd walked into this whole thing.

"Nice to meet you," she stammered. They didn't extend their hands to shake, which was lucky as she didn't want to let go of Nicky. He seemed the safest anchor in this strange, foreign world. Vasco's arm still rested on her neck, his fingers curling gently around her shoulder.

"I'll take Stella inside and show her around." He squeezed her shoulder with his fingers, which made her eyes widen, then ushered her up a wide flight of stairs and through a double door into a large foyer. A vast woven tapestry covered one stone wall—a hunting scene, lavishly decorated with foliage and flowers. Vasco walked toward a curving flight of stone stairs with a carved balustrade. "And on the way we'll pass by the library, which I suspect is far more interesting to you than your bedroom."

Another squeeze made her heart beat faster. He seemed to be giving the false impression that they were involved. Her face heated and she wondered how she could pull away without seeming rude. Anger rose inside her alongside the heat Vasco seemed to generate whenever he came near her. It wasn't fair of him to toy with her like this. She bent down, pretending to adjust Nicky's dungarees, and managed to slip from his grasp.

Vasco simply strode ahead, pointing out what lay behind each carved doorway. An attendant had taken his raincoat so she had an annoying view of his tight rear end as he marched along the hallway. She tugged her eyes to the timeworn stone carvings that lined the walls.

Nicky pulled his grip from hers and ran forward, toward Vasco. A shriek of glee bounced off the ancient stone and echoed around them. Vasco turned to her with a grin on his face. "Just what this old place needs—some youthful enthusiasm." She couldn't help smiling.

The library was every bit as awe-inspiring as she could have dreamed. Two stories of volumes lined its walls and the long oak table in the center of the room was scarred by centuries of scholars and their ink. Nicky ran up to an ancient chair and she dashed to scoop him up before he could pull it over on himself. She couldn't even begin to imagine what treasures must lurk on those high shelves, accessed by rolling ladders.

The one tall window was shaded, probably to protect the books from sun, so the room had a mystical gloom that fueled her excitement.

Nicky yawned and fidgeted, and for a second she felt guilty about wanting to be alone with all those magnificent books. "He needs a nap."

"Or a good run." Vasco took Nicky's other hand. "Come on, Nicky!" He took off toward the door, with Nicky running beside him. Stella stood staring after her son for a moment, then hurried after them, torn between her pleasure at watching Nicky so secure on his tiny feet, and fearing that the pace of everything, including her son's development, was happening way too fast for her to keep up.

With Nicky tucked up in bed, under the watchful eye of one of the "aunts," Stella joined Vasco in the grand dining room for supper. The majestic surroundings demanded elegant attire, and in anticipation she'd made sure to bring several dresses with her. Karen was a talented thrift shop hunter and had scored four lovely vintage dresses for her at her favorite shop in an expensive neighborhood, each from a different era. Tonight she wore a rather fitted 1950s dress in steel-gray silk. Its perfect condition suggested that it had never been worn, and the crisp fabric hugged her body like reassuring armor. Karen loved to choose matching accessories, so tiny clusters of 1950s paste diamonds ornamented her ears. She had one pair of shoes for all her ensembles, gunmetal silver with pointed toes and medium heels. She tucked her hair into a 1950s-style chignon and felt—if not as glamorous as the type of women Vasco was used to—pretty elegant and well put together.

Vasco rose from the table as she descended a small flight of stairs into the dining room. His gray eyes swept her from head to toe, and darkened with appreciation. He walked toward her, took her hand and kissed it.

"You look stunning." Throaty and sincere, his words made her blink.

Luckily the stiff peaks of silk hid the way her nipples tightened under his admiring gaze. "Thanks. Jeans and a T-shirt didn't feel right for dinner in such a dramatic environment."

Vasco himself wore tailored black pants and a fine-striped shirt, open at the collar. Considerably more formal than his clothes in the U.S. "I'm not sure it matters what you wear here. The palace drapes around one like a velvet robe." His white teeth flashed a grin. "But you make everything around you vanish."

Her hand tingled where his lips had touched it. Normally this kind of flattery would make her roll her eyes, but from Vasco's lips it sounded oddly sincere. He pulled out a carved chair and she sat in it. The table was elaborately set for the two of them. Glass goblets glittered with both red and white wine, and the silver cutlery shone from recent polishing. As soon as Vasco was seated, two waiters appeared carrying an array of dishes, which they offered to her one by one, spooning their contents onto her plate when she agreed.

She didn't understand the words they'd said but the aromas spoke for themselves. Crispy-skinned game hen, fragrant rice with snippets of fresh herbs and a rich ratatouille. Her mouth watered.

"It's good to be home." Vasco smiled at the feast. "I

miss the cooking almost more than anything when I'm gone."

"How long were you gone? When you were younger, I mean." She wanted to know more about his past, and the circumstances that had conspired to bring them together.

"Almost ten years." He took a swig of red wine. "I left when I was eighteen and I didn't plan to ever come back."

"Why not?" He seemed so deeply rooted in the place.

"There's only room for one male heir in Montmajor. He inherits the palace, the crown, the country and everything in it. Any other male heirs must set forth to seek their fortune elsewhere. It's a thousand-year-old tradition."

"But why?"

"To avoid conflict and struggles for the throne. One of my ancestors made it a law after he seized the throne from his own older brother. On his eighteenth birthday the younger son must leave the country with a thousand Quirils in his pocket. It's been enforced rigidly ever since."

"So they literally drove you out of the country on your eighteenth birthday."

"No one had to drive me. I knew to make myself scarce."

Stella tried not to shiver. She couldn't imagine what it would feel like growing up knowing you'd be banished one day. "And I bet one thousand Quirils doesn't go as far as it did a thousand years ago."

Vasco laughed. "Nope. Then it was the equivalent of a couple of million dollars. Now it's about seventy-five."

"What did your parents think of all this?"

He shrugged. "It's the law." The candlelight emphasized the strong planes of his face. "I suppose I thought they wouldn't enforce it. What boy thinks his own parents plan to send him away? But when the time drew near...and there was my brother." Vasco's brow lowered and his whole expression seemed to darken.

Stella gulped down a morsel of tender meat. She had the feeling she'd hit on a very sensitive topic. "I assume your brother is dead." She said it as quietly as possible. "Which is why you came home."

"Yes. He killed himself and both my parents in a car accident. Drunk at the time, as usual." He growled the words. "And it's over all of their dead bodies that I'm back here." His eyes flashed, and he took another swig of wine. "Lovely story, isn't it?"

She drew in a breath. "I'm so sorry."

"That was nine months ago, when my father's oldest friend called me up and told me to return." He raised a brow. "I flew back the following day for the first time in ten years."

Something in his expression touched her. He looked wistful. "You must have missed Montmajor while you were away."

"Like a missing part of me." His gray eyes were serious. "I didn't think I'd ever see it again."

"The laws demanded that you never even visit?"

He nodded. "In case I was tempted to lead a coup." His eyes sparkled with humor. "Paranoid country, huh?"

"Very." Stella swallowed some wine. Was Nicky heir to the throne here? The question seemed far too huge to just say out loud. "Do you plan to change the law, so that if you have several children the younger ones don't have to be turfed out at age 18?"

"Already did it." He grinned. "My first edict when I came back. People were really happy about it. That and I made it legal to have sex outside marriage."

Stella laughed. "I bet that law was broken a lot anyway."

"I know it. Sounded pretty funny when the official speaker pronounced it from the castle walls. Maybe that's why no one ever had the nerve to change it before."

"So I guess you're not under pressure to marry anyone in order to enjoy life."

"That's a fact." He smiled and lifted his glass. "Marriage and the Montoya men generally don't agree with each other."

Stella lifted her glass, but wondered what he meant. Did he not intend to marry? If Nicky was his heir he didn't need to. The next in line was already born and he hadn't had to break any ancient laws, either. "Maybe you just haven't met the right person yet."

Vasco's eyes darkened. "Or maybe I have?"

His suggestive tone sent a ripple of awareness to her core, and she shifted slightly in her fitted dress. "There must be a lot of women who'd be happy to be your queen."

"Oh yes. They've been coming out of the woodwork from all over." His dimples showed. "A crown has amazing aphrodisiac effects."

Not that he needed them. With those looks he wasn't in much danger of being lonely. But could he marry some glamorous woman and expect that she'd put up with his sperm bank son becoming king?

Frightening as it was, she needed a clearer picture of what he had in mind. "What are you hoping for, with Nicky? He's not really next in line to the throne, is he?" The whole thing sounded so ridiculous that she blushed when she said it. Maybe a lot of moms would love their child to carry a scepter, but she wasn't one of them.

"Right now he is. He's my only heir." Vasco frowned. "However, if I were to marry someone, the first son I had with her would become heir. Children born in marriage take precedence over illegitimate heirs."

"That doesn't seem fair." Indignation flared in her chest, which was insane, considering that she didn't want Nicky to be king. Still, it implied that somehow he was less important, and maybe that tugged at her sense of guilt over choosing to bring him into the world in a nontraditional family.

"You're right. It's not. I could change the law but it doesn't seem to be an urgent problem right now."

"Not like the need to have unmarried sex."

"Exactly." His eyes twinkled. "First things first."

Heat sizzled inside her and she wished his seductive gaze didn't have such a dramatic effect. She had no intention of having any kind of sex with him. She'd managed without sex for more than two years since she broke up with Trevor, and hadn't missed it at all. Of course being woken up several times a night by a baby could put a damper on anyone's libido. Maybe now that she was getting sleep again it had come back?

Not a very convenient time for lust to reappear in her life. She tugged her gaze to her plate and pushed some rice onto her fork.

"How did you get into restoring books?"

The innocuous question surprised her. What a change

of subject. "It happened by accident. My mom had an old edition of *Alice in Wonderland* that had belonged to her great-grandmother, and she gave it to me when I was in college. The spine was starting to come apart so I asked for advice at a local bookseller, who told me about a course in book restoring—and I got hooked. There's something addictive about restoring someone's treasure so it can be enjoyed by another generation of readers."

"An appreciation for the past is one thing that links us. My ancestors have lived here for more than a millennium and I grew up walking in their footsteps, using their furnishings and reading their books." He gestured at the long wood table, its surface polished to a sheen but scarred with tiny nicks by generations of diners.

"It must be nice to have such a sense of belonging."

"It is, until you're turned out of the place where you belong." He lifted a brow. "Then you search and search for somewhere else to belong."

"Did you find that place?"

He laughed. "Never. Not until I came home. Though I traveled far and wide looking for it." His expression turned serious. "I want Nicky to have that sense of belonging. To grow up breathing the air of his ancestral homeland, singing our songs and eating our food."

Stella swallowed. He was getting carried away and she'd better set some boundaries right now. "I can understand why you feel that way, but you didn't write any of that..." She leaned in and whispered. "In the sperm donor information." She put down her fork. "Because if you had I wouldn't have chosen you as the donor. You gave away the right to decide what happens to Nicky when you visited Westlake Cryobank."

His eyes narrowed. "I made a terrible mistake."

"We all have to live with our mistakes." She could say she'd made one in choosing Vasco as Nicky's father—except that now she had Nicky, the center of her world. "Don't think you can tell me and Nicky what to do." She tried to sound stern. "Just because you're a king and from a thousand-year-old dynasty…" she gestured around the elegant chamber "…doesn't mean that you're more important or special than me and Nicky or that your needs and desires come first. We were raised in American democracy where everyone is equal—at least in theory—and I intend to keep it that way."

Humor flashed in his eyes. "I like your fire. I'd never coerce you into staying. After a few days or weeks in Montmajor I doubt you'll be able to imagine living anywhere else."

"We'll see about that." Soft golden candlelight reflected in the polished glass of their goblets and illuminated the ancient sandstone walls around them. Already Montmajor was beginning its process of seduction.

And so was Vasco.

He tilted his head, smiling at her. "Let's take a walk before dessert." He rose and rounded the table, then extended his hand.

She cursed the way her fingers tingled as she slid them inside his. Still, she rose to her feet and followed him, heels clicking on the stone floor as she walked with him through a vast wooden double door into a tall gallery and out onto a veranda.

They stood high above the surrounding landscape.

The last sliver of sun was setting in the west—to their left—and the mountains fell away at their feet like crumpled tissue paper. As the peaks disappeared into the mist she almost thought she could make out the shimmering glass of the Mediterranean sea in the far distance.

Hardly any sign of human habitation was visible. Just the odd clay-tiled roof of a remote homestead, or the winding ribbon of a distant road. "Amazing," she managed when she caught her breath. "I bet it looked like this in medieval times."

"In medieval times there were more people." Vasco smiled, the sun highlighting his bronzed features and deepening the laugh lines around his eyes. "This area was a center for weaving and leatherwork. Our population is about half what it was in the tenth century. We're one of Europe's best kept secrets and I think most people here like it that way."

His thumb stroked the outside of her hand and sent heat slithering up it. Again her nipples tightened inside her gray silk dress and she sucked in a breath and pulled her hand back. "What about schools? How are the children educated?" Anything to get the conversation on some kind of prosaic track, so she wasn't falling prey to the seductive majesty of the landscape and its monarch.

"There's only one school, in the town. It's one of the finest educational institutions in Europe. Children here learn all the major European languages—now Chinese is popular, too—and go on to university at places like Harvard and Cambridge, the University of Barcelona. All over the world."

"Don't you lose a lot of well-educated people that way? When they go on to work in other countries."

"Sure, for a while. But they always come back." He gestured at the dramatic landscape around them. "Where else can you live once you've left your heart in Montmajor?"

Stella felt an odd flutter in her chest. The place was already taking hold of her. "I'd like to see the town." She glanced at him. "There is a town, isn't there?"

"We call it the city." His white teeth flashed in the setting sun. "And it would be my great pleasure to give you a tour tomorrow. Let's go finish dinner."

She stiffened as he slid his arm inside hers. Really, she should protest at all these intimate gestures, but somehow that felt petty, when he might just think he was being a gracious host. People were different in this part of the world, more demonstrative and touchy-feely, and she didn't want to come across like an uptight puritan when she'd chosen for her son to have Mediterranean heritage.

Her own elbow jostled against his soft shirt, and the hairs on her arm stood on end. In fact every inch of her body stood to attention as they strolled through a dimly illuminated forest of stone columns back to the candlelit dining room.

Their plates had been cleared and as soon as they sat—Vasco pulled out her chair, old-world style—servants appeared with gleaming platters of glazed pears and homemade ice cream.

Stella's eyes widened. "I'm not going to fit into any of my clothes after a week here."

"That would be a shame." Vasco glanced up, mischief dancing in his eyes. "That dress fits you so beautifully." His gaze flicked to her chest, which jumped in excitement.

She felt heat rising to her face. "I'll have to do some exercise."

"There's nowhere better. Tomorrow we can ride in the hills."

"On a horse? I've never ridden in my life."

"You could learn. Or we could walk."

"I like the second option. Nicky can't walk too far, though. He's only starting."

"Nicky can stay with his new aunts while you and I stride through the landscape."

She had to admit that sounded pretty good. "I used to walk in the hills all the time, but since I had Nicky it's been hard to find the time."

"Here we'll have all the time in the world." His smile broadened. "And we can do *anything* you like."

The emphasis sent a shiver down her spine. Already her body had a few suggestions, mostly involving peeling those well-cut clothes off Vasco's ripped and tanned physique.

What was it about this guy that set her on fire? Maybe his being Nicky's father had something to do with it. There was already a bond between them, forged in blood, a connection with him that went far beyond their brief acquaintance.

And maybe the strange and worrying situation had set her nerves on edge, which made her emotions and senses all the more likely to flare up in unexpected ways. She'd have to watch out for that.

"When you look out the window tomorrow and see the sunrise, you'll know you've come home." Vasco's voice startled her out of her thoughts. His eyes heavy-lidded, he looked at her over a sparkling glass of white wine.

"I'm not at all sure I'll be awake at sunrise."

"I could come rouse you." His eyes glittered.

"No, thanks!" She said it too fast, and a little too loud. She needed to keep this man out of her bedroom.

Which might be a very serious challenge.

Five

Stella had rather dreaded seeing Vasco's handsome countenance over the breakfast table the next morning, but found herself put out when he wasn't here. Apparently he'd gone off on royal business and wouldn't be back until late. So much for her tour of the town and walk in the hills.

Was she turning into a pouting, jealous girlfriend, when she wasn't even his girlfriend?

"Ma!" Nicky played with the omelet the kitchen staff had made for him. "Cheerios!"

"Hey, you can say real words when you truly need something." She wiped his chin. "But I'm not sure they have Cheerios here."

"Cheerios!" He banged his spoon on the gleaming wood surface of the table, which made Stella seize his wrist and glance over her shoulder to see if anyone else had witnessed the desecration.

"This table is very precious, sweetie. We have to be careful with it."

"Cheerios, peez." His big gray eyes now brimmed with tears. Why hadn't she thought to bring some with her? She'd had a ziplock bag of them for the plane, but she hadn't thought about people eating different foods here.

"I'll go ask the cook, okay? We'll find something."

She left him at the table and pushed open the door that the staff seemed to appear and disappear from. She was a little alarmed to find a young man hovering right behind it. "Do you have any breakfast cereal?" She spoke in Spanish. He nodded and summoned her into a tiled hallway that led to a series of pantries. One of them turned out to be lined floor to ceiling with boxes of pasta, crackers and cereals, all imported from the U.S.

"For little Nicky," he said with a smile. "His Majesty requested them."

Stella bit her lip. How thoughtful. She pointed at the giant box of Cheerios on a high shelf. "Could he have some of those in a bowl—no milk?"

"Of course, Madam."

She heaved a sigh of relief—or was it awe—and walked back to the table. Alarm filled her heart when she pushed through the door and saw Nicky's chair empty. He always sat in a high chair at home but they didn't seem to have one here.

"Nicky?" She glanced around the room. There was no sign of him. And so many doors he could have gone out through. Panic snapped through her. This palace was vast, and probably had plenty of high walls and ledges a child could fall off. It wasn't safe to leave him unattended for a single moment in such a labyrinthine and nonchildproof space, and she'd have to keep that in mind from now on. "Nicky?"

She hurried out into the main hallway, and waved to an older footman. "Excuse me, I... My son..."

He simply smiled and gestured for her to follow him. More doors and stone hallways—they all looked alike, even though they weren't—led to an interior courtyard with a large, round pool in the middle. A fountain bubbled water and her pulse began to return to normal when she saw Nicky floating a small wooden sailboat in the water under the watchful gaze of two of the "aunts."

She heaved a sigh. "Thank goodness you're here! Sweetie, please don't take off without telling me where you're going." As if he could have explained it. Still, she wanted the women to know, since they must have brought him here. "Mommy needs to know where you are at all times."

She gave the "aunts" a frosty smile. "This water looks rather deep." She spoke in Spanish. They gave no sign of having understood. The fountain was lovely, but the patterned tiles at the bottom of the pool shimmered beneath a good foot and a half of water. Quite enough for a toddler to drown in if someone's back was turned. She'd have to talk to Vasco about safety, so he could lay down some guidelines for the "aunts."

"I found you some Cheerios, Nicky. Come have some." She held out her hand. He glanced up at her, then turned his attention right back to the sailboat. It was quite an elaborate one with cotton rigging and a striped sail. "We'll come back to the boat after breakfast."

"No! Nicky sail boat."

Her eyes widened at the longest sentence he'd ever said. "Have some Cheerios first." Her eyes turned to the aunts in a silent plea.

"Don't worry, Ms. Greco. He just ate two cherry pastries." The smaller aunt—Mari—spoke in flawless, barely accented English. "And we'll take care of him while you eat your own breakfast and do anything else you like."

Cherry pastries? Not the most nutritious breakfast, but at least he'd eaten. And maybe she could go have hers quickly. "Are you sure?"

"I raised eight of my own children and there's nothing I'd like better than to spend time with little Nicky. Frida feels the same and when Lilli's back from her doctor's appointment, she'd agree, too." She beamed at Nicky. "He's such a dear child."

"Yes." Stella bit her lip. "You won't let him fall into the water." It was a statement not a question.

"Absolutely not." Frida's reply showed that she spoke perfect English, too. Stella felt embarrassed for thinking they wouldn't. Though Mari was already speaking softly to Nicky in Catalan, encouraging him to move one of the sails, from what she could gather. "Vasco tells us you restore antique books. We're so lucky to enjoy your expertise here. I used to be a professor of medieval literature at the University of Barcelona, and I know this palace is a treasure trove."

Stella swallowed. "Yes. I saw some of the library yesterday. Maybe I will go there now. We'll have to have a long chat later." She was far too flustered to talk now. These white-haired old grannies were more accomplished and educated than she'd ever be.

Never mind what they could teach her son—*she* could probably learn a lot from them. "I'll see you later."

She kissed Nicky on the forehead, trying to ignore her maternal misgivings at leaving him in such capable hands. No worse than leaving him at the local day care, which she'd used regularly for work.

She spent the day in the library fondling impressive volumes dating back to the time of Charlemagne. Vasco had arranged for a selection of the finest restoration tools, including a vast array of delicate leathers and sheets of gold leaf, to be used for repairing or replacing damaged covers.

Just touching the books was a sensual experience. Reading the words, stories, poems and dramatic tales from history brought her imagination to life. She knew French and Spanish, and quite a bit of Latin and Italian, so she could understand and enjoy much of what she read in the same way the lucky residents of this palace must have done for generations.

She made mental notes of different things she wanted to show Vasco, because she thought he'd enjoy them: tales from his own family history, intriguing Montmajor folktales, even a journal of sorts written by a young king in the 1470s.

But Vasco didn't show up that afternoon.

He was absent at dinnertime, which made her feel rather silly in the aqua vintage maxi dress Karen had chosen for her along with some pretty turquoise earrings. She ate alone in the grand dining room, wishing she'd shared Nicky's feast of scrambled eggs and toast. Nicky was now tucked up in bed under the watchful gaze of a local girl. It was awkward sitting there as waiters brought dishes to her and refilled her glass, and she stared at the empty chair on the other side of the table.

Where was Vasco? Of course it wasn't really her business. They weren't involved or anything. Even if he was out to dinner with another woman, that was absolutely fine.

She swallowed more wine. Maybe she wasn't so crazy about the idea of him carrying on with other women while she and Nicky were there. Couldn't he save that for after they'd gone? They were his guests, after all.

He was probably at a party, schmoozing with wealthy aristocrats, and had forgotten all about them. Or maybe he'd flown off somewhere in his purple-seated plane, to spend a few days on someone's yacht or attend a grand wedding.

Why did she care? She was busy and happy with the library and its amazing collection of books and manuscripts. So why did she glance up and catch her breath every time the door opened? And why did her heart sink each time she saw it was just the waiter again?

She only ate half of the pretty apricot tart in its lake of fresh cream. It seemed a shame to waste such carefully prepared and delicious food, but then it was also foolish to eat it if she wasn't hungry and no one was here to share the pleasure.

She'd removed her napkin from her lap and was about to head upstairs to her room, when the door opened again. This time her startled glance and increased pulse rate were rewarded by the appearance of the man whose presence seemed to hover everywhere in the palace.

Gray eyes flashing, and hair tousled by the wind,

Vasco swept into the room like a sirocco. "I'm so sorry I missed dinner."

He strode toward her, long legs clad in dusty black pants. A white T-shirt clung to his pecs and biceps, revealing a physique more developed and chiseled than her wildest imaginings.

She struggled to find a sensible thing to say, and failed. "Where have you been?"

He looked surprised, and she regretted her rude question. "I rode over to Monteleon, to visit an old friend. We got to talking and the hours slipped away."

So that was the "royal business" he'd been called away on? Again she felt slightly offended. She wondered if the old friend was male or female, but she didn't want to know that. "I found some interesting things in the library."

"Oh?" He'd rounded the table, where he picked up her wineglass and drank from it. Before she had time to blink, a rather flustered male waiter appeared with a filled glass for him. He thanked the waiter, but as soon as the man had disappeared he looked ruefully at his glass. "I'm sure this won't taste as good as one blessed by your lips."

Then he sipped and walked on around the table, leaving Stella staring after him. How did he get away with saying stuff like that? She glanced at her own glass back on the table, and it suddenly seemed unbearably sensual to drink from it again.

"I thought I should start the restoration project by focusing on books and papers that directly relate to the royal family. I've found quite a few interesting things buried amongst the other books, and I thought you might want to organize them into a separate archive of their own."

"Great idea." He was now at the far end of the table, where he put his glass down and stretched, which sent ripples traveling through the muscles of his broad back.

Was he trying to taunt her with his impressive physique? He should know by now that she was the bookish type and didn't notice such things. "Would you like me to show you the book I plan to work on first? After you have dinner, of course."

"I've had dinner." His eyes wandered to her cleavage, which swelled under his admiring gaze. "Though I wish I'd had it here instead. The view is much better." His gaze drifted lower, which made her belly tighten, then to her hips, which had to resist a powerful urge to sway under his intense stare.

"It was strange eating all alone in this big dining room."

"I apologize for making you do that. I'll make sure it never happens again."

She didn't quite believe him. He was a flatterer who knew the right thing to say at any moment. Like his promise of taking her for a walk today.

"Shall we head to the library now?"

"Sure." He walked back to her and slid his arm around her waist. Her eyes opened wide as a shiver of sheer arousal snapped through her. How many glasses of wine had she drunk? Surely it was only two, though it was hard to keep track when they kept refilling it for her.

"I am dusty. Maybe we should stop by my room on the way so I can change. No need to add any dust to the considerable amount that must be on the books already."

His smile made her knees weak. She cursed herself for it. "No need. Did you ride your horse there?"

"Many horses." He grinned. "My bike. It's a far better way to get around these mountains than a big royal sedan. The dirt is the only drawback. I should have showered before coming to find you, but I couldn't wait."

Her cheeks heated under his glance, and she sucked in a breath. Her pewter shoes made an impressive noise on the stone flags of the grand hallway. Vasco turned to the right, in a direction she'd never been before. The carvings on the walls grew more elaborate and the floor turned into an intricate mosaic, which led to a grand, arched doorway.

"The royal bedchamber?" She looked up at the embossed shield carved right into the stone above the door.

"Exactly." He made a courtly gesture with his hand. "Please come in."

She didn't have much choice with his arm still tucked around her waist. A vast bed rose almost to the twenty-foot high ceiling. Heavy curtains hung from a carved wood frame. Candles burned in elaborate candelabra on each side of the room, throwing off a surprising amount of light.

"They've invented something called electricity. Have you heard of it?" The host of candles made shapes and colors dance on the walls and ceiling.

"These newfangled inventions never last. Much better to stick with what's tried and true." She saw his dimples for a second before he peeled off his white T-shirt to reveal bronzed muscles that made her jaw drop.

When he unbuttoned his pants she turned away. "Maybe I should wait outside?"

"No need. I'll be ready in a moment."

He was doing this to torment her. And it was working. She couldn't resist sneaking a peak in the age-clouded mirror than hung on a nearby wall. His tight backside looked very fetching in classic white underwear. His thighs were powerful and dusted with dark hair, and she admired them for a split second before they disappeared into a crisply ironed pair of black pants that seemed to have appeared out of thin air.

He stretched again, causing her to close her eyes for a moment. No one needed that much overstimulation. When she opened them she was relieved to see his thick biceps hidden behind the creamy cotton of a collarless shirt.

"Now I'm ready. Take me to your library." He walked toward her, barefoot on the stone floor, a smile in his gray eyes.

Stella swallowed. Her library? Obviously he'd decided it was her domain for the duration of her stay, which gave her an interesting feeling of pleasure.

Vasco took her cold, rather nervous hand in his warm one, and they set off along the corridor. Even with her in heels and him barefoot she only came up to his cheekbone—and a dramatic, well-shaped cheekbone it was.

Anticipation tingled through her veins as she switched on the low hanging lights in the library, illuminating the magical kingdom of books. She led him to the table where she'd started to arrange the volumes most in need of repair. One heavy tome, its delicate leather cover almost in tatters, sat apart from the others.

Vasco ran his fingers over the rough surface, where the tooled gold had all but vanished under the wear of centuries of hands. "It's a history of Montmajor."

"Written in 1370." Stella laughed. "Rather amazing that they had so much to write already."

"We always have a lot to say about ourselves." That mischievous white grin flashed in his tanned face. "And apparently we love to read about ourselves, too."

He flipped open the book with a casual hand, which almost made Stella want to grab his wrist. This book was six hundred and fifty years old, after all. Vasco began to read, his deep, rich voice wrapping itself around the handwritten Catalan words that she could almost understand, but not quite. Something swelled inside her as Vasco spoke the ancient words aloud with obvious enjoyment.

He stopped and looked at her. "Do you know what it says?"

"I need to learn Catalan. I know French and Spanish and a little Italian and it sounds to me like it's a bit of all of them mixed together."

"It's so much more than that." His eyes narrowed into a smile. "I'll have to teach you."

"That's a big project."

"Then we'll tackle it one word at a time." He pressed a finger to his sensual mouth. "First things first. What's the most important thing in life?"

Stella frowned. "Good health?"

Vasco shook his head. "Passion. *La passio.*"

"La passio." She let the word roll off her tongue, and decided not to start a debate about how crucial passion was to people who were starving. Kings clearly lived in a rather more gilded and hedonistic reality.

"Ben fet."

"I'm guessing that means *well done,* since it sounds a bit like *bien fait* in French."

His grin widened. "You're catching on. Soon you'll be speaking it like a native."

She couldn't help a little flush of pride. "I'll do my best. I can't help but feel *la passio* for the work I'll be doing." She glanced down at the lovely book and managed to restrain herself from moving Vasco's large hand from the page. No need to bore him with her worries about natural oils seeping into ancient handmade paper and tiny microscopic creatures eating away at natural inks. "I plan to restore the cover first. I'll preserve the original then make a leather slipcover that mirrors how it would have looked when new. Then I'll go through page by page and stabilize the book. The inside is in surprisingly good shape."

"Which means it hasn't been read enough times, yet." He flipped a page and started to read again, letting his tongue wrap around the words, bringing them to life in the quiet library.

Stella watched, entranced. Even though the book was about history, it was written in some kind of verse, and Vasco's voice rode the cadence of the words in a sensual rhythm. She could figure out the meaning of enough words to recognize a description of a battle, lances flying and flags fluttering in the wind, horses galloping on an open plain. The vision of it all danced before her eyes, brought to life centuries after it was written so painstakingly in the book.

Her heart was beating fast by the time Vasco stopped, or pulled up, since it felt more as if she'd been riding along in the tale and they'd slid to a halt, dust flying and hooves clattering.

"Beautiful." Her voice was breathless, as if she'd been running alongside the riders.

"Bell." Vasco smiled. "And thank you for awakening me to it. I'd never have opened this book if you weren't here. I confess I'm not much of a reader, by nature."

"You're more action oriented." She noticed how Vasco always seemed to have the wind in his hair, even here in the quiet calm of the library. "And this book has a lot of action in it."

"It does. And plenty of *passio.*" He took her hand in his. Part of her was glad he'd removed it from the fragile old book, but the rest of her started to quiver in a mix of excitement and terror as desire rose inside her, hot and inevitable.

Was this just a friendly gesture for him? Everything about Vasco was sensual and dramatic, so maybe she read too much into his bold touches and looks. Her hand heated inside his and her fingers tingled with the desire to explore his warm skin. All the sexual feelings that had lain dormant in her for the last two years—or more if she was honest—rose up like a river after a rainstorm.

She tugged her hand back and stepped away. "Let me show you another book I plan to work on." She reached for a black leather volume, its pages coming loose from the worn binding. Her hands trembled as she heaved its weight toward Vasco, anxious to break the seductive spell he seemed to have cast over her.

She didn't dare look at him but she imagined his eyes laughing. He knew how much power he had over her and he found it amusing. Flirtation came naturally to him and he used it like a weapon. She'd better find some good armor, possibly the polished set of inlaid sixteenth century armor in the great hall. That looked about her size.

"What's so funny?" His voice tickled her ears.

"Just wondering how I'd look in a suit of armor."

"It's easy to find out. I used to try them on myself when I was a kid—even rode my horse in one, which wasn't too comfortable." He laughed. "But none of them fit me now. Our ancestors were smaller than we are." His daring eyes swept over her again. "Though you're about the right size for Francesca's. Come on."

He'd been leaning on the table with one hip, but he rose and headed for the door, beckoning her.

Stella swallowed. Did he really intend for her to try on some armor? She had to admit the idea had some appeal. How often did you have an opportunity to peek into the experiences of people in another era? Now she'd know how a nervous eighteen-year-old count might feel as he dressed for battle with a neighboring fiefdom.

Her pace quickened as she followed him. She wasn't exactly dressed for battle, medieval or otherwise. Her long dress swept around her legs as she hurried down the hallway. Would he expect her to take it off? Karen had convinced her to buy new lingerie for her trip on the pretext that if servants would be arranging her belongings, they should fit in with a royal household, not scream "bargain bin."

She wasn't sure how many royal guests wore skimpy pale silver satin and lace, but at least her underwear drawer did look smart and she felt glamorous when she put them on.

Vasco led her along a gloomy passageway, il-luminated by a single lamp, and into a vast chamber with no lighting of any kind. He flicked a switch and spotlights in the ceiling splashed over a startling display of weaponry arranged on the walls in intricate patterns. Swords crisscrossed each other and muskets fanned out like lace petticoats. Armaments covered most of three walls, shining and polished as if ready for immediate use.

"My ancestors liked to keep their defenses at hand." Vasco grinned. "But they also liked things to be pretty."

"Does someone take these down to polish them?"

"Only once a year. They haven't been pressed into service for quite some time."

"That's a relief. Besides, it can't be easy to buy ammunition for a seventeenth century musket these days."

"You'd be surprised…" he winked "…at what you can find on eBay."

Spotlights also illuminated three suits of armor, each standing in a corner. Two were silver metal with tooled decoration, the other was black and bronze, very elaborate and slightly smaller than the others.

"It's so pretty." She walked toward the unusual one. "Is it Italian?"

"It is." He sounded surprised that she knew. "My ancestor Francesc Turmeda Montoya had it made in Genoa and brought here over the mountains. By the time it arrived he'd grown and it didn't fit."

"What a waste. So it was never worn?"

"Not by him. I'd imagine it was pressed into service over the years from time to time." His long, strong fingers caressed the tooled metal. "But it's possible that it's never experienced the pleasure of encasing a woman's body."

Stella felt every inch a woman as Vasco's gaze met hers. "It does look like it might fit."

He reached behind the torso and unbuckled something. The breastplate, arms still attached, loosened from the stand. "I think you'd better slip out of your dress."

Stella fought the urge to laugh. "What if someone comes?"

"They won't."

"What if war breaks out and all the staff comes running to find the weapons?"

"Then you'll be dressed for battle." His dimples deepened. "Let me help you." He pulled his hands away from the armor and stepped behind her. The sound of her zipper sliding down her back made tiny hairs stand on end all over her body. She shrugged out of the arms and let the dress slide to the floor.

"Lucky thing I'm not self-conscious," she said, wishing she really wasn't. At least the spotlights focused on the armaments, so she stood in relative shadow outside the pool of light on the armor.

She glanced at Vasco to find his eyes feasting unashamedly on her bare skin. Her nipples thickened inside her elegant bra and she felt an urgent need to hide behind the black and gold metal. "Hold it out for me."

He lifted the breastplate off the stand. The arms clanked against the torso with a sound that could wake the dead, and she glanced behind her before sliding her arms into the dark holes and letting Vasco step behind her to fasten the straps. His fingers brushed her back as he closed the armor and she tried not to shiver.

The legs fastened individually, strapping over her thighs and attaching to the main body, so Vasco's fingers had a lot of intimate contact with her skin. The mere touch of his hands made her breath catch at the bottom of her lungs. At last she was entirely encased in metal except her head. "Let's see if I can walk." She felt precarious. The armor was heavy and with her hands in metal gauntlets she wasn't sure she could catch herself if she fell.

"You look like a very elegant Joan of Arc."

She took a tentative step forward. Surprisingly, the armor moved with her like a second, if heavyweight, skin, though the shoe part was too large and clanked on the stone floor. "It's not easy to walk in these things."

"That's why you need a horse." Vasco smiled. "No one marched into battle in that getup. Want to try the helmet?" He lifted the tooled headpiece.

Stella nodded, and let Vasco lower it over her head. She'd worn her hair loose tonight, curling around her neck, and she tucked in the bottom ends so they wouldn't stick out. It was dark inside the helmet, and had an interesting smell, more like wood than metal. She wondered about the people who'd stood in here before. Were they preparing for battle and fighting their fears, or were they like her, just trying it on for fun?

She couldn't see Vasco at all. The eye slits weren't quite in the right place so she could only see the floor and up to his knees. They must work better up on a horse.

She pulled off the helmet, and even the spare illumination in the armaments chamber seemed blinding after the darkness inside. "Phew. It's nice to be able to breathe again. I can picture you riding around the countryside carrying a lance. Rescuing a fair maiden or two."

One dark brow lifted. "What makes you think I would be rescuing them?"

"Okay, endangering their virtue."

"Probably closer to the truth." Even the way the skin around his eyes crinkled only made him more handsome. "But I would mean well." His seductive smile and tilted head seemed to gently ask forgiveness.

"I'll bet." Even in the armor she didn't feel at all safe around Vasco. And it was getting uncomfortably hot in here. "I'd better get this off."

Vasco's slow smile crept across his mouth again. "Let me help you with that."

Six

Vasco had noticed that Stella's hair changed color depending on the light. Right now the spotlight that usually shone on the armor picked out bright gold and red strands from the silky bob.

Sweet and excited but slightly hesitant, her smile tormented him. Her pink lips were mobile, soft and tempting. He could almost imagine how it would feel to kiss her.

But not quite. There was only one way to find out what her mouth would feel like pressed against his.

His knuckles caressed her back as he unbuckled the armor. Soft and warm, her skin begged to be touched. The clasp on her bra beckoned him like the key to a hidden chamber, and with difficulty he managed to prevent himself from unlocking it.

Stella slid out of the armor and he lifted it back onto its armature, irked that he had to drag his eyes from the inviting vision of her body. Luckily the legs required some assistance to remove. The darkness hid his appreciative gaze as he released her deliciously athletic thighs from their metal casing, and pulled the heavy shoes from her delicate feet with their coral-tipped toes.

Her silky underwear didn't help matters. It took all his self-control not to cup the sweet roundness of her backside. Instead he held up her dress and helped her back into it. Her cheeks were pink, even in the dim light. He'd like to see them flushed deeper, with exertion and desire.

Good things come to those who wait.

"I enjoyed that." She fastened the matching belt back around her waist. "Although it's heavy, it's also surprisingly flexible. I'd never have imagined that."

"This armor was cutting-edge technology in its time. No expense would have been spared in kitting out the son and heir to defend the family lands and honor and live to tell the tale."

Stella's eyes looked golden in the half-light of the chamber. "Do you wish you'd lived back then?"

"What man wouldn't?"

"The ones who'd rather play battle games on a computer, I suppose."

"I don't have the patience for those. I'd rather feel the blood pulsing in my veins."

"Or pulsing right out of them if it was a real battle. I'm glad Nicky won't be expected to ride into battle on a galloping horse. That would scare the life out of me."

"I'd imagine mothers have felt the same throughout history." He picked up her hand, an instinctive gesture.

"However, they haven't often had the final say in such matters."

She raised a brow. "Luckily women do have an equal say now. At least in civilized countries." He saw the glint of a challenge in her eyes.

"I suppose it remains to be seen whether Montmajor is civilized in your eyes." He couldn't keep a smile from his lips. "Though it's a hard thing to quantify. We do bathe somewhat regularly and use utensils at the table."

"I'll make up my own mind." A smile tugged at her soft, pink mouth. "I certainly have my doubts about their king."

"I imagine a lot of people do." He loved that she wasn't intimidated by his titles and all the pomp and circumstance that came with them. "I do my best to convince them that under this rough exterior beats a heart of gold."

Her laugh bounced off the weapon-laden walls and filled the air with its soft music. "No one could accuse you of being modest."

"Modesty is not a quality people seek in their king." He let his hungry eyes feast for a moment on Stella's delicious body. Her dress wrapped snugly around her waist, then flared out, concealing the curve of her hips and those silky thighs. Lucky thing the memory of them—and her seductively elegant underwear—was imprinted on his brain like a freshly switched-off lightbulb.

"I suppose arrogance and a sense of entitlement are more appropriate to a monarch." She lifted her neat chin.

"But only in measured doses, otherwise people might

want to rise up and overthrow me." He grinned. "We don't want them storming the castle."

"No, it would take too long to get all these weapons down off the wall."

"Don't worry. The palace staff is trained in kung fu."

"Really?"

"No." He took her hand and kissed it. Couldn't help himself. He knew it would be soft and warm and feel sensational against his lips.

The color in her cheeks deepened. She was ready. He could tell she was interested. Hell, he'd seen the first sparks of it in her eyes during his first surprise visit, somewhere behind the alarm and fear. Now she'd had time to get to know him and his world a little, to relax and realize that he wanted the best for her and Nicky. Even if she was still wary, she was open-minded and prepared to like both him and his country.

Now he needed to apply a little glue.

He stepped toward her and her eyes widened. Before she had a chance to move, he cupped her head with his free hand and kissed her gently but firmly on the lips.

She tasted fresh, like summer wine. A jolt of arousal crashed through him, and his fingers sank into the softness of her hair. His tongue slid between her lips, prying them open, and he longed to press his body against hers.

But two small hands on his chest pushed him back.

He blinked, aching as the intoxicating kiss came to an abrupt end.

"I don't think we should do this." Stella sounded breathless. Her eyes sparkled with a mix of shock and arousal. "Things are so complicated already."

"Then let's make them simple." He stroked her cheek. The hot, flushed skin begged to be cooled by kisses.

"This doesn't make anything simple. We barely know each other."

"We share the strongest bond any man and woman can enjoy—a child."

"That's what worries me. We owe it to Nicky to keep things harmonious between us. Once...romance comes into the picture, that's when problems start."

"Has that been your experience?" He raised a brow. Maybe she was single with good reason.

"I was in a long relationship that I ultimately decided wasn't what I wanted."

"What made you decide that?"

She hesitated, blinked. "Partly, at least, because he didn't want children."

He smiled. "So, problem solved in this case." Her mouth looked so lush, and now that he'd tasted it he couldn't bear to simply look at it.

"But what if we decide we hate each other?"

"Impossible."

"So you think we'll just kiss and live happily ever after?"

"Why not?" Happily ever after was an awfully long time, but the sight of her tempting body a few hot inches away made him ready to promise almost anything. He liked Stella immensely. She'd gone to a lot of trouble to come here and adjust herself to Montmajor for Nicky's sake and his sake, and he could tell she was a woman with a big heart as well as a lovely face.

"Why not?" She blew out a sharp breath. "I'd love to live in a world of fairy tales but reality does keep poking its ugly head back up. What will the other people at the palace say?"

"Who cares? I'm the king. I don't trouble myself with the thoughts of other people." He grinned. He hadn't troubled himself all that much with them when he wasn't king, either, but no need to mention that.

He trailed his fingers down her neck and to her shoulder. Her collarbone disappeared into the pretty aqua dress and he followed it with his fingertips. Stella shivered slightly, and he watched her chest rise and fall.

She wanted him.

His own arousal strained uncomfortably against his pants. His need to seduce her into bed tonight was becoming urgent. He slid his arms around her waist. "Trust your instincts."

"My instincts are telling me to run a mile." The smile dancing around the corners of her mouth made him doubt her statement.

"No, that's some silly part of your brain that wants to prevent you from enjoying too much pleasure."

"Is it really?" Her eyes twinkled.

Almost there.

"Absolutely. You need to switch it off."

"How do I do that?" She raised a brow.

"Like this." He pulled her close and pressed his lips to hers again, this time deepening the kiss right away, enjoying the hot softness of her mouth with his tongue.

Her arms rose around his neck and he felt her sink into his embrace. A tiny sigh rose in her throat as their bodies bumped together, her nipples brushed against his chest through the fabric of their clothes. He let his hands roam lower, to enjoy the curve of her backside and thigh.

Stella writhed against him, pulling him closer, her hot cheek against his and her eyes closed tight. Desire built inside him almost to the boiling point as her lush body tempted him into a state of rock-hard arousal.

With great difficulty he pulled back an inch or two. It was time to transfer this scene to a room with a comfortable surface of some kind. Like a bed.

"Come with me." He was half-tempted to pick her up and carry her, to reduce the chance of her changing her mind, but he managed to resist. Holding her hand tightly, he led her out of the armaments chamber and up the flight of stairs into the east tower.

He'd ordered fresh sheets for the round bedroom in happy anticipation of this moment. With windows on all sides, but no one outside to see in, this room was the most private in the whole palace and had no doubt been used for royal trysts for hundreds of years.

He pushed open the door and was pleased to see a vase filled with fresh flowers glowing under an already lit lamp. The grand hangings on the bed shone, the embroidery shimmering with gold thread, and the covers were turned back to reveal soft, freshly laundered linen.

"What a lovely room." Stella hesitated in the doorway. "It's not your bedroom, is it?" She'd seen him change clothes in his own bedroom.

"It's *our* bedroom." He pulled her into his arms and shoved the door closed behind them with his foot, then drew her into a kiss that silenced all thought, let alone conversation.

Stella couldn't believe she was able to kiss Vasco and breathe at the same time, but it must be happening because the kiss went on and on, drawing her deeper into a sensual trance.

She'd never experienced anything like this kiss. Sensation cascaded through her, bringing every inch of her alive and making her aware of her body in an entirely new way. Colors danced behind her eyelids and her fingers and toes tingled with awareness as Vasco's tongue jousted with hers.

When he finally pulled back—she would have been totally unable to—she emerged blinking and breathless back into reality like a creature startled out of hibernation.

So *this* is what people made such a fuss about. She'd always wondered about the poems and songs and all the drama surrounding romance and sex. Her own love life had been prosaic enough that she thought they were all exaggerating for effect. Now she could see she'd been missing out on the more exciting aspects of the experience.

And they hadn't even had sex yet...

Vasco's eyes shone with passion that mirrored her own and electricity crackled in the air around them. This was the chemistry people talked about, she could feel it like an explosive reaction about to happen, heating her blood and stirring her senses into a witches' brew of excitement.

Vasco reached behind him and switched off the light. A fat pale-gold moon hung outside the windows, bathing them both in its soft glow, turning the dramatic round room into a magical space.

Her hands were buried in the soft cotton of Vasco's shirt, clutching at the muscle beneath. She longed to pull the fabric from his body, but some vestige of modesty prevented her. Vasco had no such scruples. He undid the tie that held the waist of her dress together and unwrapped her like a gift. For the second time that night her dress descended to the floor and she stood before him in her underwear. This time, however, she had no armor to hide in.

His eyes roamed over her body, heating her skin with their warm admiration. His fingers followed, stirring currents of sensation wherever they touched. She let herself move under his hands, enjoying their sensual touch as she ran her fingers over his shirt, feeling the muscle beneath.

Soon enough her fingers found themselves plucking the buttons from their holes and pushing the fabric back over his shoulders. She'd had a glimpse of Vasco's chest earlier—surely that was his real bedroom?—and it was even firmer and more enticing at close range. A shadow of dark hair disappeared into his belt buckle, and soon she found herself sliding the leather out of it and unzipping his black pants.

It was glaringly obvious that he was every bit as aroused as her. His erection jutted against his briefs. She let her knuckles graze against it as she pushed his pants down past his thighs, and the hardness of it made her shiver. Trevor had always needed a good deal of coaxing to get ready, by which point her interest had sometimes waned. Clearly Vasco did not need any encouragement.

She glanced up at his face, and his predatory gaze only deepened the intensity of her desire. His lips were parted and she could feel his breathing, watch his chest rise and fall as anticipation jumped between them like a spark. Her own heart thumped so loud she could almost hear it in the still nighttime silence. It grew louder and faster as Vasco reached around her back and unhooked her bra.

She could pretend it was the cool night air that tightened her nipples, but they both knew better. Vasco lowered his head and licked one, then looked up at her, eyes shining with desire. She pushed his underwear down and he kicked it away. Glazed with moonlight, his hard body looked like an ancient statue. She could hardly believe such a gorgeous vision was interested in her.

Vasco plucked at her scanty lace briefs, then slid them down her thighs, leaving them both naked. The moonlight felt like a warm robe around her, making her unselfconscious and hungry for the feel of his body against hers. She stepped forward, until the tips of her breasts brushed his chest. The tickling sensation almost made her laugh and step back, but Vasco's big hands caught her around the waist and pulled her closer.

Their bellies met, Vasco's fierce arousal trapped between them. He captured her mouth in a kiss that made her head spin and ran his fingers through her hair. Stella's hands wandered over his muscled back, enjoying the athletic perfection of his body as the pressure of their desire built between them like water held behind a dam.

Stella felt the soft edge of the mattress behind her thighs, and realized they'd been moving backward to the bed. Vasco's hands cupped her buttocks and lifted her onto the high surface, without breaking their kiss. The soft fabric felt cool beneath her hot skin, and she wriggled a little, enjoying the sensation. Vasco laid her backward, easing himself over her. He pulled back enough to look into her eyes. "You're a very sensual woman."

"Who knew?" She sounded as surprised as she felt. Her senses were alight with wonder and excitement she'd never imagined. She'd not given sex more than a passing thought in so long she almost wondered if she'd ever have it again. Or if she even cared.

Now she craved it like her next breath.

Vasco slid into her slowly and she arched her back to take him deep. A groan of sheer pleasure slid from her lips and flew into his mouth as it covered hers again. He moved with creativity and elegance, shifting his body over hers and drawing her closer into a tangle of delight.

As they writhed together on the bed, she felt like the partner of an expert dancer who knew how to bring out her own innate talent. She found herself guiding them, too, climbing on top to deepen the dramatic sensations coursing through her, then letting him tilt her body to daring angles and roll with her in perfectly executed moments that made her gasp for breath as passion crashed through her.

Vasco's warm skin against hers felt so right. His arms around her waist or her shoulders, his fingers in her hair or caressing the skin of her face, every touch was gloriously perfect. When her climax reached the point of no return she let herself disappear into the ecstatic madness of the moment, clinging to him while the real world fell away.

In his arms afterward, wrung out by the intensity of the experience, she could barely remember her name or even breathe. His mouth and hands and tongue had explored every inch of her, making her whole body quiver with desire and anticipation, then giving her satisfaction she'd never known before. Now she felt soft and pliable, relaxed and content. Happy.

Vasco whispered to her, sometimes in English, sometimes in Catalan, telling her how beautiful she was, what a sensual lover, what a fantastic mother and how pleased he was to have her here in Montmajor. And in his bed.

Everything he said seemed normal and natural and made her smile though she could rarely summon the energy to reply. That didn't seem to matter. She rested her head on the firm pillow of his chest and drifted off to sleep, lulled by the rhythm of his big heart.

Her dreams were surreal visions of their imagined life in the palace. Walking, laughing and talking together. The perfect happy family living a comfortable and enjoyable life amidst the sandstone walls of a thousand-year-old castle. Normal and natural and predictable as the sunrise—which poked its bright harsh fingers through all those windows around the room and jolted her from sleep with alarming suddenness.

Only then did she realize what she'd done.

Seven

Stella sat up in bed and raised a hand to keep the bright sun out of her eyes. A quick glance at the pillow next to hers confirmed that Vasco was gone. When had he left? Did he sleep with her all night or disappear the moment she fell asleep?

Had he used a condom? She hadn't spared a thought for contraception. Trevor had always been the one to worry about that, since he was so terrified of having children and the responsibility and expense it would entail. He'd always come armed with condoms despite the fact he'd convinced her to have an IUD fitted. She'd had the IUD removed to conceive Nicky, and hadn't bothered with birth control since because she hadn't been on a single date.

She swallowed. Her insides still pulsed with traces of the fierce contractions she'd enjoyed at the peak of their lovemaking. Vasco had turned her inside and out, guiding her to feats of sexual acrobatics that made her blink as she remembered them. Wow. Who knew there was a whole new world of sexual pleasure out there that she'd barely even dipped her toes in?

Now she'd dived in headfirst, with a man she barely knew, who just happened to be the father of her son.

She climbed out of bed, scanning the room for her clothes. Light blazed in through the windows, leaving her naked and exposed. She found her dress in a crumpled heap on the floor, and her skimpy lingerie under the bed, where it must have been kicked by eager feet. She fished them out and tugged them back on with shaky hands.

How easy it had been for Vasco to seduce her. Her face heated. She hadn't even been here a week. Or all of three days. She'd leaped into bed with him the first time he even kissed her.

Her dress was crumpled, but she pulled it on and fastened the tie at the waist. She'd wanted him to see her as attractive, desirable. She didn't want him to think that the woman who'd bought his sperm was someone who couldn't find a man the old-fashioned way. Had she bent over backwards to convince herself she could tempt Vasco?

She certainly had put effort into looking nice and attempting to be a charming guest. He must know she wanted him to like her, and now he'd obliged by taking her to bed.

The large four-poster bed with its long curtains loomed over her. Whose bed was this? Not Vasco's, for sure. Was this room reserved for sexual escapades with visiting women? There were no signs of habitation, no pictures or bits of clothing or toiletries. It looked like a museum recreation of an ancient castle bedroom. Except that it was the real thing.

The sun had just lifted over the horizon, so hopefully Nicky was still asleep, but what if he'd woken up in the night, wanting her? He could have been calling for her for hours and no one knew where she was.

Heartbeat quickening, she picked up her shoes from under a chair and hurried to the door. Hopefully most of the staff was still asleep and she could sneak back to her room without being seen.

She pulled open the tall, heavy wood door and peered outside. The lightless hallway looked like a black hole after the blinding light of dawn illuminating the bedroom. She hadn't paid close attention on the way here, so she wasn't even sure which part of the palace she was in.

The cold stone stung her feet as she tiptoed into a narrow corridor which led to a flight of spiral stone stairs heading up and down. She went down, and out through the next arched doorway into a small courtyard where dew clung to ornate iron railings. Had she come this way last night? She'd been so wrapped up in Vasco she hadn't noticed. No doubt she'd assumed he'd be escorting her back, as well.

She should have known better than to think Vasco so predictable.

The courtyard had two doors leading out the other side, and she picked the one on the right, only to find it locked. The door on the left was open, and she crept through it with relief, but didn't recognize the wide hall she found herself in. A large, rather faded tapestry covered one wall, and an ancient wooden chair stood in one corner. There were doors at both ends, but no clue which one led to the busier part of the castle.

Stella hurried to the nearest door and peeped through it. It scraped on the floor as she pushed it open a crack and her heart almost stopped when she found herself peering into what was obviously a chapel. Tall candles burned on a small altar and the smell of incense wafted from a censer above it. The morning sun lit up a series of jewellike stained-glass windows, strung amid carved columns like stones in a necklace.

Worse yet, three black-clothed bodies knelt at the altar—the "aunts"—deep in morning prayer. She shrank back from the door, but it was too late. One of them—Lilli—had already turned.

"Stella." Her voice rang through the sacred space, rooting Stella to the spot like one of the carved statues above the altar.

Shoes in hand, she felt her face flush purple as all three heads turned to stare at her.

"Come join us for Matins." For the first time she noticed the priest, a shadowy figure near the altar. Was this the right time to explain that she'd been raised Lutheran? She gulped and smiled. She was probably supposed to cross herself or curtsy or some of the things she'd seen in films, but right now she just wanted to die.

"Sorry, wrong room." She backed away, shame pulsing through her veins, hoping they hadn't seen too much of her crumpled dress. Maybe they wouldn't put two and two together. What kind of woman would they think her if they knew she'd slept with Vasco on her second night at the palace?

She ran a hand through her tangled hair and scurried in the opposite direction, where she found herself in the great armaments chamber, facing the suit of armor she'd so readily stripped to don last night. What happened to her when Vasco was around? Normally she was a modest and reasonably sensible person.

Footsteps on the stone outside the room made her sink into a corner. Luckily the spotlights were turned off and she pressed herself against the wall beside a polished silver suit of armor until the sound disappeared into the distance.

This time she put her shoes on before venturing out again. At least then she could pretend she was up and dressed—if inappropriately—for the day, rather than creeping about in last night's rumpled finery. She found her way back to the suite she shared with Nicky without too much trouble. The door to Nicky's adjoining room was open and the sitter—a girl who worked in events planning—was asleep in an armchair next to the bed. Stella cringed at the realization that at least this one person would know exactly what she'd been up to last night.

Nicky was still sweetly asleep in the bed they'd made up for him, clutching the dinosaur Vasco gave him.

I'm so sorry, Nicky. I don't know what I was thinking. What happened last night would certainly complicate things. Would it develop into some kind of romantic relationship? Or was it just a one night fling?

The latter would be awful. She'd rather not have known how astonishing and enjoyable good sex could be. And the thought of not being able to kiss Vasco again...

She shook her head, trying to clear it, as she walked back into her room. For now she had to keep going. She ruffled the bed, as if she'd just climbed out of it, then went into the adjoining bathroom for a shower. She almost laughed but the sight of her flushed face and wild hair in the mirror made it shrivel in her throat.

Everyone would know. And she couldn't help thinking that's exactly what Vasco intended. He'd been hugging her and fondling her and flirting with her since they got here, apparently keen for people to think they were an item. Maybe he didn't want anyone to find out that he donated the royal seed to a sperm bank. That wouldn't go over too well with his devout Catholic "aunties."

Stella climbed into the stream of steamy water and wished she could scrub away her guilt and embarrassment at being so quick to jump into bed with him. He started it!

This time she did laugh, and when she emerged from the shower, she felt much better. She was also relieved to see that the sitter had left, so who knew, maybe her rumpled sheet ruse could have worked, too?

She took Nicky down for breakfast, hoping to finish quickly and go hide among the books—even though that would mean facing the "aunts" again so she could place Nicky in their care—before Vasco came down. She gulped hard when she saw him sitting at the table, biting into a slice of melon.

He rose to his feet with a mischievous smile when she entered. He held her gaze just a little longer than appropriate, then glanced down at Nicky and said something in Catalan.

Nicky smiled. "*Hola,* Papa."

Stella stared at him. Now he was saying complete sentences in a foreign language? Not to mention calling this virtual stranger Dad. Vasco grinned, those inviting dimples puckering his tanned skin.

"Come join me." He gestured at the chair beside his for Stella. "I bet you're hungry." His eyes flashed in a way that made her belly quiver and her face heat. Was he trying to embarrass her? Probably not. He was just being Vasco.

She rounded the table, still holding Nicky's hand, and settled him into the chair next to Vasco. Better to have some distance between them. As soon as the child was seated, however, Vasco moved up to her and pressed his lips to hers. Too startled to protest, she found herself kissing him right over Nicky's head. Desire roared to life inside her, and she was blinking and breathless when she finally managed to pull back.

She couldn't help glancing nervously about to see if any of the staff were there.

"You look radiant."

Hopefully that's not because I'm pregnant. Now was not the time to ask if he'd used anything, though. She was furious with him for kissing her in front of Nicky—not that he'd noticed—and anyone else who might walk in.

"I'm not sure what got into me," she murmured, avoiding his gaze.

"I am." His secretive smile only stoked the infuriating fires burning inside her. He handed her a plate of fruit. "You need to rebuild your strength."

"My stamina is just fine, thank you." She took a seat on the far side of Nicky and primly spread her napkin on her lap.

"I'm tempted to make you prove it." He took another

bite of melon, sinking his teeth in with obvious gusto. The gesture made her hips wriggle.

How could he carry on like this in front of his own innocent son? Obviously the man had no scruples. She reached for a piece of toasted muffin from a plate in the center of the table and spread it with butter. Vasco chattered away to Nicky in Catalan as if they were having a conversation. Stella almost dropped her knife when Nicky replied, "*Sì,* Papa."

"Nicky, that's fantastic. You're learning to speak a new language."

"Of course he is." Vasco rubbed Nicky's blond hair, messing it up. "It's his native tongue."

"He does seem to be picking it up surprisingly fast. He barely said a word until this month."

"Because he was speaking the wrong language." He spoke to Nicky again in Catalan. Stella couldn't make out what he said, but Nicky laughed.

A knot formed in her stomach and she realized she felt left out. Which was ridiculous. She could learn Catalan, too, even if it wasn't intricately woven into her DNA.

"Today I'll take Nicky for a tour of the town while you work on your books." Vasco took another bite of melon. It was a declaration rather than a suggestion.

She tensed. "He might get anxious being away from me."

"Don't worry. If he fusses I'll bring him right back." He stroked Nicky's tiny chin with his thumb and spooned in a mouthful of Nicky's favorite oatmeal that one of the staff had magically appeared with. "And we'll come play with your books."

"Great. Bring some crayons. Nicky can decorate you with gold leaf."

"I like that idea. This shirt is a bit dull." He glanced down at his well-cut black shirt. "But we'll let you get some work done first."

Why did she trust him completely with Nicky? She wanted to be nervous, or suspicious, but it was hard. She knew that most of the reservations she had concerned herself, not Nicky.

And if this morning's kiss was anything to go by, last night was not a one-night stand.

A week later, little had changed. Nicky was now babbling complete nursery rhymes in Catalan. Stella had plenty of time to lose herself in the demanding but exhilarating world of the ancient library. And she'd slept with Vasco every night.

They always slept in the same room. She'd asked again whose room it was, and he always replied that it was "theirs." Vasco was never there when she awoke. Her feelings on this had developed from surprise into disappointment, but she didn't like to whine about it. They'd only been involved for one week, so she was hardly in a position to ask him to adjust his lifestyle to her needs. Or maybe she didn't want to make waves when she enjoyed their time together so much. Now at least she knew the way back to her room.

During the day Vasco was flirtatious and affectionate, treating her like his lover, regardless of who was around. They'd even strolled through the town with Nicky twice, as if they were a real family.

Stella's ears burned all the time. She could imagine the gossip that must result when the nation's dashing young king showed up with a woman and child and no wedding ring in sight. The "aunts" said nothing, just smiled sweetly and doted over Nicky. The staff members were polite and somewhat deferent, treating her as a guest rather than one of themselves, though theoretically at least she was there to do a job.

And there was no discussion about the future. Vasco seemed to operate under the assumption that she and Nicky were there for good, and since it was too early to decide whether they were or not, she didn't ask any pointed questions. Most of the time they were together they were either within earshot of the staff, at dinner for example, or in bed. Neither was the ideal place for a "state of the state" conversation.

The moment Vasco kissed her, all practical concerns melted away and she floated on a cloud of bliss that could be temporary or eternal, her mind and body didn't seem to care. The palace was like a little country in its own right and—busy with Nicky and Vasco and the library—she almost forgot about the rest of the world chugging along all around them.

So it was a rude awakening when a former work colleague in L.A. sent her an abrupt email with the heading "OMG Stella—this you?" and a link to *CelebCrush* magazine's website. Stella clicked the link wondering if she had a job lead. She and the sender had been out for lunch a few times and she knew Elaine, an archivist, had found a new position at the Getty Museum.

The link took her to a headline blaring "Royal Romance?" The tone of the article was breathless. "Dashing King of Montmajor Vasco Montoya has been spotted out on the town with a mysterious

American—and her young child. Rumors are buzzing that he's the dad. Royal mistress, or future wife?" Stella blinked. There was a large picture of her and Vasco, each of them holding one of Nicky's hands, as they walked past a fruit stall in the main square of the town. She was staring at Vasco with a goofy grin on her face, while he looked boldly ahead, all windswept good looks and photogenic charm.

There wasn't any more to the story. Apparently that's what passed for journalism at *CelebCrush* magazine. Not that there was much more to the story in real life.

Her heart pounded beneath her neat yellow blouse as she sat in the library in full view of the elderly caretaker who dusted the volumes daily. Who else might see this? She was tempted to email back, "Nope, not me!" but she couldn't.

Royal mistress or future wife? Cringeworthy. What if Vasco saw this? She clicked away from the page and back to her Yahoo! homepage. At least she'd never heard of this magazine. A little research told her it was based out of Luxembourg, and for all she knew had a circulation of about twenty-five. Still, the fact that Elaine had stumbled across the website out in California was a bit alarming, since she hadn't mentioned Vasco to anyone except her best friend, Karen. She'd told other friends and neighbors she was taking Nicky to Europe for a vacation.

She typed back the words "Out of office autoreply—Stella is busy sleeping with a European monarch, and will attend to your email as soon as possible. Until then, please mind your own business." She wanted to laugh hysterically. Or cry. Then she deleted it all except the first phrase, wrote a more prosaic version and sent it out right away. That at least would keep Elaine from asking for more details.

She slammed the laptop and hurried from the library, unable to sit still, let alone do delicate restoration work. Maybe it was time to ask Vasco where this whole thing was going. It might be nice to know the answer for when a reporter thrust a microphone in her face.

At least she wasn't likely to be pregnant. He'd used condoms on all the subsequent trysts so she probably just hadn't noticed him rolling it deftly on in the excitement of their first encounter.

"Stella." Vasco's voice behind her stopped her in her tracks. "Where are you rushing?" He walked up behind her and slid his arms around her waist. Her belly shuddered with awareness. "To find me, I hope." His deep voice curled into her ear. It was hard to think straight and be practical around Vasco.

"Can we talk about something?" She drew in a breath, trying to steady her nerves.

"We can talk about anything. Astrophysics, the Holy Grail, the works of J.D. Salinger, what to eat for lunch…" He pressed a kiss to the back of her neck and she felt her knees turn to jelly.

"Let's go somewhere private."

"An excellent idea. Let's go to our room."

"No, somewhere without a bed." She couldn't stop the smile that tugged at her mouth even as she spun around to extricate herself from his embrace.

"Tired of beds?" A piratical grin lit his features. "Then we'll head outside. Follow me." He hooked his arm through hers and marched her along the corridor. They exited the palace through a side door and headed down a long, curving flight of stairs onto the hillside below the castle walls.

Grassy hills dotted with sheep and cattle unfurled around them like a rumpled blanket. "Where are we going?" She was glad she wore ballet flats, not heels, as they set out on a narrow track.

"Nowhere." Vasco marched ahead, holding her hand. "Which is one of my favorite places."

"Oh." Now would be a good time for discussion. Nicky was with two of the "aunts" and almost due for his nap, so he wouldn't miss her if she was gone for a while. She cleared her throat. "I'm a little confused about my status here."

"Really? Right now I'd say you're walking." He flashed that pearly grin before turning around to stride ahead again.

"Very funny. I mean the status of me and you."

"Intimate, definitely." He squeezed her hand.

"I know that, but am I..." How did you put this stuff without sounding like a middle schooler? "...your girlfriend?"

"Most definitely."

"Oh." Relief filled her chest. So they were dating. That was something she could understand.

"And much more than that. You're the mother of my child. We're a family." His dark gaze was meaningful, serious.

The complicated part again. Vasco seemed to assume that Nicky tied them together permanently, no matter what else happened. Which he did, of course, but did that mean they were going to get married?

On less than a month's acquaintance she wasn't brave

enough to ask that. Did she even want to marry him and abandon her freewheeling single life?

Yes, of course she did. Her heart sank as she realized how much she'd fallen in love with him in such a short time. He'd swept her right off her sensible shoes and deposited her here in his fairy kingdom, where he spent hours seducing her to shocking new heights and depths of sensual pleasure. Montmajor was a peaceful and lovely place, with seemingly no poverty or social unrest, and was less than two hours by plane to nearly every capital in Europe. And then there was a lifetime of satisfying work—probably several lifetimes, in fact—restoring all those magnificent books.

But did Vasco intend to make her his queen, or was the "royal mistress" scenario more realistic?

In her heart, she knew the answer. "Why don't we sleep in my room or your room? Why the round chamber?"

"That's a special place just for us."

"But my bedroom is lovely, and I wouldn't need anyone to listen for Nicky overnight if we were right next door."

"You might get tired of finding me in your bed."

Or you might get tired of me. "Why do you always leave in the night?" She'd never dared to ask before.

Vasco squeezed her hand again, still walking. "I do business in Asia, and that's the best time to make phone calls. I wouldn't want to disturb you."

She frowned. It was a good reason, but not entirely convincing. "I can sleep through anything, you really don't need to leave."

"It's easier if I'm in my office." He picked up the

pace a bit as they climbed a small hill, and she had to struggle to keep up. "It's all quite tiresome."

"If it was tiresome, you wouldn't do it. I know you too well already."

He laughed. "Okay, I enjoy my businesses. I can't just sit around on the throne all day gassing with the citizens. I need new challenges."

That's what worries me.

The round room with all its windows was their room—which he could leave at any time to take up in a different room with someone else.

"Is the palace always this quiet? I mean, do you not have to entertain foreign dignitaries and that kind of thing?"

Vasco slowed. "I didn't want to scare you off by thrusting you into the middle of a social whirl, so I told my events planner to keep things light while you settled in. Are you ready for some more excitement?"

"Um, I don't know." She wasn't wild about the prospect of being surrounded by medal-laden dignitaries or glossy-haired princesses. What would they think of a simple girl from suburban L.A.?

She straightened her back. She didn't have anything to be embarrassed about. She was educated and intelligent and could hold a conversation. As an American, she wasn't intimidated by blue blood or piles of wealth. It would be interesting to meet different people. "Sure, why not?"

At a social event he'd have to introduce her as something. Then maybe she'd know where she stood. *My fiancée,* perhaps?

"Then we'll send out some invitations." Vasco

raised a brow. "Though I admit I'd rather keep you all to myself."

He pulled her gently along with him as they climbed another small slope, then they paused at the top. The view was incredible. Hills and mountains all around, including the castle-topped one behind them. There was no sign of civilization.

Stella stared around them. Not even a distant plane in the sky. "I feel like we're all alone in the world." The sun glazed peaks and valleys with pale gold light.

"We are, for now." Vasco's strong features glowed in the warm light.

For now. Those words rang a little ominous in her ears. She'd asked her question about her status and received an answer. She was his girlfriend as well as the mother of his child.

That would just have to do. For now.

She'd been here barely a week, so who was she to start making demands and asking pointed questions when she didn't even know what she wanted. She might tire of Vasco and Montmajor and decide to head home, so it didn't make sense to demand a commitment from him when she wasn't ready to offer one herself.

Why was it so hard to be patient and let events evolve naturally? They'd just started dating. Okay, so it was a little more intense than usual since they lived under the same roof—and had a son—but any relationship was a delicate thing that could suffocate and die under too much pressure. She needed to relax and go with the flow a bit, enjoy the moment, live in the present and let their relationship grow in its own way.

Eight

Nicky was safely tucked up in bed when the first guests arrived. Stella had spent hours getting ready, or at least it seemed like hours. She'd bought a new dress and shoes in the town, with a credit card Vasco gave her and told her to "enjoy." She felt appallingly self-conscious flicking through racks of dresses at the local boutique under the watchful eye of the proprietor, who must know exactly what she was doing with Vasco every night.

She'd said "No, thank you," to the more flirty dresses with low-cut cleavage and plunging backs, and picked a rather demure ice-blue satin dress that fell to her ankles. It draped flatteringly over her curves but didn't reveal too much. Why give them more to gossip about?

"You look beautiful." Vasco's warm breath on her neck made her jump. She stood at the top of the stairs looking down into the foyer, as a well-dressed crowd of visitors trickled in, removing velvet capes and even furs despite the warm fall temperatures. All of the women were stunning, including the older ones, and dressed with the elaborate elegance of people who took seeing and being seen seriously.

"I'm a little nervous." Her palms were sweating and she didn't dare wipe them on her delicate dress.

"Don't be. Everyone's thrilled to meet you."

"Do they know, about Nicky and you and…"

"Only that you're my guest of honor." He kissed her hand, which made the tiny hairs on her skin stand on end. If only this were all over and she could lie in his arms in "their" bed.

She wasn't sure whether to be relieved that the guests didn't know the truth or worried that this meant they could therefore guess and speculate in all directions.

Vasco slid his arm into hers and guided her down the stairs. His proprietary touch silently introduced her as his girlfriend. The bright, winning stares of richly dressed females raked her skin like sharp nails and their tinkling laughter hurt her ears. Still she made her best effort at conversation—people spoke in English most of the time, presumably for her benefit—and managed to keep a smile plastered on her face.

Vasco looked devastatingly handsome in black tie. Somehow he made even the formal dinner jacket look rakish and daring. He touched her whenever they were near, just a brush of his knuckles along her hip, or a dusting of fingers over her wrist. Each time it made her heart leap into her mouth and her skin tingle with awareness.

Hushed voices, especially in Spanish or Catalan, made Stella's face heat. She knew they were wondering and whispering. Did they think her too plain and ordinary for Vasco? Did they suspect a "compelling reason" of some sort to explain his interest in her?

"What brings you to Montmajor?" asked a woman about her age, with short dark hair swept into a glossy updo and a curious expression on her carefully made-up face.

"The library." Stella smiled as sweetly as possible. "I'm a book restorer and the chance to work with these ancient volumes is a dream come true." Ha. Didn't even have to fib.

The woman smoothed an imaginary wrinkle out of her black lace dress. "Are you enjoying our local hotel?"

Stella swallowed. "Actually it's easier for me to stay here at the palace. Closer to the library." She cleared her throat.

"Of course it is." A slim eyebrow arched upward. "Such a lovely building. With so many bedrooms." Her voice dropped slightly for the last phrase. "I've seen some of them myself." Her dark eyes sparkled a challenge.

"Really?" Stella tried to sound amused. "Are you one of Vasco's old girlfriends?"

A crease appeared between the carefully plucked eyebrows. "Vasco and I are very old friends, but he could never claim I was simply his girlfriend." She said the word as if it tasted nasty.

Stella felt herself shrink a couple of inches. She'd been so pleased and proud to have Vasco call her his girlfriend. "Oh, you were just lovers, then?" She couldn't believe how bold she was being.

And it backfired again.

"Yes." The woman glanced across the room, and

her eyes darkened. Stella ventured a guess that she was looking right at Vasco. "Lovers." A lascivious grin crept across her reddened lips. "That's exactly what we are."

The use of the present tense dried Stella's response on her tongue. She took a hasty swig of champagne.

"Have I embarrassed you?" The velvety voice seemed to mock her. "I am accused of being blunt sometimes. But nothing embarrasses Vasco, I assure you."

She turned and walked away, leaving Stella staring, openmouthed. This woman obviously considered herself to be Vasco's current lover. Or one of them, at least. Maybe she was housed in some other well-appointed room at the palace. A square turret, perhaps, or an octagon.

She glanced around, looking for Vasco, and spotted him laughing with a bubbly redhead, whose pale breasts practically poured out of her red bustier. Now, that was what a royal mistress should look like.

Stella glanced down at her frosty-colored ensemble. Maybe she would have been better off with more *va-va-voom* so these women might see her as competition. She hated the pointy little spears of jealousy that pricked her as he took the woman's hand and kissed it, just as he'd done with hers earlier that evening.

Vasco was a charmer. A ladies' man. He couldn't help flirting and teasing and seducing women. Which made him utterly unsuited to any kind of lasting relationship.

A rather chinless young man asked her to dance and she accepted, glad of the opportunity to keep busy. They chatted about books and the local language and culture in his halting English while he whirled her around the floor to a brisk waltz. Stella inadvertently looked at Vasco a couple of times, but was never gratified by him staring jealously back. He seemed to be enjoying himself and had probably forgotten she was there.

After midnight and the end of a multicourse buffet dinner she was tempted to sneak upstairs on the pretext of checking on Nicky and not come back. As she slipped out a side door of the ballroom into a quiet corridor, a hand on her arm made her jump.

"I've missed you tonight." Vasco's eyes glittered. "I prefer being alone with you."

"Me, too," she said honestly.

"Let's go to our room."

Her whole body said yes. In the privacy of the round chamber, Vasco peeled off her dress and devoured her with a ravenous gaze that made her feel like the most gorgeous woman on earth. He feasted on her with his tongue and she enjoyed caressing and tasting his whole body. A banquet much more tempting and satisfying than the one downstairs.

By the time they finally made love she was so aroused she thought she'd climax immediately, but Vasco made a meal of delaying and slowing his movements, taking her right to the brink, then pulling back, until she was almost hysterical with passion. They climaxed together then lay breathless and happy in each other's arms.

No one else mattered. How could they? When she was alone with Vasco everything was perfect.

But when she woke up later in the night he'd gone. Did he go back to join the party? Possibly even to share his advanced lovemaking skills with another woman? She'd left her son in the care of a sitter night after night for a man who claimed they were a family but offered no permanent commitment.

Sooner or later riding this emotional roller coaster was going to catch up with her.

Vasco returned to the party feeling a buzz that didn't come from the vintage Montmajor wines they enjoyed. Time with Stella always left him feeling refreshed and glowing with good cheer.

"Hey, Vasco." His old friend Tomy called to him from near the bar. "I thought we'd lost you for a while there."

"I had some urgent business." He took a glass of champagne from a waiter.

"I noticed. The American girl seems to have quite a hold on you." Tomy raised a blond brow.

"She does indeed." He sipped the bubbly liquid, which only echoed the fizzing of arousal that still pumped through his system. "She's the mother of my son."

Tomy's eyes widened. "So the rumors are true."

"Every word of them. Little Nicky has brought life to the palace and so much joy to all of us."

"Why didn't any of us know about him?"

"It's complicated. I didn't know about the boy until recently. I'm having to move carefully and take my time."

"You will marry her, won't you?" Tomy looked skeptical even as he asked the question.

Vasco's muscles tightened. "You know the Montoya men aren't cut out for marriage."

"That's never stopped them before. You know the people of Montmajor will expect it of you."

"I've spent my life defying expectations and I don't plan to stop now. I have no wish to marry anyone."

"What does the girl think about this?"

Vasco frowned. "We haven't discussed it. Like I said, it's early days, and she's a freethinking American who values her independence. She's not looking for a man to marry."

They hadn't discussed it, mostly because despite the intimate tie of Nicky, they were just getting to know each other. How many people started discussing marriage after a month? Usually people dated for years before committing these days. She probably didn't know what she wanted yet any better than he did.

Tomy's lips curved into a smile. "So you intend to keep her here as some kind of concubine?"

"No!" He took a swig of his champagne. "Of course not."

"A lover, then."

Vasco took in his friend's amused expression. "Yes, a lover. Why not?"

"Because women are never satisfied with simply being a lover. Maybe it won't happen this week, or this month, or even this year, but sooner or later she'll want some kind of commitment from you, in the form of a ring. Especially since there's a child involved."

"I'll keep her happy." He'd found that a kiss soon dissolved any tension or confusion that arose between him and Stella.

Tomy gave him a wry smile. "For a while you will, then she'll want to marry you."

"A fate to be avoided at all costs." Vasco glanced around at the crowded room. At five in the morning the party was still going strong. "Marriage ruins all good relationships. How many of the married couples in this room don't despise each other? They all go out to parties so they can dance and flirt with other people. The wedding day is when a relationship starts a perilous downhill journey to hatred and resentment."

"Your parents were married for more than forty years."

"And despised each other for every second of it. They only married because my dad was forced into it when she became pregnant with my brother. They may have even loved each other once but there was no evidence of that during my childhood."

"Your father did like to share his affections."

Vasco snorted. "With every woman in Montmajor. My mother only put up with it because she hated scandal and drama."

Tomy shrugged. "That's how it goes. You marry the pretty mother, then continue to enjoy extracurricular activities. No need for the fun to end because you find a queen. Have your cake and eat it too, as the Americans say."

Vasco shuddered. "No, thanks. Too much cake will rot your teeth and clog your arteries. There are some Montoya traditions I mean to break with."

"We noticed when we saw your proclamation making relations legal between unmarried couples." Tomy grinned. "Very romantic."

"There's no reason to make the mother of my child a criminal."

"You're such a sweet guy." Tomy shoved him playfully. "No wonder every woman in Western Europe has the hots for you. You do know all the other girls will take your unmarried status to be an open invitation."

"If I got married they'd just see it as an intriguing

challenge." Vasco raised a brow. "I think I'm safer single."

Tomy shook his head. "If only I was you."

The ball, with its large and gossipy guest list, set rumors buzzing round Europe. Stella found herself drawn to the websites of paparazzi rags which linked her name with Vasco's and speculated openly about Nicky.

It was humiliating to know that people all over the world could ooh and ahh and guess over their romance—and she didn't know any more about where it was headed than they did.

"You're taking it too seriously," protested Karen, when she phoned her late one night. She knew Vasco would be waiting for her in "their room" and she hated herself for being so eager to head there. "Let loose and enjoy yourself."

"Trust me, I have been. That's half the problem. If I had any discipline I'd confront him and ask him where this is going."

"Why don't you just let things take their own course?"

"I'm trying." She sighed. "But I have a feeling we'll carry on like this forever."

Karen laughed. "What's wrong with that? It sounds like you're having a fabulous time."

"I came here to Montmajor so Vasco could get to know his son. I've done everything his way and I've even discovered that I love it here. But I can't stay here, sleeping with him every night, as some kind of live-in girlfriend."

"Why not? Sounds perfect to me."

Stella stretched herself out on the bed in her own room. "I guess I'm not cut out for prolonged dating. I must be old-fashioned. Remember how I was always trying to get Trevor to go one step further?"

"That's because you wanted kids."

"Yes, but I also wanted to get engaged, and married. Does that make me strange?"

"No, it makes you boringly normal. Don't be boringly normal. Seize life by the horns and Vasco by the...well, whichever bit sticks out most."

"You're horrible. I don't know why I even called you." She couldn't help smiling as she let her head rest on the pillows. "And of course that's exactly what I'll go do the moment I hang up this phone."

"Thank goodness. I'd hate to think of him going to waste. I saw the pics of you on the *Hello* website and he's seriously droolworthy."

"You're looking at those websites, too?"

"Human interest. Those of us who don't have a life of our own live vicariously through the exploits of lucky ladies like you."

"All I wanted was to quietly raise my son and restore books."

"Now you're doing both of those and sleeping with the hottest guy in Europe. Oh, and he's a king. I'm crying into my coffee for you."

"Be serious. I have to decide whether to stay here with Nicky, or bring him back to the States. Vasco wants me to stay, but I've already decided that I can't live here as his lover indefinitely. It's not fair to me or to Nicky. We've been here a month and I'm sure it's starting to feel like home to Nicky. I need to know

whether it will be our permanent home, or if I'm just
another in a long line of girlfriends."

"A month isn't a very long time."

"It's been long enough for me…" *To fall in love.* She
didn't want to say it out loud. Right now it was just her
secret.

A month might not be much in a conventional relationship where you meet the person for a date once or
twice a week, but they were living together and saw
each other all day long, not to mention all night long.
Well, except those lonely early mornings. It was a fast-
forward kind of relationship, and in the public eye, too.
If total strangers wondered and gossiped about where
they were headed, she'd be foolish not to want some
concrete answers, too.

"What, you're bored with him as a boy toy already?"

"I wish."

"Uh-oh. I think I get it now. You're getting in deeper
than you imagined and you want to know whether to
go all the way or pull back while you can still save
yourself."

"You have amazing insight. I've never felt like this
about anyone, including Trevor." Not even close. "And
I know from my years of living on this planet that this
kind of relationship ends in marriage or tears."

"Or both."

"Thanks for your support." Stella rolled over. Vasco
would wonder where she was if she didn't leave soon.
Maybe she should keep him guessing for a change, so
he wouldn't take her for granted.

"Just ask him."

Stella laughed. "You make it sound so easy. Hey,

Vasco, will we be getting married or are you saving yourself for someone hotter?"

"Leave out the last part and you'll be fine. Or ask him to marry you."

Stella sucked in a breath. She could never do that. The prospect of rejection was far too agonizing. But there was another possibility. "Maybe I could ask him if he intends for Nicky to be his heir. If he doesn't marry me, then Nicky doesn't inherit. At least not if Vasco has another child."

"Go for it. That could be a good deciding factor on whether you stay. Does Nicky seem happy there?"

"Very. He's gone from being shy and almost nonverbal to the most babbling and outgoing little boy. I think he loves being doted on by caring relatives rather than competing with lots of little go-getters in day care. The slower pace of life here works nicely for him."

"And for you."

She hesitated. "I do love it here. It's a bit like living in a five-star hotel all the time. The people are so lovely and I have work most restorers could only dream of."

"And Vasco."

"For now."

"Go ask him." Karen sounded firm. "Just find out what's in his mind. And don't call me back until you do!"

The abrupt dial tone sent a frisson of anxiety through Stella. She peeled herself off the bed and slipped her feet into her shoes. Vasco would be waiting for her with that warm, seductive smile on his sensual mouth and a twinkle of mischief in his eyes. She had to get her question—whatever it might be—out before she fell under the spell of his touch and his kiss and all sensible thought retreated into oblivion.

She passed one of the porters in the hallway and nodded a greeting. She wasn't even too embarrassed anymore about running into people on her nightly perambulations. Surely everyone in the palace knew what went on between her and Vasco. No doubt they accepted it as a normal and natural part of life in a royal house.

With a royal mistress.

She didn't feel like a "girlfriend," whatever that was. She lived in his palace and ate his food and wore designer clothes he paid for. Girlfriends took care of their own rent and phone bills and went out for nights on the town with their other friends. She was a kept woman right now, even if she did have a job that paid far more than the going rate.

"El meu amor." Vasco's deep voice greeted her from the darkness of the round chamber. *My love.* Did he feel the same way she did?

She closed the door behind her and searched for Vasco's moonlit outline on the four-poster bed. Silver rays picked out his muscled torso and proud, handsome face. He lay naked on the covers, arms outstretched to welcome her. "Come here, I'll undress you."

She steeled herself against a desire to climb right into his embrace and surrender herself. "I've been here a month." Better spit it out before she succumbed. "I want to know where Nicky and I stand. Long-term, I mean."

"You live here and it's your home."

Her heart beat faster and her courage started to fail

her. Did she want to risk losing what they had? "I can't be your girlfriend forever."

"You're far more than that."

"I know, I'm the mother of your son, but what does that mean for us in the future?" She straightened her shoulders. "Will we marry? Will Nicky be king one day?"

He laughed. "Already looking ahead to when I'm dead and gone?"

"No." The word shot out. How rude she seemed with her demands. "No, not at all." The prospect of Vasco dying was unimaginable. A more vital and indestructible man would be hard to find. "It's just that…I want us to be a real family and…"

Her words trailed off. *I want us to live happily ever after.* Her face heated and she was grateful for the darkness. There, she'd said it. Put all her pathetic hopes and dreams out into the dark air, where they now hung in silence that stung her ears.

"Stella." He rose off the bed and moved toward her. "We are partners in every way."

She braced herself as he came close. The warm masculine scent of him drifted into her nostrils, taunting her. "I don't want to be a royal mistress. People are talking. All the papers are speculating. It's embarrassing."

"People always talk and write about members of the royal family. It's just part of life in the public eye. There's no need to read that stuff or trouble yourself with it. Our life is ours alone and no one else matters."

He slid a powerful arm around her waist and her belly shuddered in response. Why did he always sound so sensible and make her feel she was being silly?

She tried to picture the worst-case scenario. "Do you plan to marry someone else one day? Another aristocrat perhaps?"

Vasco's throaty laugh filled her ears. "Never. Never, never, never. Our son will be king and you will always be my queen." He pressed his lips to hers and a flash of desire scattered her thoughts. "Let's enjoy tonight."

His hand covered her breast through her thin blouse. Her nipple thickened under his palm and her head tilted back to meet his kiss. How did he always do this to her? Already her hands roamed over the warm, thick muscle of his chest. Again she was intoxicated by the sheer pleasure of the moment.

Maybe she wanted too much. Couldn't it be enough to enjoy life here in this lovely place with a man she was crazy about? Vasco undressed her slowly, working over her body with his tongue. She arched her back, letting herself slide into the ocean of pleasure he created around her. Most women would kill for a lover this sensitive and creative, let alone all the other things she enjoyed in the palace.

She ran her fingertips over the hard line of his jaw, enjoying the slight stubble that roughened his skin. Vasco's eyes gleamed with desire as he looked up at her while sliding her pants off. The chemistry between them was undeniable. She'd never felt anything like it. Would she seriously walk away from Vasco because he didn't plan to marry her?

Her whole body shouted "No!" Vasco took her in his arms and they rolled on the bed together, wrapped up in each other. Her body craved his and judging from his arousal and the soft words he breathed in her ear, the feeling was mutual.

She exhaled with relief as he entered her, and they moved together in a dance of erotic joy that swept them both up into their own world of bliss, where no one else existed. Afterward, she was too tired to think, let alone speak.

But she phoned Karen the next day, as promised.

"He said I'll always be his queen." It sounded pretty promising when you said it out loud like that.

"What more could you want?"

"A wedding date. You remember how Trevor always put me off with excuses and reasons for delay. All that *We're too young. We have our whole lives ahead of us. You can't rush these things.* Maybe he even meant it at first, but he got comfortable with the way things were and decided not the change them."

"Vasco's not Trevor, thank goodness."

"If there's one thing I've learned in the last decade, it's that a man who's determined to dig his feet in can stand like that forever. After we broke up, Trevor got more honest and admitted that he'd never have married me or had a child. He didn't want the responsibility."

"I always told you he was a creep."

"He's comfortable living in a pleasant limbo between carefree boyhood and the responsibilities of family life. He wanted the reassurance of knowing he had a date on Friday, but not the commitment of diapers to change or college fees to pay."

"Or a wife to still cherish and adore when she had silver hair and crow's-feet." Karen chimed in. "He's like my ex. They like to keep the escape clause open."

"I can't live like that. Not anymore. I decided that when I broke up with him and made the choice to start a family by myself. I chose a life on my own terms and embraced it, and I'm not going to turn around and live life on someone else's terms that I don't agree with, and that's what I'm doing right now."

"One month, Stella. It's not exactly the same as nine years."

"That nine years happened one month at a time, because I just kept waiting. Never again. It's worse now because people I don't even know are curious. You should see the headlines—'Royal wife or royal mistress?' It's totally humiliating."

Karen sighed. "I think I could get used to being a royal mistress, if there were enough diamonds involved."

"Oh, stop."

"But I have a crazy idea."

"Knowing you it really will be crazy."

"Listen, if you asked him whether you're getting married and he fobbed you off with some fluff about being his queen, then maybe you can call his bluff."

"How so?" Already a nasty sense of misgiving writhed in her gut.

"If you told one of those gossip rags that you and Vasco were getting married, would he deny it?"

Stella shrugged. "Probably not. He'd just nod and smile and say 'one day' or something like that."

"But what would he do if you told them you definitely weren't getting married?" Her voice had a calculating tone.

"You've lost me."

"He's used to running his life the way he wants it and having everyone follow along nicely. If you, the mother of his child and heir and the woman he sees as his queen, says she won't marry him, he's bound to protest, right? Men always want what they can't have. It's reverse psychology."

"Well…" Karen had a point. He probably would be upset by an outright refusal.

"And he'll want to prove you wrong."

"By proposing and making me his wife within the week?" She laughed, but the idea was oddly intriguing. "I don't know, Karen. It's not my style."

"You've tried your style and it's not working. If he won't discuss your future with you in private, flush him out in the open. At least then you'll get your answer one way or the other. If you really want it, that is."

Stella bit her lip. "You're right. If he's not going to marry me I'd rather know now, so I can move on with my life. Your idea is crazy, but it just might work."

Nine

Getting the information to the press was easy. Stella had figured out that the "mystery" gossip editor of the local paper was a rather glamorous older widow who lived on an estate near the town. Anything she printed had a way of getting out into the mainstream media, too. Probably because she couldn't resist telling everyone she knew when she found a piece of actual gossip.

Since this woman, Mimi Reyauld, was constantly fishing for new items, she would be easy to leak it to. After only three expeditions to the local town for magazines or a new toy for Nicky, Stella managed to "run into" her in the market square.

"Stella, my dear, don't you look lovely?" Mimi had a bouffant blond 'do that didn't move in the wind. "How is that gorgeous boy of yours?"

"Nicky's having his afternoon nap. It's a great time for me to come stretch my legs and do some shopping."

Mimi's gaze raked her hand. "He's such a dear. I'm sure he'll be the spitting image of his father one day."

Stella smiled. She hadn't openly acknowledged Nicky as Vasco's, but she knew people assumed he was. Clearly Mimi was fishing. "I'm sure he will. Are you coming to the masked ball on Friday?" Almost every adult in Montmajor was invited to the legendary annual festivities and the palace was abuzz with preparations.

"I wouldn't miss it for anything. Vasco throws such wonderful parties." She leaned in and her expensive scent stung Stella's nostrils. "When will we be celebrating your engagement?"

"Engagement?" Fear made her pulse skitter and she pushed back her hair with her ringless hand. "Vasco and I have no plans to be married." So far she'd said nothing but the honest and sad truth.

Mimi's eyes widened. "Come now, dear. Don't be modest. Everyone in Montmajor can see the two of you are madly in love."

Stella's tongue dried. They could? How embarrassing. She knew it was true for her, if not for Vasco. "I'm not sure where they're getting that idea. Vasco and I won't be getting married." It hurt to say it out loud, but if that was going to be the truth, better to find out now rather than months, or years, down the road when it would be harder to extricate herself from the awkward situation.

"Oh." Mimi's mouth formed a red circle of surprise. No doubt she'd been hoping to be the first with the engagement scoop because she looked disappointed.

"I imagine there will be a lot of other ladies who'll be happy to hear that." She hoisted her chic little bag higher on her shoulder. "And I look forward to seeing you at the ball, though I dare you to try to recognize me in my mask." Mimi air kissed and walked away, leaving Stella feeling a little stunned.

She'd done it. Other things she'd mentioned to Mimi even in passing had almost invariably shown up in print—there just wasn't that much good gossip in Montmajor—so it was inevitable this latest tidbit would, too. It seemed very European to have the local gossip columnist be an old friend of the family.

That night with Vasco she felt like a traitor. He hadn't sworn her to secrecy about their relationship but she'd been very discreet until now, not telling anyone except Karen what was—or wasn't—going on. Even his inviting embrace and his spine-tingling kisses didn't entirely banish the sense of guilt she felt for talking about their relationship in public.

The next morning, sure enough, the story had made it into the gossip column, and by the afternoon it had spread like wildfire through the European tabloids, culminating in headlines like "Dashing Vasco Montoya Still Europe's Most Eligible Bachelor."

It didn't take long until Vasco noticed.

"What's the meaning of this?" He brandished the local paper. "You told Mimi we're not getting married."

"Mimi?" She played innocent. "What does she have to do with the local paper?"

"She's Senyora Rivel, the gossip columnist. Everyone in Montmajor knows that."

"And you still invite her to the palace?"

"She's a sweet old lady who never writes anything harmful. But why did you say this?" His eyes flashed. She'd never seen him look so serious. Not exactly angry, but…annoyed.

Part of her was excited and grateful that he cared. "It's the truth. We're not getting married."

"Says who?" He strode toward her.

"We've made no plans. Every time I ask you about the future you start kissing me or change the subject." She couldn't believe how bold she was being. She'd never be capable of it if Nicky's future wasn't at stake, too. "Since apparently everyone else is talking about our marriage plans, I thought I'd better start setting them straight."

Confusion furrowed his noble brow. "I think our relationship should be between us, and not anyone else's business."

"I didn't make a proclamation, I just had a short chat with Mimi at the market. Since it's the truth, there's no harm done."

His eyes narrowed slightly. "Now everyone will want to know why we're not getting married."

Her heart contracted. He'd now confirmed what she said. Part of her wanted to die right now on the spot, or sink into the stone floor. She managed to keep a straight face. At least now she knew where she really stood.

"Then tell them the truth." She swallowed hard. "Tell them we're not in love." She held her breath, while her chest ached with hope and despair and she silently begged him to argue with her and say that he loved her with all his heart and soul.

But he didn't. He simply stared at her for one long, searing moment, then turned and sauntered away.

Crushed, Stella shrank against the nearest wall as she heard his footsteps recede into the distance. She'd hoped her little media revelation would be the catalyst that would draw them together. Instead it had just the opposite effect. At least she had an elaborate silver-sequined mask to hide her tears behind at the ball that night.

Vasco, masked like everyone else, stood amidst the flow of arriving guests. Anonymity added a certain feverish excitement to the occasion, and champagne flowed like a summer rainstorm. Anger still thudded through him like distant thunder. He'd been surprised by how much Stella's words wounded him.

He hadn't held up a magnifying glass to his feelings for Stella, but they were intricate and involving. She'd come here as the mother of his son but transformed into far more. Their nights together wove a web of passion that bound them tightly, even when Nicky was asleep on the other side of the castle. He loved her company and craved it when he was busy working or held up with other tasks.

Stella had quickly become the center of his existence and he shared his life with her in the most intimate way imaginable. Only to have her coldly deny their relationship in public.

There was no denying that he'd pushed back a little when she'd asked about the future. They'd known each other a short while and the future was a very long time. There'd be plenty of time to make decisions about that later. He'd been overwhelmed by the new emotions crowding him since he learned about Nicky, let alone his feelings for Stella. He needed time to adjust to the reality that his family had expanded and these new people were now closer to him than his own parents or siblings had been.

Then she came right out and said that they didn't love

each other? Something unfamiliar and painful gnawed at his gut.

He took a swig of his champagne and listened for the strains of music flowing over the crowds from the adjoining ballroom.

"Cavaller." A female masked in shimmering green sequins greeted him in the old style.

"At your service, madame." He kissed her hand, which was soft and scented, but not Stella's.

He knew exactly where Stella was right now. Standing on the far side of the room in a blue dress and matching mask. He'd determined to ignore her all night—shame he couldn't take his eyes off her.

The hurt and fury raging in his blood made him almost want her to flirt with another man so he could be angry and call her a tease and despise her for cheating on him. But so far she'd spoken only to women and men over the age of seventy.

"Your masked ball is a sensation, as always." The lady in green had a deep, seductive voice that he didn't quite recognize.

"You're too kind. Would you honor me with a dance?"

Her dark eyes glittered behind her mask. "I'd be delighted."

He slid his arm through hers and risked a glance at Stella to see if she'd noticed. Irritation rippled through him that she was deep in conversation with one of the town's elderly librarians and not paying any attention to him.

He tightened his arm around the waist of his companion's green silk dress and guided her to the dance floor. He gave the band's conductor the cue for a tango, and led her into the middle of the crowd as the first sultry strains swept through the room. He didn't need Stella. He'd always enjoyed a full and exciting life and there was nothing to stop him continuing that. Stella had as much as given him permission.

He twirled his partner and dipped her, and she flowed with the movements like hot butter, a smile curving on her red-painted mouth. Another lightning-fast glance at Stella revealed that she was watching him.

Ha. He pressed his partner against him and executed several quick steps and another turn that made her dress sweep around him. His muscles hummed with the sheer joy of movement. Another glance confirmed that Stella's eyes were still fixed on them, and he fought a triumphant smile. She might not love him, but she was certainly paying attention.

After the dance his green-masked partner gratefully accepted a glass of champagne and offered to remove her mask and reveal her face.

"Don't take off your mask," he murmured. "Tonight is for mysteries and magic."

"But I know who you are," she protested. "Doesn't it seem fair that you should know who I am?"

"Perhaps life isn't supposed to be fair."

"I suppose that's a good attitude for a king. Not everyone can inherit a nation." She hesitated and leaned closer. "Is it true that you've already sired an heir?"

"It is." He'd never deny Nicky.

"Then you've chosen your bride, as well." Her eyes shone with curiosity.

"Who knows what the future will bring." He picked up her hand and kissed it. His intention was to taunt Stella, though he managed to resist glancing at her to see if she was watching. He could feel her gaze on him like a touch.

Even if she didn't love him, Stella was deeply attracted to him and he'd be sure to stoke the fire of her passion when they were alone later tonight. In the meantime, apparently flirting and dancing with other women was an excellent aid to focusing her attention.

"Hello." A statuesque girl in silver with a long fall of blond hair and a pouting mouth touched his arm. "What a wonderful party."

He turned readily away from Ms. Green. "I'm pleased you're enjoying yourself."

"Very much so." Her eyes lit up inside her mask. "And I've always wanted to meet you. I'm—" She had a French accent.

He pressed a finger to her lips. "Don't spoil the enigma. Let's dance." He didn't want to know who she was. He took her hand and led her into the crowd of dancers, where he whirled around with her, losing himself in the pleasure of the dance. Stella was only one woman in a world of millions.

So why was she the only one he wanted?

Stella shrank further into the shadows each time she saw Vasco smile at another woman, or kiss her hand. At first she couldn't take her eyes off him when he danced. He moved with muscular grace and the skill of a professional dancer. Women seemed to melt into his embrace, and their besotted smiles dazzled her like car headlights when she made the mistake of looking at them.

Did she really think she could be his one and only? Even if she hadn't infuriated him with her little press leak, he'd still be dancing and flirting with other girls in his role as host. Women flocked to him like iron filings to a magnet. He wasn't just rich and royal, he was gorgeous and mischievous and charming and obviously enjoyed their company. No wonder he didn't want to marry her. Why would he give up all this to spend his life with her?

Far too much to hope for. She was an ordinary book restorer from an ordinary suburb who lived a quiet, humdrum and happy existence until Vasco swept into it like the Santa Ana winds and made her realize how much she'd been missing until now.

Thank goodness for the mask. It was hot and itchy but at least it hid her expression of despair. She'd been shamefully lax about looking for jobs—too busy enjoying her work here—and had barely kept in touch with anyone because she didn't want to reveal too much about her situation. Maybe she just couldn't bear to think about leaving.

And there was Nicky. Instead of being gone eight hours at a stretch with him in day care, she could spend time with him every hour or two when she took a break, and in the meantime he received individual attention from people who adored him. They'd even arranged for some staff to bring their young children to the palace so he had playmates to laugh and sail his boat with. His vocabulary had gone from less than five words to full sentences in both English and Catalan, and his joy in his daily existence was undeniable. No more tears as she left him at day care, or endless colds that he picked up from the other kids.

Could she pull him from this peaceful existence that

suited him perfectly and drop him back into their old hectic routine again? If she could even find a job.

A waiter offered her champagne and she shook her head. She needed to keep it clear as both of their lives depended on the decisions she'd make now.

She didn't relish the idea of Nicky being king, but it didn't seem like such a hard life either, if things did work out that way. And if they didn't, because Vasco married another woman...

Fierce jealousy twisted her insides. It was physically painful to watch him laughing and talking with other girls, let alone marrying them and having children. At least if she went back to the States she wouldn't have to see him and be tormented by what she wanted but couldn't have. She knew Vasco had no legal rights to claim Nicky or even see him again. If she chose to, she could leave here tonight with her son and never look back.

The prospect made her cold. She knew in her heart she could never do that to Nicky, or to Vasco. Now that the father she hadn't intended for her son to have had manifested himself in their lives, she could see how much Nicky adored and looked up to him. Vasco himself had opened his home to them with such generosity and goodwill, and had thrown himself wholeheartedly into the role of father. In all honesty that was one of the reasons she'd fallen so hard in love with him, and she'd rather die than take his son away from him.

So she and Nicky had to stay.

A furtive glance across the crowded room found Vasco in the arms of yet another woman. Tall and wrapped in a slinky purple dress, her white mask flashing bright as her smile. Stella grimaced beneath her own festive disguise. She'd have to tell him that from now on they could no longer be intimate. She'd be an employee, like all the others, not his lover. She wasn't cut out to be a royal mistress and she should know by now that she'd never be anything else if she stayed here.

Clutching her sadness like a cloak about her, she slipped out of the room and into a quiet corridor. Vasco wouldn't even notice she was gone. He hadn't said a word to her since the party began. No doubt he wanted to put an end to any rumors about them being involved, let alone married.

She pulled off her mask, climbed up to her room and peered into Nicky's adjoining one where tonight's sitter, one of the palace cleaning staff, sat in a chair reading a thriller. "You can head off for the night. I'll be here." She managed a shaky smile.

"Are you sure? I don't mind staying until morning." The young girl looked a little bashful. Everyone in the palace knew that all-night sitters were the order of the day because Stella spent her nights in the round tower with Vasco.

But no more. "No thanks, I'll be here."

She washed her face and put on the cotton pajamas she hadn't worn in as long as she could remember. The bed felt cold as she climbed into it. She'd grown so used to having a warm body next to her that the sheets seemed empty and uninviting without one.

She'd get used to it. She hugged her arms around herself and tried not to picture Vasco downstairs dancing with beautiful masked women. Would he take another of them to the round tower tonight? Or would he expect her to meet him there regardless of their argument?

Rolling over, she pulled the covers over her head to block out the strains of music that crept into the room from the party. She'd managed just fine without Vasco for most of her life, and she'd be fine without him for the rest of it. Maybe she'd even find another man, a more sensible and reliable and ordinary guy with whom she could have a real relationship. Kings weren't really cut out for modern relationships. They too readily expected everyone to be at their beck and call, and she'd certainly obliged so far.

Though after Vasco it could prove very challenging to find anyone else appealing.

She tossed and turned, listening over the faint music for Nicky's sleeping sounds, but she couldn't hear anything. He'd been in bed for hours and was a solid sleeper, so she couldn't even distract herself by humming lullabies or stroking him to sleep. She needed someone to hum her lullabies, but clearly she'd have to make do without.

There was usually a half-finished novel next to her bed for her to dip into at moments like this, but she hadn't slept here for so long that she'd neglected to find one. She could sneak off to the library and bring back something to read—not all the books were ancient manuscripts—but then she'd run the risk of encountering party guests in her pajamas. Or worse, seeing Vasco creeping off to some turret with his mistress-of-the-minute.

No. She'd have to tough it out here in bed. She'd resolved to stare at the dark ceiling until she either fell asleep or passed out, when she heard the door open.

"Who's there?" She sat up in a panic. Hadn't she locked it?

"You didn't come to our room." Vasco's deep voice penetrated the darkness.

Her chest tightened. He'd really expected her to go there after they argued and stayed apart all evening? "I thought I'd better sleep here."

"You're angry with me."

Was that was he wanted? A jealous rage to gratify his male ego? "No, just sleepy." She didn't want him to know how upset she'd been by seeing him with those other women. She didn't even know why. He hadn't done anything but dance with them. She certainly didn't want to give him the satisfaction of letting him know she cared.

"Me too. It's been a tiring night."

The room was too dark for her to see more than his outline, but she heard the sliding sounds of clothing being removed. She held her breath. Did he intend to come climb into her bed without an invitation? Her skin tingled under her cotton pajamas.

She heard something hit the floor—his pants? Her heartbeat quickened and she scanned the darkness. His warm, masculine presence moved through the room toward her. She clutched the covers.

"You can't just come get in bed with me." Her voice sounded shrill, like she was trying to convince herself.

"Why not?"

"I came here to be alone."

"Every time I danced with someone, I was thinking about you." His soft voice crept through the darkness and caressed her. "I pretended I was holding you, moving with you. The masks made it a little easier, but nothing compares with the real thing."

She bit her lip in the dark. Already her muscles softened, forgiving him everything, wanting him close. When she felt his weight tip the mattress, she couldn't bring herself to push him away. Then the covers lifted and he slid underneath. His thighs were warm, rough with hair, and his arms wrapped around her before she could summon the energy to resist. How arrogant of him to assume he'd be welcome! Yet the scent of him disturbed her senses and sent lust sizzling through her.

"You need to take these off." His fingers plucked at the buttons of her PJs. What if she didn't want to take them off? Maybe she did want to sleep?

Her body said otherwise. Already her muscles relaxed and her nipples tightened into peaks. Vasco slid her top off and kissed her firmly on the mouth before licking each nipple with his tongue. Passion stirred deep inside her and she found her hands clutching at his muscle and drawing him closer. Hard and ready, his erection only intensified her arousal.

He'd danced with all those other women, but it was her he came looking for in the darkness, to spend the night with. Her heart sang at the truth of it, and their kisses filled her with feverish hope and joy.

I love you. She wanted to say it but common sense prevented her. Vasco feared commitment—that was obvious—so he might be scared off by declarations of undying love. Still, what wouldn't she give to hear it from him?

He entered her slowly, kissing her with measured passion. His movements were restrained, slow, his hips barely shifting and his hands holding her still, so that she could feel every beat of both their hearts and feel each breath that filled their lungs. They lay there, suspended in time, senses fully engaged and aroused, bodies moving as one. Her anger and hurt had evaporated, replaced by joy and excitement that stirred her body and mind.

Her demand for marriage felt foolish now. What did some official piece of paper matter when it was so obvious they were meant to be together? Vasco didn't have to tell her in mere words that he loved her. She could feel it in his touch, in a language much more subtle and ancient than any of the ones she'd learned to speak.

They started to move again, this time with a fevered energy that made her gasp and shiver with desire. They rolled together on the bed, taking turns driving each other to new heights of arousal and intense emotion. The music from downstairs now seemed an accompaniment to their erotic dance, a celebration of their private passion. None of those people downstairs mattered anymore, just the two of them, traveling further and further out onto a peninsula of bliss.

Her climax swept over her in a cool shiver of ecstasy, and she felt Vasco explode inside her, gripping her with force and murmuring her name over and over again.

I love you. Again the words hovered behind her lips, but she didn't need to say it. She'd told him with her body, as he'd told her. There was no mistaking the connection that joined them. They shared a child, but more they shared something less tangible but just as precious in its own way.

"I missed you tonight." His whispered confession made her smile.

"I missed you, too. I thought you were mad at me."

"I was. Mad at you, mad about you." He kissed her lips softly. "I wanted to make you jealous."

"It worked. I wanted to dance with you."

She gasped as Vasco's strong arms whipped her out of bed and onto her feet. The cool stone shocked her soles, but his arms wrapped around her like a blanket as he guided her into a dance in the dark bedroom. Music still swirled in through the doors and windows, caressing them with its delicate notes. A strong partner, Vasco pressed her against him as he moved across the floor of the large bedroom, whirling her round and round, so light on his feet they might be floating.

With her chest pressed against his, naked and still warm from lovemaking, she followed his motion effortlessly. Eyes closed, she imagined them gliding through the crowds, then through the clouds, a perfect partnership.

"Whatever you wish, my lady." He twirled her one last time, then pulled up her hand to kiss it.

"Except marriage." The words flew out before she could stop them. Immediately she wished she could inhale them back inside her.

Vasco stiffened, still holding her. She felt him draw away, even though he didn't move. She'd broken the spell that held them together with her petty worldly concerns. "You should be glad. You've made it clear that we won't be getting married." His voice was quiet.

She was tempted to say she'd only done it in the hopes that he'd change his mind, but that would just make her look pathetic. If Vasco wanted to marry her, it would just happen. He was like that, a thunderstorm in motion. She'd been swept along on its high winds and pierced by its lightning bolts enough to know that. How else had she ended up living here in a strange country within weeks—days, really—of meeting him?

Now he did pull back a little, putting a couple of inches of darkness between them. "I'd like to formalize my relationship with Nicky. I want to be his true father in the eyes of the law."

Her chest tightened. "I don't imagine that will be too hard since you can change the laws anytime you feel like it."

She could swear she saw his smile gleam, despite the lack of light. It must be quite something to have that much power. Tempting to abuse it. She knew Vasco wasn't a cruel man, but he could be arrogant and demanding. No doubt that came with the territory of being king.

"I think a simple declaration will suffice. And perhaps a law confirming that children born out of wedlock can inherit the throne." He sounded thoughtful.

"I suppose that's just keeping up with the times." He wouldn't even need her consent. The DNA tests had confirmed that he was Nicky's father. She wouldn't try to take Nicky away from him now. Her son adored his tireless and playful father.

"Indeed. And it ensures that one day Nicky will be king."

They weren't even touching now. Their bodies had slipped away from each other, and goose bumps rose on her skin in the night air coming in through the open window. Perhaps it was simply his love for Nicky that brought him to her? Maybe he wanted to make sure she'd stay and this was the only way he knew how. He paid for her loyalty—and for his son's presence in his life—with passion that fired her heart but left his cold.

An ache of despair and loneliness crept over her, extinguishing the joy she'd felt only moments earlier. She turned away from him and climbed back into the bed. "We'd both better get some sleep." He must be anxious to slip away, as he did every night, back to his own realm. Away from her.

She heard him don his clothes in the darkness, even his mask, because she saw the sequins that edged it shimmer in the pale moonbeams that crept around the curtains. "Good night, Stella. Sleep well."

His kiss made her lips hum, and she hated the way her heart squeezed at his touch.

Of course now she wouldn't be able to sleep at all. Not that she could earlier. Being around Vasco was driving her crazy. One minute she was drifting on a tide of joy, sure that she was the happiest woman alive. The next she was alone and filled with anguish, sure that he didn't love her and never would. She could make all the plans and conditions she liked when she was alone, but as soon as she was in Vasco's presence all common sense and resolve evaporated in the heat of passion.

There was no way she could stay here in the palace with him and remain sane.

Ten

The local librarian put her in touch with some owners of nearby private libraries who might want a restorer. She didn't mention that she was also looking to live in. She struck gold with a nearby family who spent most of the year in Paris but had a small estate in Montmajor only a ten-minute drive from the palace. After a phone call and a reference from her old boss in California, they hired her to restore some rare volumes over the next three months. Most importantly, she could live in their villa, which would buy her time to find somewhere permanent to move and give her space to think about her life.

She waited a few days until Vasco went out of town. She knew that if she tried to confront him he'd just wear her down, probably with nothing more than a meaningful look. She'd tried too many times to stand up to him and failed more miserably each time. She needed to make her break when he wasn't there to cajole her out of her decision.

While she waited for him to leave she slept in her own bedroom, alone, with the convenient excuse that it was "that time of the month." She'd felt a mix of relief and disappointment at the realization that she wasn't carrying another of Vasco's babies. And her monthly visitor was welcome protection. If she slept in Vasco's arms at night, she'd lose every last ounce of conviction.

With no possessions other than those in her suitcase, the move required no planning beyond packing some of Nicky's toys into a box and calling a taxi.

"What do you mean, you're leaving?" Aunt Lilli's eyes widened with alarm. Her arms reached for Nicky, who ran immediately into them.

"I'm only moving up the road, to Castell Blanc. I'll be working in their library and living in the house. If you agree, and if Vasco is okay with it, I'd like to bring Nicky here every day to spend time with you."

"Vasco's not going to like this." Aunt Frida pursed her lips and shook her head. "Not at all."

Stella swallowed. "I know, but's too difficult for me to live here. It complicates matters."

"How is it complicated? Vasco is crazy about you." Aunt Mari crossed her arms. "You must marry him."

Stella blinked. "He's made it clear that he won't marry me. Or anyone else, I think. He doesn't like the idea of marriage and said it ruins relationships."

"But you're the one who told Mimi you'd never marry him."

"Only because I knew his opinion already. To be honest I was hoping he'd see it differently, but he's as determined as ever to remain single and I can't live here as some kind of..." She glanced around, then lowered her voice. "Concubine."

Lilli sucked in a breath. "I've had words with him. I've tried to explain to him that you're a nice girl." She hesitated.

Stella pondered that if she was such a nice girl she wouldn't be in a position to be called his mistress.

"He's stubborn," Lilli continued. "Obstinate."

"A typical man," cut in Aunt Frida.

"Perhaps you moving out is for the best. He'll realize what he's missing."

Stella shrugged. She wasn't going to get carried away hoping things would change. People rarely changed. "I want Nicky to grow up with his family, including all of you. I intend for us to stay here in Montmajor, but I need to leave the palace right now, today."

Lilli nodded. "I understand." Still, she looked very sad as she stroked Nicky's cheek. "You'll bring him tomorrow?"

"Without fail. Unless Vasco barricades the castle against me."

"He's not that foolish." Aunt Mari looked down at Nicky. "I do hope he'll see sense before it's too late."

Her feet and her heart felt heavier than her suitcase as she walked through the grand archway out of the palace. Silly, as she hadn't come here to marry him. She also hadn't planned to fall madly in love with him. That was the real reason she had to go. It was just too painful to fall asleep in his arms dreaming of them as a real family, knowing all the while he saw her only as his girlfriend—enjoyable and potentially disposable— and that he had no plans to ever commit to a permanent relationship.

Heck, he wasn't even there when she woke up in the morning!

Maybe if she hadn't waited nine years for a commitment from Trevor—which never came—she'd feel differently, but her life had made her who she was, and she'd sworn she'd never let anyone do that to her again.

"What do you mean she's gone?" Vasco scanned the hallway behind Aunt Lilli. He'd returned from his short trip to Switzerland midday on Sunday, and the palace was eerily silent.

"She moved out four days ago." Lilli pursed her mouth in that disapproving way he remembered from his childhood. "She said it was a personal matter." She raised her brow on the word *personal*. No doubt she didn't want to reveal too many details in front of the staff.

"Come to my study." He strode past her. How could Stella do this? She was happy here in the palace, he knew it.

Though she had been avoiding him for the last week. Her excuse about having her period was convincing at the time but now he grew skeptical. She'd known all along that she was leaving and she wanted to keep her distance.

He flung open the door of his office and ushered Lilli in, then slammed it again. "Nicky, where is he?"

"He's with Stella, of course."

He blew out a curse. "She said she'd stay here. That she liked Montmajor and she knew it was a good place for Nicky to grow up."

"She hasn't left the country. She's living at Castell Blanc."

"Oscar Mayoral's old place? Why is she there?"

"She's working on books in the library. And living there."

"How does she even know Mayoral?"

Lilli shrugged.

At least the landowner was in his seventies. And married, with several children and grandchildren, so there was no immediate risk of losing Stella to him. "Doesn't he live abroad?"

"Yes."

He frowned. "So she's there alone?"

"There's a housekeeper, a handyman and a gardener."

He inhaled and tried to wrap his mind around Stella living anywhere other than right here in the palace. It felt wrong. "I must bring her back home."

"She no longer wishes to live here as your...lover." His elderly "aunt" narrowed her eyes slightly as she said the last word.

"She told you that?"

"In so many words. She knows you won't marry her and she's too principled a lady to live here in sin with you, especially with her son to consider."

Vasco snorted. "Live in sin? Not everyone has the same outdated moral code as my aunts."

Lilli lifted her pointed chin and crossed her arms. "No. They don't." Her gaze accused him. She clearly felt that he was at fault. "She wants to marry you."

"She told the press she'd never marry me."

His "aunt" clucked. "Nonsense. She told Mimi she knew *you'd* never marry her. That may not be how she phrased it but we all know it's the truth." She walked up to him and adjusted his collar, which made him feel like a naughty schoolboy again. "And she won't live here anymore unless you marry her."

Something deep in Vasco's gut recoiled from the implied ultimatum. "Marriage is not for me."

Lilli shook her head and clucked her tongue in that infuriating way of hers. "Then apparently Stella is not for you, either. Or Nicky."

Panic flashed through him for a second, then he calmed. "She agreed to let me become Nicky's legal parent. He'll officially be next in line to the throne."

His aunt snorted. "After you're dead? How consoling. Don't you want to enjoy him in your life right now?"

"Of course I do." Why did Stella have to mess things up when they were going so well? "Are you trying to say that Stella won't let me see Nicky unless I marry her?"

"Stella brings Nicky here in the mornings during the week to spend the day with us. She has no intention of keeping Nicky away. Just herself."

He frowned. "So she'll still be coming to the palace." He'd see her every day. He could tempt her. He'd already proved that.

"I know what you're thinking, young man. If you try to seduce her you'll only drive her further away. Stop thinking like a lover and start thinking like a father."

Vasco wheeled away. That's exactly what he didn't want to do. If he started planning his love life around domestic practicalities, it would end up as loveless and unromantic as his ancestors'. Passion and duty just didn't go together.

"Do you love her?" Lilli's quiet question penetrated

his thoughts and almost made a sweat break out on his brow.

"What kind of question is that to ask a king?"

"Don't make light of it. It's a question you need to ask yourself."

"I don't know what love is. I'm a Montoya man, remember?"

She snorted. "That's the trouble with you. Montoya men keep their brains in their breeches, that's why they've relied on women to keep this good country going all these years."

"I should have you thrown in the dungeons for such a treasonous statement."

She raised a stern penciled brow, but humor twinkled in her eyes. "I can see I'm making you think."

"Nonsense. You're making me annoyed. And hungry. Do they not serve lunch around here anymore?" He needed to end this conversation. "Please ask Joseph to serve it immediately." He turned away and pulled out his phone to signal that the conversation was over.

His aunt Lilli didn't budge. Barely more than five feet tall, she seemed to occupy the entire space of his office with her willful presence. "Bring her back home, Vasco. For all of us."

"Ms. Greco, there's someone very important here to see you." The elderly caretaker wiped her hands anxiously on her flowered housedress. Her wide eyes said it all.

"His majesty." Stella managed not to look up from the large letter *E* she was touching up on a seventeenth-century bible. It was Sunday and she was trying to squeeze some work in during Nicky's afternoon nap.

"Yes. He's at the door right now. Which room should I bring him into?"

Stella swallowed and put down her tiny paintbrush, sure she wouldn't be able to keep her hand steady enough not to destroy the precious book. She would have loved to say, "Send him away!" but that would have scandalized and horrified the housekeeper, and wasn't fair.

"I'll come to the door."

"I can't leave him standing there." Already the old lady was shocked.

"I'll go right now." She closed up her bottle of ink. The most important thing was not to weaken and fall into his arms. Not that he'd want her to. If he thought chatting with a gossip columnist about her lack of marriage prospects was a breach of trust, then moving out had probably set his hair on fire.

She hurried past the flushed housekeeper and headed for the front door. The housekeeper's gnarled husband, who was the live-in handyman, hovered hidden behind an archway.

"The king!" he sputtered, as she went by. Apparently they hadn't been reading the gossip columns or they might have expected his majesty to show up. Castell Blanc was a very quiet place. She'd been here four days—since Vasco left for his trip—and no one had visited at all, not even a Jehovah's Witness. Now suddenly the local monarch was cooling his heels on the doorstep.

She managed to prevent a hysterical giggle from rising to her throat. It was late afternoon and warm amber light brightened the foyer and poured through the half-open door. She could see Vasco silhouetted against it, standing just inside the doorway.

"What does this mean?" His deep voice greeted her before she could even see his face.

"Let's go outside."

"No, I'd like to come in."

"It's not my house so that's not appropriate." Her heart beat like a freight train. She didn't want the elderly couple to hear their conversation. He might be king but that didn't mean he could just march in anywhere like it was his own palace.

She walked past him, avoiding his glance, and out the front door. Unfortunately his spicy masculine scent tickled her nostrils as she passed, and sent darts of misgiving prickling through her.

He followed her down the wide steps. Castell Blanc was a large house, maybe three hundred years old, built of mellow golden stone. It had the air of a summer residence, not well updated or overly maintained, which suited its rustic charm. She hadn't even met the owner. He'd hired her over the phone on the strength of her Pacific College references and her acquaintance with a respected local librarian, who was too discreet to mention her circumstances. What would Senyor Mayoral think if he knew his new book restorer was angering royalty on his front doorstep?

A vast paved courtyard, surrounded by disused stable buildings, sprawled in front of the house.

"You're not going to let me in?" He looked both amused and astonished. Vasco had probably never been denied entry anywhere. She'd even let him into her L.A. house eventually.

"I can't."

"I'm sure Oscar wouldn't mind."

"I came here to get away from you." She felt indignant that he didn't even seem to be listening to her. "I need some space."

"There's plenty of space at the palace. You could have your own wing."

She felt the urge to growl. "And you'd be able to saunter into it whenever you pleased. That's what I'm trying to get away from."

Why did he have to be even more handsome and good-humored than she remembered? He looked striking and quite unroyal in jeans and a dark green shirt. The thin layer of dust suggested he'd arrived on his motorbike, which was just so...Vasco. It was hard to be mad at him in the flesh.

Which, of course, was the whole reason she needed distance between her flesh and his. "I don't want a relationship where I'm at your beck and call but there's no permanent commitment between us. You may find that bizarre, especially since we haven't been together very long, but that's just how I feel. I've been there already with my ex, and it's not for me. I'm sorry, but I can't do it again."

"Your ex and I are totally different people."

"On the surface, this is true. On the other hand, you're both men and neither of you wanted to commit, so maybe you have more in common than you think."

"This is all about marriage, for you?" He frowned.

She inhaled a breath. "That makes it sound like I'm making an ultimatum, but I guess it is about marriage, when you come right down to it. If I choose to be in a relationship, then it's because I am seeking the kind of lifetime partnership that I think all of us deserve.

I'm not a teenager looking to experiment, or a college student interested in playing the field. I'm a mature woman and the mother of a young child. At this point in my life I either want a committed relationship, or I'd rather be single."

She'd made that decision when she told Trevor she wouldn't be available on Friday nights anymore. No more dating "just for fun." Once she realized a relationship wasn't going anywhere, she wanted out. Which was probably why she hadn't taken a chance on one since. Was she a freak because she wanted a committed, loving relationship?

"We can be committed without being married." Vasco's gray gaze implored her. "Marriage doesn't work out well for the Montoyas."

Again desire warred with fierce irritation. Why did his eyes have such an infuriating sparkle to them? "You aren't your ancestors, you're you. We can't just live together in our situation. You're a king. We have a child. No one knows the true details but right now I have 'live-in royal mistress' stamped on my forehead like a supermarket chicken. Nell Gwynn may have been happy with that arrangement, as long as Charles II gave her enough money and houses, but I'm more old-fashioned and can't live like that."

She glanced around, suddenly worried the elderly caretakers might be listening. "I don't want people talking about me. About us."

"But they will anyway, because Nicky is our child."

"They don't know the truth about his conception." An idea made her stand up straight. "Maybe we should tell them? We're not lovers at all, simply strangers brought together by the freezers of a California sperm bank."

Vasco shivered. "No."

"Why not? It's the truth. You made the choice to leave your deposit there. It's not like you didn't know what you were doing."

"I wasn't the king then, and didn't think I ever would be."

"I don't see the difference." She tilted her head. "You made the generous act of donating your DNA—for a small fee—and I made the choice to buy it. Why does it matter if you're the king or just some bored teenager with a grudge against his family."

"Because as king my children inherit the throne of Montmajor."

"As you've pointed out, that can happen anyway. Wave your magic wand and change whatever laws you need to." Speaking to him like this was liberating. Now that they were out of the castle—his domain—she felt freer and able to be irreverent and argumentative in a way that she couldn't while she was his guest.

"If people knew they'd be shocked."

"So shock them." She smiled sweetly. "I never intended to conceal the truth when I made a choice to use a sperm bank. I don't think it's any different than adopting, you're just doing it at an earlier stage of life."

"You're saying I put my sperm up for adoption?" Vasco squinted in the sun.

"Exactly. Nothing embarrassing about it."

He snorted. "I'm ashamed of doing it. I was young and stupid."

"But if you hadn't done it, Nicky wouldn't exist."

"True, and I'll always be grateful for him, but…" He turned and stared into the distance for a moment.

"But you'd rather have people think he was conceived during a moment of breathless passion." She narrowed her eyes.

His dimples reappeared and that infuriating twinkle lit his eyes. "Exactly." He walked toward her, and she crossed her arms and braced herself against the appeal of his outstretched hands.

"How come there isn't a male word for *mistress?* It doesn't seem fair that I get to be the naughty one in everyone's eyes. I could tell the papers you're my royal boy toy."

He laughed. "Go right ahead. Happy to oblige. Now if you'll just invite me inside…" He stepped closer, until his warm, intoxicating scent crept into her nose.

"No, thanks. I have books to restore."

"Including the ones at my library. Surely you haven't abandoned your duties?"

"I'd be happy to continue my work once relations between us are settled." Ack. That sounded like another ultimatum. At least she knew he'd never agree to anything just to get his books restored. He wasn't that much of a bibliophile. Still this whole situation was mortifying.

"My aunts told me you'll bring Nicky to spend the day with them." His gaze softened. He looked almost apprehensive, if such a thing was possible.

"I will. I have. I don't want to take Nicky away from you. That's why I'm still in Montmajor. I can see that this is his home and he loves it here."

"And you?" Again, his eyes shone with something different from their usual mischievous sparkle.

"I love it here, too." Her heart ached.

I love you, too. But he knew that already. It didn't matter. He knew she'd drop everything and rush back to the palace to marry him if he offered. But he didn't want that.

"So you're staying." He shifted his weight, arms hanging by his sides, but with tension in them as if he wanted to reach out and hold her there.

"I'm staying, but on my own terms. If I'm going to live here I'll have to build a life that suits me. I've been a guest in your house for long enough. Lovely as it is, it's not my home."

"Nor is Castell Blanc." He gestured at the big house behind her.

"No, but it's a good place to stay while I figure out my long-term plan. I need to settle in and assess my employment prospects and what kind of house I can afford."

Vasco laughed. "You have the coffers of Montmajor at your disposal and you're worried about finding a job?"

She wrapped her arms around herself. "My independence is important to me. I don't want to be a kept woman."

He frowned. It was clear he had trouble understanding her point of view at all, which was exactly why she needed to keep distance between them. She suspected that under his thoughtful exterior he was just waiting for another opportunity to seduce her back to his lotus-eating isle of pleasure where she didn't care about the future but only the blissful present.

Which would undoubtedly happen if she let him get too close.

"Stella." He said her name softly. His gaze rested on hers for a long moment that made her breathing shallow. She had the feeling he was about to say something powerful and important. Maybe he would ask her to marry him? Her heart quickened and she felt blood rise to her face.

How quickly that would solve everything. She could accept his offer and return right home with him. Oscar Mayoral wouldn't mind very much if his books didn't get restored, at least not right away. They'd been in the same condition for at least two hundred years, so what was another year or two?

Vasco still hadn't said anything. Emotion passed over his face, deepening a tiny groove between his brows. His mouth twitched slightly, which reminded her of how it felt pressed to hers. Her palms heated, itching to reach out and hold him.

"Come home with me now." He stepped toward her until she could almost feel his body heat through her clothes. How easy it would have been to say yes.

But she stepped back. "Have you not been listening to me at all?" Tears hovered at the edges of her voice. "Next you'll come out and issue a law that I have to come live with you at the palace. You can't have things all your own way. I've been very obliging so far, in moving across the world with my son—who is probably standing in his crib wondering where I am right now—and settling into a brand-new country and culture. But I have my limits. You can't just seduce me into fitting into your life on your terms twenty-four hours a day. I'm staying here and that's final."

Why did he not look more shocked? He seemed almost amused, as if he was contemplating her idea of enacting a law to keep her at his side. Anger fired her mind and body. "If you try any sneaky moves I'll tell the press how Nicky was conceived."

She watched his Adam's apple move as he swallowed. "I'll respect your wishes." *For now.* The unspoken words hung between them. Vasco was not used to having his plans thwarted. She had a feeling he'd be back with some new scheme to wrap her up in his palace cocoon and keep her and Nicky there on his terms.

She'd have to be strong.

Which was so hard when she wanted nothing more than to run into Vasco's warm embrace.

"Please leave. I need to check on Nicky and you can't come in. I'll bring him to the palace on Monday as usual." She turned away, feeling rude and cruel even though she knew he deserved it.

She half expected to hear his footsteps behind her on the courtyard, but he didn't move. Suddenly chilly, she ran up the steps and in through the door. She didn't stop running until she got to Nicky's bright bedroom on the second floor, to see him still peacefully asleep in the antique crib.

"Oh, Nicky." Unable to resist, she picked him up and squeezed him. He snuffled and rubbed his eyes, not quite ready to wake up. "You're the only man in my life who matters." She held him close, his big head heavy on her shoulder, and his warm, sweet-smelling body filling her arms and soothing the tension in her limbs.

He was the reason she couldn't stay at the palace as Vasco's concubine. He was too young to understand now, but in only two or three years he'd know about moms and dads and marriages. She was well prepared to be a single mom. That she'd planned for and eagerly anticipated. But when her son asked why she and Daddy weren't married, she wanted to be able to answer truthfully, and say it simply wasn't meant to be, rather than still be sleeping in Vasco's bed and hoping and praying that one day he'd finally ask her to be his bride.

She was cured of that kind of false hope. If a man wanted to marry a woman he came out and asked her. If he didn't...well, then the woman moved on, no matter how hard it was to make that break.

Eleven

"So you admit I was right." Still astride his Yamaha, Tomy pulled off his helmet.

"About what?" Vasco removed his own helmet. Hot and sweaty, he didn't feel any more relaxed after burning fuel up and down the Pyrenees all day.

"That your lady would want a ring on her finger."

"You're supposed to be taking my mind off the situation." He shot his friend a scowl. The sun was high in the sky, scouring both them and the mountaintops with harsh light. Tomy's blond hair stuck up in spikes.

"How does that help? The situation is still there when you go home."

"I wish it was. I told you Stella moved out." Just saying it out loud made him feel hollow inside. The palace seemed like the loneliest place on earth since she'd been gone.

"Are you just going to give up on her?"

Every nerve in Vasco's body recoiled with a snap. "No way!"

Tomy laughed. "You are in love."

"I have no idea what love is." It couldn't be this painful ache that haunted him every time he thought of Stella.

"Sure you do. It's like the feeling you have for your Kawasaki." He gestured at Vasco's dark blue bike, which was covered in a thick layer of dust.

"I have three of these. And two Hondas and a Suzuki."

"Okay, then the feeling you have for Montmajor."

"That's pride, and passion. And a whole bunch of stuff that's probably twisted into my DNA. Not love."

"Hmm." Tomy's mouth twisted with amusement. "Methinks he doth protest too much."

"Lust, I know all about. That's a powerful emotion." It stirred inside him right now, as he let Stella's face drift into his imagination. He wanted nothing more than to hold her in his arms, kiss her...

"Lust is a sensation, not an emotion, so if you're feeling it in your heart, it's probably love."

His heart just plain hurt. And talking about it made it worse. Usually he could count on Tomy to distract him from serious matters. "Are we really having this conversation?" He wiped a grimy sleeve across his face to mop up the sweat. "Because if we are I think some alien has seized my friend's body and is holding him hostage somewhere."

"Entirely possible." Tomy glanced down at his big hand, sprinkled with pale hairs. "I hope the alien chicks are having fun with me."

Vasco snorted. "See? What do you know about love? You're with a different girl every time I see you."

"And I love each and every one of them." Tomy smiled and stared at the horizon. "Especially Felicia. I'm seeing her tonight."

"You're a bad influence."

"I know. You shouldn't associate with me." Tomy drew a heart in the dust on his engine casing. "Something's different since you met Stella."

"Since I learned about Nicky, you mean." Was that when everything changed? His life hadn't been the same since he laid eyes on his son.

"That too. Stella and Nicky come as a package, but I can tell it's not just the kid you're crazy about."

Vasco inhaled a long, deep draught of mountain air. Shame the air was hot, and somewhat smoky from a nearby fire. "Stella's an amazing woman. She's bright and funny and gorgeous. I love that she restores books and that she was prepared to do anything to fulfill her dream of having a child."

"So marry her."

"Marriage is the death of fun. Suddenly we'll be bickering about palace protocol or what to have for dinner and everything will seem like a chore."

"Says who? I can't see you arguing with anyone about palace protocol."

"This is an observation. Not just of my parents but other married couples both of their generation and ours. Once you marry, the relationship becomes a job."

"They're not you, Vasco. Even your job is play. Look at you, for crying out loud." He gestured at Vasco seated on his bike high on a sunny hilltop. "You're not only king of a small nation but you have a large stone mining company with offices on several continents. You manage to turn any work into play."

"Or maybe I've figured out how to keep work where it belongs and play where it belongs." That's what he'd always told himself. Why didn't it seem a satisfying answer anymore?

"Is that why you don't ever have women in your bedroom?"

"I told you that?"

Tomy nodded. "You want to be able to skip off at a moment's notice."

"Exactly. See? Stella is better off without me." Why hadn't he invited her into his own room when he had the chance? Now his attempt to keep his life ordered and compartmentalized seemed petty and foolish.

"You might find you like waking up with her."

Vasco shoved a hand through his damp hair. It certainly was hell spending all night alone and waking up without her. "I might." Right now nothing seemed more appealing than the prospect of waking to Stella's sweet face.

"So marry her."

"But I know marriage will ruin everything."

Tomy laughed, then shook his head. "Vasco, my friend, you've already ruined everything. She's moved out and taken your son with her. How much worse can it get?"

"Good point."

"Besides, you're a king. If it doesn't work out you can always lock her up in a tower and have some fresh maidens delivered." Tomy's eyes twinkled.

Vasco's muscles tightened. This was no laughing matter. "If I wasn't sitting on a bike I'd…"

"What?" Tomy climbed back astride his own bike. "How about you race me down to the river instead."

Adrenaline surged through his veins. "You're on."

Vasco had paced the halls all night trying to decide if he should marry Stella. Whenever he decided "yes," it felt strange and frightening—not feelings he had much acquaintance with.

Whenever he decided "no," it felt wrong. The prospect of spending the next few decades without Stella in his bed, or at his dining room table, or by his side made his soul rattle.

Which meant he should do it.

But would she even say yes? He was pretty sure she had wanted to marry him. She'd even said as much. She was attracted to him, she seemed to like him a lot, and he was Nicky's father.

On the other hand, he'd done enough wrong to drive her out of the palace and he'd come right out and said that he didn't believe in marriage. Not very confidence-inspiring words for a potential fiancé.

The prospect of her rejection made him realize how much he desperately wanted her to say yes. Just think, she could be back in the palace by tomorrow night, with his ring on her finger and a smile on her lovely face as she climbed into his bed.

In his bedroom.

He marched through the palace, heels thundering over the stone. Dawn was just beginning to throw daggers of light onto the vast array of weapons in the armaments hall when he came up with his plan. He paused in front of the ornate armor that had recently encased Stella's lovely body. Stella loved pageantry, all the old medieval stories of knights and maidens. He'd get dressed up as a knight and ride over to Castell Blanc, where he'd serenade her and ask for her hand.

How could she resist that?

There was no sign of Vasco that morning when Stella dropped Nicky off at the palace. Her son looked so happy to be back in the loving arms of his aunts, who had planned a picnic for him and a playdate with two children from the village. Still, she felt a little empty leaving the palace without even seeing him.

He must be angry that she wouldn't come back and slot into the routine he'd planned, especially after her threat that she'd reveal the truth about how Nicky was conceived.

It was the truth, after all.

She left the palace feeling a little downcast, but determined to throw herself into her work and enjoy the sunny day. The car she drove belonged to Castell Blanc, and the owner had agreed to let her share it with the caretakers. It had turned out that neither of them could or would drive—they cycled into town for what minor supplies were needed—so it was hers alone. Everything was working out almost too well to be believed. She had a lovely, if temporary, home for her and Nicky, a job doing what she loved, and she could bring Nicky to see Vasco and his other relatives every day.

Yes, she felt a little empty inside, but that was just the wrench of leaving the only romantic relationship she'd ever really enjoyed, and because she didn't have any other friends here. She'd been so wrapped up in Vasco she hadn't bothered to make any. Now that she'd found her backbone and taken her life back, she resolved to join an evening class at the local school—there was one about Catalan poetry, and a series on sushi preparation—and get more settled into the local community. Sure, they might look at her strangely at first, but as long as she didn't confirm or deny anything they'd soon realize she was a person, not a tabloid headline.

She bought a baguette in the bakery and some of the local cheese, along with some olives and salami, and made herself a pleasant brunch on the terrace outside Castell Blanc. After a cup of coffee she settled into the enjoyable work of restitching the worn binding of an eighteenth-century book about the Roman conquest of Europe.

It had not been easy for Vasco to squeeze himself into the largest suit of armor in the palace. People were a lot smaller back then. There was no way the leg pieces would fit, but he managed to buckle the breast piece and arms on loosely and jam his feet into the crazy metal shoes. The big problems started when the horse saw him.

"Tinto, it's just me." He clanked over the cobbles toward the terrified beast. "Your ancestors would think nothing of this getup."

The pretty gray mare snorted and jerked her head up, eyes staring. The groom held tight to her bridle, but couldn't keep her feet still. Vasco propped up the visor, and looked at her. "I need you to work with me, Tinto. I have a maiden to woo."

The groom tried to disguise a grin.

"Once I get on her she'll be fine." He tried to reassure himself as much as the horse and her handler. Tinto herself was wearing fancy ceremonial tack, including an embroidered saddlecloth and tasseled reins. They'd make quite the romantic picture together—if he could just mount up.

He clanked a few steps closer, but the horse only skittered farther away across the stone courtyard. The groom tried to reason with her but she looked like she was about to turn and bolt for her field. Riding her would be interesting, under the circumstances. Still, he knew Stella would love it, and surely the armor functioned much like safety gear, right?

"Lead her to me while I stand still. Maybe that will work." He smiled reassuringly at the mare, who responded by snorting and pawing at the ground. Jaume, the groom, tried to lead her closer, but she planted her feet and peered suspiciously at him down the length of her proud nose. "Maybe give me some treats. Some of those mints she likes."

Jaume called out to Luis, who came running over with a fistful of candies and placed them awkwardly in Vasco's armored hand. Lucky the metal cased gloves were leather underneath and surprisingly flexible. He managed to get the wrapper off and place one on his other palm, then reach out his hand. "Here, Tinto. It's your favorite."

Tinto looked interested, but wary. She tossed her head and sent her white mane flying. After about a minute she took a hesitant step toward him, then another, and took the treat. "See, I knew you'd figure out it's me. You're part of a very important plan." He spoke softly to the mare. "Now we just have to figure out how to get me up on your back." He looked from his metal clad foot to the wide, ceremonial stirrup. This armor must weigh a good seventy-five pounds. It wouldn't be easy to get airborne. "Luis, could you give me a hand?"

Luis, who was neither young nor tall, shuffled over and wove his fingers together into a kind of human stirrup. Vasco knew he'd probably cripple the man if he stepped on his hand. "How about Luis holds Tinto and Jaume gives me a leg up." Jaume was young and strapping. A relieved Luis took hold of the reins and Jaume strode boldly over, in turn looking relieved not to be holding one thousand pounds of potentially explosive horse.

"One, two..." Tinto neatly sidestepped out of the way before Jaume could give him a leg up. "Oh, come on. No more mints until I'm up." He frowned meaningfully at the horse. "It's barely a fifteen-minute ride. You'll be home eating hay before you know it."

Luis maneuvered Tinto back into position. Lightning-fast, Jaume helped heave Vasco up into the saddle and he slung his leg over and came down as lightly as possible on Tinto's back. Tinto immediately wrenched free of Luis's grasp and took off bucking across the courtyard. "Easy!" Vasco grabbed the reins and tried to bend her neck to get control. He clanked and rattled like a bag of bolts as she skated over the cobblestones. "All right, we're off." He had the ring in his pocket. As long as that didn't fall out he was good.

He managed to steer her toward the gate that led from the stable yard out to the fields beyond, and all went surprisingly well until they got through the gate. Once they were outside the palace, Tinto threw in one more almighty buck, which pitched Vasco over her head. He landed on the ground with a loud series of clanks—and some very nasty sensations in his muscles—and managed to get his visor up in time to see her galloping off over the crest of the nearest hill.

He cursed. Luis and Jaume came running and helped him to his feet. The breast plate was dented and he felt pretty dinged, as well.

"You okay?"

"Still alive in here, I think. We need to catch her before she trips on the reins." He peeled off the armor and they spend most of the next hour following Tinto's trail until they caught up with her grazing quietly under an oak in a disused sheep pen. She had a small cut to one of her legs, so they led her back quietly and bandaged her up.

"Guess I'd better ride one of my other faithful steeds." He had enough bruises for one day. He changed into different clothes, this time a Chevalier costume he wore for parties sometimes. With the ring safely in the new pocket, he went and mounted his trusty Kawasaki. Not quite as romantic as a horse, but much more predictable. Within minutes he rode up to the entrance of Castell Blanc, propped his bike, and launched into song.

The roar of an engine made Stella look up from her sewing. It sounded like a motorcycle engine. Her heart started to rev and she put down her needle and moved to the window. The first strains of a male voice—singing—stopped her in her tracks.

Powerful and haunting, the raw music stole in through the open window and rooted her to the spot. Was it Vasco?

She stepped forward and peered gingerly outside. Her eyes widened as she looked down on Vasco dressed in embroidered silk breeches like a character from a

Cervantes story. Windswept and rugged as usual, and with his dark motorcycle only a few feet away, he looked impossibly masculine in the ornate costume.

But his voice… Deep and rich, it wrapped around the unfamiliar Catalan words and filled the air. Sound reverberated off the stone facade of the house and bounced back to the surrounding hills, growing and swelling around them.

"Oh, Vasco." She said it quietly, to herself. Just when she thought he couldn't be any more outrageous or adorable, he pulled some new stunt like this. Her heart squeezed and she wanted nothing more than to run into his arms.

Resisting that impulse, she had a sudden urge to show Nicky the fantastical vision of his father singing like an ancient troubador, then she remembered he was still at the palace with his aunts. Vasco was singing for her alone.

As she listened, she could make out a few of the words. Impassioned and heartfelt, the song seemed to tell of a heartbroken man who'd lost his true love and would never see her again. Tears almost rose in her eyes, not because of the lyrics, but because of the raw emotion in Vasco's melodious voice. Could he do everything? It didn't seem fair. How was anyone supposed to stand a chance around him?

He'd spotted her at the window, and even from the second floor she could see his eyes light up as he launched into another verse. Her own heart beat faster and excitement swelled in her chest. She soon found herself leaning out the casement window to fully enjoy the rapturous sound. Even a cappella, Vasco gave off more energy and intent than an entire orchestra of professional musicians.

And he was doing it all for her.

As a way to get into a woman's underwear, she had to recommend it. Right now she had chills and hot flashes going on at the same time. Still, she had to remain strong. This was about the rest of her life here, not some steamy afternoon scandalizing the housekeeper and her husband while their boss was away.

Tempting as that seemed.

Vasco reached the end of the song and made a dramatic bow and flourish. Stella clapped and couldn't help smiling. "Beautiful," she murmured, not even loud enough for him to hear.

"Would you do me the honor of coming to the door?" His courtly attitude amused and pleased her. Normally he'd just storm through the door without asking.

She nodded, and hurried away, pulse pounding. She dashed down the steps, telling herself over and over again to be strong. *Don't fall into his arms. Just say hello and tell him he's a good singer.*

"Hi," was the best she could manage, with a goofy grin, when she pulled open the front door to greet her dashing cavalier.

Vasco immediately got down on one knee and bowed his head. Stella froze. He reached into his pocket and fumbled for a moment, then pulled out a ring.

She almost fell down the steps. Surely he wasn't…?

He raised his head, and his gray eyes met hers with intensity that felt like a punch to the stomach. "Stella, I love you. I've thought about nothing but you since the moment I heard you were gone. I'm miserable without you and I know with agonizing certainty that I want to spend the rest of my life with you. Will you marry me?"

She stood rooted to the spot. Was she dreaming? She wanted to pinch herself but couldn't seem to move.

Vasco's gaze searched hers. She could swear she even saw a trace of anxiety cross his handsome face. He held out the ring a little farther. "Please Stella, be my wife."

"Yes." The word fled her lips without any permission from her brain. Why had she said that? His sudden change of heart was shocking and not entirely convincing. Still...

Vasco rose and slid the ring on her finger. The metal felt cool and sensual on her skin. He kissed her hand with deliberate passion, eyes closed. Then, face taut with emotion, he took her in his arms and pressed his lips to hers.

Her body went limp under the force of his kiss. If he weren't holding her close she'd have fallen to the ground. The whole situation was too amazing to be real.

When they finally pulled apart she looked down at his elaborate and historically accurate costume. Her doubts crowded back over her. "Is this a scene from a play that you're acting?"

"No, the words and emotions are entirely my own."

She frowned. "But yesterday you said..."

"Yesterday was an age ago. I had all night to contemplate the prospect of living without you and to realize how miserable I'd be if I lost you." His eyes shone with conviction that echoed deep inside her. "I've behaved like a spoiled child who wants to have everything his way, and ignore the feelings of others. Nicky needs a father who's a family man." He lifted his chin proudly.

Stella hesitated for a moment. "You're marrying me so that Nicky can have a proper family." An official marriage, without emotion. Something that looked good on paper, like all the Montmajor marriages before it. Her stomach tightened.

He took her hand, the one with the ring. "I said I love you and I mean it. You should know me well enough to understand that I'd never marry simply out of duty. I made it clear from the beginning that was out of the question." He paused and looked down for a moment, before his eyes fixed on hers with a penetrating stare. "It took some soul-searching to realize that what I feel for you has nothing to do with duty, or responsibilities, or anything else other than the joy I feel when I'm with you."

A strange warm sensation rose inside her. "I love you, too." It was a sweet release to let the truth out. "I think I've loved you almost from the start, when you showed up on my doorstep demanding a place in your son's life and unwilling to take no for an answer."

"Guess I'm lucky you didn't boot me out on my ear." He grinned.

"Well, I did try, but you're not easy to get rid of." She smiled, too. "And I'm glad of that, now." She glanced down at the ring. It was unusual, with an ornate tooled gold setting, and the stone was a bright blue sapphire rather than the more conventional diamond. "Is this an old ring from your family?"

Vasco faked a shudder. "No way. I don't want us following down their dreary path in marriage. I had it flown in from Barcelona overnight. Given your love of history I thought you might like something dramatic and historical looking, rather than an ordinary diamond solitaire like everyone else."

"You're so right. I adore it." The clear blue stone reflected the bright sky above.

"The stone was mined by my company in Madagascar, and I had it tooled by my favorite jeweler. I bet if you look closely enough you can see the whole universe in there."

She lifted the ring. It sparkled with astonishing brilliance and drew her eye to its depths. "I've never seen anything like it. I keep forgetting that you have a whole company out there in addition to being king."

"Comes in useful at times like this."

"And you're the type of person who needs to keep busy."

"Like yourself. I don't see you wanting to sit around all day staring out the window. Still, I do think you should be restoring the royal collection rather than a few tatty old novels here at Castell Blanc." His dimples showed as he made a dismissive gesture at the house behind her.

"Mr. Mayoral has a wonderful collection. Not as large as yours, of course, but every bit as distinguished in its own way." She smiled. "Still, I admit that I miss the lovely palace library. There isn't enough room for me to set up my tools in the library here so I have to bring the books into a spare bedroom."

Vasco looked pleased. "Perhaps you can bring his books to the palace to work on, if you still want to restore them."

"Maybe I will." Her muscles tingled with excitement at the thought of moving back to the beautiful palace with Nicky. It must be almost time to go pick him up.

Except that she didn't have to pick him up. The thought struck her hard and she glanced at her ring just to check again that she wasn't dreaming. "Are we really getting married?"

"You still don't believe me?" He stroked her chin, humor in his eyes.

"I want to, it's just a bit much for me."

"We're one hundred percent absolutely definitely getting married. As soon as possible. Today would be fine, in fact."

"Today?" She glanced down at her jeans and plain blue shirt.

"Or tomorrow. Or the next day. Or next month. I'll leave it entirely up to you. It depends on what kind of wedding you'd like to have. I vote for big and fancy with everyone we've ever met in attendance." His teeth gleamed as he smiled. "Just so they know we really mean it."

She laughed. "You know, you might have a point there. A big, fancy, over-the-top royal wedding with all the trimmings would give the paparazzi what they're looking for, and then maybe they'll leave us in peace."

"Never happen." He grinned.

"Oh, well. Maybe we should seize some peace right now." She glanced back at the house. A week and a half of abstinence from Vasco's lovemaking was catching up with her. His intoxicating male presence, especially in the dashing musketeer outfit, made her want to rip his clothes off right there. "Would you care to come inside?"

Her courtly invitation made him laugh. "I certainly would. I'm so glad I'm now permitted entry."

"We'd better not tell Mr. Mayoral about what we're about to do."

He raised a brow. "My lips are sealed. And I can't wait to find out what we are about to do."

Twelve

The carriage wheels rattled over the ancient cobbled streets as crowds cheered the wedding procession. Stella didn't need to worry about smiling for all the people watching. She'd had a grin plastered to her face all morning.

"I'm amazed the horses aren't spooked by all the helicopters." A fleet of them had hovered overhead since dawn, filming the wedding party as they emerged from the cathedral, and the long, colorful procession as it wound through the streets of Montmajor.

"They're used to them." Vasco beamed, as well. "Much less scary than a man in a suit of armor."

"Suits of armor seem to be a theme in our relationship." She murmured the words in his ear.

"So true. We'll have to get the horses acclimatized to them so we can try jousting." His arm rested around her waist and he pulled her closer. Arousal sizzled through her. How long would it be until they were alone again? The aunts had hovered over them all morning, and hairdressers and dressmakers had fussed and prodded and poked her until she was ready to scream. Now it was torture being right next to Vasco—in full view of the entire world.

Nicky sat opposite them in the carriage, with aunt Lilli holding tightly to the sash of his waistcoat to prevent him from jumping out into the throng. He even waved along with the grownups, and people called out "*Hola,* Nicky!" as he passed, much to his delight.

At last the carriage pulled up at the palace, where preparations were underway for the biggest party in Europe. Friends and family and thousands of diplomats and dignitaries had flown in from all over the world. Every room in the palace had been pressed into service as accommodation, and guests were billeted throughout the town.

A red carpet of rose petals covered the ground between where the carriage stopped and their entrance to the palace, and their sweet scent filled the air. A hundred white doves flapped and pecked around the petals and gravel and glided silently overhead. "Why don't they just fly away?" Stella whispered, as she alighted from the carriage and looked around her in awe.

"They prefer caviar on toast to grubbing for insects." Vasco grinned and waved to the assembled palace staff, who launched into some ancient Montmajorian greeting, half spoken, half sung. Vasco led her into the castle. Her lush ivory dress had a train nearly fifty feet long, and the six little train-bearers—boys of only seven or eight—rushed forward to gather and lift it behind her.

"I really do feel like a queen in this getup." She smiled at their serious expressions.

"You look like one." Vasco kissed her hand. "A coronet suits you." The tiny crown, tipped with rubies, was pinned to her elaborate hairstyle. If anyone had ever told her she'd wear an outfit this outrageous to any occasion, she'd have laughed, but the palace staff and wedding planners had snuck each detail in gradually until it was far too late to protest. Vasco simply laughed and said that if people enjoyed a bit of pomp and ceremony, why not give it to them?

Vasco himself was in a rather dashing getup that made him look like a nineteenth-century cavalryman. It even had tall shiny boots and acres of gold braid. His hair, of course, still looked windblown and wild, which only made him even more gorgeous. She could imagine women all over the world sighing and smiling as they looked at the pictures, and wishing they were her.

And who wouldn't?

Vasco lifted Nicky into his arms, and she squinted against the glare of flashbulbs. There seemed to be an insatiable appetite for pictures of Europe's most eligible bachelor as a family man. She hadn't told anyone that Nicky was conceived in a lab. It didn't seem relevant now they'd long since made up for the lack of sex during his conception.

Her skin tingled as Vasco took her hand and led her into the grand ballroom. A large glass fountain in the middle of the room bubbled with champagne. A waiter scooped two slender glasses of it for her and Vasco, and they turned to face the crowds—and yet more media— to raise a toast to their marriage.

"I'm the luckiest man in the world." Vasco lifted

his glass. "I live in the best country, I'm married to the kindest, loveliest woman and I have a wonderful son. Who could ask for more?"

Stella wanted to laugh. Even if they did ask for more, Vasco had that, too, starting with the fountain of champagne. The crowd cheered and the guests flocked around them with congratulations. Champagne poured late into the night and the guests enjoyed a feast of Montmajor specialties and hours of rousing traditional dances. By the time the guests finally trickled away to their beds, Stella was exhausted.

"I think you might have to carry me upstairs."

Vasco seemed tireless, as usual. "I'd be delighted."

"I may even have to actually sleep tonight." She raised a brow.

"Sleep?" Vasco whisked her off her feet. The train had been removed from her dress shortly after the toast, but she still wore about an acre of frothy taffeta that threatened to swallow him. "Sleep can be such a waste of time."

He lowered his lips to hers, and stirred a sudden rush of energy with his kiss. "Okay, maybe you have a point there," she gasped, when he finally pulled his mouth away. "I feel strangely invigorated." A funny thought occurred to her. "Wouldn't it be something if our second child was conceived on our wedding night?"

Vasco's eyes met hers, wide with surprise. "A second child?"

"Why not? Nicky would enjoy having a playmate." A tiny flame of fear licked inside her. Did he not want more children? They hadn't discussed it at all, and of course Vasco had never intended to have Nicky. Still, he seemed to enjoy fatherhood.

His expression turned thoughtful. Still holding her in his arms he strode for the stairs. He carried her into his old bedroom, which now truly was their room, and closed the door. They'd slept here since the night he proposed and brought her back to the castle. Her clothes had been moved into the large wardrobes that day, Nicky's things and child-safe bed were moved into one of the adjoining chambers, and there was no more talk of trysts in the round tower.

He laid her gently on the grand four-poster bed and tugged at the fastenings on her elegant dress. "You're so right. Tonight would be the perfect time to make Nicky's little brother or sister." A warm twinkle in his eyes warred with his serious expression. She wriggled slightly as he eased the bodice of her dress down past her waist.

She tugged at his cravat, then realized she needed to take out the gold pin that held it in place. It was hard removing all this crisp formal clothing when you were addled by lust and exhaustion. Probably in the old days they had servants standing around the bed to help.

"What are you laughing at?" Vasco's eyes crinkled into a smile.

"Just wondering if we'll get all these clothes off before dawn."

He pretended to tear at her fancy bra with his teeth. "We can always resort to scissors."

When she finally got his buttons undone she sighed at the sight of his hard, bronzed torso. Vasco really was hers, to have and to hold. Since she'd come back to the palace with the ring on her finger, their lovemaking had a whole new dimension. Gone were the nagging worries that she was making a huge mistake sleeping with her son's father.

And now they truly were married. She pressed her cheek to his chest, enjoying the strong beat of his heart. For a long time she thought she'd never know the joy of joining her life with another person. She'd achieved it in part when she had Nicky, but marrying Vasco made her life complete. They were a real family now, an inseparable unit. For the first time she could remember, she felt safe and protected, able to relax and enjoy the present without harboring doubts and fears about an uncertain future.

She gasped as Vasco pushed his fingers inside her delicate panties. Hot and wet, she shuddered against his touch. She'd never known her body could enjoy so many different sensations. There seemed to be no limit to the new feelings and emotions that crowded her mind since they became engaged. She could love Vasco, adore and enjoy him, without wondering what tomorrow would bring.

She wriggled under his sensual touch, suddenly aching to feel him inside her, to move with him and lose herself in the fevered intensity of the moment.

She reached for his erection and guided him in, and he let out a shuddering groan as he sank deep inside her. A wave of relief swept over her as it had every time since she'd come back. For those few brief but agonizing days at Castell Blanc she thought she'd never know this sensation again. She knew it would never be the same with anyone else after Vasco. He was a tornado that tore into her life and left it changed forever. Without him the aftermath would have been drab and lonely, but with him…

She arched her back and took him deeper still, then climbed over him and guided him into a fast rhythm. She felt no sense of self-consciousness making love with Vasco, just pure pleasure. He rose and fell with her, holding her close and kissing her face when she leaned forward, then flipping her under him and pinning her to the bed while he tormented her with his tongue and hands.

"Which would you prefer, a boy or a girl?" He whispered, at one intensely pleasurable moment.

Stella hugged him tight. "I don't care at all. I never did."

"I never even knew I wanted children." Vasco kissed her, holding her tight. "I didn't even think I wanted a wife. Thank heaven I found you."

They played in bed for hours, bringing each other to climax, pulling back, then starting over, in a rapturous exploration of their bodies and free-spirited baring of their souls. Somehow knowing that they could do this every night for the rest of their lives didn't diminish their hunger to enjoy each moment.

By the time dawn peeked in around the curtains they lay snoozing in each other's arms. "How long until we know if Nicky will have a new sibling soon?" Vasco's deep voice tickled her ear.

"About a month. It was an agonizing wait to find out if I was pregnant with him the first time. And the conception wasn't nearly as enjoyable."

"I'm not even going to ask how that happened, since I know I wasn't there in person." He stroked her cheek. "I should have been."

"We would never have met if it hadn't been for Westlake Cryobank." Stella grew thoughtful. "Instead of suing them for giving out my information I should send them flowers."

"Thank heavens for corruptible employees." Vasco grinned.

"You did pay someone off, didn't you?" They hadn't talked about it once. Somehow it was off-limits, too sensitive. Now that they were married, however, no topic seemed too touchy.

"Of course. Wouldn't you?"

She laughed. "No, probably not. But then I'm not a European monarch."

"Yes, you are." His steady gray gaze sparkled with humor.

Stella blinked. "You're right. How extremely weird."

"Queen Stella." He kissed her on the mouth. "Of Montmajor."

She shivered slightly. How strange. That's who she really was now. And her son—their son—was Prince Nicholas of Montmajor. It seemed a very dramatic title for a little boy who still loved to mash Cheerios with his fingers. "I suppose I'll get used to it eventually." She ran her fingers into his hair, then along his stubble-roughened cheekbone. "You've been married a whole day, almost. Is it as dreadful as you thought?"

His dimples appeared and he squeezed her with his strong, warm arms. "So far, so good. I think that since we broke with royal tradition by conceiving a child together before we even met, it's safe to say everything else will be different, and wonderful."

"I agree. And we'd better try to get a few minutes of sleep before our son wakes up."

Epilogue

One year and eight months later

"Blow, sweetie, blow!" Aunt Lilli held little Francesca up in front of her cake.

Stella laughed. "She doesn't understand. I bet she can extinguish the candles with her drool, though." She leaned forward to help blow out the single candle flickering amidst the shiny frosted decorations. They all sat around a big wooden table in the palace gardens, afternoon sun warming their glasses of fruit punch and sparkling over the silver cutlery.

Stella and Vasco had been thrilled to find out that they were indeed pregnant within the first month of their marriage. When little Francesca emerged a month before they expected, they realized that in fact she might have been conceived even before the wedding, though no one could be sure as Francesca was quite petite and it wasn't so unusual for a baby to be born a month early. Unlike Nicky she had silky dark hair, but she did have those big, gray eyes that marked her unmistakably as a Montoya.

She waved her chubby arms and her plump fingers danced dangerously near the elaborate icing. "I think she wants a slice." Vasco picked up the knife and handed it to Nicky. Now almost three, he took great pride in being an older brother and helping his baby sister.

"I'll cut her a big one, since it's her birthday." Guided by Vasco, Nicky plunged the knife into the rose-covered frosting with gusto. "And then I'll cut myself an even bigger one, because I'm older." He looked up with a toothy grin.

"What about us? We're even older." Vasco ruffled Nicky's blond hair.

"I think that means you have to save the biggest pieces of all for your aunties." Aunt Mari clapped her hands. "We're so old we don't even remember how many birthdays we've had."

Stella found it hard to remember how she'd coped without a large extended family to help. She still spent time every day working with the books in the library, and she and Mari had started to catalog the books, making several intriguing discoveries along the way. Her duties as queen were pretty light. Being a monarch in Montmajor mostly consisted of holding large parties and inviting everyone for miles around. Nice work if you could get it.

Vasco passed out the slices of cake, then lifted his glass. "A toast to our little princess." Francesca waved her sippy cup around with flair, giggling and slapping her other palm on the table. "Who will never have to leave Montmajor unless she wants to."

His words surprised Stella for a moment, then she remembered the strange ancient law that had driven Vasco from his homeland when he was still a boy.

"It's good to travel and see the world." Aunt Frida waved a forkful of cake in the air. "I spent three years touring Africa when I was in my twenties. And I ran a catering company in Paris for a while, too." The aunts— who did seem to have lived for several centuries—were constantly surprising her with their life stories. "But you always want to come back home to Montmajor."

"There's nowhere as peaceful," agreed Aunt Lilli.

"Or as beautiful," sighed Aunt Mari.

"Or with such good food," exclaimed Nicky, through a mouthful of cake.

"I have to agree." Stella smiled. "Though I think it's the people that make it so special. I don't know of anywhere on earth that's so quick to welcome strangers and make them feel like they've always lived here."

Vasco slid his arm around her waist. "Every now and then we have to venture into the outside world and find some more special people to come live here." He pressed a soft kiss to her cheek—which still tingled with excitement like it was the first time.

She sighed and smiled at her husband, and their growing extended family. "I'm glad you found us."

* * * * *

A sneaky peek at next month...

Desire

PASSIONATE AND DRAMATIC LOVE STORIES

My wish list for next month's titles...

2 stories in each book - only £5.30!

In stores from 16th December 2011:

❑ Have Baby, Need Billionaire — Maureen Child

& The Boss's Baby Affair — Tessa Radley

❑ His Heir, Her Honour — Catherine Mann

& Meddling with a Millionaire — Cat Schield

❑ Seducing His Opposition — Katherine Garbera

& Secret Nights at Nine Oaks — Amy J. Fetzer

❑ Texas-Sized Temptation — Sara Orwig

& Star of His Heart — Brenda Jackson

Available at WHSmith, Tesco, Asda, Eason, Amazon and Apple

Just can't wait?

Visit us Online

You can buy our books online a month before they hit the shops! **www.millsandboon.co.uk**

1211/51

Have Your Say

You've just finished your book.
So what did you think?

We'd love to hear your thoughts on our
'Have your say' online panel
www.millsandboon.co.uk/haveyoursa

- 🌹 Easy to use
- 🌹 Short questionnaire
- 🌹 Chance to win Mills & Boon®
  goodies

Tell us what you thought of this book now at
www.millsandboon.co.uk/haveyoursay

YOUR_S

Mills & Boon® Online

Discover more romance at
www.millsandboon.co.uk

- 🌹 **FREE** online reads
- 🌹 **Books** up to one
  month before shops
- 🌹 **Browse our books**
  before you buy

...and much more!

Special Offers

Every month we put together collections and longer reads written by your favourite authors.

Here are some of next month's highlights— and don't miss our fabulous discount online!

On sale 16th December

On sale 16th December

On sale 6th January

Save 20%
on all Special Releases

Find out more at
www.millsandboon.co.uk/specialreleases

Visit us
Online

Special Offers
Great Value Collection

eet these kings of seduction under the sizzling ustralian sun!

On sale
16th December 2011

On sale
6th January 2012

Save 20%
on all Special Releases

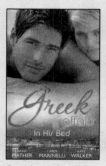